LIVE THE DREAM

Josephine Cox

WINDSOR
PARAGON

First published 2004
by
HarperCollins Publishers
This Large Print edition published 2005
by
BBC Audiobooks Ltd by arrangement with
HarperCollins Publishers Ltd

ISBN 1 4056 1118 9   (Windsor Hardcover)
ISBN 1 4056 2105 2   (Paragon Softcover)

British Library Cataloguing in Publication Data available

Printed and bound in Great Britain by
Antony Rowe Ltd., Chippenham, Wiltshire

For my darling Ken, as ever

To
Mary Jane

You were a fine friend, and a wonderful mother. You always taught me that if I believed in myself, my dreams might one day come true.

I will never forget how through all your own troubles, you always understood and encouraged me.
Thanks Mam.
God bless.
Luv you.
Your wayward daughter, Josie.

CONTENTS

PART ONE
February 1932
The Way It Was

CHAPTER ONE

For a long, regretful moment he leaned against the back wall, his tall, strong figure merging into the shadows, his heart aching, and his dark, thoughtful gaze intent on the house. It was such a beautiful house, he thought . . . so warm and inviting. *Like she used to be.*

His thoughts shifted to the woman inside. She was still beautiful, and sometimes, when she was afraid, her warm hand would slip into his. But that was all. There was rarely any passion in her gesture. Seldom a smile or welcome in her eyes.

She neither loved nor wanted him. But it wasn't her fault—he knew that. He still loved her, but he didn't know her any more, not in the way he used to.

He felt such deep regret, and yet, in a strange way, he was also relieved, as though he no longer needed to prove anything. There was no need. *There was no one to care.*

He had loved this fine house since that first day, seven years ago, when he had carried his wife through the wide, oaken doors and swung her round while she held on to him, laughing and happy, her beautiful face glowing with love for him and, oh, how he had adored her in return. *But that was then.* Now all he had left were the memories.

His heart ached for things to be how they once were. But however much he wished it, there could be no going back.

With a deep sigh he made his way across the delightful garden, with its pretty, meandering paths

3

and multitude of shrubs and trees. It was early February now, and here and there the buds were already forming. In another month or so, they would open and the garden would be filled with colour. Walking through it, you could imagine yourself to be in paradise.

Sometimes, when the symptoms of her illness became too much for him, he would come out here, and walk and think until his spirit was refreshed. Then he would go back inside, ready to deal with whatever came his way.

Today was Tuesday, and Tuesdays were very special. For a time he was free to follow his heart, to do what he wanted, to be whoever he wanted to be. Tuesday was *his* day. *His sanctuary.*

He quickened his steps towards the outbuilding. Here, he took out a bunch of keys, unlocked the door and let himself in. He threw back the makeshift curtain at the window, and a shaft of sunlight fell on the cloth-covered easel at the back of the room.

Sliding away the cloth, he revealed the painting of a beautiful, slender woman with chestnut-coloured hair flowing to her waist, and dark, sultry eyes. For a while he stood there, thoughtfully observing the face, with its exquisite features and soft, smiling mouth.

Reaching out, he traced the tip of his finger around her inviting, sensuous mouth. A great sadness took hold of him.

'I'm so sorry,' he murmured. 'If I could only change things, you know I would.'

A moment longer, then he covered the painting and strode to a large wooden chest and opened the lid. From where it was hidden beneath layers of paint-trays and brushes, he took out a heavy iron key. It was his passport to another world.

He slid the key into his jacket pocket and left, securing the door behind him. Then he quickly made his way through the gardens and out of the side gate.

*   *   *

From the bedroom window she watched him leave . . . that same woman he had painted so lovingly and whose portrait was hidden in the outhouse. She saw him carefully close the gate; she heard the familiar turning over of the engine, and in her mind's eye she imagined him driving the long black saloon he had bought only a few months ago. She heard the engine swell as it was driven away, and through the beech trees that lined the road she caught a fleeting glimpse of the car as it went from the house.

Even when she could no longer hear the engine, she remained, thinking and wishing, until, startling her, a voice from the door called her name.

'Sylvia! I've been looking for you everywhere.'

With a smile, she turned from the window. 'It's such a lovely day, don't you think, Edna?' But the smile was forced, because now he was gone and already she was lonely.

She often felt alone now—detached from her husband, from her sister, from dear Edna. No one came to visit. Too scared of her moods. The medication helped suppress the anger, but often her moods got the better of her. Sometimes the anger was preferable to the dulling effect of the drugs, and so on occasion she would hide the medicine and only pretend to take it. But there were days when she had no choice but to take it or lose control.

*   *   *

As the distance lengthened between them, Luke's thoughts remained with her, the further he got from the house, the more he felt as though a great weight was being lifted from his shoulders. The frowns eased and his face softened; his dark eyes began to twinkle and his whole body relaxed into the seat. It was Tuesday, he was heading away, and a sense of freedom flooded his soul.

Today he would drive by way of the coast, some twenty-odd miles away. He liked the open sea and sky after the neat residential street in Blackburn, and the noise and sootiness of the factory on other weekdays. Afterwards, he would turn inland, to enjoy the special pleasures and freedom of his precious day off.

As he neared the beach, a flock of screaming seagulls descended, effectively blinding him as they flew across the windscreen of his car.

'Jesus!' Startled, he slammed on his brakes and screeched to a halt. Drawing on the handbrake, he climbed out of the car and watched the birds as they flew away, throwing their shadows over the morning sun. Anger subsided; a smile flitting across his thoughtful features. 'Free as a bird.' When they were mere specks in the faraway sky he momentarily closed his eyes, wishing he was up there with them.

His gaze flowed across the beach to the horizon. The sea was unusually quiet.

6

In the far distance, on the beach, a woman strolled with her two Labradors, one running ahead, the other trailing behind. She was a regular walker here. He had seen her tall, slim silhouette many times before.

His gaze travelled: to his left where the man was already opening up his tea-stall, and beyond him the flower shop was ablaze with spring flowers. Life goes on, he thought. *If only they knew.*

Getting back into his car he reminded himself that it was Tuesday. Put the dark thoughts out of your mind, he thought. He'd best get going, or the day would be gone before he knew it.

At the end of the road, he turned from the seafront and headed inland towards the fells and the Ribble Valley, every familiar curve and landmark a comfort to him.

The lanes became narrower and more meandering, until at length they disappeared altogether and he was bumping along a rough track that carried him deeper and deeper into the woods, beyond civilisation . . . beyond the burden of his duty and responsibility.

*   *   *

Almost a full hour after leaving the house, he arrived at his destination, where thick woodland hid him from the world and high trees almost blocked out the skies above.

The winding, babbling stream glittered in the morning light, and look there! Excited, he inched forward to see two small deer drinking at the water's edge. This was what he needed. Through the week when he was driven by work and duties,

7

this was the magic his soul craved.

He made his way towards the little log cabin, built by his own hand over two long, wonderful years. Afterwards, when it was finished he would sit on the covered veranda for many an hour, lazing and thinking, and though his troubles were heavy, he always found time to thank the Lord for his many blessings. The land had been owned by his family for generations, and he had spent happy childhood summer holidays riding, fishing and picnicking here, when visiting his grandparents nearby.

Taking the key from his pocket he slid it into the keyhole and opened the door. As always, when he came back after a week away, the clammy, damp air instantly wrapped itself around him. Impatiently he threw back the wooden shutters and opened the windows to let the fresh air in. When that was done, he took a box of matches from his pocket and struck it against the stone wall surrounding the fireplace. When the match-head flickered into life, he set light to the carefully laid pyramid of paper and wood in the grate.

Soon, the fire was cheerily blazing, airing and warming the whole cabin.

He felt a sense of pride in his achievement. The place was strong, built to last, with a tiny bedroom, makeshift bathroom, and a large centre area providing a sitting room and kitchen. Serviceable and attractive, the cabin was ideal for his own modest needs.

The furniture itself had been hewn from the trees outside, before being lovingly shaped by his own hand, to provide all that was needed: a small, square table and two chairs; a strong, deep chest of drawers; a long settle against the fireplace, where he would sit of an evening and dream of a life he would never have.

Then there was the bed. Square and sturdy enough to take a man's weight, it was a handsome thing. Covered in a wine-coloured eiderdown, it was roomy enough for two. After all, he could dream . . .

Beside the bed stood a narrow wardrobe, not spacious by any standards, but enough to hold his most cherished possessions.

To use the bath and washbasin he would carry bucketfuls of water from the stream, and there was an earth closet in a separate little shack.

If he got hungry there was always a supply of tinned food in the larder, and titbits to be gathered in the woods, depending on the time of year. Running wild in those idyllic childhood holidays had been excellent training for cabin life.

Now, with the fire crackling and spitting, he was ever mindful of the falling sparks, any one of which could burn the cabin to the ground; which was why he had built the deep stone hearth. He had also fashioned a makeshift wire cage, which he now placed in front of the leaping flames.

Having placed the guard before the now crackling fire, he went to the wardrobe. He took out the canvas and easel and carried them to the corner of the room. He did not uncover the painting. Instead he held it for a moment, his thoughts going to a cosy little café in the centre of Blackburn. That was another part of his secret life. Then he set the frame on the easel.

From the chest he took out a pile of clothes and draped them over the wire cage of the fire guard to warm and air, while he stripped off his suit, shirt and tie.

When he was dressed again the businessman was gone and in his place was an ordinary workman, dressed casually in brown cords, green check shirt and heavy black boots. The uniform of duty was discarded, and he was now a man at ease with himself.

Now was the moment he'd anticipated with pleasure since his last visit. With great care he slipped the cover from the painting.

When it was laid bare he gazed at it for a long, wondrous moment, his dark, smiling eyes roving its every feature.

Smiling back at him, the young woman with the tumble of hazel hair seemed almost alive. Her laughing eyes, blue as the darkest sapphire, were painted in such a way as to be looking at him wherever he went in the room. Her pretty, slightly parted lips seemed so real he felt she would suddenly talk to him. But she never did, except in his dreams. She probably never would.

Yet he knew her well, that small, vibrant woman who had invaded his thoughts. A special part of his Tuesday life, she hardly knew of his existence.

Returning to the wardrobe he collected his paints and brushes. A few moments later he was stroking the tip of the brush over the curling ends of her brown hair. 'You don't know me,' he murmured fondly, 'but I feel I know you. I've seen how you light up a room when you walk into it . . .' Images of her came into his mind—going about her own Tuesday life, laughing with her friend—making him smile. 'And I know you have a wonderful sense of humour.'

Changing his brush, he worked on her cheekbones. 'You can't imagine how much I've been looking forward to seeing you.'

He paused, his thoughts going back to the house and the woman who waited there. 'Maybe it's just as well you don't even notice me,' he sighed. 'You see, Amy . . . a man might dream and hope, but dreams are not real, and life can drag you down. I do my best, but I'm hopelessly trapped. If only I can find a way to change how things are.'

*   *   *

That night as he sat on his veranda watching the stars twinkle and dance, a glass of wine in his hand and a great loneliness in his heart, he had no way of knowing how Amy was watching those same stars, and that in her heart were the same impossible dreams, and sense of awful loneliness.

Leaning on the windowsill, arms folded, her gaze raised to the skies, she wondered where Don was, and whether he ever thought of her. She did not wonder whether he might come back, because his parting words had been that she would never see him again. And although for many months after he'd gone, she had prayed he might change his mind and come back, he never had. Now the pain had settled to a sense of loss and disappointment with the acceptance that what he had said was true. Earlier, when he had asked her to marry him, she had been filled with such joy; not knowing that it would end in her heart being broken. There had been weeks of planning and excitement when the date was set and the church booked. The bridesmaids were chosen, the bridal gown ordered

11

and even the honeymoon arranged, before he confessed to her that he had never really wanted family or responsibilities.

Sometimes she wondered if that had been a kind excuse—a way of letting her down gently. He had been so handsome and such fun. Maybe she hadn't been good enough for him . . .

Amy had been devastated when he left, and even now the love she had felt for him still lingered.

Pressing her nose to the window she recalled the happy times they had shared.

'I don't hate you, Don,' she murmured. 'I could never hate you.'

She remembered his smile and the way he would hold her in his arms, and her heart was heavy. But she no longer fooled herself. It was over.

'Good night, Amy.' That was her mammy on the landing.

'Good night, Mam.'

'Don't forget we've an early start in the morning.'

'I won't.'

The sound of passing footsteps, then the closing of a door, and the house was quiet again.

Leaving the curtains open so she could see the stars, Amy went softly across the room and slid into bed.

She closed her eyes, shut out the memories and was quickly asleep.

CHAPTER TWO

'Don't look now, but our mystery man is here again!'

Having seen her come up the street, the young waitress flung open the door, grabbed Amy by the arm and yanked her inside the café.

'It's driving me crazy, not knowing who he is!' She stole a glance at the far table. 'He's been here half an hour,' she whispered, drawing Amy to the back of the café, 'and I *still* don't know any more about him than I did three months ago.'

'For God's sake, Daisy! Let me get my coat off.' Amy had already noticed the man as she passed the window and, as always, her own curiosity was aroused—though she would never admit it to Daisy. 'It's bitter cold out there and, if you don't mind, I need to sit down.'

Loaded with shopping bags and a face bright pink from the biting wind, she resisted Daisy's pushing and shoving. 'Get off!'

Daisy stepped back a pace. 'He hasn't said a word, except to order bacon and eggs.' She dropped her voice until it was almost inaudible. 'I'd say he were a film star . . . God knows, he's handsome enough.' She sighed. 'But you can tell he's not, because of his clothes. I reckon he must work in a factory, wearing them boots and with a flat cap.'

'Honestly, Daisy, you're becoming obsessed with the poor fella,' Amy groaned. 'Why don't you leave him alone to get on with his breakfast, instead of gawping at him every two minutes?'

13

Sliding her bags onto the nearest table, she dropped her weary self into the chair. 'God, my feet are aching.' Slipping off her shoes, she wiggled her toes. 'These new shoes don't help either! I knew I should have worn them round the bedroom a few times before going out in them.'

Daisy was incredulous. 'Listen to you, lass! Talking about shopping and shoes and moaning about the weather . . . you sound like your mam!'

'You're right,' Amy agreed with a soft laugh. 'I do, don't I?'

'I know you're curious about him too, so don't deny it!'

Leaning forward, Amy was disturbed to find the man's gaze on her. 'I'm not denying it,' she answered softly, 'I *am* curious.'

Daisy beamed with satisfaction. 'Well there you are then.'

'There I am . . . *what?*'

'You want to know about him as much as I do, so stop lecturing me.'

'I'm not "lecturing" you.'

'You are!'

'All right then, I am, and for good reason.'

'And what might that be?'

'Two things.' Taking off the pretty dark blue hat with its tiny brim and blue cotton band, Amy ran her fingers through her short brown hair. 'For all we know, he could be a really dangerous man, and he must know how much you're attracted to him, the way you keep sneaking a look at him with those big, moony cow eyes. You could be playing with fire. That's the first thing.'

'And what's the second?'

Lazily placing the hat on the nearby chair, Amy

warned, 'If there's nothing sinister about him, and he's just a man who likes to be left alone, you should leave him be. If you frighten him off, you'll lose one of your best customers—and then you'll never find out who he is.'

While Daisy considered her remarks, Amy took off her coat. 'Now then, are you going to serve me or what?'

Daisy gave a long, impatient sigh. 'Being as we're quiet, can I sit with you? It's time for my break anyway.'

'All right. If you promise not to drive me mad.'

Daisy rolled her 'moony cow eyes'. 'What d'you want to eat—same as usual, is it?'

While Amy glanced quickly through the one-page menu of fry-ups, barm cakes and pie-and-peas, Daisy's attention drifted to the man, then back again to Amy, her one and only friend.

She had taken to Amy the first minute she'd wandered into the café some two years ago. It had been a grim, wet day and Amy had got caught in a downpour. Having sought refuge in Tooley's Café, she had brought it alive with her bright friendly chatter and warm engaging smile. She had a streak of mischievousness that often caught Daisy off guard and made her laugh till she ached. But Daisy had also discovered her own mothering instincts when her friend's fiancé had left her, practically at the altar.

Amy was now a regular customer, always loaded down with shopping, always ready for a chat, with her down-to-earth and lovely manner. It was on Tuesdays that Amy went to pay a couple of the smaller wholesalers who supplied Atkinsons' Corner Shop, owned by her parents, and where

15

Amy herself worked. She also did the weekly shop then, her parents being too busy working to find the time. Daisy looked forward to Tuesday more than any other day of the week. In between serving customers, she would press her nose to the window, watching for Amy, knowing that when she came through that door the whole room would light up and so would Daisy's heart.

Amy had her serious side too. A good listener, she was kind and considerate, and when Daisy came to work saddened by the acrimonious situation at home between her parents, Amy gave her hope for the future, and Daisy had come to see her as the sister she never had.

Although, at twenty-four, Amy was just two years older than Daisy, she had a calmer, deeper nature, and that special ability to put people at their ease; whether it be through her engaging smile, or her easy, friendly manner.

She was not dazzlingly attractive, but she had a certain magnetism that seemed to draw people to her. Her face was small and heart-shaped, with a halo of light brown hair that fell in natural waves about her ears, and her mouth was generous, with full lips upturned at the corners, like a smile waiting to happen. Her eyes were her best feature, though—deepest blue with a naughty twinkle. Small of build, she had a slight figure, and it only took a few minutes of knowing her to realise she had a warm, open heart.

Daisy knew what Amy would order, but she asked all the same. 'You'd best make your mind up,' she urged. 'Any minute now, I could be rushed off my feet.'

Amy looked about the half-empty café: there

16

was the man by the window; a little old couple in the corner, Daisy and herself. 'I don't think there's any danger of that just yet,' she teased, 'but just in case, I'll have a pot of tea . . . and one of your toasted barm cakes.'

Daisy shook her head. 'Sorry, no can do. The toaster blew up. We're waiting for the fella to come and mend it.' She laughed. 'You should have seen it this time . . . there was a big bang and the bloody toast went flying in all directions. Come and look.'

Amused, Amy followed her. 'Not again? That's the third time!'

Daisy shrugged. 'There must be a fault somewhere.'

Smiling, Amy shook her head in disbelief. 'It's you. *You're* the "fault". You're not supposed to snatch the plug from the wall every time you think the toast is done enough. You have to switch it off first.'

'Then it burns the toast!'

'That's because you haven't got the setting right.'

'It's a nuisance! I don't like the bloody thing. I never have.'

'So, use the grill instead.'

'Mrs Tooley won't let me. She says she's not spending good money on new things for me to ignore them. That toaster is her pride and joy. I'm to use it, and that's an end to it. I did use the grill once, when the toaster went wrong and she tore me off a strip for making a mess everywhere.'

'But Mrs Tooley only comes of an evening to collect her takings.'

'What's that got to do with it?'

Amy explained, 'Well, now that she's got her new fancy man, she hardly ever shows up here during

the day, so she won't know you're using the grill—
not if you clean it up half an hour before she
arrives.'

As the possibilities dawned on her, Daisy's frown
became a wide, cunning grin. 'You're right!' she
gasped. 'I'll use the old things and clean 'em up
before she gets here!'

'I'm glad that's settled!' Amy knew how to put a
smile on Daisy's face. 'So now, can I please have
my tea and barm cake?' Feeling mischievous, she
teased, 'And while you're gone, I'll have a word
with the stranger. I'll find out who he is and where
he's from. Oh, and you'll want to know if he's
married or if he's got a girlfriend, and whether he's
well off or stony-broke, in which case you won't
want to know any more about him and we'll all get
some peace. OK?'

Daisy knew she was being teased and went along
with it. 'While you're at it, happen you'd best ask if
he lives local, 'cos I followed him one time and he
suddenly disappeared—went down a side street
and was gone like will-o'-the-wisp.' She threw her
arms wide and opened her hands to demonstrate.

Amy was surprised. 'You never told me you
followed him!'

'No, because you'd have told me off good and
proper.'

'Quite right too.' Amy put on her most severe,
reprimanding look. 'Following men down alleyways
. . . what if he'd turned round and attacked you?'

Daisy chuckled. 'I should be so lucky!' She
glanced through the kitchen door at the man.
'Anyhow, does he look like the sort who would
attack anyone?'

Amy followed her glance. 'Maybe not, but you

never know.'

He was certainly a mystery, she thought. Although as Daisy said, he didn't seem like the sort who would turn on a woman. There was a kind of gentle strength about him that would protect rather than hurt.

'I'll get your order,' Daisy said, adding hopefully, 'I bet you won't dare speak to him while I'm gone.'

Amy continued the charade. 'If I do, and providing he gives all the right answers, I'll ask him if he'll take you on a date, because you fancy him summat rotten.'

'Oh, I wish you would,' Daisy sighed. 'Three whole months he's been coming here. Almost every Tuesday without fail, and I don't even know his name!'

Realising she would have to wait for her breakfast, Amy resigned herself to listening while Daisy chatted on about the 'Tuesday man'.

Taking a moment to observe this busy, bumbling person she had come to know so well, Amy took in the big brown eyes, the shock of wild auburn hair and the pretty face with its multitude of freckles over a pretty, pert nose. Short and voluptuous, outgoing and friendly, Daisy was once seen never forgotten.

Amy thought of Daisy's miserable home life, with the constantly feuding parents.

For as long as Amy had known her, Daisy had suffered wretchedly at the hands of her selfish, boorish parents. Their noisy, sometimes violent, arguments, often fuelled by drink, meant that Daisy could never invite Amy to her home. In Mrs Tooley's fuggy little café, Daisy could escape the unhappiness of her home by chatting with the customers, teasing and joking with the friendly regulars, and even flirting a little with the men. In this way, Daisy could create some much-needed fun in her life.

'Look, Daisy . . . don't get too infatuated with your Tuesday man,' Amy warned. 'If he'd wanted you to know who he is, I'm sure he would have told you.'

'But he *wants* to talk,' Daisy confided, 'I can tell that much. Sometimes he looks so sad, and sometimes he smiles at me and I want to sit next to him like I'm sitting next to you, only he looks away, just when I think I'm getting through to him.'

Amy shook her head. 'Maybe he's not such a "mystery",' she said quietly. 'Maybe he comes in here because he lives alone and needs to be amongst people. Or maybe he comes in here because he's got a wife and ten children and he can't get any peace at home. Either way, if he needs to be quiet and alone for whatever reason, it's his choice and you should respect that.'

Casting a sideways glance out at the man, Amy sensed his loneliness. Daisy was right: he *was* a mystery—always preoccupied, head bent to his newspaper, while not seeming to be actually reading it. Instead he appeared to be deep in thought. Sometimes he would raise his head and gaze out of the window, before eventually returning to his newspaper or thoughtfully sipping his tea.

He never looked at the other customers; in fact it was as though he was totally oblivious to them. It was a curious thing.

'What are you thinking?' Daisy's voice cut through her thoughts.

Amy looked up, her voice quiet as she answered,

'I just think he deserves to be left alone.' She smiled fondly at the other young woman. 'Not everybody's like you, Daisy,' she pointed out. 'Some people really do like their own company.'

Daisy shifted her gaze to the man. For a long moment she didn't say anything, but there was a troubled look in her eyes.

'Daisy, are you all right?' Reaching out, Amy closed her hand over Daisy's. 'Has something happened at home?'

Daisy shook her head. 'It's the same,' she confided with a sad little smile, 'always the same.' Drawing away her hand she added brightly, 'Here's me chatting away and you cold and famished. Sorry, love. I'll go an' get yer breakfast.'

'But something's wrong, isn't it?' Amy had learned to read the signs. 'Do you want to talk about it?'

Daisy shook her head.

'All right, but I'm a good listener if you need me.'

Daisy gave that little smile again. 'I know that.' With a roll of her eyes, she looked over to where the man was closing his newspaper. 'If only a man like that could sweep me up and carry me off, it would solve everything.'

'Oh, Daisy. You can't mean that!'

'Why not?'

'Well . . .'

Amy took another discreet look at him. He was certainly handsome, there was no denying that, with his long easy limbs, fine sensual lips and that dark brown tumble of hair. Once, when he looked up at the clock over the counter, Amy had caught sight of his dark, brooding eyes. There was something about him that stirred the senses.

21

'Hey!' Daisy gave her a prod. 'You were saying . . .?'

Ashamed and startled at her own thoughts, Amy returned, 'I just don't think it would solve your problems to run off with some stranger and, besides, like you said yourself, you don't know the first thing about him.'

'But if he carried me off, I'd soon find out, wouldn't I? Anyway, what's to know? He pays his bill with proper money, and he always treats me with respect. Leaves a tip he does, and smiles up at me when I serve him.' She gave a girlish giggle. 'Anyway, even if it turned out he was some sort of rogue, he's so good-looking it wouldn't matter a bugger! A man like that . . . I could forgive him anything!'

Amy was alarmed. 'You're too trusting.'

'And *you're* too bloody suspicious!'

Amy changed tack. 'I'm also cold and hungry, and I've changed my mind about the barm cake. I fancy a hot meat-and-tatty pie . . . with a helping of mushy peas and a dollop of that awful gravy you make.'

Daisy bounced over to the fridge. 'Don't get cheeky, lass,' she wagged a warning finger, 'or I might refuse to serve you. In fact, I might shut up shop and lock myself in . . . with *him*!' She winked as she went. 'And it's no good you getting jealous, 'cos I'm the manager here and what I say goes.' With that she sauntered off to open a tin of peas and suddenly, softly started to sing.

'Whatever makes you happy,' Amy chuckled, resuming a seat at her table.

She looked across at the man and when he unexpectedly smiled at her, her heart took a leap.

For what seemed an age he held her gaze before turning away.

Confused and embarrassed, she fumbled in her shopping bag. Drawing out this month's *Woman and Home*, she opened it up and spreading it across the table, pretended to read. In her mind's eye she saw his smile, soft and friendly, reaching out to her . . . and those wonderful dark eyes! Daisy was right. He was devilishly handsome, and yet, there was such sadness about him—a kind of lost look that had touched her deeply.

'What you got there?' Daisy was back. Placing Amy's order in front of her, she turned the page of the magazine. 'Heck! Look at that!' Pointing to the elegant model in centre-page, she called Amy's attention to the blue spotted dress with thick belt and flared hem, *'How much!'* Her look of rapture turned to one of horror. 'One and ten! I'd have to work a whole month before I could buy that!'

Amy wasn't listening. Something else had alerted her. Strangely uneasy, she turned to see the man looking straight at her again. He held her gaze for a second or two, then he stood up and walked towards the door with long easy strides. 'I think your mystery man is leaving,' Amy told Daisy quietly.

'What!' Looking up, Daisy saw the door close behind him. 'Damn! He *always* does that to me!'

Amy tutted mischievously. 'What? You mean he sneaks off without paying?'

'No, you daft ha'pporth!' Daisy groaned. 'He always leaves his money on the table. I wish he'd pay at the counter, then I might get chance to quiz him a bit.'

Amy's curious gaze followed him as he went past

23

the window and away down the street. 'Maybe next time,' she said quietly. 'But I wouldn't count on it if I were you.' Because there was a man who had a lot on his mind, she thought, and he wasn't about to share his secrets with anyone at Tooley's Café.

Just then two more customers arrived, a middle-aged woman with a younger woman who, judging by the argument going on, appeared to be her daughter. 'What in God's name d'yer think you're playing at?' demanded the older woman. 'By! If your dad knew, he'd hit the roof!'

'I don't give a bugger what he says!' snapped the younger woman. 'It's *his* fault I'm leaving. Miserable old git, I don't know how you've put up with him all these years!'

Daisy groaned. 'Bleedin' Nora! It's them two! Argue all the time, they do. I've a good mind to bar the pair of 'em.'

Amy couldn't help but laugh. 'Good customers, are they?'

Daisy nodded. 'Three times a week, regular as clockwork: two full breakfasts and gallons of tea.'

'Right!' Amy gave her a shove. 'What you do is shut your ears . . . if you can bear not to eavesdrop. Then you smile, and serve them and take their money when they've finished. And now if you please, I'd like my breakfast.' With that she gave Daisy another shove and Daisy toddled off to ask the other customers, 'What can I get you, ladies?' And back came the swift answer, 'Piss orf. Can't yer see we're not ready yet!'

Cursing under her breath, Daisy quickened her steps to the kitchen; while Amy, having heard the whole thing, found it hard not to laugh out loud.

When behind her, the argument raged on

24

between the two women, she looked up to see Daisy, elbows resting on the counter, ears pricked and eavesdropping like a good 'un. 'That's my Daisy!' she chuckled. 'Can't resist a good argument.'

Amy loved her Tuesday shopping, and her regular stop-off at Tooley's Café because rain or shine, there was always something going on.

Then, as thoughts of the man came into her mind, her amusement turned to concern. What made him so afraid to reach out, she wondered. What was it in his life that put the sadness in those deep, dark eyes?

Like Daisy she would have loved to know more about him.

She glanced out the window but he was long gone. 'A burden shared is a burden halved,' she murmured. And he had seemed to want to talk, she thought. Just for that split second or two when he held her gaze, he had seemed to be reaching out to her.

But then again, maybe it was only her imagination.

CHAPTER THREE

'What plans have you got for tonight, lass?' Strikingly pretty, small-built like Amy, and with the same bright smile and brown hair, Marie Atkinson was mild-tempered and of a kindly nature. 'Off somewhere exciting are you?'

It was a Friday evening and Amy was busy emptying the till in the shop. She glanced up at her mother. 'I might go to the pictures with Daisy.'

'Hmm! Sounds like a good idea.' When she was younger, Marie had always fancied herself as a film star. 'What's on?'

Concentrating on separating the silver coins from the less valuable copper ones, Amy said, 'I think it's Charles King in *The Broadway Melody*.'

Marie liked the sound of that. 'By! If your dad weren't coming home tonight, I might have joined you,' she said dreamily. 'Ooh! I do like Charles King.' She tap-danced on the spot. 'Feet of magic and a smile that turns you inside out. I wouldn't mind a little twirl with him.'

Amy laughed. 'Don't give me that! If it was a choice between Dad and Charles King, you'd pick Dad every time.'

Marie kept on dancing. 'Happen I'll let your dad get his own dinner. Happen I'd rather put on my glad rags and go to the pictures with you and Daisy.'

Knowing how devoted to her father Marie was, Amy laughed. 'I can't see you letting Dad come home to an empty house, not even for Charles King! Besides, you've always said how nobody could ever take Dad's place.'

Exhausted, Marie stopped dancing and leaned over the counter. 'You're right, lass,' she said breathlessly. 'There's not a man in this world can ever tek the place of your father.'

Her face wreathed in a smile, she let her mind wander back over the years. 'Me and your dad have been wed almost twenty-five years, and I wouldn't swap a single minute.'

In fact their anniversary was only eight months away. 'I were just turned eighteen when we walked down the aisle,' she confirmed. 'Your father was twenty . . . though o' course he weren't your father then . . . he were just my Dave.' She sighed. 'I loved him with all my heart then. And I've loved him the same ever since.'

Amy sighed longingly. 'I wish I could find someone to love like that.' All her life Amy had witnessed the love and devotion between her mam and dad, and it was a wonderful thing. She had thought that marriage to Don would have been just the same—had envisaged a life of devotion to her gorgeous husband—and even now flashes of that golden future that would never be occasionally passed through her mind. She couldn't see how she could ever love that way again. Her parents' happiness was a living example of an idyllic marriage Amy now feared she might never have. She shrugged away the thought.

Having bagged up the takings, she came across the room and, placing the bags on the counter, she wrapped her arms round that small, delightful figure. 'After all this time you still adore him, don't you, Mam? What woman in her right mind would give up a night with Charles King to be with "your Dave", as you call him?'

Marie gave it some thought. 'Well, I'll admit your father's not as slim as Charles King and it's no wonder, with all that dancing an' tapping an' flinging himself about. By! It's a marvel he's not worn down to his kneecaps.'

Amy loved to tease and she did so now. 'Whereas Dad can't dance; and he can't tap, although I have known him "fling himself about" a bit, when he comes home three sheets to the wind.'

'No!' Marie flew to his defence. 'You've never

27

seen your father three sheets to the wind!' she protested, half smiling. 'He's only ever been the worse for drink once in the whole of his life, and that was when Grandad Atkinson got wed for the second time. Even then he didn't have the strength to "fling himself about a bit".' She chuckled. 'Though he did manage to fall down the coal-hole and bruise himself from top to bottom.'

Amy laughed. 'I bet that sobered him up.'

'It did, yes. It weren't the first time he'd fallen down the coal-hole,' she revealed. 'A natural disaster, that's your dad.'

Marie told a tale or two about what Amy's dad had got up to before she was even born, and for the next few minutes the two of them rolled about with laughter. 'On the night I decided I loved your father we were holding hands as we walked from Atkinson Street. A horse and cart ran through a puddle and splashed him from top to bottom. How could I not want to marry him after that?'

'A couple of old romantics, that's what you are.' As always, Amy's heart went out to Daisy, whose own parents were forever feuding and fighting. Tonight would be as much an escape as an entertainment for poor Daisy.

'I wish he hadn't gone driving for Hammonds, though,' Marie said thoughtfully. 'I really miss him. Why in God's name did he have to take on that delivery work? He was offered work inside the factory, but he said he didn't fancy "being cooped up". All the same, I wish he'd taken it. At least he'd have been home of a night-time.' Her frown deepened. 'I do hate him being away all week!'

Hammonds had two lines of business: a brush factory, and delivery of their own and other people's goods in a small fleet of motor lorries.

In an effort to bring back the smile to her mother's face, Amy quipped, 'Why d'you need Dad, when you've got *me*?'

Collecting up the money bags, Marie groaned. 'That's another thing. I feel guilty about you giving up your job at Wittons factory, so you could come and help run this place. *And* you were about to be promoted to the office.'

Amy was astounded. 'How did you know that?'

'Rosie Salter told me a few days after you left.'

'She should never have done that!'

'Well, she did, and I've felt bad about it ever since. I mean, you can't deny, it's a bit of a come-down for you.'

'Oh, Mam! You're not to feel guilty.' Amy enjoyed working in the shop and she told her mother so. 'Do you know what I think?'

'What?'

'I think you're sorry you asked me to come and work with you, because now you think I'm no good at shop-keeping.' By deliberately going on the defensive, Amy cunningly turned the tables on her mother. 'The truth is, you want rid of me, and you don't like to say. That's it, isn't it?'

Just as Amy suspected, Marie was mortified. 'Aw, lass, nothing could be further from the truth! I love having you here and, what's more, you've learned the business like you've been at it all your life. As a matter of fact I don't know what I'd do without you.' Collecting the money bags and the ledger into her arms, she sighed. 'It's just that, well, I really loved working with your dad, and I miss him terrible when he's not around.'

'He'll be home soon.' Amy gave her a hug. 'You

go and make yourself beautiful for him, while I mop the floor and clear up in here.'

'You'll do no such thing, my girl!' Marie insisted. 'We'll clear up together, same as always.'

A short time later, having cleared up, swept the floor and tidied away the large blocks of butter and cheese, and canisters of loose tea and broken biscuits, Marie walked with her daughter to the living quarters at the back.

'When me and your father started this business, I thought we'd be doing it together until we retired, but he just got more and more restless. He'd always been a driver, y'see, lass—first with the horse and carts, then the beer wagons, and now with these new-fangled motor vehicles . . . dangerous things if you ask me!'

At first Amy's father had seemed to settle into his new life as a grocer. Then a few months back, he'd spotted an advert in the post office for a driver at Hammonds distribution business. He applied for the job and got it. 'I'm fed up of being behind a counter all day,' he'd told Marie. 'I need to get back on the road. I'd rather not be staying away nights, but it's all they've got for the minute.' Once he'd decided, there'd been no dissuading him.

'I miss him too,' Amy confessed, 'but he's a lot happier now he's away from the shop. He loves the driving, and anyway, the week goes by quickly enough.' Amy glanced at the kitchen wall-clock. 'Look! It's already half-past five. Another hour and he'll be home,' she winked, 'with another present for you, I expect.'

Every Friday was the same. He would bounce through the door, beaming from ear to ear, with a little present in his pocket for his beloved wife, and a small posy of flowers for Amy.

Talking of her husband and knowing how sometimes Amy was lonely for the same kind of love, Marie grew serious. 'Do you ever think of Don?'

Surprised by her mammy's unexpected question, Amy nodded. 'Sometimes, yes, but it doesn't hurt in quite the same way as it did. There was a time when I would have had him back with open arms, but not any more.' When her fiancé dropped her only a few days before they were due to be wed she had thought she would never get over it, but somehow she'd survived. The pain had faded; maybe one day it would go altogether. 'I'm over it now, Mam. If he walked in that door right now, I'd speak to him, yes, but I wouldn't feel anything. Not any more.' This was in part true: nothing for it but to move forward. The love she once felt for him had long since gone.

Marie slid an arm round her. 'I'm glad about that, lass,' she said softly, before quickly changing the subject by asking brightly, 'And you're absolutely sure you don't regret giving up promotion to come here and work with me?'

'I'm content enough here,' Amy answered. And she was.

In truth, Amy had not been too keen to give up her job, and at first had missed the banter and comradeship of her factory mates. But much to her astonishment she had come to enjoy working in the corner shop. It was easy enough work, and the tasks were always varied: selling tobacco, weighing out dried peas or potatoes, unwrapping the fragrant sacks of sugar and tea, or stacking the shelves with fresh eggs or that day's newspapers.

Her mother was great company; though the wages were not as good as Amy had been used to, but there were other compensations—no journey to work, the pleasant work and the friendliness of the customers—and so she had settled into the job surprisingly well.

*   *   *

By six thirty, just as Amy had predicted, Dave arrived home. A man with no airs or graces, he was of good build, with a shock of fair hair and a homely smile, which he now bestowed on them. 'By! Summat smells good.'

Coming into the back parlour he kissed Marie first. 'Don't tell me . . .' throwing off his coat he draped it over the chair and sniffed the air, '. . . meat pie, roast potatoes and baked parsnips, am I right?'

Amy came for her kiss. 'I don't know when you've ever been wrong,' she laughed.

He joined in, then assumed an apologetic expression. 'Look, I'm sorry, but we've had such a rush on, I didn't have time to find you a present.'

'Aw, never mind, love.' Marie was philosophical. 'You've brought yourself home and that's all that matters.'

He gave her a kiss. 'You're a very understanding woman,' he said gratefully. 'There's not many men can say that about their wives.'

Marie gave him a little shove. 'You go and get your wash,' she said, 'while me and Amy get the dinner on the table.'

When he was gone into the scullery, Marie gave Amy a knowing wink. 'I've learned to be crafty as

32

him over the years,' she whispered.

Amy whispered back, 'What d'you mean?'

In answer, Marie tiptoed to her husband's jacket and, dipping her hand inside it, withdrew two small packages.

Just then, Dave shouted for a towel. 'Hurry up, Marie. I'm dripping wet!'

'Here,' handing Amy the two small packages, Marie instructed mischievously, 'hide 'em, quick!'

Dave's frantic voice sailed in from the scullery, 'MARIE!'

'All right, all right, I'm on my way!' And off she went, chuckling at their innocent deception.

A few minutes later, washed and changed and ready for his dinner, Dave returned to the parlour. 'By! A feast fit for a king!' he said, his hungry eyes roving the table. Right in the centre was the deep-dish meat pie with a brown crusty pastry and a wash of egg to make it shine.

There were two earthenware bowls: one filled with roasted potatoes, the other brimming with quartered parsnips. For Dave there was a welcome jug of beer, a glass of stout for Marie, and a tumbler of home-made elderberry wine for Amy.

'Well, don't just look at it!' Marie told him. 'Sit yourself down and eat.'

'One minute,' he said, reaching into his jacket pocket. 'I've summat here for the pair of you . . .' Chuckling, he confessed, 'I were just winding you up when I said I hadn't got you a present.'

Marie feigned excitement. 'So you brought us one after all? Oh, sweetheart, I knew you would.'

The grin on Dave's face faded as he felt in the pocket for the third time, fumbling this way, then that. 'They've gone!' he cried. 'Some thieving bugger's 'ad 'em away!'

At the look of horror on his face, Amy couldn't bear it. 'Here they are, Dad.' Collecting them from behind the clock on the sideboard she handed them to him.

When his mouth fell open with surprise, Marie laughed. 'It serves you right for teasing us. Come on then, let's see what you've brought?'

Marie's present was the prettiest brooch, shaped like a butterfly and made out of enamel. 'Aw, Dave . . .' She gave him a hug. 'It's lovely . . . *you're* lovely!'

Grinning like a Cheshire cat, he seemed embarrassed, though he enjoyed her fussing round him. 'You know how I like to give you nice things,' he said proudly. 'It's only what you deserve.' He glanced at Amy. 'Come on, lass . . . open your present.'

Amy was thrilled with hers too. The necklace was a tiny heart, shaped in silver, and when she put it on, both Marie and Dave said how pretty it looked on her.

'Thanks, Dad.' She too gave him a fond hug. 'But you shouldn't spend your money on us like that.'

Indignant, he asked sombrely, 'If I can't spend it on the two most important people in my life, who *can* I spend it on?'

There was no answer to that, except for Marie to say, 'Let's eat our dinners, afore they go cold!'

*   *   *

As they ate, the three of them chatted and laughed, and Dave told of his latest disaster.

34

'For the life of me, I don't know how it happened,' he began excitedly. 'Soonever I was given the address, I knew straight off there were a good many narrow little streets in that area, some of 'em virtually impassable, especially with a lorry that size. The new foreman assured me there was no problem as the road widened out at the end and I could drive straight through. But when I got halfway down, I knew some bugger had been playing silly devils with me, 'cos instead of the road getting wider, it got narrower. In the end I couldn't go forrard and it seemed there were too many twists and turns to go backards.'

'Sounds frightening.' Against all odds, but urged on by Daisy, Amy had once secretly considered learning to drive, but the tales her dad came home with had put her off altogether. Dave had a little car, his pride and joy, but now Amy couldn't envisage being one of the pioneer female drivers of Blackburn.

'Aye, it *were* frightening an' all, lass!' Rolling his eyes he groaned. 'In fact it were a bloody nightmare!'

Marie was horrified. 'So what did you do?'

'Well, I had no option, did I? All I could do was to feel my way back inch by inch. Unfortunately I badly scraped the side of the wagon and almost demolished a wall on the way.'

Once he got into the swing of it, Dave could tell a tale as well as any man, and on this particular occasion he had a riveted audience.

'Not content with that, soonever I got the back end out I swung my front round to avoid a lamppost,' he continued. 'I missed the lamppost all right, but knocked down two bollards in the

35

process, and ran over some poor bloke's bicycle.'

Amy could see it all so vividly in her mind, she couldn't stop laughing. 'You're a one-man demolition party!'

'It weren't my fault,' Dave protested, indignant. 'The buggers should have had more sense than sending me there in the first place!'

'But that poor man . . . what did he have to say about his bike?'

'Well, he weren't too pleased, I can tell yer that. Yelled and shouted he did—went bright red in the face; said as how I should be locked up for my own safety, the cheeky article! On top o' that, he wanted me to pay for a new bike, but I told him, I said, "If you're daft enough to park it by the kerbside, you expect to get it run over."'

Marie was curious. 'And was he content with that?'

'Were he buggery! Threatened to fetch the police if I didn't pay up, but I'm no pushover. I stuck to my guns.' He puffed out his chest. 'As you know, I'm not a man who's easily threatened!'

'So what did you do?'

With a defiant look, he explained, 'Well, what d'yer think I did? I paid him half what he said. I mean, what else could I do under the circumstances? I had no intention o' paying him the full whack, I can tell you that. But y'see, I didn't want no police on the scene. They'd have only made me later coming home to you, my darling.' The expression on his face was a picture. 'And we couldn't be having that, could we now?'

All three laughed at his antics. It had been a good day, and an excellent meal, and as Dave went for his evening 'constitutional', Marie and Amy

36

cleared away the dinner things. 'It's good to have him home,' Marie said, and Amy agreed. Such contentment—she had envisaged such a marriage for herself, but she knew, even so, that she was fortunate to share in her parents' happy lives. After all, what would Daisy give for this much love?

Dave returned just as Amy came down the stairs, having gone to get ready. 'By! You look lovely, lass.' He beamed with pride. 'Off somewhere nice, are you?'

'Me and Daisy are going to the pictures.' Amy blushed at his compliment, but then she had taken a lot of trouble to look especially nice.

The long dark skirt had been a birthday present from her mother, and to go with it, Amy had bought a pale blue blouse and close-fitting jacket of darker blue. With her small-heeled ankle-strap shoes and the pretty spotted scarf at her throat she looked and felt good.

'Your dad's right,' Marie agreed. 'You look beautiful in that outfit.'

Aware that she was no beauty, but grateful for their compliments, Amy kissed her parents cheerio and promised not to be too late home.

'And mind them roads!' Dave warned. 'It won't be long afore the motor vehicles outnumber the horse and carts. Mind you, some of them drivers couldn't even control a dog on a lead, let alone a thing with an engine in it.'

'You worry too much,' Amy chided as she hurried out the door. 'I'll be fine.'

Marie waved her daughter off at the door, then returned to the parlour and her beloved husband. 'She's a good lass, don't you think?'

'Aye.' He smiled and nodded. 'She teks after her

mammy.'

Winking meaningfully, he patted his knee. 'Look here, lass. There's a sizeable lap going begging,' he said invitingly. 'All it needs is a pretty woman to plonk her bare bottom on it, and I'll be happy as a pig in muck.'

Softly laughing, she went to him. 'You're a randy old thing, Dave Atkinson,' she said, nibbling his ear.

'And who can blame me, eh,' hugging her tight, he kissed her full on the mouth, 'when I've got the best-looking woman in the whole o' Lancashire?'

Marie laughed, and as her smile met his, there was no doubting her love for him. 'Are you after my body?'

'What do *you* think?'

Marie smiled softly. 'I think the same as you,' she whispered. 'What's more, I think we ought to do summat about it.'

He kissed her again. 'A woman after my own heart, that's what you are, Marie Atkinson.'

A moment later the two of them went up the stairs together.

With Dave away all week it seemed such an age since they had made love.

CHAPTER FOUR

A trip to the pictures was always a treat, and tonight was no exception.

'Am I glad to see you!' Daisy was already waiting in Blackburn town centre as Amy disembarked from the tram. 'I've been waiting here for ages.'

38

Linking arms with her friend, Daisy was talkative as usual. 'You should have seen this good-looking fella just now,' she sighed. 'He weren't nearly as handsome as our Tuesday man, but I wouldn't mind having him for a sweetheart.'

Amy laughed. 'How do you know he hasn't already got a sweetheart?'

'I expect he has,' Daisy groaned. 'I expect every decent, good-looking man has already been claimed.' The long-drawn-out sigh came from her very soul. 'I can see I'm destined to grow old and miserable and never know what it's like to have a fella of my own.'

Something in Daisy's voice and manner told Amy things weren't right. 'What's the matter?' Drawing her to a halt, Amy asked gently, 'There's something wrong at home, isn't there?' She remembered Daisy's barely concealed unhappiness at the café last Tuesday morning.

Daisy lowered her gaze. 'How do you know that?'

Amy always knew. 'Well, for one thing, I got here at the time we arranged, and yet you said you'd been waiting ages for me.'

Daisy nodded. 'Well, if you must know, there's hell going on at home,' she admitted in a trembling voice. 'That's why I came out early, to wait for you.'

'Have you had anything to eat?'

Daisy shook her head.

'OK!' Glancing about, Amy was relieved to see the hot-potato stand was here as usual. 'The first thing we do is get you something to eat. Then we'll skip the pictures and find a quiet little place where we can sit and talk.'

Daisy was emphatic. 'I don't want to talk.'

39

'So, what do you want to do?'

'Go to the pictures, like we said.'

'Are you hungry?'

'I might be.'

'Well then, we've time enough, so it's hot potatoes first, then the pictures. All right?'

In fact everything was 'all right' to Daisy whenever she was with Amy. It was only when she was home with her parents that life was unbearable. The sound of their angry screaming voices still rang in her head. No, she'd make an effort; she wouldn't let them spoil her evening. Pulling her shoulders back, she straightened her coat and tossed her auburn curls. 'All right,' she grinned.

Linking arms again, the two of them went towards the hot-potato stand.

'Evening, girls.' A short, round little man in a grey coat, the stallholder resembled one of his own potatoes. 'Off to the pictures, are you?'

While he served them, he chatted about the weather and told them how pretty they were and flirted outrageously. Daisy responded in a like manner and earned herself an extra large potato, while Amy laughed to see her friend determined to enjoy herself.

Amy paid for the two bags of hot potatoes smothered in salt, and butter, which dripped from the bottom of the bag. 'Mind it doesn't get on your coat,' she urged Daisy, who was tucking in as she walked. 'You'll have a terrible job getting it out.'

Seating themselves on a nearby bench, they sat and enjoyed their meal; though Amy was full to bursting, having already had a good dinner. Still, she didn't confess that to Daisy. Instead, under

40

Daisy's watchful eye, she ate every bit of her delicious potato.

Delighted to see how Daisy wolfed her food, Amy laughed at the way her friend puffed and blew and complained about how hot it was—'It's burning my bloody mouth!' But she soon devoured it, skin and all.

Afterwards, with Daisy seeming more content, the two of them took off for the picture house and, feeling too full for words, Amy was thankful for the brisk walk across the square.

The Roxy was a grand-looking place, with plush red seats in the auditorium, thick carpet underfoot, and a man softly playing the organ at the front.

'There's two seats along there.'

The usherette shone her torch along the dimly lit row, and carefully as she could, Amy led the way, while behind her she could hear chaos unfolding. When she glanced back it was carnage, with everyone they'd passed bending forward, clutching their poor mangled feet where Daisy had trodden on them.

The silent, hateful glances that followed hastened them to their seats, and Amy, for one, was thankful to sit down.

'Clumsy devils!' The last poor man they'd passed appeared to be in agony. 'If folks would only get here in good time, there'd be none o' this!'

'Oh, stop moaning, you miserable sod!' Giving him a withering glance, Daisy flicked down her seat and almost fell on the floor when it sprang back up. 'Damned thing!' By now, Daisy was ready to take on the world.

Amy held the seat down while Daisy plonked her backside on it. 'Sit down and behave,' she chuckled, 'unless you want us to get thrown out.'

Then all was quiet. For the moment.

As always the picture house was full. There were little old folk at the front, families in the middle and sweethearts at the back.

Once or twice Daisy glanced at the sweethearts kissing and canoodling, and twining themselves round each other. 'Look at them! It's disgusting!' she said. But Amy knew how much Daisy would have loved to be seated at the back with a sweetheart wrapped round her.

'Ssh!' The woman behind wagged a finger at Daisy. 'Be quiet!'

Daisy fell silent and for a moment she seemed to be deep in thought; though Amy suspected she was thinking about her parents and the way it was at home.

Luckily, the organ music soon swelled in a crescendo and the film started.

To Amy's relief, Daisy was soon tapping her feet along with the master of dance, Charles King, and as the film progressed, her whole mood changed. Her eyes shone and her whole body twitched to the music, and for a time she was content and happy in a different world.

Amy too enjoyed the film. It was fast and furious, and all too soon it was the interval.

'What d'you want, lass?' Standing up ready to queue for refreshments, Daisy waited for Amy's answer.

'Nothing for me, thanks,' Amy told her. She was still full to bursting.

Daisy shrugged, 'Suit yourself,' and off she went, leaving another trail of broken toes and complaining voices as she made her way through.

Having stood in the queue for what seemed an age, Daisy was next to be served. 'A bag of popcorn please, gal,' she told the usherette.

'No popcorn, sorry.' Grim-faced and fed up, the young woman had no interest in her work. As it happened that very morning, she had been turned down for a job as train-driver. Consequently, she was not in the best of moods.

Brought down by her own problems, Daisy was ready for anything the other woman had to throw at her. 'So what have yer got then?' she demanded impatiently.

Adjusting the strap round her neck so as to relieve the weight of her tray, the usherette ran both hands through the array of goodies, muttering as she searched, 'No popcorn . . . and I've just sold the last of the chocolate bars.' Wiping her nose with the back end of her cuff, she said wearily, 'There's only ice cream left now.'

'Haven't yer got no nuts?' Hopeful, Daisy peered into the tray. 'I don't fancy ice cream.'

Angrily making another quick search of the tray, the usherette shook her head. 'Ice cream. Take it or leave it.'

'Are you sure there are no nuts in the back-room?'

Laughing aloud at Daisy's suggestion, the usherette told her, 'The only "nuts" in there are the manager and his fancy-bit.'

She leaned forward. 'I don't think they'd thank me for barging in . . . if you know what I mean?' Her sly little wink left nothing to the imagination.

'Lucky them!' Daisy laughed.

'HEY!' The angry voice sailed up the queue. 'The damned picture will be started soon! Cut the chatter and get on with it, will you?'

Fearing for her job, the usherette demanded of Daisy, 'So do you want an ice cream or not?'

Daisy held out her loose change. 'Go on then, gal. If that's all there is, I've got no choice, have I?'

Clutching a tub of ice cream, Daisy fought her way back, amused to see how, in the ten minutes since she'd joined it, the queue was now snaking along the aisle.

'So, it's *you* who's been holding up the queue, is it?' Lolling on the back of a seat, the brash young man turned Daisy's heart over with his winning smile. 'Can't make up your mind what you want, eh?' Fair-haired and of small build, he had a wiriness that made her think of a terrier.

Returning his cheeky smile, Daisy held up the ice-cream tub. 'I wanted popcorn,' she said, 'but this was all she had left.'

'Got a hankering for popcorn, have you?' He moved an inch or two closer, but not so far that he might lose his place in the queue.

'I might have.' Touching the tip of her nose with her finger she gave him a haughty glance. 'Though it's none o' your business.'

Undeterred, he shifted back into the queue. 'With your boyfriend, are you?'

Daisy smiled. 'I've not got no boyfriend at the minute.'

The young man licked his lips. 'All alone then, eh?'

'No.'

'Oh?' Disappointment coloured his voice.

'Who've you got with you then?' He glanced about, but quickly returned his attention to her. 'Not your mam and dad, is it?' he asked warily.

Daisy bristled. 'I wouldn't even cross the street with them two!'

'Is that so?' As the queue shifted, he went with it. 'Like that, is it?'

'Like *what*?' On the defensive now, Daisy didn't care for the way the conversation was going.

'Looks to me like you don't get on with your parents.' Taking hold of her arm, he held her there, a gleam of mischief in his small, bright eyes. 'Been a naughty girl, have you?'

Daisy shook him off. 'Like I said, it's none of your damned business!'

When she hurried away, he tried to follow her, but the picture was starting and the dispersing queue blocked his path. 'Wait for me at the main doors,' he called after her, and, secretly thrilled, Daisy pretended not to hear.

She returned to her seat, irritated by the medley of voices threatening to have her chucked out. 'You've mangled my toes once too often!' cried one irate woman.

'If you shifted your bloody great feet out the way,' Daisy snapped back, 'I wouldn't be able to "mangle" 'em, would I?'

Throwing herself into the seat, she was horrified when the randy old codger in the next seat stroked her knee suggestively. 'Take no notice of them,' he urged.

When she glared at him, he leered at her. 'You're a pretty young thing,' he whispered, curling his fingers tighter about her thigh. 'What say you and me leave for a while, eh?'

45

Daisy smiled her best, at the same time spilling her tub of ice cream all over his trousers. 'Whoops!' Digging Amy in the ribs, she said, feigning innocence, 'Oh dear, look what I've just done to this poor *old* man!'

Unaware of what had gone before, Amy was astonished to see the man leap out of his seat, his trousers dripping ice cream, and a wet patch forming round his flies.

'YOU DID THAT ON PURPOSE!'

He caused such a fuss that the usherette came running. 'What the devil's going on here?'

'Ask *him*!' Grabbing Amy's arm, Daisy forced her way past. 'You should be careful who you let in here,' she informed the usherette. 'The dirty old git needed cooling off. A dollop of ice cream round his old what-not seems to have done the trick, though.'

Outside, the two girls collapsed laughing.

'Did you see the look on his face?' Amy chuckled.

'Serves him right!' Daisy replied. 'Filthy old sod.'

'I hope you're not talking about *me*?' It was the young man who had tried chatting up Daisy earlier. He was leaning against the wall, another man, of about the same age, with him.

'No, I didn't mean you.' Her ready smile told how she was pleased to see him. 'Some randy old bugger and his wandering hands. I had to teach him a lesson!'

'So it was *you* causing all that fuss?'

'It was.' In truth she was quite proud to have dealt with the matter so efficiently.

'Put him in his place, did you?'

Daisy grinned. 'I dropped a tub of ice cream in his lap . . . that cooled him off all right.'

The young man laughed. 'I'd best watch my p's and q's when you're around.'

'That's right . . . you had.'

He sidled closer. 'Are we on for a date then?'

Daisy decided to play it casual. 'We might be.'

He persisted. 'Well, are we or not?'

Daisy glanced at his mate. A quiet man with lean figure and intense gaze, he seemed well taken with Amy. 'Who's your friend?'

'This is Jack . . .' beckoning his friend forward, he introduced him, '. . . Jack Tomlinson. We work together and we're good pals.' He half smiled. 'Jack never has much to say, but he thinks a lot. Not like me. I take things as they come.'

His gaze fixing Amy, Jack stepped forward. 'Pleased to meet you . . .' he hesitated, '. . . I don't know your name.'

Amy held out her hand. 'I'm Amy.' Ever cautious, she saw no need to elaborate on that, at least for now.

Holding her hand for a moment longer than she would have liked, he smiled down on her. 'Pretty name.'

'Thank you.' He seemed a nice enough fella.

'And I'm Roy.' The sharp little man stepped forward, addressing himself to Daisy. 'Let me guess . . . you've got to be a Joanne . . . or mebbe Ruth, am I right?'

She giggled. 'I'm Daisy. Pretty as a flower.'

Feeling uncomfortable about the way the young man was eyeing Daisy, Amy intervened. 'Lovely meeting you both, but we've a tram to catch.'

Daisy, though, was already infatuated. 'Oh, Amy, we've time to find a chippie first,' she protested. 'Don't forget we left the flicks early, so we've got

47

some extra time.'

Amy, horrified at the idea of yet more food, was about to disagree, but the young man called Roy pounced on the idea at once. 'I know where there's a good chippie!' Grabbing Daisy by the arm, he suggested, 'We could have fish and chips, then find a quiet place to talk . . . if that's what you'd like?'

Before Amy could say anything, Daisy had agreed and the four of them were on their way, in the direction of the docks, being led by Daisy and her chatty companion.

'They seem to have hit it off together, don't they?' Bringing up the rear, Jack walked at a more sedate pace with Amy. 'I wish I was more like him. He makes friends so easily, while I've always found it difficult.'

Amy smiled at that. 'Daisy's the same,' she said, adding cautiously, 'Is he all right though, your friend?'

'How d'you mean?' Jack gave her a curious glance.

'He won't take advantage of her, will he?'

'In what way?'

'Daisy is going through a bad time at the minute, and I wouldn't like to see her hurt.' There was no point beating about the bush. 'It's just that, well, your friend seems a bit of a flirt . . . too full of himself for my liking.'

Jack smiled knowingly. 'You're right. He can be a bit of a flirt, but it's just his manner. He doesn't mean anything by it.'

They walked on, the night closing in around them, and Amy growing slightly alarmed at the way in which Roy was all over Daisy. When they turned down a darkened side street, her fears grew.

'Daisy, where do you think you're going?'

Laughing, Daisy called back, 'To the chippie, o' course . . . where d'you think?'

'There's no chippie down here.' Amy knew the streets of Blackburn like the back of her hand. 'We'd best turn back . . . we don't want to miss the last tram.'

'Oh, stop your worrying!' came the reply. 'We're going the long way round, that's all.'

As they walked on, Amy and her companion chatted about this and that, and she began to think he was a nice enough bloke; though she kept a wary eye on Daisy, who by now was loudly laughing and shrieking.

The tall fellow chuckled. 'Your friend seems to be enjoying herself.'

For just that split second, Amy took her eyes off Daisy. When she looked up again, they were gone. 'Where are they?' Beginning to panic, she quickened her steps, with the young man striding out beside her. 'Don't worry!' he told her. 'They can't be far.'

Amy wasn't convinced. Something told her that Daisy was out of her depth. Her fears were confirmed when she heard Daisy calling her name. 'That's Daisy! Maybe she's in trouble.' Beginning to panic, she looked this way and that, trying hard to pinpoint where the shouts were coming from, in the maze of alleys. 'DAISY! WHERE ARE YOU?'

She set off at a run, in the direction of Daisy's voice, with the young man coming up behind her. Fear gripped her heart. *She didn't trust him either.*

When Amy came running into the alley she saw Daisy struggling against Roy. He had her pinned against the wall and his mouth was clamped to

49

hers, while one hand groped inside her coat. Daisy was struggling against him, moaning and trying to push him away.

Amy misunderstood. Thinking Daisy was in real trouble, she kicked out and caught Daisy's attacker a nasty blow on the shin. He went down with a look of agony on his face. Amy was briefly aware of Daisy's astonished expression, but then the other man, Jack, darted forward and grabbed Amy's arm.

'Leave him. It's OK,' he said, but his hand on her arm only served to panic her.

Twisting away from him, she grabbed a half-brick that was lying in the alley. She aimed for his head but the brick bounced off his shoulder and fell at his feet, delivering no more than a bruise.

Meanwhile, Daisy had caught her breath and was buttoning her blouse. While Roy moaned at her feet, Jack looked shocked.

'Now just a minute . . .' he began.

'It's OK,' Daisy promised Amy. 'No harm done.' She giggled. 'It were a bit heavy for a first kiss, though.' Her hair was dishevelled and her lipstick smudged, but her eyes were mischievously twinkling in the light of a nearby streetlamp.

'But . . . I thought . . .' When realisation dawned Amy was embarrassed. Oh, no, this was awful. She began her way back down the alley. 'I think we'd best be off home,' she said lamely.

'I think we had,' chuckled Daisy, winking at Roy.

'But you said—' he began.

'Never mind what I said,' replied Daisy. 'Perhaps you'd better learn some manners, rushing a girl like that.' She patted her hair in place, straightened her coat and trotted back up the alley behind Amy.

'Time to cool off!' Daisy quipped as she went.

Softly laughing, she grabbed Amy's hand and they were soon running back towards the main road, their heels pounding the cold pavement, and the sound of their laughter echoing through the night air.

The street was relatively quiet, with the exception of a big black saloon motor car which passed them, slowing briefly before accelerating away, as they turned towards the tram stop and raced to meet the oncoming lights. He couldn't be certain but Luke wondered if they were the young women from Tooley's Cafe.

In the lamplight, Amy took a good look at her friend. 'My God, Daisy . . . look at the state of you!' Amy was horrified. 'We'll have to try and tidy you up. They'll never let you on the tram like that.' With her dishevelled hair and rumpled clothes, Daisy looked like a refugee from hell. 'The tram's coming now—quick!' She took Daisy by the shoulders. 'Let's see if we can make you presentable.'

'Been in a fight, 'ave yer?' The conductor gawped with open mouth as they boarded the tram.

'You could say that,' Amy replied, stifling her laughter.

'Sit yourself down then, and don't start anything.' Convinced they'd been drinking, the conductor warned, 'These are decent, God-fearing passengers, so mind you behave! I want no trouble on my tram!'

During the journey they relived the night's events. 'By! You went for him like a blinking Jack Russell,' Daisy said. 'That'll teach him to get fresh with me without a by your leave. The look on his face . . .' When she laughed loudly, the conductor,

51

who had been eyeing the red-faced pair suspiciously, came to give her a warning. 'Start trouble and I'll put you off!'

'I'm not "starting trouble"!' Daisy protested, and would have said more, were it not for the dig in the ribs she got from Amy, who was herself beginning to giggle; which then set Daisy off.

Somehow managing to remain fairly composed until disembarking at their stop, the two of them were helpless with laughter. 'You're a bad 'un, you are!' Amy spluttered.

'I've had the best night o' my life.' Swinging her arms round Amy, Daisy marched her forward at a galloping pace.

'Get off!' Amy shrugged her away. 'You'll have us both arse over tip!'

Daisy was astounded. 'Language, my girl.' She feigned indignation. 'I'll thank you to mind your tongue when you're in my company.' To which they both started laughing again.

Some short distance away, a strolling constable gave them a knowing wink. 'Evening, girls.'

'Evening, officer,' Amy replied.

'You two look like you've had a good night.'

'Not so's you'd notice,' Daisy replied.

On looking closer, he saw how tousled they were. His tone grew serious. 'All right, are you?'

'Right as rain,' Amy replied.

'Aye, well, you'd best get off home,' he advised. 'There are some strange folks hanging about this time of night.'

They watched him go, shaking his head as he went.

As they wended their way home, the streets echoed with their merry laughter.

52

One thing was certain, Amy thought. Life was never dull with Daisy about.

CHAPTER FIVE

Switching off the engine, Luke Hammond climbed out of the car. His business meeting had overrun and then he'd had to entertain clients. 'I'm sure that was Amy with the young woman from the café,' he murmured. But the lamplight played strange tricks on the eye, so he couldn't be absolutely certain. He'd learned Amy's name by eavesdropping at Tooley's, and now it was a name inextricably linked to Tuesdays—those days of freedom and dreams.

He closed the car door and made his way to the house. As he walked on, the image of Amy's face was bright in his mind.

There was something irresistible about her. She had a warm, magical, memorable smile, and those bluest of eyes. It was the face of a woman you could trust. That was why he had a need to paint her: so he might capture that special something, and keep it for ever. Smiling, gentle, constant, her portrait brought him nearer to living the dream he conjured up on Tuesdays. Whenever he was feeling low, he thought of Amy and his heart was lifted.

His reverie was, however, suddenly shattered as he approached the house. Through the kitchen window he could see a woman frantically pacing the floor and, judging from her manner, she seemed to be in a dark, dangerous mood.

'Oh God, that's all I need . . . *Georgina!*' A slim,

attractive woman with thick, dark hair, she was his wife's sister. He didn't care much for her, a scheming, greedy woman. 'What the devil can she want?' Because of her, he was able to enjoy his one day of freedom and keep his sanity. But he knew her well enough to be certain that she never did anything out of the goodness of her heart, and for that reason his suspicions were aroused. 'I can be sure of one thing,' he mused, 'she won't be here for any good reason.'

Growing anxious, he quickened his steps.

Sensing his nearness, the woman peered out of the window, delighted to see him there. Before he had even opened the door, she was there to greet him.

'Oh, Luke, I'm so glad you're back!' Her voice was entreating; her wide dark eyes glittering with excitement. 'It's been awful. I didn't know which way to turn.'

At once he was on his guard. 'What do you mean?' Looking about he asked pointedly, 'Where's Sylvia?'

'In the bedroom.' Casting her gaze to the upper reaches of the house she told him in a whisper, 'She's sound asleep.'

'Is she all right?'

'She is *now*.'

He began to understand. 'Is Edna with her?' Edna, originally employed as housekeeper, was a good and loyal friend who had seen him and his wife through thick and thin.

'No.' Bristling at his question, she snapped, 'She is *not*!'

'So, where is she? She promised to stay until I got home. The meeting went on longer than was planned.'

With eyebrows raised and a marbling of anger in her voice, she asked sweetly, 'What kind of meeting . . . or am I not allowed to ask?'

'A meeting of business minds,' Luke answered sharply. 'A long-awaited meeting, too important to miss.'

'Really?' Again the eyebrows were raised, the smile devious. 'I thought you might have a secret rendezvous with some attractive female,' she suggested softly. 'After all . . . the way things are, who would blame you?'

'If you thought that, then you were wrong. There is no other woman. There never has been, nor is there likely to be.' Bitterly he cast all lingering thoughts of Amy from his mind.

Taking a long, deep breath he squared his shoulders. 'Now . . . will you tell me what's been going on?' he asked quietly. 'You say Sylvia is asleep?'

'That's right. And, as you well know, it would be best if she was not disturbed.'

He nodded. 'So, if Edna is not with my wife, where *is* she?'

Georgina gave a cunning half-smile. 'I sent her home of course.' Her expression changed to one of disgust. 'To tell you the truth, I'd sack her if I had my way.'

Anger darkened Luke's face. 'Then it's just as well you *don't* have your way!' he snapped. 'That dear soul is a godsend to us. She's been with us through very difficult times. Anyone else would have been long gone, but not Edna. She's a good woman . . . and, thank God, she's made of sterner stuff than most. What's more, she knows as much about what's happening as any one of us.' His voice trembled with anger. 'You had no right to send her home.'

'Sylvia is my sister. I had every right! I've said it before and I'll say it again. Sylvia needs a proper nurse, not an old has-been like Edna!'

'You've got a short memory, Georgina.'

'What do you mean?'

'Cast your mind back to when Sylvia came home from hospital.' With his eyes burning into hers, he explained the situation for the umpteenth time. 'She had bruises and marks where she'd taken that terrible beating, but to look into her eyes, you'd think she was recovering well. Oh, yes, the doctor warned us that it was a possibility, but we hoped beyond hope for her sake that he was wrong. But he wasn't, was he? What was it—a month, maybe two—before the fits started; the unpredictable violence, the depression and amnesia.'

'I know all that!'

'Then you also know how I got Sylvia the best nurses money could buy. First one then another. They had all the certificates and experience. They came with the finest references, but Sylvia sent them packing.' He paused, allowing the words to sink in. 'She would have nothing to do with any of them, and worse, nothing to do with the medication they administered. And then, when I'm about to despair, we discover that the finest nurse of all is our own housekeeper, Edna—fully trained, qualified, and with years of experience. What was even better was that she already had Sylvia's complete and absolute trust . . . mine too. I can go to work during the week and know that Sylvia is in safe, loving hands, and that she isn't hiding her

56

tablets or pouring her medicine away.'

Georgina knew how every word Luke uttered was right, but she still had her say. 'Except for Tuesdays.'

He nodded. 'Yes, except for Tuesdays, but then Edna has to have at least one day off and she visits her aged mother. They go to the old lady's whist club. But then you kindly offered to stay with her on that one day, and the arrangement seems to have worked out really well. Like you say, Sylvia always seems content in your company.'

Eaten with jealousy, Georgina persisted. 'If you ask me, Edna is far too familiar. It never pays to let the servants know too much.'

'Why don't you let *me* worry about that?' Finishing the conversation, he turned away with the parting words, 'Besides, you know we never think of Edna as a "servant".'

'Then you *should* . . . because that's exactly what she is. A housekeeper pretending to be a nurse again!'

'To be honest, the fact that you sent her away is neither here nor there, because if I know Edna, the minute she realises I'm home, she'll be back again . . . if only to make certain Sylvia is all right.' He smiled knowingly. 'In fact, I suspect our Edna has nothing but dislike for you.'

'Hmm!' Georgina narrowed her eyes and spat, 'The feeling is mutual, because I can't stand the sight of the damned woman!'

Treating her remark with the contempt it deserved, Luke made no reply. Instead, he went out of the room and on up the stairs.

At the top of the stairs he turned left towards his wife's room. He knew from experience that it was best to leave her sleeping, but he had a deep-down need to check on her. He had to be certain she was all right.

Lingering outside her door, he listened. There was no sound. There never was. Gingerly he turned the handle, opened the door and, ever so softly, let himself inside.

Standing by her bed, he studied her sleeping face. Sylvia never liked complete darkness, and in the kindly haze of light from the standard lamp, her quiet, pale features took on a ghostly aspect. With her soft skin and long, tousled chestnut hair, she seemed almost like a child lying there. He stayed a moment longer, thinking how beautiful she was, and how fortunate he had been.

Raising the blanket to cover her arms, he tenderly stroked the strands of rich-coloured hair from about her face. When she was sleeping like this, everything seemed so perfect. *Yet he knew it was not.*

Beside the bed, her supper plate lay untouched: two small, plain biscuits, and a dainty wedge of cheese with the knife lying beside it; all exactly as it was when brought up by Edna. Untouched, unwanted.

The empty tumbler was on its side, half drunk, half spilled. As he carefully uprighted it, the dregs ran down his wrist. He wiped it away, but the stale milk remained, sticky and uncomfortable. It occurred to him it might well contain something medicinal, but it was spilled now, and anyway, she was sound asleep.

'Good night, my love.' Leaning over, he whispered assurances with the softest of kisses before, collecting the supper plate, he left the room as softly as he had arrived.

Once outside on the landing, he made his way to the bathroom; a large converted bedroom with high ceilings and stripped wooden floor, it always struck him as strangely cold and bleak.

Setting the supper plate on the cupboard, he went to the basin where he splashed a handful of cold water over his wrist, then another over his face. After hours of talking business he was wearied. The shock of cold water felt refreshingly good.

When, eyes half closed, he turned to find the towel, she was suddenly on him like a fiend.

'YOU'VE BEEN WITH *HER*!' Shrieking like a demented soul she grabbed the cheese knife; lashing out, wanting to hurt him, needing to maim him, just as she felt maimed. 'You don't want me any more. I'm no good to you . . . don't lie to me!' With one swipe of the knife she caught him down the cheekbone. When the blood spurted out she lunged at him again, but this time he caught her arm to fend her off.

'Sylvia! Drop the knife! Sylvia, please!'

'Let me go, you bastard . . . I HATE YOU!' There was no stopping her now. Raising her arm she brought it down, the small curved blade targeting his face. He ducked, grabbed her by the waist and, drawing her towards him, pinned her arms by her sides. 'It's all right, Sylvia,' he gasped, '. . . it's all right. There is no one else in my life but you.' He struggled to regain his breath, to ignore the blood he could feel oozing down his face.

Her dark eyes calmer now, she looked up. 'Promise me?'

He nodded, his forced smile seeming to settle

59

her fears. 'I promise.'

When she began sobbing, he gently took away the knife and, at that moment, something made him glance towards the door. Shocked to see Georgina leaning against the door-jamb, he asked harshly, 'How long have you been there?'

Smiling triumphantly, she replied, 'Long enough.' In fact she had witnessed the whole thing.

'Did you wake her?' Suspicion trembled in his voice.

'Shame on you, Luke.' Her small, mean mouth opened in disbelief. 'Do you really believe I would do such a thing?'

His voice hardened. 'I *know* you would . . . if it suited your purpose.'

Just then, a plump woman of homely face and grey hair appeared.

'Is Mrs Hammond all right, sir?' She was obviously distressed.

Relieved to see her, Luke reassured her. 'Yes, Edna, she's all right.'

Clinging to him, Sylvia looked up at her husband. 'I'm tired,' she said wearily. 'Can I go back to my bed now?'

Kissing her tenderly on the forehead, Luke nodded. 'Come on . . . I'll take you back.'

As he moved forward, she saw the blood trickling from his cheekbone. A look of astonishment came over her features. 'Your face is cut!' Horrified, she reeled from him. 'I want Edna.' Her voice rising to a shriek, she demanded, 'Edna! I need *you* to take me back. Please, Edna . . .'

Like a frightened child she entreated the older woman, and the older woman loved her as she would her own flesh and blood. 'You must calm

60

yourself, my dear,' she said soothingly. 'O' course I'll take you back.' She shifted an inquisitive gaze to Luke. 'If it's all right with Mr Hammond, that is?'

Luke gave the nod she needed, and now, as Sylvia went to her with open arms, Edna quickly but gently led Sylvia back to the safety of her bed.

Reaching out for the towel, Luke dipped a corner into the wash-bowl and dabbed at the blood trickling from his wounds, but all the while his wary eyes were fixed on Georgina. 'If I thought you'd woken her,' he warned, shaking his head, 'I would have to think twice about banning you from this house.'

'You couldn't do that! I'm her sister.'

'And I'm her husband—so I could, and I would. My only concern is for Sylvia.' His voice thickened. 'My God! If I knew you'd deliberately upset her . . .'

Afraid now, she stepped forward. 'I *didn't*. I love her!' There was a measure of sincerity in her voice. 'I would never hurt her . . . you must know that.'

Using what she considered to be her best card, she taunted, 'If you thought me capable of hurting her, you would never trust me to stay with her on a Tuesday.'

Taken aback, Luke spoke firmly. 'And you think it would bother me if I didn't have my Tuesday freedom, do you?'

'I know how much you treasure your Tuesdays, that's all,' she retaliated. 'Or am I wrong?'

'No, you're not wrong.' Once more wiping the towel over the wound on his cheekbone, he reminded her, 'However much I treasure my little freedom, Sylvia will always be my first concern.'

61

A moment passed while Georgina silently considered his answer. She knew that, in spite of the way things were, he was speaking the truth, and to her mind it was a shocking waste of a man's devotion. Deep down she resented the love he felt for her sister. 'On these Tuesdays, when I come over to take care of her, *where do you go*?'

'That's my business.' He gave her a warning glance. 'We've had this conversation once too often, Georgina. Make this the last time, will you?'

Not being a woman who gave in easily, she persisted, 'I know you don't go to the factory.'

Angry and worried, he demanded, 'And how could you possibly know that?'

'Ah! I have my ways and means,' she said with a sly little grin. 'But don't worry. I won't give your secret away.'

'Do what you think fit,' he advised casually. 'It makes no difference to me.'

She took a step closer. 'I really am curious. What do you do? Where do you go?'

Throwing the towel into the washbasin he told her, 'That's enough talk for now!'

'All right. Like you say, it's none of my business.' She wisely backed off. When he had that look about him she knew it was impossible to get answers so, instead of riling him, she changed tack. 'I meant what I said, though. I do love Sylvia and, whatever you might think, I would never hurt her.'

Luke nodded. 'I don't know why, but I'm inclined to believe you.'

He knew there had always been a measure of love between the two sisters, but: 'All the same, I wish I could be certain of you.'

'Oh, but you can!' Tears swam in her dark eyes.

'You really can.'

He nodded, but made no move towards her. One thing he had learned about her was that she could turn on the tears at will.

She bowed her head. 'I know there are times when you don't trust me, but it's just that . . . I'm saddened by what's happened to her, and there's nothing I can do about it. Sometimes, it cripples me . . .' she tapped her chest, '. . . inside here.'

He understood how that felt, and deep down, where the pain lived, he felt a kind of sympathy with her. 'Oh, look, I'm sorry if sometimes I seem unfeeling.' Ashamed, he reminded himself of the hours he and Georgina had spent together at the hospital, not knowing whether Sylvia would live or die. It had been the worst time of his life and she had been there for him when he needed her. 'But she's so precious to me. I can't risk her being damaged again . . . not by *anyone*!'

Unmoved, she gave another glimpse of her cruel nature in her comment: 'What about *Arnold Stratton*?'

He gave her a withering look. 'I don't want to hear that name.'

'Will you tell me something?' There was a look in her eye that disturbed his peace of mind.

'Depends?' Just when he was beginning to trust her she made him wary as always.

'Why did you never go after him?'

For a long, awkward moment he remained silent; the past swirling through his mind, taking him back to a place he did not want to be. 'I *did* go after him.'

'What!' She stepped forward, her eyes wide with astonishment. 'I never knew *that*!'

63

He smiled, a sad, telling smile that showed the scars inside. 'That's because I never told anyone.'

'Not even Sylvia?' There was no end to her cruelty.

'*Especially* not Sylvia.'

Excitement trembled in Georgina's voice. 'What happened?'

'Nothing. I went there with the intention of tearing him limb from limb . . .'

The telling brought it all back with a vengeance, and he walked across the room, his fists rubbing one into the other as though they were itching to hit something, or someone. 'The police got there before me. When I turned the corner he was being arrested. After that, it was out of my hands.' His features stiffened. 'More's the pity! A ten-year gaol sentence is so little for what he did.'

Needing to end the conversation, he swung round on her. 'What are you doing here anyway?'

'I was worried about Sylvia.' Venturing closer, she lied, 'I couldn't sleep. I got to thinking how that bastard Stratton beat her so bad she almost died. As it was, he damaged her brain so much she'll never be whole again.' Her voice dropped to a baby whine. 'Is it her punishment, do you think . . . for having relations with him . . . cheating on you, when you've always been such a wonderful husband?'

'That's enough, Georgina. I think it's time you went.'

'Oh, Luke, I'm sorry. I know how painful it is for you to think about what happened.' Making the sign of the cross on herself she whispered solemnly, 'I promise I'll never speak of it again.'

'I'd appreciate that.'

Georgina was a strange person, he thought. And he could never fathom her. Sometimes she couldn't do enough for himself and Sylvia, and other times she seemed to take satisfaction in torturing him.

Walking to the door he expected her to follow. Instead she went on talking. 'It was just as well I got here when I did,' she assured him. 'By the time I arrived, Sylvia was already being difficult. Ask Edna, if you don't believe me. Between us, we managed to calm her and get her to bed. Edna insisted on going in to check on her, but I wouldn't let her. I sent her home instead.'

A thought occurred to her. 'What was she doing here just now? I told her not to come back. I told her I was going to have a word with you—that it must have been her who upset Sylvia in the first place, otherwise why was she in such a state when I got here? And just now, how did she get into the house? You can't get into the house without a key.'

Luke enlightened her. 'Edna has a key. And before you say anything, she will continue to have a key. For Sylvia's sake I need to know that Edna can let herself in at any time.'

Georgina saw her opportunity. 'Think about it, Luke! I have some experience of looking after sick people—I nursed my mother when she was ill—and the doctor said I would have made an excellent nurse.'

'And you would,' Luke agreed. 'I've seen how gentle and good you can be with Sylvia.'

'There you are!' she cried jubilantly. 'So, why don't I sell my house and come to live here? Then you'd have no need of Edna.'

He swiftly dismissed her idea. 'Thank you all the same, but I really don't think that's necessary.

65

Besides, Edna might be a little slower than she once was, but she's more than capable and, as well you know, Sylvia trusts her implicitly.'

'She trusts me too. I mean, on Tuesdays when Edna has her day off and you're away working on your "secret" project . . .' she waited for an explanation, and when there was none, she continued, '. . . well, she always enjoys my company. We get on well together. We always have.'

'Yes. I know that.'

He had seen how the two of them laughed and chatted together, about their childhood and other things that women were interested in, such as the latest fashion designs and favourite film stars.

They really did seem to enjoy each other's company, and on the one occasion when Sylvia had a bad turn, Georgina quickly got the doctor out and everything was under control.

She was a sensible, intelligent woman. That was the reason he was content enough to leave them together while he enjoyed his own company on that one special day.

All the same, his small, sneaking distrust of Georgina remained. Now, though, he thought it best to remind her of something. 'Just now, when Sylvia saw what she'd done to my face, she was upset. But did you notice, it wasn't you she turned to? It was Edna. No, Georgina, it's kind of you to offer, but it's best we leave things the way they are.' His instincts told him it would be a very bad idea to have Georgina in the house at all times.

Opening the door, he offered, 'I'll have a word with Edna . . . see if she wouldn't mind me running you home.'

But Georgina would not hear of it. 'No. I'll get a

cab. I'd prefer that.'

'All right,' Luke conceded, 'if that's what you want.'

Going to the hallstand, he took down two coats: a long dark, woollen coat with belt and deep pockets, and a black astrakhan three-quarter one with black bone buttons and fur collar.

First helping her on with the astrakhan, he then shrugged on his own coat. 'I'll walk you to the bottom of the street. We'll flag down a cab there.'

It was a matter of only five minutes or less, before a cab pulled over. 'Mind you go straight indoors once you get home.'

'It's all right,' she answered with the sweetest of smiles, 'I know how to look after myself.'

Helping her into her seat, he kissed her dutifully on the cheek. 'Good night, Georgina.'

Before settling back into her seat, she clung to him a moment longer than he was comfortable with. 'Good night, Georgina!' Taking her by the shoulders he gently but firmly pushed her away and closed the door. 'Eighteen, Park Street.' He thrust a handful of coins into the driver's hand. 'There's a bit extra there,' he pointed out. 'Mind you wait until she's safely inside.'

A smile from her, a wave and she was gone.

Somewhat dejected, Luke made his way back to the house. 'I'll never understand it,' he muttered. 'How could two sisters be so different?'

But then he reminded himself of how Sylvia had been having an affair with Arnold Stratton, before they found her beaten and battered in the alley.

It had been the worst shock of all, and even now Luke found it hard to believe that she had deceived him with another man. He had adored Sylvia since the first day they met; with every fibre in his body. Without question or reservation. Time and again, she had told him how she never wanted or needed anyone else, and he believed her.

In the early years theirs had been the ideal romance, the meeting, the courtship, the sharing and growing together. Then the cracks had begun to show, with Sylvia's waywardness and selfishness. She was bored; she didn't want Luke to go to the factory; she wanted to travel . . . She started spending every evening out—with friends, but they were not friends he knew—and she was drinking a lot. Luke tolerated all this because he still had his dreams of their growing old together, with maybe a son who would one day take over the business from him. Then Sylvia met Arnold Stratton . . .

Luke still loved her now in spite of her cheating, but not in the way he had loved her before. Not with his heart and soul. Not blindly. But he had made his vows and he held her close to his heart. She was his wife, his responsibility and he would take care of her until the end of her days . . . or the end of his! Whichever came first.

His thoughts returned briefly to Amy as he had seen her that evening—young, care-free, laughing in the street. She was his dream, but Sylvia was his reality.

*   *   *

The portly cab driver was a chatty sort. 'I'll soon have you home, miss,' he assured Georgina proudly, 'safe and sound, just like the good man wanted.'

Deep in thoughts of a devious kind, Georgina

68

didn't hear him.

'Decent fella . . . seems concerned to keep you from harm,' the cabbie went on. 'Your intended, is he?'

Coming out of her reverie with her mind made up, Georgina didn't catch his last remark. 'What's that you say?'

Half-turning his head, the cabbie apologised. 'Sorry if I offended you. I were only asking if the fella was your intended?'

Georgina smiled. 'Not officially,' she answered coyly, 'I mean, he doesn't know it yet, but I intend for us to be man and wife one day.'

The cabbie laughed out loud. 'You women!' he chuckled. 'Once you get your claws into us men, we've got no chance at all.'

He was only minutes from Park Street when she instructed, 'Turn down the next street left.'

Confused, he advised her, 'But that's Johnson Street. I were told you wanted Park Street.'

'Well, now I want Johnson Street!' she snapped. 'Keep moving until I tell you when to stop.'

Swinging the vehicle into Johnson Street, the cabbie was guided by the streetlamps. 'What number?' He peered at the door: 'This is fifteen . . . seventeen . . .' As instructed, he moved slowly on.

'Here!' Perched on the edge of her seat and ready to open the door, she screeched at him, 'STOP HERE!'

Made to halt in a dark, shadowy spot between two streetlamps, he wondered what she was up to. 'Do you want me to wait?' he asked as she climbed from the cab.

'Well, of course I want you to wait,' she replied impatiently. 'The trams have stopped running and I certainly don't intend walking home in the dark.'

He nodded. 'How long will you be?'

'I don't know,' she snapped. 'Anyway, what does it matter to you?'

'Well, if it's only a few minutes it'll make no difference. But if it's gonna be some time, then I might have to charge you a bit more.'

Georgina rounded on him. 'You'll do no such thing!' she told him. 'I saw the handful of coins he gave you, and it was more than enough. You're getting no more—not even if I'm in there till morning!'

'I see.' He had taken a real dislike to her. 'And are you likely to be in there "till morning"?'

'Well, now . . .' giving a sly little wink, she leaned towards him, '. . . we'll just have to wait and see, won't we?' With that she sauntered off, glancing up at the house numbers as she went.

Curious, he watched as she knocked on a door. Smartly groomed and dressed in expensive clothes, she was quite an eye-opener, he thought. But it didn't always follow that what looked good on the outside was good on the inside.

A naturally wary man, he decided that when she came back out, he would take her home quick as he could, and never a word of conversation between them.

Cabbies should keep their traps shut and just do their job, he decided, or who knew what trouble they might find themselves in.

After a few moments the door opened. Casting a glance up and down the street, she hurried inside.

The cab driver also glanced up and down the street. 'It's a far cry from Park Street,' he muttered thoughtfully.

70

A long meandering street on a deep slope towards the town, Johnson Street was typical of the roads in those parts. It was the kind of ordinary, serviceable place where folks like himself lived out their days—hard-working, God-fearing folks who worked long, back-breaking hours in the cotton-mills or the nearby factories.

One thing was certain: it was nothing like the beautifully kept, wide open streets, with their big posh houses, that ran up alongside the park. Those were reserved for wealthy folk—employers, bank managers, that kind of contented, fortunate soul.

He settled himself into the seat, closed his eyes and yawned. 'One thing's for sure, she's up to no good.' He thought about the man who had paid for her cab. 'Some women don't know when they're well off!' he muttered. 'That fella seemed a decent sort, but if he's not careful, he'll find himself hooked up to a bad lot, an' no mistake!'

*   *   *

Georgina followed the man into the sitting room.

'I didn't expect you tonight, Helen. What you doing 'ere at this late hour anyway?' A rough-looking fellow, but well-endowed, clad only in underpants he made a fetching sight to her eager eyes.

'Aren't you pleased to see me?' A flush of disappointment coloured her face, but she pouted seductively and slowly slipped her coat off, her eyes full of suggestion.

He gave a wily grin. 'Depends, don't it?' Looking her up and down he licked his lips. 'It's been a while since we got together.'

71

'I was on my way home and thought I'd come and pay a visit,' she purred.

His blue eyes coveting her, he smiled. 'If I knew where you lived, I might be able to repay the favour now and then.'

Shaking her head, she took a step forward. 'I'll *never* tell you where I live.'

'Hmm! Sometimes I wonder if your name really is Helen.' He gave her a wry little smile. 'Is it?'

She laughed. 'That's for me to know and you to find out.'

'You're a secretive bugger and no mistake.' Now, as he moved towards her, the light from the flickering gas-mantle played shadows on his unshaven face. 'And why is that, I wonder?'

Stroking her hands through his tousled brown hair, she murmured, 'Because I don't trust you. I don't trust anyone, but I especially don't trust men.'

Through hostile, narrowed eyes he studied her. 'All the same, it would make things easier if I knew a bit more about you. After all, you know my name, and you know where I live.'

Staring him out, she answered emphatically, 'Only because I had to bring you home when you were drunk out of your mind. You couldn't stop talking.'

They had met in the town one afternoon when Georgina's high heel had become caught between paving stones and he'd freed her. Each had liked the look of the other. He admired her bold manner and her expensive perfume, and she had always secretly lusted after rough-looking men. Good manners, she found, so often took the excitement out of sex. Sylvia must have found the same, Georgina thought. Why else had she had an affair with Arnold Stratton?

Neither had anything better to do so they'd found a hotel bar; then, when they'd drunk a fair amount, gone on to a pub he knew. There he'd become ridiculously drunk and she'd had to take him home in a taxi. She'd stayed the night and their affair had started when his hangover abated.

'And besides, you don't need to know my real name and address,' she now added.

'Oh, but you're wrong. As a rule I know all about my women after the first meeting.'

'I'm not one of "your women".'

'So, what are you doing here?' Leering into her face, he laughed. 'Can't resist me, is that it?'

She batted her eyelashes. 'I get lonely sometimes,' she answered. 'Is that so hard to understand?'

He took a long, slow breath. 'It is, yeah. You're an attractive woman . . . not short of a bob or two, by the looks of it, and here you are, slumming through the back streets to see an old lag like me.'

Smiling, she observed his muscular figure, with the first signs of a rounded stomach, and that unkempt face with its peculiar, rough appeal and, stepping forward, she stroked his bare arm. 'You're not an "old lag",' she murmured.

'Oh, but I am.' He was deliberately taunting her. 'When a man's been in prison, what else would you call him, but an old lag? I'm a bad man, Helen.' His eyes were hard like two bright marbles. 'Some of us are locked up because we deserve to be.' '

She touched him tenderly, her fingers curling round the hairs on his broad chest. 'If you'd rather I left . . .' her voice was like silk in his ear, 'I'll go now . . . if that's what you really want?'

'O' course it's not what I want.' His features softened. 'You don't know how glad I am that you took me home that night,' he said gratefully. 'I were in a bad state—drunker than I've ever been in my life.'

She gave a soft, knowing laugh. 'You were in need of help.'

With a wicked look in his eye, he asked meaningfully, 'And are *you* in need of help?'

'You know I am. Why else would I be here?'

Grabbing her to him, he kissed her hard on the mouth, one hand undoing her dress, the other snaking round her waist.

There was little foreplay and even less tenderness. It wasn't long before they were naked and locked together, writhing on the floor in ecstasy. The coupling was fast and furious, leaving them collapsed into each other, gasping and breathless.

*　　　*　　　*

A short time later, the cabbie almost leaped out of his skin when she banged on the window. 'Open the door, dammit!' In the streetlight, with her face pressed to the window, she made a frightening sight to a poor wakening man.

Scrambling across the seat, he opened the door. 'What time is it?'

She was smiling like a cat who'd got the cream. 'It's time to take me home,' she said.

And because his every instinct told him she was trouble, he lost no time in taking her home as fast as he could.

74

Edna hurried home to Peter Street.

'I've kept the kettle on to boil.' A small, round figure with balding head and pot belly, Harry had been wed to Edna these past forty years, and he loved her now as much as he had ever done. 'Sit yerself down, lass.' Scrambling out of the chair, he began his way to the kitchen. 'I'll mek yer a brew.'

When the tea was made, the two of them sat before the fire, comfortable in each other's company, and as always, the low-burning fire making them drowsy. 'Everything all right when you got back there, lass?'

'Aye, in the end,' she replied.

'Don't let that woman upset you, lass. She's not worth losing a minute's sleep over.' Sliding down in the chair he closed his eyes.

Seemingly unaware that her husband was ready for his bed, Edna remarked on what she had overheard. 'That devil were calling me names again.'

Looking up, Harry scratched his head. 'What's that you say, lass?'

Edna tutted. 'Sylvia's awful sister. She were calling me names to Mr Hammond.'

He shook his head in disgust. 'She's a bad lot, is that one. Anyway, how d'yer know she were calling yer names? Did Mr Hammond mention it then?'

'Naw, course he didn't. He would never do that. He doesn't like trouble, doesn't Mr Hammond; he prefers a peaceful life. No, I overheard the two of them talking about Sylvia, and I heard her say as how I weren't fit to be looking after her. She reckons he should get somebody more suited.'

75

'Huh! He'll not get nobody more suited than you, lass. By! You've got more qualifications an' experience than she'll ever have!'

Edna smiled at that. 'You allus did credit me with more than I deserve.' Though she did allow herself a little pat on the back. 'But you're right o' course,' she conceded. 'I worked long and hard over the years, and if I say so meself, I look after Sylvia better than anyone else ever could . . . matter o' fact I don't think she'd ever agree to anybody else taking care of her. Y'see, she's come to rely on me for everything.'

Harry couldn't agree more. 'Aye! An' that's 'cos she loves you like you were her own mammy,' he retorted. 'Look, lass. You tek no notice o' that sister of hers. She's an out-and-out troublemaker. Like you say, she's got her eye on Luke Hammond, and soonever his wife is out of it, she'll be in there afore yer can thread a needle.'

Edna laughed at his boldness. 'And you're right,' she told him, with a loving pat on the hand. 'But I mentioned that to you in confidence, so you must never repeat it to another soul, or I'll be sent packing for good, and no mistake.'

By the time she'd finished speaking, he was beginning to nod off. 'Hey! Come on, you.' Shaking him fully awake, she urged, 'Off to bed with you, an' I'll be up alongside you in a few minutes.

After he'd gone, she thought about the conversation between Luke Hammond and his scheming sister-in-law. Harry's right she thought. That sister of hers is a devil in the making!

She thought of Sylvia's predicament. 'I do love that poor lass, though,' she muttered. 'By! If her sister had her way, Sylvia would be shut away in some institution or another by now, leaving the coast clear for that madam Georgina to work her wiles. But thankfully, the lass will be safe enough.' She comforted herself with the thought. While Luke Hammond has the final say, his wife will be well looked after, God willing. With me there to tend her every need.

CHAPTER SIX

'Come on, you lazy pair!' Dave's voice sailed through the house. 'Let's be having you.'

'What's up?' Sleepy-eyed, Amy leaned over the banister. 'Is there a fire or what?'

'There will be if you don't get your backsides down here.' Positioning himself on the second stair, Dave told her, 'It's ten past six. I've made the fire, boiled the kettle and now I'm ready for my breakfast.'

Amy glanced at her parents' bedroom door. 'Where's Mam? Why didn't she get up with you?'

'Because she likes her bed too much, that's why.' Banging the banister again he pleaded, 'Go and knock the door . . . tell her I'm ready for off.'

Amy groaned. 'It's surely not that time yet, is it?' So far there had not been one day when the shop was late opening.

'Happen not. But it soon will be if you don't get a move on. So shift yourself, lass. And wake your mam up, will you?'

Grumbling and moaning, he lumbered into the kitchen where he checked the gas-ring. 'Damn thing, it's allus going out.' Striking a match on the range, he lit it again. 'One o' these days I'll chuck the bloody thing in the river and be rid of it once and for all!'

Glancing at the mantelpiece clock, he groaned. 'Jesus! I'm getting nowhere at this rate.'

Making his way to the bottom of the stairs, he called up again, 'MARIE . . . AMY! What the devil's keeping you?'

Halfway to her parents' room, Amy turned and came back. 'What now?'

'Did you wake your mam up?'

'Not yet, but I will if you'll give me a chance.'

'Look, lass . . . get her out, will you? I can't be going to work without summat inside me . . . I'd make my own breakfast, but you know what happened the last time I tried cooking on that blessed gas stove!'

'And how could we ever forget?' Having been woken by the yelling and shouting, Marie emerged fully dressed from her bedroom. 'By! You should be ashamed . . . a grown man who can't fry an egg without setting fire to the kitchen.' Coming along the landing, she winked at Amy who by now was wide awake.

Relieved to see Marie already out and fighting fit, he called up, 'Come on, lass. I don't want to be late.'

'Stop your moithering. I'm on my way.' Starting down the stairs, Marie noticed how Amy was shivering. 'Aw, lass, you'll catch your death o' cold. You go and get yerself dressed,' she instructed in her best no-nonsense voice, 'while I make a start on the breakfast.' She feverishly rubbed her hands together. 'By! It's bitter cold! I hope your dad's got a good fire going.' Giving Amy a little push, she

78

urged, 'Go on, lass. Get dressed.'

'Thanks, Mam.' Drawing her robe tight about her, Amy felt the cold right through to her bones. 'Don't worry about my breakfast,' she told Marie, 'I'll do myself a boiled egg and toast when I get down.'

Marie wagged a finger. 'Your breakfast will be on the table soonever you're ready,' she promised. 'Now go on. Be off with you.'

Amy didn't argue. It would not have made any difference anyway. 'All right, Mam, thanks. I'll not be long.'

Hurrying back to her bedroom, Amy winced as the bare feet struck against the cold lino. It was November now, and the winter's cold seeped into every corner, yet even in summer the warmth of the sunshine could not seem to find its way in, not even when every window in the house was open.

Grabbing her clothes, she went along to the bathroom, where she quickly cleaned her teeth and washed herself. A few minutes to brush her hair and she was ready for the day ahead.

Humming a tune to herself, she danced down the stairs and burst into the kitchen, where her parents were already seated at the table.

'You look nice, love.' Always ready with compliments for his two women, Dave looked up from his forkful of bacon. Taking note of Amy's pretty blue jumper and the dark flared skirt that fell to just below the knees, he saw how her eyes sparkled and her brown hair shone, and he was curious. 'Off somewhere special, are we?'

'Only as far as the shop.' She sat down, her egg and toast already on the table. 'Why do you ask?'

'No reason.' He winked mischievously. 'You

79

wouldn't be seeing a fella would you, lass? I mean, in my experience, when a young lady has that particular sparkle in her eye, it's usually because she's found herself a fella.'

'Well, I'm sorry to disappoint you,' Amy answered with a shy little smile, 'but I haven't "found a fella", and nor am I likely to . . . unless he comes into the shop for a packet of drawing-pins or a pound of cheese.' Strange she thought, how her father's words made her think of the handsome man who visited the café on a Tuesday.

'No fella, eh?' Dave sighed. 'Ah, well, it's a terrible shame, that's all I can say . . . especially when you look pretty as a picture this morning.' Dave had never fooled himself about his darling daughter. Amy was a kind and wonderful young woman with a beautiful way about her that attracted all manner of compliments, but she was not what you might describe as pretty. She was *more* than that, he thought proudly, and he would not have her any other way. That rogue Don Carson had let her down badly, but she was probably well out of it. Don had been a bit too slick for Dave's liking—he'd always suspected there was something not quite trustworthy about him. Shame he'd broken his little girl's heart, though. Her confidence had been badly shaken. It'd take a special fella to make her trust again.

'You may not know it, lass,' he went on, 'but you're a real head-turner—bright and winsome, like a ray of sunshine, that's what you are.' He was inwardly pleased when she flushed with embarrassment.

Having heard and seen the exchange between husband and daughter, Marie chuckled through

80

her toast. 'Tek no notice, lass,' she told Amy. 'Your father's allus had a silken tongue. He's the world's best flatterer . . . Matter of fact it wouldn't surprise me if he doesn't chat up the girls wherever he goes.'

'Nonsense!' Dave took umbrage at her remarks. 'Why would I do a thing like that?'

She gave Amy a sly little wink. 'One pretty smile from some wayward girl, and he'd be putty in her hands.'

Dave would have none of it. 'There's only two girls in my life,' he declared sombrely, 'and they're right here at this table!'

It wasn't long before the conversation turned to more serious matters. 'Anyway, what are you doing up so early?' Chopping off the top of her egg, Amy cut her toast into long thin soldiers. 'You don't have to be at work until eight.'

Taking a deep gulp of his tea, Dave pushed back his chair. 'Mr Hammond is giving us a pep talk this morning and he wants us all in by half-past seven.'

Marie looked up. 'What kind of pep talk?'

'God only knows.' He frowned. 'We shall just have to wait and see.'

'Are you worried about your job, Dad?'

Dave shrugged. 'We've all been worried, Amy,' he imparted quietly. 'Work seems to be slowing down of late, and I'm told that two of the wagons were parked up for the best part of last week. On top of that, half the factory floor is completely empty.' He looked from one to the other. 'Some of the lads who've been there since Hammonds started up say they've never seen it like that before.'

'Oh, Dave, I hope he's not setting some of you

81

off. I know how much you like your job.' Marie knew that when work ran short, the rule was always last in first out.

'I'm sure it won't come to that, lass.' Seeing their worried faces he assured them, 'It'll be summat and nowt, you'll see. And besides, the brush production side of it has never been busier. While the two wagons have been parked up, the brush delivery vans have been on the go as usual. Look, don't worry. I'm sure there'll be an explanation for the slow-down on the other side.'

Marie nodded. 'Happen you're right, love.'

But she was uneasy all the same.

Dave left in plenty of time. 'I'll see you both later,' he said and, with a twinkle in his eye, he told Amy, 'This fella you've got in your sights, don't keep him all to yourself, lass. Me and your mam would like a glimpse of him some time or another.' And with that, he went away whistling.

However, when he got out of earshot, the whistling stopped. 'I hope Hammond's not about to finish some of the workforce,' he muttered. 'I don't want to lose my job. I can't go back working in the shop, not now our Amy's given up her own job to help her mam. And, oh, I did hate being cooped up.'

Striding along in the cold morning air, he felt like a free man. There was something about being outside, even when he was driving along in his wagon—something so natural and satisfying, he would be greatly sad to lose it.

'Morning, Dave.' The big man was a loader at Hammonds. 'I'm not looking forward to this 'ere meeting, I can tell you.'

'Morning, Bert.' Dave greeted him with a

82

friendly nod, though his voice carried a worried tone. 'Do you reckon we're in for the chop then?'

'Oh, aye.' The big man's expression said it all. 'I reckon some of us are bound to be finished. What with the building half empty and two wagons stood off, we must be losing orders. I can't see Hammond keeping a full workforce on, however good a man he is. Can you?'

As they turned the corner of Montague Street, they saw the tram about to pull out. Setting off at a run, they leaped onto the platform and hurried to sit down.

'I think you might well be right,' Dave said, squashing himself next to the big man who was taking up two-thirds of the slatted seat. 'And if he is getting shut of some of us, I'll surely be one of 'em,' he contemplated. 'Last in first out, isn't that what they say?'

'Mmm.' Preoccupied with his own predicament and the missus with a new babby on the way, Bert didn't answer straight off. Instead he stared absent-mindedly out the window, his mind turning over what Dave had said. 'It doesn't allus work out that way,' he replied presently. 'Sometimes they get rid of the older ones first. And that'll be me included.'

They spent the rest of the journey in silence. There was much to think about, and the more they thought, the more anxious they became.

*   *   *

While Luke straightened his tie at the hall mirror, Sylvia looked on.

'Why are you going so early this morning?' Drawing near, she looked proudly at his reflection in the mirror. Immaculate in a dark blue suit, with white shirt and dark tie, he looked every inch the employer gentleman. 'You look especially smart today.'

She reminded herself that he looked smart every day when he was going to his work. But on a Tuesday, he didn't go to his work. She knew that because she had given Georgina the slip when they were out shopping and gone to his factory once, and he hadn't been there. 'He never comes in of a Tuesday, miss,' some helpful, misguided lad had told her.

So, in spite of her enquiries and much to her consternation, she still did not know where he went on Tuesdays. She had asked him many times, but he always fobbed her off. 'Work doesn't present itself,' he told her. 'I need to put time aside to go looking for it.' Which, even Sylvia knew, was no lie.

'I have to be at work for seven fifteen,' he answered her question.

'Why?' She hated it when he left in the mornings.

Used to her inquisitions, Luke answered her again. 'Because I've called the men together for a special meeting.' Leaning sideways he gave her a sound kiss. 'It wouldn't go down well if I was late, would it now?'

'And what about me?'

'What do you mean?'

'I don't want you to leave me, that's all.'

Concern showed on his face. 'What's wrong? Is there something you're not telling me?' He had tried hard to read the signs but her moods were so unpredictable, it was impossible to know.

'No there isn't!' She began to grow agitated. 'I

know what you're thinking, though,' she snapped sulkily. 'Go on then. Why don't you ask me if I'm about to go crazy?' She was painfully aware of the times when she lost control, and afterwards, filled with shame and fear, she knew little about what had taken place. During that dark period when her mind went into some kind of chaos, she was totally helpless.

Lately, because of something her sister said, she had convinced herself it was the price she had to pay for taking a lover outside her marriage. Sometimes Georgina said things like that—things that made Sylvia feel bad, and which she found hard to forget. Georgina had always had a spiteful streak. Sometimes they were such friends—like sisters ought to be—and then Georgina would be mean. When they were little, Mummy had said Georgina was just jealous, when Sylvia told tales of her, and to take no notice. But now Sylvia found it hard to cope with her sister's unkindness, which, as ever, could strike out of the blue.

Now as she goaded him, the fear was etched in her face. 'Go on, Luke! Ask me if I'm about to lose control!'

Turning, he took her gently by the shoulders, his voice soft with compassion. 'And are you,' he asked, 'about to lose control?' There were times when she took him by surprise. One minute she would be perfectly normal, and the next she would be like a raving lunatic, hitting out at anything and anybody; smashing whatever she could lay her hands on.

It was at times like that, when he feared she might harm herself.

'Stop fussing.' Pushing him away, she suddenly smiled. 'I'm fine,' she lied. 'In fact, I've never felt better.'

'So, what did you mean just now when you said, "What about me?"'

'Like I said . . . I don't want to be left alone, that's all.' A little flurry of fear turned her insides over.

Astonished, he asked, 'Do you really think I would leave you alone?'

Just then the rear door opened and Edna popped her head round. 'Seven o'clock, Mr Hammond,' she said with a homely grin. 'And here I am, as promised.'

Sylvia's face lit up. 'Edna, it's *you!*'

'Well, it isn't anybody else, you can be sure o' that,' came the chirpy reply. 'Now then, who wants a brew?'

'Not for me, thanks.' Concerned about the time, Luke told her, 'I'd best be off or I'll be late.'

'Well, it won't be because I let you down,' she declared. 'I were out of my bed a full hour afore time on account o' you.' She wagged a finger as she told him mischievously, 'O' course, I'll be wanting overtime money, you understand?'

He tutted. 'Oh, I'm not sure I can promise anything like that,' he teased. He and Edna understood each other very well.

Having already removed her coat and slung it over her arm, she pretended to put it back on. 'I'm sorry, sir.' Her voice was firm but her smile was growing. 'If you aren't going to treat me right, I shall take leave of you.'

Sylvia chuckled. 'Behave yourselves! Stop teasing her,' she chided Luke. And turning to Edna, she told her firmly, 'And you're just as bad. "Overtime money", indeed. We've always looked after you and always will.'

Looking mortified, Edna curtsied. 'Sorry, ma'am,' she stuttered contritely. 'Please don't sack me. I won't do it again.'

With a little laugh, Sylvia asked, 'Didn't you say something about "making a brew"?'

Edna laughed out loud. 'I'll make it right away,' and she departed the room in a burst of merry laughter.

'Edna is pure gold,' Luke said. 'She'll take good care of you, and before you know it I'll be back home.'

Sylvia nodded. 'I should have known you wouldn't leave me on my own,' she apologised. 'I'm sorry I was surly before.'

He slid his arm round her waist. 'It's all right.'

'You're so patient with me,' she answered softly. 'Any other man would have left long since.'

'No they wouldn't,' he assured her, 'not if they loved you as much as I do.' Yet though he loved her, he was not *in* love with her. Sadly, with her affair with Arnold Stratton, and its consequences, she had severed that very special bond that held them together as man and wife.

It had been of her choosing, when she'd taken another man in place of Luke. But she was still his wife and, as far as he was concerned, that gave him certain responsibilities.

'Kiss me, Luke . . . please.' Like a spoiled child, she gave up her face for a kiss and he obliged. 'I'll come to the door with you.' Taking hold of his hand, Sylvia went with him to the front door. 'What's this meeting about?'

'I'll tell you when I come home,' he promised.

'Tell me *now*!'

'There's no time now.'

'I won't let you go until you tell me!' The smile remained, but the voice began to quiver.

Edna appeared on cue. 'Now, now, dear. Let your husband get off,' she urged gently. 'He has important things to see to. Let's you and me go and sit down for a few minutes, eh? I'll make you some toast and marmalade, what about that?'

For a long, worrying moment, the younger woman stared at Edna, then she smiled at Luke, a coy little smile. 'I'll let you go,' she told him, 'for another kiss.'

Bending to kiss her on the mouth, he assured her, 'We'll talk when I get home. All right?'

Her smile widened. 'Yes . . . all right.'

'That's my girl!'

'Come on then, my dear,' Edna said. 'I hope you haven't forgotten, we're going shopping today.'

Sylvia appeared not to be listening. Instead she was standing at the open door, her gaze following Luke as he went to the car. A moment later he was gone and she was still waving. 'It's all right, he's gone now.' Edna would have closed the door but Sylvia put her foot there.

'Why did he have to go early?'

'He's promised to tell you all about it when he gets home, and you told me yourself, he's never yet broken a promise. Come on now, let's go and get that toast on, eh?' Edna had learned to read the signs. 'Close the door, then we'll go into the kitchen you and me.'

Ignoring her, Sylvia waved after Luke until her arm ached and when she turned it was with an expression of disbelief. 'He's gone!'

Edna quietly smiled. 'That's right, my dear . . .

he's gone to his work. So don't you think you should close the door now?' When Sylvia made no move, she stepped forward to shut out the cold morning air.

'NO!' Catching her heavily across the shoulder with a fist, Sylvia hissed through clenched teeth, 'You leave it!'

Clutching her shoulder, Edna gave her a hardened stare. 'Keep hold of yourself, child,' she chastised harshly. 'I meant only to close the door.'

'There's no need. Look, I can do it myself.'

With a sly little grin, Sylvia took a step sideways, then, gripping the edge of the door, she slammed it shut with all her might. The shuddering impact rattled the nearby shelf, sending ornaments crashing to the floor.

For a long, nerve-racking moment both women stared at the broken china.

Suddenly, the silence was broken with what sounded like a child sobbing, 'Don't punish me . . . please. I didn't mean it.'

Before Edna could stop her, Sylvia had picked up a long shard of broken glass, crying out in pain when the sharp edges cut into her flesh. 'Oh, Edna, look what I've done.' All sense of reason had gone and in its place was the innocent fear of a child hurt. Holding the offending arm up for Edna to see, she began wailing. 'I've done something bad, haven't I?' She appealed to the older woman with sorry eyes, 'What's wrong with me, Edna?'

Her cries collapsed into sobs and Edna's heart went out to her. 'It's all right, my dear,' she murmured. 'You'll be all right.' But she would never 'be all right'. Both Luke and Edna knew that, and maybe, deep down in the darkest corner of her mind, Sylvia knew it too.

The tears of remorse were genuine, as Edna knew all too well. 'I'll take care of it, child,' she soothed, leading her away. 'Once it's washed and cleaned, it'll be good as new.'

A swift examination told her that this time the wound was only flesh deep, thank God.

*   *   *

It was Luke Hammond's father who had started the brush-making factory. Twice it had almost gone under and twice he brought it back to profit.

Luke grew up with it. He learned the art of business at an early age and had been groomed to deal with men on all levels. Like his father he respected his workers and was well trusted. Also, like his father he had a tireless passion for the business.

After his father was gone, he had taken up the reins and developed the business further. Now it was two businesses rolled into one. On the one side was the production of brushes: scrubbing brushes; horse brushes; yard sweepers, and anything that cleaned as long as it had bristles. Brushes of any kind had been the original backbone of the Hammond business and they still were.

But now there was another business growing alongside; a business started by Luke and which served others. There were many other companies in industrial Lancashire—some small and just starting out, and which had neither the capital nor premises to store the goods they produced. This was where, only a few years back, Luke had seen an opportunity.

90

Thanks to his father, he was fortunate to own a warehouse and factory premises of sizeable proportions, with room to spare for the brush-making business. 'I have ample space,' he told the owners of the small businesses at various meetings he'd arranged. 'And I intend purchasing a fleet of wagons, so if we can close a deal, I'll not only take your goods for storage, but I'll deliver them as well. We can agree a long-term contract, or a short one that will let you out should you decide to expand your own concern.'

His intention was to provide such a good service that they would have no reason to sever relations.

Just as he had hoped, the idea was well received. Terms were agreed, and deals made, and it had turned out to be the best thing Luke had ever done.

News of the success of the arrangement spread, and it wasn't long before larger, more established company men were knocking on Luke's door. 'We need to diversify,' they said. 'Our factory space is desperately needed for production and right now we have no wish to purchase other premises, but if we could utilise our present storage area and sell off our wagon fleet, we could grow our businesses overnight.'

Deals were struck that allowed Luke to take over old wagons, which had since been exchanged for newer ones.

Luke's distribution business prospered, though its downside was that whenever one of his customers took a wrong turn and went under, Luke lost a sizeable slice of his business's turnover. This had happened a few times, and on each occasion it threatened a serious step back.

This was what his employees now feared: that

there had been others who had taken that 'wrong turn' and now it was themselves who were about to lose their livelihoods.

And so this morning, when they would learn their fate, they gathered from all parts of the factory: from the brush-making side, where the machines clattered all day and both men and women worked them with expertise, some cutting out the wooden shapes that would make the brush-tops, some feeding the bristles into the holes that were ready drilled and cleaned, and others fashioning and painting the handles.

When the production line produced the finished articles, the packers would neatly set them into boxes and the boxes would be carted away for delivery.

By nature, this was a dusty, untidy area, with the smell of dry horsehair assailing the nostrils, and the fall of bristles mounting high round the workers' feet. Yet they loved their work and many a time the sound of song would fill the air.

The other side of the premises was cleaner, with mountainous stacks of boxes and parcels from other factories as well as Hammonds, all labelled and ready for delivery, and the four wagons in a neat row outside waiting to be loaded.

For the past few days, however, there had been only two wagons waiting, with the other two stationary further up the yard. Rumours had circulated, unease had settled in, and now, the mood of worried workers was so palpable, it settled over the factory like a suffocating blanket.

From his office at the top of the factory, Luke watched the workforce gather in the front yard. 'They're in a sombre mood,' he told the clerk.

'Aye, they are that, Mr Hammond.' A ruddy-faced Irishman with tiny spectacles and tufts of hair sprouting from his balding head, old Thomas kept his nose glued to his accounts book.

Luke had some fifty people in his employ, and seeing them gathering in one place like now, it made a daunting sight, which filled him with pride and a sense of achievement, and also with apprehension. 'They're a good lot,' he told the clerk.

'Aye, they are that, Mr Hammond.' Licking his pencil Thomas made another entry in his ledger.

Luke turned from the window to address him. 'I expect they'll be wondering why I've called them together like this.'

This time, Thomas glanced up. 'Aye, they will that, Mr Hammond.' The old man had been with Luke's father before him, and was a loyal, trustworthy man who knew everything there was to know about the Hammond business.

Looking away, Luke smiled. 'You're a man of few words, Thomas.'

Thomas gave a long-drawn-out sigh. 'Aye, I am that, Mr Hammond.' Now as he glanced up, he smiled a wrinkly smile. 'A man o' few words, that's me, so it is.'

Realising all the workforce were now gathered and waiting, Luke straightened his tie and fastened the buttons on his jacket. 'It's time,' he said, opening the door. 'I'd best tell them why they're here.'

Downstairs, the atmosphere was one of apprehension. There were those who expected to be finished on the day, and others who prayed they might be allowed another few years of work and

93

pay before they were put out to pasture.

'Ssh! Here he comes!' The word went round, a hush came down, and, hearts in mouths, they watched Luke's progress as he came down the staircase.

'If I'm for the chop, I'll sweep the streets rather than be cooped up in the shop, a grand little place though it is.' Being a man with an appetite for fresh air, Dave Atkinson was adamant he would find outdoor work.

'I'm sixty-two year old,' said another man. 'Who in their right mind will tek me on at my time o' life?'

'Ssh!' The ruddy-faced man in front turned round. 'He's here now.'

When the muttering was ended and the workers' attention was on him, Luke revealed the reason for their being there. 'Firstly, I want to thank every one of you for your loyal service and dedication to this company . . .'

'Bloody hell!' Half-turning to Dave, the ruddy-faced driver whispered, 'That sounds a bit final, if you ask me.'

'Ssh.' Dave gestured towards Luke. 'We'd best listen to what he has to say.'

Luke went on: about how proud he was of them all, and how, 'I would have told you before but I had to wait and be sure.'

Recalling the endless meetings and frustrations of the past weeks, he took a moment to formulate his words. 'I've had to do some hard talking these past few weeks and I don't mind admitting there were times when I despaired. But I got there in the end, and now I can tell you that the future looks good, and we're about to expand. The premises will

94

be doubled in size and the fleet increased to eight wagons—the old ones going two at a time, until we have all eight exchanged for brand-new ones.'

With the workforce's full attention, he continued, 'All this will take time but, as you can see, two of the wagons have already been set aside for a ready buyer. I've secured two long-term contracts with sizeable companies based in Birmingham, and the hope of another in the pipeline.'

For a long, breathless minute, the silence was deafening.

Clenching his fist, Luke punched the air. 'That's it, folks! GO TO IT!'

He may have said more, but his voice was suddenly deafened by the biggest cheer ever to have been heard in that yard.

'GOD BLESS YER, SON!' Like many others, delighted and relieved, the ruddy-faced driver was leaping in the air, fists clenched and tears swimming in his eyes. 'We all thought we were for the bloody chop!'

Tears turned to laughter, and Luke went amongst them, with congratulations coming from all sides. He was deeply moved by the loyalty of these ordinary, wonderful people.

'Back to work now,' he told them, and with smiles and much chatter they ambled away and, well satisfied with his own considerable achievements, Luke returned to the office.

'These good people have made this business what it is today,' he told the old Irishman.

'Aye, they have that, Mr Hammond.' Thomas wondered what Luke's father would have had to say about what had happened just now, because in all the years he'd sat at this desk, he had never witnessed such a great surge of devotion as he'd seen today.

'If you don't mind me saying, Mr Hammond, I think you've forgotten something, so yer have.'

'Oh?' Turning from the window where he was enjoying his employees' good humour, he asked, 'What's that then, Thomas?'

Thomas took off his spectacles, as he habitually did when about to say something serious. 'The men may well have "made" the business, as you so put it. But it's *you* they look up to, and it's *you* that inspires them, so it is.'

Having said his piece, he smiled to himself, discreetly blinked away a tear, and got on with his paperwork.

Later, Luke discreetly observed his employees, content at their work. He wondered what his father would think about this new turn of events. A twist of regret spiralled up in him as he reflected, and not for the first time, how he had no son to hand the business on to. Somehow, a child had not happened, and now it seemed all too late.

His thoughts turned to Sylvia.

Why had she given herself to a man like Arnold Stratton? Had he himself let her down as a husband? Had he worked too long and hard, sometimes building the business, sometimes trying to keep it afloat? Had she been lonely? Was it all his fault? Time and again, he had asked himself that.

And yet when he looked back, he had not seen any real signs that she was unhappy or lonely. At that time she had many friends; all of whom had since deserted her when she needed them most.

96

She had been a busy, fulfilled woman who lived life to the full. He made sure they spent a great deal of time together. Since the day he met her, he had loved her with all his heart and had believed she loved him the same.

And yet she had found the need to seek out a man like Arnold Stratton. It was a sobering thought. He could not understand. Had she never really loved him? Did she secretly yearn for the greater excitement he could not give her?

And now, with the lovemaking ended and her injuries taking their toll, there would never be a child and she was like a child herself: helpless; frightened. All she had in the world were the two people who really cared: himself, and the devoted Edna. But, though they would do anything for her, they could not perform the miracle she needed.

In his mind's eye he could see his painting of Sylvia. In that painting he had captured her beauty and serenity. If he was to paint her now, the fear and madness, however slight, would show in her eyes and mar her beauty. *Arnold Stratton had done that and now he was in prison for what had happened to Sylvia. And rightly so!*

The feeling of sorrow turned to a cold and terrible rage. If only he could have stopped it happening. If he could get his hands on that bastard, he'd make him pay for every minute he and Sylvia had been together. He imagined them in bed, naked, and his mind was frantic.

Stratton was where he belonged. A long spell in prison was not punishment enough for what that monster had done.

His unsettled thoughts shifted to another painting, hidden away in his sanctuary. It was a painting of another young woman. A woman with mischief in her eyes and the brightest, most endearing smile. A woman not of the same kind of beauty as his wife, but with something he could not easily define, not even in the painting of her.

She was *alive*! He only had to glance at the painting and it would make him smile. Her very essence leaped off the canvas. She warmed to the eye and her image lingered in the mind.

Thinking of her now, he smiled freely.

'Amy,' he murmured.

Her name on his lips was like a song.

PART TWO
May 1933
The Child

CHAPTER SEVEN

'So, have you caught sight of her yet?' Though harmless enough, old Alice was one of those women who was never happier than when somebody else was miserable.

Amy looked up from wrapping the two slices of bacon. 'Who are we talking about now?' She was used to Alice's gossiping tongue.

'The woman who's just moved in, next door but one to me.' Leaning forward she imparted in a harsh whisper, 'There's summat very strange about a woman who moves house in the middle of the night, don't you think?'

'Happen she works a late shift.' Marie emerged from the back room just in time to catch Alice's remark. 'From what I hear, the poor woman arrived bag and baggage at half-past nine. I'd hardly call that the "middle of the night".'

'Well, *I* would!' Alice retorted. 'I'm away to my bed at nine o'clock, and I don't take kindly to being woken by the slamming of doors. As for "bag and baggage", I can tell you, all she had with her was a little lad in arms and a portmanteau no bigger than this 'ere shopping bag!' Holding her canvas bag up high, she declared jubilantly, 'Now then! You tell me that isn't suspicious—arriving at half-past nine of an evening, with a hankie-sized portmanteau and a child in arms.' Sliding her bag onto the counter, she folded her chubby arms and waited for an answer. 'Well?'

Amy voiced what her mother was also thinking. 'She wouldn't have any need for much, would she?'

101

'Oh, and why's that, then?'

Amy shrugged. 'Well, I mean . . . the house is fully furnished, isn't it? Mac Robinson hasn't sold up. Apparently, he intends coming back from Scotland at some point, and from what he told me, he left everything intact for the prospective tenant. Cutlery, crockery, furniture and such. He even had new sheets put on the beds.'

'So?' Alice was not impressed. 'That doesn't change anything. Even if Mac Robinson left the sheets and towels, you'd think a mother and child would need more than just the clothes on their backs. Because as far as I could tell when looking through the window, that's more or less all they had with them.'

Her interest growing, Marie leaned on the counter. 'Aye, well, if that's the case, she deserves my sympathy. It sounds to me as though the poor soul is down on her luck.'

Amy was curious. 'What does she look like?'

'Well, I wouldn't say she was anything special.' In a superior voice, Alice described her in detail. 'Short woman, narrow face and iron-red hair. Not her natural colour, I shouldn't wonder. And if anything, she seemed a bit tatty, if you know what I mean?' Squaring her shoulders with authority, she begrudgingly added, 'Mind you, having said all that, she's not a bad-looking woman, I suppose.'

Amy had a mental picture of this new neighbour and she felt a little sad. 'I don't think we should be talking about her like this.' Reaching up to the shelf, she rearranged the boxes of Omo washing powder. 'I think we should accept her for what she is, and count our own blessings.'

'That's what I say an' all, lass.' Cutting off a

small square of butter, Marie carefully wrapped it before placing it on the counter. 'There you are, Alice.' Licking her pencil she totted up the amount on a notepad. 'That'll be one and ninepence, please.'

'Hmm!'

Alice quickly paid and, after stuffing the groceries into her bag, she made for the door with a parting piece of advice. 'You should be very careful who you make friends with.' She cast a wary glance towards the door. 'If you ask me, people like her need to be watched. There's summat very fishy about that woman,' she warned. 'I've said it now, and I'll say it again, anybody who moves house late at night, with a child in tow and hardly any belongings, has got summat to hide.'

Having said her piece, she marched out.

As she left, little Bob Ainsworth stumbled in. 'Bloody hell!' he chuckled. 'The way she's gone down that street, it's like her knickers are on fire.' A man in his seventies, he seemed to shrink with every passing day.

Marie and Amy both laughed. 'Morning, Bob.' Marie was already reaching under the counter. 'After your baccy, is it?'

'Aye . . . unless you've summat more appetising to offer a poor, lonely old fella?'

'What did you have in mind then?' As if she didn't know. In varying forms, Marie had gone through this conversation with him every day since the shop opened.

He licked his lips. 'Well now, being as you asked, you wouldn't have a nice young lady under that counter, would you? Plump and merry, with a mind to keeping an old man happy.'

'Sorry, Bob, we're out of nice young ladies today . . . present company excepted, of course.' In a more serious voice she warned, 'You want to be careful. You know what happens to older men who take young ladies into their homes.'

Embarrassed, he made light of her remark. 'Say what you like, there's only one thing that could happen, and that's me and her having a good time.'

Marie persisted, 'I'm telling you, Bob, I've known it happen many a time. An old man takes a young woman into his home and, before you know it, she's got her feet under the table and he's out on the street, homeless and penniless.'

The widower gave a nervous grin. 'D'you think I'm gullible enough to let that happen?'

'You're on your own, Bob, and from what you keep telling me, you'd welcome some young woman with open arms,' Marie said kindly. 'But think about it. Any young lady would want a man her own age. Unless o' course she's waiting for some gullible, randy old fool to come along; some poor bloke she can flutter her eyelashes at, before she robs him blind and walks away with everything he's got.'

Bob took a minute to dwell on her words, and when he spoke, it was in a panic-stricken voice. 'You heard me wrong, lass. I never said . . .' He shook his head so hard, his eyes swivelled in their sockets. 'I don't know what you thought I meant, but you got it all wrong. All I meant to say was, I just thought it would be nice to have a bit of company, that's all.'

To save his dignity, Marie went along with his bluff. 'Oh, Bob, I am sorry,' she said penitently. 'You're right. I must have misheard.'

104

'Aye, you bloody well did, an' all.' Bristling with indignation he told her, 'Just give me my baccy and I'll be off. And mind what you say in future . . . I'm a respectable pillar of society and allus have been.'

A moment later, clutching his precious wad of baccy, he tumbled out of the shop, leaving Marie unusually quiet and Amy softly laughing, though when she caught sight of Marie deep in thought, she wondered if her mother was already regretting her harsh words to the old man.

Amy asked her now, 'Why did you do that?'

'Do what?' Marie seemed agitated. 'I didn't "do" anything.'

'Aw! Come off it, Mam,' Amy chided. 'You put the fear of God in him.'

'I'm glad I did!' Marie sharply rebuked her. 'Anyway, it serves him right.'

Amy couldn't agree. 'You know Bob,' Amy replied. 'He's a bit of a dreamer. If a woman threw herself at him, he'd run a mile.'

'You could be right,' Marie admitted. 'Happen I were a bit hard on him.' Her voice dropped to a softer tone, 'Aw, look, lass. It was for his own good. Bob is a smashing bloke who's worked hard all his life. He had fifty happy years of marriage with a good woman, and for most men that would be sufficient. He must be seventy-five if he's a day, and here he is, talking about some young thing who would happily rob him of his life savings and even the roof over his head.'

'But you don't know that.' Amy had never seen her mother so agitated. 'And if you don't mind me saying, Mam, it's not like you to interfere in somebody else's life.'

Marie fell silent for a time before confessing in a

quiet voice. 'I do know what I'm talking about, lass,' she revealed quietly. 'I've never spoken of it before but two years after we lost your grandma . . . my mother . . .' she paused a moment, '. . . your grandad was terrible lonely. He was still a fair-looking fella, with a decent enough house . . . all paid for, and a few shilling in the bank. After a while he did what old Bob's in danger of doing. When some young woman cocked her hat at him, he was flattered. Common sense flew out the window and eventually he took her into his house.'

Amy was astonished. 'What happened?'

'Your grandad doted on her, but it was never enough. She led him a right merry dance, I can tell you! Your father and me tried hard to persuade him to be rid of her, before she ruined him altogether. But would he listen . . . no! Until one night, when she thought he was asleep, he caught her going through his wallet.

'He realised what a fool he'd been and he threw her on the streets where she'd come from. But not before she'd managed to spend every penny he'd put by, and sold a multitude of precious things which he'd got hidden away in the cupboards.'

She shook her head sadly. 'He never saw them, or her again.'

Amy was horrified. 'Why did you never tell me?'

Marie explained, 'You were only a few month old at the time, and when you were older there was no point raking it all up. Me and your father thought it best to leave it all in the past where it belongs. Besides, it's not summat you shout from the rooftops, is it? I for one didn't want folks to know what a silly old fool your grandad had been.'

She gave a little chuckle. 'God only knows what

your grandma said to him when he got up there.' She rolled her eyes to Heaven.

Amy began to understand. 'Oh, Mam, I wish I'd known my grandparents.'

'You do, lass,' Marie reminded her. 'You've got pictures of them and I've told you as much as I know, so you know them almost as well as I did.' She tutted loudly. 'And now you know the grubby little secret I've been keeping all these years.'

'And it'll stay a "secret",' Amy promised.

'And I'm sorry if I frightened old Bob.' Marie jerked a thumb towards the door. 'But he's treading on dangerous ground if he goes looking for some young flighty thing. I had to give him a little warning.'

'You did right, Mam.' In view of what she'd just been told, Amy agreed. 'I would love to see him find a good woman . . . we both would. But what you said might just make him think twice before he does anything foolish.'

*   *   *

The day quickly passed, and customers came and went, and it was just an hour to closing before Marie and Amy found time to catch their breath.

Then Amy began replenishing the shelves, while Marie went into the back room and made them each a cup of tea. 'I've brought us a slice of cake,' she told Amy, emerging with a tray and a smile.

'Just what the doctor ordered.'

Pulling up a stool, Amy sat beside her mother at the counter. 'When we've had this, you can start the cashing up, while I finish filling up the shelves.'

'That's a good idea,' Marie agreed. 'I doubt if

107

we'll get any more customers now. We can't shut up shop just in case, but we can take a minute or two to enjoy a well-deserved break.'

They had no sooner started tucking into the refreshments than the door opened and in came a woman with a child at her side.

At once, because of her appearance, both Amy and her mother thought this might be the new neighbour Alice had complained about. Seemingly in her mid-thirties, she looked a weary soul, and if, as Alice claimed, the clothes on their backs were all they had, then both woman and child were in a sorry state.

While Marie returned the tray to the kitchen, complete with half-eaten cake, Amy addressed the child, a small, scraggy thing with wild fair hair and an angelic-looking face.

'Hello. What's your name then?'

Reaching down to chuck the child under the chin, she was disappointed when he drew away and hid behind his mammy's skirt.

'His name's Johnny.' Putting an arm round his tiny shoulders, the woman explained, 'He'll not talk to you. He never talks to anybody but me.'

Amy smiled at the toddler. 'He's a fine-looking boy.' Though she thought he could do with fattening up a bit. 'How old is he?'

'He'll be three come July. I won't have to think about putting him in school for a bit yet.'

'We've a good school round here,' Amy informed her. 'According to what the customers tell me, their children seem to be doing all right.'

'I'm not interested in what other folks might say,' the woman informed Amy.

Fearing she might have overstepped the mark,

Amy apologised. 'I'm sorry. I was just trying to help.'

'Well, there's no need, thank you. Now, what can I get for that?' She slapped a handful of coins on the counter.

Amy glanced at the coins. 'What is it you want exactly?'

Pushing the coins towards Amy, the woman asked, 'Is there enough for bread, butter, and a half-pint o' milk?'

Amy collected up the coins. 'You've more than enough,' she said, sliding two halfpennies back to her.

'Are you sure? I don't want charity!' the customer declared proudly.

'It isn't charity.' Giving the halfpennies another push towards the woman, Amy added kindly, 'This is your change. There really is enough money for what you want.'

There was a curious moment when the woman and Amy looked at each other, and a kind of deep-seated understanding passed between them.

'Thank you.' The woman nodded gratefully.

It took only a minute for Amy to gather the few items and, as the woman dropped them into her bag, Amy noticed the boy's longing glance at the sweet jars. Wary of being too familiar with the child, she asked the woman, 'Is it all right if I give Johnny a sweetie?'

'And how much will that cost me?'

'No, please . . . let it be a small gift from me to him. It's nothing much.'

The woman looked at the boy and the boy smiled up at her. 'Sweetie,' he whispered shyly, his eyes lit up, and her heart melted.

'All right, son. But we'd best not make a habit of it,' she added to Amy.

Taking a sweet from the jar, Amy held it down to the boy. 'There you are, Johnny.'

But before the boy could take the sweet, Marie returned and the woman seemed to panic. 'It's time we were off!' Taking Johnny by the hand, she propelled him across the shop.

'No, Mammy,' the boy began to cry, 'the lady's got my sweetie.'

'Please . . . I have it here.' Running across the shop, Amy blocked their way, but not in a threatening manner. 'It's just a sweet,' she pleaded. 'Please?'

There was that long, intimate moment again, when the older woman and the young one seemed to understand each other and when the woman spoke now, it was with gratitude. 'Thank you. But you'd best give it to me. You're a stranger. He'll not come anywhere near strangers.'

When the boy backed away, once more hiding behind his mammy's skirt, Amy stooped down, keeping her distance but all the while smiling at his peeping face. 'This is for you. Take it, Johnny.' Holding out the sweet, she coaxed, 'It's liquorice, all soft and chewy, but if you don't like this one, we can choose another. What do you say?'

Slowly, hesitantly, the boy came forward and took the sweet from her, and to everyone's amazement, he reached up, kissed Amy on the face and ran back to his mammy, with the sweet clutched tightly in his hand.

'Well, I never!' The woman couldn't believe it. 'That's the first time he's ever done a thing like that. It seems he's took a liking to you.' Now, as she

110

smiled, the years and weariness fell from her face and she looked ten years younger. 'What's your name?'

'Amy.'

'Well, Amy, it would seem you have a way with children. Do you have any of your own?'

Amy shook her head, 'No. I'm not married.'

'Got a regular fella, have you?'

Amy rolled her eyes in frustration. 'Not so's you'd notice.' She supposed the Tuesday man at Tooley's Café didn't count. She had come to look forward to seeing him there despite the frustration of having, even yet, not discovered even his name. In a way that made it easier—he could be anyone—and she would find herself thinking about him and wondering.

'Hmm! All I can say is, the men round these parts must be a wagonload o' fools.'

Amy laughed. 'Happen they're just not interested in me.'

'Oh, and why would that be?'

'Because I'm not the prettiest girl around.' Amy had never fooled herself on that score.

'I don't know who told you that, because you look all right to me. But it means nothing anyway,' the woman assured her. 'Prettiness is on the outside, and anyway, after a time it begins to fade.' She wagged a finger. 'It's what's on the *inside* that counts. A man might cast his eyes over a pretty girl, and for a time he might have his head turned, but when he comes to settling down and wanting to raise a family, he looks for a bit more than prettiness. He looks for a kind heart and common sense—somebody as can cook and mend, and keep him content . . . if you know what I mean?' A brief

111

uplift of the eyebrows spoke volumes.

Turning to Marie, she asked in a softer voice, 'Are you the mother?'

Marie took a pace forward. 'That's right, and I'm proud of it.' She wasn't altogether sure what to make of their new neighbour.

'You've a good lass here.'

'I know that, but thank you anyway.'

'She's wasted in this shop.'

'I know that as well, and though she's everything you said, she is also stubborn and determined. When she makes up her mind there's no reasoning with her.'

The woman laughed out loud. 'A girl after my own heart. I dare say you'll miss her when some man comes and snatches her away, and they will. You mark my words. There aren't many decent young women left, but this one seems a good 'un.' In harsher voice she finished, 'There are some bad buggers out there, I can tell you!'

Amy thought she sounded as though she'd met a few. 'I'm sure there are,' she agreed, 'but you'll not find them round these parts.'

'Is that so?' Giving them each a wary glance the newcomer declared firmly, 'I think I've said enough.'

Taking Johnny by the hand she opened the door and was going through it when she felt a tug. Looking down, she saw how the boy was turning back to smile at Amy.

'Bye, Johnny.' She gave him an affectionate, mischievous wink.

Returning Amy's smile, the woman nodded appreciatively. 'Thank you.'

When they were gone, Marie stepped forward.

'The lad seemed to have taken a shine to you,' she said. 'He's such a quiet, nervous little thing . . . hardly said a word. Is he backward, do you think?'

Amy shook her head. 'No.' She had thought that herself at first but now she knew different. 'I just think he's shy and he doesn't know how to deal with people around him.'

Marie tutted. '*She's* a strange one, though.'

Amy had to disagree. 'I think she's just frightened.'

'Frightened of what?'

'I don't know.' Amy couldn't quite put her finger on it. 'Did Alice mention anything about a man being with them when they arrived?'

'No. There was no mention of any man.'

'So where is he then? I mean, there must be a man somewhere . . . a husband. The boy must have a father. So, why isn't he with them?'

'Happen she's a widow. Or they're split up, lass. We know it happens.'

Amy was made to think of Daisy's parents, and she couldn't help but wonder whether it might be better for a warring couple like that to go their separate ways.

'It does seem an odd thing, though—woman and child, moving into a house with apparently nothing to call their own, and no man in sight. So, where have they come from? Why haven't they got anything of any value?' A thought occurred to her. 'Mam?'

'Yes?'

'Do you think they're on the run?'

Marie chuckled. 'By! What an imagination you've got. Why in God's name should they be "on the run"?'

'I don't know, but I reckon there's something wrong.' For both their sakes, Amy hoped they weren't in any kind of trouble.

Marie ended the conversation. 'Didn't you say Daisy was coming round?'

'Oh, yes!' Her mind taken up with the woman and boy, Amy had almost forgotten. 'She promised to help sew up my new curtains.'

'And I've the dinner to get on. Your father's home tonight and he'll be dying of starvation. So now then, my girl, put our new neighbours out of your mind, 'cos we've work to do.' Marie observed the half-empty shelves. 'We'd best get the shelves restocked and call it a day.'

And that was what they did; although, as much as she tried hard to forget them, Amy's thoughts kept coming back to the woman and child.

There was something about them that troubled her.

*   *   *

May was such a beautiful time of year, Luke thought as he drove out to his cabin. The leaves on the trees were bright green and tender, and the blackbirds were singing extra loudly. The glorious sunshine softened the rugged landscape of the fells to the north of Blackburn so that the countryside seemed to be welcoming him with a broad smile.

Above the track to the cabin the canopy of trees was not yet thick enough to exclude the sun, and its beams slanted like spotlights across the track. A large rabbit ran ahead of the car, then bounded off into the undergrowth with a flash of white scut. Soft-furred baby rabbits grazed the shorter grass beside the track with intense concentration,

114

ignoring Luke's car.

The winter mustiness of the cabin had almost vanished with the late spring sun, and when Luke arrived he immediately threw all the windows wide to take advantage of the warm fresh air and today's exceptional light. This was a day for painting, and he'd come to the cabin especially early, forgoing the attractions of Tooley's Café. He aimed to finish Amy's portrait before he returned to Blackburn, having progressed only slowly over winter, with the poor light.

He'd laid a fire in the grate before he left last week, and now he put a match to it. Then he went straight to the wardrobe for the covered canvas, and the easel, which he set up by a window.

As usual, he didn't uncover the painting immediately, but held it, still wrapped, while he thought of Amy, as he had seen her last Tuesday at Tooley's.

She was looking happier these days, more confident somehow, and this complemented her gentleness. Unlike her friend Daisy, Amy was not bold and brassy, and Luke found that sweetness very appealing. He concentrated on her face as he remembered it, trying to distil that exact slight element of bright assurance she'd developed. Then he unwrapped the canvas and set it on the easel.

Yes, yes . . . he'd almost captured it. A little lift at the corner of her mouth, maybe . . .

He gazed at the portrait for several minutes until he realised he was no longer looking with critical faculties, but rather with adoration. Oh God, she was gorgeous. If only the picture were really Amy, and not merely her likeness. Mad thought, but then Tuesdays were for dreams, however farfetched, and

115

Luke allowed himself this indulgence increasingly now that the portrait was almost finished.

He went to collect his paints and brushes from the wardrobe and set to work.

Only when he stopped to rest his painting arm did he realise that the sun was now very high. He looked at his watch: three hours had passed in total concentration without his realising. Suddenly he was thirsty and remembered he hadn't had a drink since arriving at the cabin. First he went to wring out a rag in the brook to cover the open paints. Then he went back out with the kettle.

As Luke stooped on the bank, the filled kettle in his hand, he heard a quiet rustling of undergrowth. He'd seen deer in these woods, of course, or maybe it was a rabbit, or a bird scratching for nesting material. Very slowly Luke turned, half crouched, and looked behind him from where the noise had come.

There stood a small brown deer, exquisitely pretty, with large dark eyes and a velvety nose. Luke kept absolutely still—and so did the deer. They eyed each other for a long moment, and still neither moved. As slowly as he could, Luke straightened, willing the creature not to dart away. But when he was almost upright, she flicked her pointed ears, turned quite calmly, it seemed to him, and trotted back among the trees and out of sight.

Luke laughed in delight at the deer's inquisitiveness. For a wild creature she was pretty bold. Maybe she'd visit again and he could entice her closer to the cabin. When he was a child, that had been the ambition of his school holidays—to tame a wild deer in these very woods. Well, now he'd try again. Velvet, she'd be called, and she'd feed out of his hands. He smiled at his foolishness and shrugged. Well, why not? Some dreams could come true, couldn't they?

The portrait of Amy greeted him on the easel as he re-entered the cabin, and after a few minutes away from it, he saw it with fresh eyes. All at once he knew that it was finished, that adding anything more would detract from what was there already. This was the best he could do and he was pleased with it.

He stood for a long time gazing at Amy—his Amy—while the sun moved round and the light in the cabin changed, and Amy's smile met his.

*   *   *

A month later on a beautiful June morning, Maureen Langdon came into the shop with the boy at her side. Now a regular customer and somewhat mellowed, she was on first-name terms with both Marie and Amy.

'Are you sure you don't mind?' she asked Amy, 'only he won't stay with anybody else and, like I told you, I really have to go on this errand.'

Amy assured her it was fine. 'Don't worry, Maureen. He can help me fill up the shelves.' Being as they had taken delivery that very morning, there was any amount of packets to be put away.

'I'll be back inside of two hours,' Maureen promised, 'and look, I can't tell you how grateful I am.'

Ushering the boy forward, she smiled at how easily he went to Amy, and how, when he slipped his hand into hers, Amy drew him close, as if to keep him safe. Knowing how frightened and unsure

117

he was around people, Maureen had been astonished at how quickly little Johnny had taken to Amy.

After everything bad that had happened to them it was comforting to know that she and her son had found a real friend in this warm-hearted young woman. She wasn't altogether yet sure of Amy's mother, Marie, because though she was friendly and interested in them, Maureen sensed a certain wariness that put her on guard.

'Take as long as you like,' Amy told her. 'He'll be all right here with us.'

'If I didn't think that,' Maureen answered, 'I wouldn't be leaving him with you.'

Amy had come to love the little boy, yet she had never been asked to take care of him before, and now she was really looking forward to it.

'Would you mind if I took him to the park?' she asked. 'I've kept back a loaf of stale bread so we can feed the ducks.'

'All right then, but mind you keep him well away from the water!' Opening her arms to him, she asked with a smile, 'Well, are you gonna give your mammy a cuddle or not?'

Running to her, Johnny was swung up high and held tight, before a moment later he was given back to Amy. 'Take good care of him, won't you?' Maureen said meaningfully. 'He's all I've got right now.'

Knowing how lonely she was, Amy took a pace forward. 'You've got me, and my mother,' she said. 'We'll be here whenever you need us.'

Maureen nodded. 'You're good people. I'm lucky to have you as friends.' Enjoying any kind of friendship was a new experience for her.

118

'You look very special today, if you don't mind me saying.' Amy observed how Maureen's short red hair shone. Her lips were painted soft pink and her high cheekbones touched with rouge.

Though slightly ill-fitting, the pretty green cotton dress was in stark contrast to the well-used clothes she usually wore. 'The dress really suits you,' Amy remarked. 'You should wear green more often.'

Blushing pink at Amy's kind comments, Maureen confessed in a whisper, 'It cost me tuppence from the rag-and-bone shop. They had a little jacket to go with it, but that was another tuppence and I couldn't quite stretch to it.'

Amy was quick to offer. 'I'd like to help you with that.'

'No, thank you!' Maureen Langdon was a proud woman. 'If I can't afford it, I won't have it.'

'Our Amy's right.' Entering from the back in time to hear the last conversation, Marie agreed with her daughter. 'You really should wear green more often.'

A moment or two later, and feeling like a million dollars, Maureen bade them goodbye. 'Two hours,' she said. 'Then I'll take him off your hands.'

'Take all the time you want,' Amy told her. 'Me and little Johnny are going to have a good time, aren't we, Johnny?' Bending to tweak his nose, she laughed out loud when he reached up and did the same to her.

When Maureen was gone and Johnny was busy refilling the shelves, Marie quietly voiced her concern. 'Aren't you getting a bit too fond of the lad?'

'How can you say that?' Amy was taken aback. 'I

119

thought you liked him?'

'Well, of course I like him!' came the sharp rebuke. 'It's just that we still don't know anything about the lad and his mammy—where they came from, or why they turned up out of the blue like that. What happens if they leave the same way?'

'Out with it, Mam,' Amy urged. 'What are you getting at?'

'You think about it, lass. Here you are, getting more and more fond of the lad—and don't deny it because I've seen you, nose pressed to the window when you think they might show their faces. So, what if one afternoon he's here, and the next minute, without warning, they're gone as quickly as they arrived?'

'But they won't. Not now.' Amy had thought about it often of late, and somehow had managed to convince herself how Maureen Langdon and the boy would be around for a long time to come. 'They're settled here now,' she argued. 'Maureen says herself how much she likes living in Derwent Street.'

A little flurry of concern made her turn to watch Johnny busying himself. 'But if, for any reason, they were to leave now, I know Maureen would keep in touch.'

Marie sighed. 'I don't want you hurt, lass. That's all.'

'Amy! Amy!' Excited, the boy came running to tell Amy how he'd finished the work she'd set him. 'No more boxes. Come look!'

Discreetly sending him before her, Amy quietly assured her mother, 'You've no need to worry. They won't be leaving. You've only got to see how well Johnny's come on since they came to Derwent

Street. Maureen too. You saw how she was when they first arrived—defensive; afraid even. They won't leave. They're settled here now.'

'I hope you're right,' Marie announced. 'For your sake.'

In a troubled voice she gave a kindly warning. 'Maureen Langdon was right about you,' she said. 'You are a good 'un. Warm-hearted and kind. But don't let the lad creep too far into your affections. Remember, lass . . . the deeper you love, the deeper can be the hurt.'

'Oh, Mam!' Throwing her arms round that dear soul, Amy held her for a long, reassuring moment. 'All right, Mam. I'll bear in mind what you said,' she promised.

A moment later, she and the boy were laughing at the way he had mixed all the buttons together; large, small and multi-coloured all in the same drawer.

From a discreet distance, Marie watched them, and the way that darling little boy was looking up at Amy with adoration only served to fuel her fears.

In spite of Amy's promise, it was all too clear that these two were already deep in each other's affections.

∗   ∗   ∗

Having travelled some distance, Maureen joined the other passengers and clambered from the tram.

Going at a fast pace down the street she turned the corner and there right before her the building blocked the way, its grim high walls sending a shard of apprehension through her insides.

Approaching the tall iron gates, she was aware

of other women all heading in the same direction. 'I hate this bloody journey!' The small weary-eyed woman was about Maureen's age. 'Every week for the past four years,' she groaned, 'and no end in sight. Knowing him and his troublemaking ways, I expect it'll be the same for *another* four years.' Pushing on, she added angrily, 'It's not just his life he's wasting. It's mine too . . . mine and the kids'. In the end it's always us who pays the price!'

Maureen nodded. She knew what it was like.

Now, as she neared the gates, she prepared herself for the ordeal ahead.

'Here they come!' Straight-faced, legs astride and arms folded, the two prison officers waited. 'The sooner this is over the better,' exclaimed the taller of the two.

'Poor devils,' replied the other. 'It can't be easy for them.'

'Listen to yourself, man! Not getting soft, are you?'

'Nope. Just getting older, I guess.'

While one prison officer opened the gate, his colleague kept an eye on the long line of visitors as they filed by him.

When the last was inside, the two of them followed behind. 'Straight ahead if you please.' A swift but careful search of belongings and one by one the visitors were allowed through. 'No canoodling, and no devious whispering.'

Spying the familiar cap of fair hair, Maureen hurried to be with her husband.

'Arnold . . .'

'Oh, Maureen, you don't know how good it is to see you!' The man's broad shoulders were slightly stooped, his blue eyes sad, and now, when he

122

spoke, his voice trembled with a deep-down regret. 'It's like I've been in this place for a hundred years,' he said. 'You can't imagine how I count the minutes till you're here.'

Under the watchful eye of the officer, they exchanged a brief kiss, but it was a kiss that spanned the emptiness between them; a kiss that said, 'In spite of everything, I love you still.'

'SIT DOWN!' The officer's voice rang out, and everyone who had been standing quickly sat down, including Maureen and her husband.

Glancing warily at the officer, he wrapped his long fingers round Maureen's. 'Are you well?'

'Well enough, I expect.' There was a certain bitterness in her tone, but he either did not detect it, or chose to ignore it.

'And the boy . . . is he well?'

Maureen's quick smile warmed his heart. 'Johnny's doing fine,' she answered. 'You'll be amazed at how confident he's grown.' All thanks to Amy, she thought proudly.

The man's eyes lit up at her news. 'Aw, Maureen, that's wonderful news!' His gaze went instinctively to the door. 'Where've you left him?'

'He's with Amy, the young woman from the corner shop. Remember I told you about her? You should see them together. It's a joy to watch.'

He dwelled on her words for a moment. 'How in God's name did *she* get through to him, when nobody else could?' He knew how painfully shy Johnny had always been. 'Anyway, what's she like, this Amy?'

'I already told you. She's about twenty-five, I reckon . . . not what you might call a natural beauty, but pretty enough, with her thick mop of brown hair and those twinkling eyes. Lovely nature, though . . .'

'Are you sure you can trust her with the boy?' he asked warily.

'Absolutely. Or I wouldn't leave him, you know that.'

'You haven't told her about me, have you?'

'No.'

'You mustn't tell anyone.'

'I won't.'

'When the boy eventually gets to school, his life won't be worth living if word gets round that his daddy's a gaolbird.'

'You don't need to tell me that, Arnold,' she replied.

Momentarily silent, he bowed his head. When he looked up there were tears in his eyes. 'I didn't do it,' he said. 'You do believe that, don't you?'

She nodded. Of course Arnold had done nothing *on purpose*. But that wasn't really the point. She felt she had to say something. 'Well, I don't think you *meant* to do anything, Arnie. But you have been known to lose your temper—get carried away. But I'll always be waiting for you when you come out, you know that.'

He held her hand. 'What would I do without you, eh?'

She chuckled. 'Fall apart at the seams, I dare say.'

In a serious voice he told her, 'I do love you.'

'Only because I'm fool enough to stand by you.'

He shook his head. 'No. It's because whatever I've done and however many women I've bedded, there's never been anybody like you.'

'Does that mean I'm stupid and gullible?'

124

'Not gullible, no. Loyal and long-suffering, and true to your marriage vows. Not like me, and not like the flippant women who take me to their beds behind their husbands' backs.'

'Tell me the truth,' she asked quietly, 'have you ever loved any of them?'

'Never!'

'Not even Sylvia Hammond?'

'Especially not her.'

'Did she love you?'

'Good God, Maureen. A woman like that! She doesn't know the meaning of the word "love".'

'You sound disappointed.' Something in his voice, some regret or anger, made her curious.

He dismissed her implication with a vague answer. 'Women like her are two a penny,' he said. 'She was no different from any of the others. Just another woman looking for a bit of excitement.'

Maureen had seen the pictures in the paper and had her own opinion. 'She's very stylish, and beautiful . . . not like me.'

He touched her hand gently. 'You're right,' he murmured, 'she's nothing like you. Stylish and beautiful maybe, but there's nothing worthwhile on the inside. She's just a greedy, selfish woman, never satisfied with the grand life she leads, and with never a thought for the good man who works his guts out to provide it all. And look at you! You're left on your own, caring for Johnny and the pair of you struggling to make ends meet. And it's all thanks to me and my bloody wandering!'

Maureen couldn't argue with that. 'I hope after this you'll mend your ways when you get out?'

He took a deep angry breath. 'I'll be an old man with whiskers before you see me on the outside!'

Maureen changed the subject slightly. 'It's tragic what happened to her, all the same. They say her mind is gone, and there's nothing they can do about it.' She had often wondered, 'What made her say it was you that did it?'

'I've no idea.' He sounded puzzled as well. 'All I know is, I was well fitted up.'

'Even so, you must try and put it out of your mind, or it'll drive you crazy.' She didn't like the way his fist was clenching against the table. 'Let it go, Arnie. *Please!* Just let it go.'

'I can't "let it go"!' This time he banged the table. 'When I find the bastard who put me in the frame, I swear to God, I'll swing for him.'

'Ssh!' Pressing her finger to her lips, she warned, 'The officer's watching you.'

In a moment the officer was at the table. 'All right, Stratton, on your feet. NOW!'

Watching him being taken away, Maureen despaired. 'Dear God! What'll become of us?'

With a heavy heart she followed the wives outside.

'They all claim to be innocent, that they've been fitted up, or that somebody had it in for them, or they couldn't help themselves.' Walking back to the tram-stop, the same woman who had walked alongside her on the way in fell into step with her now. 'They're all guilty as buggery, yet they'll deny the responsibility time and again, right up to when the rope tightens round their lying necks!'

'No, that's not true!' Realising everyone must have heard Arnold's outburst, Maureen protested vehemently, 'My Arnie really *was* "fitted up",' she said.

'Oh, really? So why is he inside then?'

126

Ashamed, Maureen hesitated. 'He *was* guilty of having an affair with her, but he swears it wasn't serious. He says he was about to finish it any day, and that she was growing agitated . . . didn't want it to end, y'see? Later, when she was attacked, she pointed him out as the culprit. He said he wasn't even with her that particular night. He was out playing cards in a mate's house, but his mate didn't want to get mixed up in it, so he denied that Arnie was ever there.'

The woman was not convinced. 'All I can say is, if your fella really did beat that woman senseless, he deserves to be where he is. They say she can be mad as a crazed dog—has these frightening fits and doesn't know what she's doing.'

'I've heard the same, but who knows what truth there is in it?' Maureen had retorted. 'Happen she's not ill at all. Happen she's seeking attention, like kids do when they can't have their own way.'

'Oh, it's true all right!' The woman drew Maureen to a halt. 'She's the wife of Luke Hammond, ain't she?'

'That's right.'

'Well, my brother works for Luke Hammond and he says it's the talk of the factory—how she drives her poor husband to distraction at times . . . half crazed and doesn't know what she's doing, that's how they describe her. She's followed the poor bugger into work before now, went from one man to another, asking questions about where he is, and who he's with. And even though it's a known fact that she cheated on him, he won't hear a word said against her. She has the best of everything, and he's always there for her day and night . . . That's what they say.'

127

A short time later the tram stopped outside Corporation Park. 'All off that's getting off,' the conductor called, and two men disembarked.

Through the window, Maureen glanced along the entrance to the park, and there, just disappearing from sight towards the lake, she spied Amy and Johnny.

'WAIT!' Rushing down the gangway she told the conductor, 'I'll get off here!'

With his finger already poised on the bell to send them forward, he gave her a wry little glance. 'I thought you were headed for Henry Street?'

'I was,' she admitted, 'but now I've changed my mind.'

'We don't give refunds,' he chided.

'I don't want a refund,' she replied. 'I just want to get off if that's all right with you?'

'Off you go then, missus.' Stepping obligingly aside to let her disembark, he said cheekily, 'Don't get lost, will you?'

Maureen wagged a finger. 'You behave yourself. I know exactly where I'm going.'

Once she was off the tram, she went away at a fast pace up the main walkway to the park, and with quickening steps, hurried towards the lake at the top of the hill, where she had seen Amy and little Johnny.

It was a long walk and with the sun belting down, she was soon made to slow her pace.

*　　　*　　　*

Amy held Johnny in a firm grip. 'Remember what your mammy said,' she told him. 'You're to keep away from the water.' The lake was notoriously

128

deep in places.

The boy tugged hard on her hand. 'Ducks!' Pointing with his other hand he gestured to Amy's bag. 'They want their dinner.'

'Be patient,' she laughed. 'They won't go far when they know there's food about.'

Seating the boy on the bench, Amy took out the bread and, breaking it into small bites, gave him a fistful. 'Come on then,' she said. 'Mind you stay back when you throw it, and keep a hold of my hand.'

Amy helped the boy to throw out the breadcrumbs.

The ducks came forward at full speed, making long, spreading patterns in the water as they swam in formation.

'Look, Amy, look!' As the last of the bread was taken, little Johnny laughed, which Amy took great delight hearing.

'Sounds like somebody's having fun.' As Maureen came through the shrubbery, the boy ran towards her. Maureen opened her arms to him and, yet again, was amazed by the change in him that had occurred over these past weeks. Now confident, he was quick to laugh, and his eyes shone with the joy of life. It was a wonderful thing to see.

Taking him into her embrace, she smiled at Amy, who had collected their belongings and was now coming towards her. 'He must have been enjoying himself,' Maureen said gratefully. 'I heard him laughing as I came round the corner.'

'He's been having a great time,' Amy told her. 'We've climbed the banks to the top of the world— we could see the whole of Blackburn town and all the church spires—and afterwards we played hide and seek in the gardens.'

'I don't know how to thank you,' Maureen told her as they headed back down along the main walkway.

'There's nothing to thank me for,' Amy said. 'I've had a wonderful time. Johnny is a delight to be with.'

Maureen watched her son bouncing and skipping down the path, and her heart filled with gratitude. 'You don't know what you've done for us,' she told Amy. 'There was a time when I thought he might never smile again. He was timid and unsure, and treated everybody with suspicion. At one time he even gave up talking, and it was a trial to get him to eat.' Her voice shook with emotion. 'They were dark days.' She looked to where the boy was happily playing. 'And just look at him now!' Grabbing Amy by the hand she drew her to a halt, her eyes suddenly brimming with tears. '"Thank you" isn't enough,' she murmured. 'You can't know how you've changed our lives.'

Closing her hand over the other woman's, Amy told her how she was glad to have been of some help. It was a curious thing, she thought, how this woman and her son had not only moved into the street, but had also moved into her own heart.

Amy realised that there must have been something very bad in their lives to have brought them down to where they were now. And what was it that had affected the boy in such a way that he had become so afraid of people?

As they meandered their way down the lane, Amy mustered the courage to ask, 'Did something happen that caused Johnny to shy away from

130

people?'

Taken aback by Amy's direct question, Maureen took a moment to answer. 'I don't really know.' She had learned to lie convincingly. 'He was all right, and then he wasn't.'

Amy realised she was not telling the whole truth. As she'd spoken, Maureen had glanced about as though she were afraid somebody might be listening. 'Are you all right, Maureen?'

Maureen nodded, but rather than lie to Amy again, she remained silent.

'Look, Maureen, if you ever need a friend, I'm here for you,' Amy told her. 'Always remember that.'

It was only slight, almost inaudible, but Amy was certain she heard a smothered sob. 'I wish I had the courage to confide in you,' Maureen answered sadly, 'and I do need a friend.'

'Whenever you're ready,' Amy assured her. 'I want to help . . . if I can.'

They continued on their way, to the sound of birdsong, and the boy's hearty laughter as he went roly-poly down the grass bank.

It was such a glorious day, Amy thought. The hot sun beat down on them and the mingling scents of flowers created a pleasant aura around them. They went on quietly a little further, and still there was that air of mystery and secrets.

After a while, Amy was compelled to speak. 'You needn't be afraid to confide in me,' she told Maureen. 'I want you to know that whatever you tell me will always stay a secret.'

For one mad, unthinking minute, Maureen almost confided in Amy. But then Arnold's words echoed in her mind: 'You mustn't tell anyone!' and

131

her courage disappeared.

She looked away. 'Thank you,' she said brightly, 'but there's nothing to tell.'

In that desperate moment she felt more lonely than she had felt at any time in her life. She desperately needed to speak with Amy, about the things that played on her mind. She needed to open her heart and tell of the things that haunted her; and the other things that had made little Johnny the frightened shadow he had been, before Amy had won his trust and his love.

But however much she wanted to open her mouth and let the words come out, they stuck fast in her throat. She would have left Arnie years back and for many reasons, but where would she go? And, besides, she loved him. That was the trouble.

As they neared the gate, Amy saw how even in the warmth of the day, Maureen's face was drained of colour. 'You'd best sit down,' she urged, leading her to the bench. 'You look so tired, Maureen.'

For a moment, Amy sat beside the older woman, and together they watched Johnny as he played on the grass. Suddenly Amy realised that Maureen was softly crying, the tears rolling down her face and her whole body shaking.

'Tell me what's haunting you?' she urged tenderly. 'Whatever it is, you need to share it.' She could feel Maureen's pain. 'Please, Maureen, for your own sake, let me help.'

Wiping away her tears with the cuff of her sleeve, Maureen nodded. 'Will you promise not to tell anyone?'

Without hesitation Amy agreed, and as Maureen told her the whole sorry tale, she learned why Johnny had become the way he was.

Maureen told her how some years ago her husband, a man of uncertain temper, had thrown her out on the streets and taken another woman into his bed. 'For a long time I was awfully lonely . . . even suicidal at one stage. But I pulled myself up and found a little job with a room as well. Then I met a new man, and everything was going along nicely.'

'So what happened?' Maureen had not mentioned the name of any man, not once in all their conversation. That was a curious thing.

'Then I became pregnant and right from the day Johnny was born, his father resented him. Sometimes, when he came home drunk, he would stand over Johnny's cot and stare at him for ages. He wouldn't do or say anything, he would just stand at the foot of the cot and stare at him. It used to frighten me so much, that as soon as his daddy had gone to his bed, I'd sneak Johnny out of the cot and take him with me, to the spare room.'

Amy thought Johnny's father must be mad and said so.

'There were times when I thought that too,' Maureen admitted, 'but things did get better, and as Johnny started walking and looking more like a boy than a baby, and had learned to say "Daddy", they seemed to get closer.'

Lowering her voice so the boy wouldn't hear, she went on, 'I found out later, it was just an act.'

Amy wasn't surprised at that. 'What do you mean? How did you find out?'

'It was a day much like today,' Maureen explained. 'The sun was shining and the boy was restless. I'd been poorly that night—tummy upset or something. Anyway, I was feeling under the

133

weather. He offered to take the boy out of my way for a while . . . down to the bridge, where they could watch the barges passing underneath. This is what, I learned later, happened.

'They were heading down the street towards the bridge with Johnny running ahead, and suddenly he fell over. He started crying and wouldn't stop, and that was when his father laid into Johnny with his fist.'

'My God, that's awful!'

'Luckily, a man who was passing witnessed it all, rescued Johnny and saw his father off. This man was, by the greatest good fortune, Arnie, my husband. He was alone again, regretting what he'd done, and had been watching over us. It was fate— I know it was. He brought Johnny to me and that was when I knew we were meant to be together.'

A look of shame shadowed her homely face. 'You see, I still loved him. I never stopped loving him, not once. But pride had stopped me contacting him. And with another man's child in tow, I was certain he'd want nothing to do with me anyway.'

Amy could hear Maureen's love for this man shining in her voice as she spoke. 'So you went back to him in the end?'

'I had to.' Maureen's quiet smile was evidence enough of the way she felt towards her husband. 'He had always been my life and always would be. The time when we were apart was the worst time of my life. But there have been bad times since.' Her voice quivered. 'Sometimes I wonder if it might have been wise not to have gone back to him. But he's never laid a hand on Johnny, and whatever else he's guilty of I'm grateful for that.'

'And Johnny . . . ?' Only now was Amy beginning to realise the extent of worry Maureen had endured.

'He was black and blue. I realised after that bruises I'd taken to be the result of tumbles while playing had probably been caused all along by his father hitting him.'

Maureen finished, 'He would shy away from strangers and even though Arnie did the best he could to get close to the boy, Johnny cowered away from him. He became terrified of all men. From that day to this, he's never forgotten.'

She looked at Johnny and a shine came into her eyes that told Amy how much she loved the child. '*I've* never forgotten either,' she murmured. 'I never will.'

Amy was curious. 'And how are things between you and your husband now?' She didn't want to pry, but she wondered if the husband being absent had anything to do with what had happened to Johnny. Maybe the child had been unable to cope with the presence of any man.

Maureen was tempted to tell her the truth. She trusted Amy, but was it fair to burden her with the facts? How would Amy take it if she knew that Arnie was in prison for beating Sylvia Hammond half to death?

She decided not to mention it at all. More than anything, she did not want to risk losing Amy's friendship.

'We went through a bad patch,' she told Amy now. 'The landlord sold the house from under us, and Arnie got a job working down South.' She hated lying to Amy, but it had to be done. 'Meanwhile, I had to find a place for me and the

135

boy. That's when I heard about the house on Derwent Street. It's only two bedrooms, but that's all we need, and the rent is cheap. We got a bit of money from the sale of our furniture and belongings when we left the other house, so we'll manage all right, as long as I count the pennies. I'm keeping a lookout for work in a hotel kitchen, or a shop, where I might be able to take Johnny with me.'

'Have you seen anything yet?' Amy would have offered to look after Johnny while Maureen went off to work, but the shop was busy most times and she didn't think her mother would welcome a small child under her feet while trying to serve the customers. Still, if she could help Maureen in any other way, she would. 'If you got a little job, I'd always be willing to take Johnny off your hands,' she offered. 'I'd even change my day off, if that suited.'

'Aw, that's lovely of you to offer,' Maureen said gratefully, 'but I know how hard you work, and I would never dream of taking up your one day off. Don't you worry, I'll find something suitable, I'm sure. There might even be somebody on the Saturday market that would let me help run the stall and take Johnny along.'

That idea had been playing on her mind these past few days. 'I'll go through the market this Saturday,' she said hopefully. 'Who knows, I might just be lucky?'

'When will your husband be coming back?'

'I've no idea.' Maureen gauged her answer carefully. 'Like I say, he's working for a developer, and they're building right across the South. So there's no telling how long it might be before he

136

comes back.'

Such lies! But, if she and Johnny were to lead normal lives, the truth must be kept from everyone . . . even the lovely Amy. 'He's got our new address, so I'm sure he'll let me know when he's on his way back.'

Amy knew instinctively that Maureen had not confided everything in her. There was a great deal more, she could tell, but it was not for her to press this poor woman, who had been through so much. Besides, it was not her business. All that mattered was that whenever Maureen and Johnny needed her, she would be there.

For Amy's part, she was glad that Maureen had found the courage to confide this much in her. Now Maureen seemed easier with herself; her smile was brighter and she was more relaxed than Amy had ever seen her.

As for Johnny, he had been in his element at the park and now, hand in hand with them both, he was as carefree and happy as any young child should be. It was heart-warming to see.

CHAPTER EIGHT

'Are you sure you don't mind me going early?' In the last hour there had been a continuous flow of customers, and Amy was concerned about leaving her mother to deal with them on her own. 'With four people to serve and probably more on the way, it wouldn't be fair to leave you on your own, Mam.'

Marie waved aside her concern. 'I'm more than capable.' She lifted the bag of dolly-blues from the

137

cupboard. 'You get off and meet Daisy.' She glanced at the wall clock. 'If you don't get away now, you'll miss the tram and she'll think you've let her down.' Giving her a gentle prod she added cautiously, 'With the way things are between her parents, you're the only light in that girl's life, so be off with you!'

'Only if you're sure.' Amy couldn't help but feel guilty.

A sharp voice interrupted them. 'Are you serving us, or what? We've been waiting ages and I need to get back. My sister's coming up from Buckingham, and I've not even got her bed ready!' That was old Alice, complaining as usual.

'Well, you are a lazy bugger, Alice.' That was John Tupp, a wily old fellow from Whalley Banks, on the way to Clitheroe; he often came into the shop to have a chat. 'It were Monday last when you told me your sister were coming to stay, and here you are not even got her bed ready. By! What the devil do you do with your time, eh? That's what I'd like to know.'

'I reckon she's got a man tucked away somewhere.' Tiny Mrs Jacobs was the pawnbroker's wife. 'If you ask me, there's more to Alice than any of us know.'

'Gerraway!' A bit of a randy devil himself, Ronnie Leatherhead had been through more relationships than all the neighbours put together. 'A man would have more sense than to link up with Alice. She's too bloody mean and crotchety.'

'One thing's for sure,' Alice bit back, *'you'd* never get the chance to "link up" with me, not in a month o' Sundays!'

Chuckling at Alice's remarks, Marie propelled

138

Amy to the end of the counter. 'Get yourself ready and catch that tram,' she said. 'I'll be fine on my own. Just you go and enjoy yourself, lass. Lord knows, you've earned it.' She was amazed at how hard Amy worked, from the minute they opened the shop, to the minute they cashed up. Tireless, she was, and thorough with it.

As Amy went out of the shop and into the living quarters, she heard her mother chiding the customers, 'Hey! That's enough of the arguing. Now then, who's first?'

There was a span of shocked silence, before the arguing started again.

A short time later, Amy returned to the shop, to find the customers quietly behaved and her mother dealing with them in her own calm, collected manner. 'Give Daisy my love.' She gave Amy a peck on the cheek. 'And mind you don't spend all your hard-earned money.'

'You look nice, lass.' Old John's eyes lit up. 'By! I wish I were young again. Off to see young Daisy Robertson, are you?'

'Yes, she is!' Marie pushed Amy towards the end of the counter. 'And if you keep her talking, she'll never catch her tram.'

To Amy she murmured, 'He's right though, lass. You do look lovely.' Amy had on a pale pink blouse with loose neck and long sleeves, and a brown straight skirt that showed off her curves. Her hair was bouncy and her eyes were shining, and altogether she looked lovely.

'Thanks, Mam.'

Amy was really looking forward to spending a few hours with Daisy. 'I wonder if she remembers where we're meeting this time?' she remarked with

139

a hearty chuckle. 'Last time we arranged to meet, she waited on Ackeroyd Street instead of under the market-clock. It was nearly an hour before she remembered. Then it started raining and by the time she got to me, the pair of us were all wet and bedraggled.'

Marie laughed out loud. 'That's Daisy for you!'

As Amy went out the door, she heard the old man telling Marie, 'I feel for that young Robertson lass. Her father is a right bad lot, and as for the mother, well . . . every man in Blackburn knows how she earns her spending money.'

When the other customers joined in to condemn Daisy's parents, Marie wisely and light-heartedly put a stop to it. She knew what they were saying was the hard truth, but it wasn't the kind of banter she wanted to hear; especially not when Daisy was her daughter's best friend.

*   *   *

The shouting and screaming had gone on for a full hour.

'Get your hands off her, you bastard!' Painted with rouge and lipstick, her hair bleached to the roots and wearing a dress that revealed too much for comfort, Daisy's mother knew how to handle herself.

Taking the poker from its stand, she confronted Daisy's father. A mountain of a man, he had Daisy pinned to the door, his two arms folded across her neck and his considerable weight pressing against her. 'You're going nowhere!' he growled. 'Not till you tell me who was in here last night. And don't try lying through your teeth, because I know she had a bloke in here. I might be thick, but I'm not bloody stupid!'

Her face stained with tears, Daisy stared him out. 'I've already told you,' her words came out in a strangled muffle, 'I don't know anything.'

'You're a madman! Let go of her!' Daisy's mother screamed, prodding him repeatedly with the poker. 'There's been no fella in here . . . not last night or any other sodding night! There were only me and Daisy. Now let her go, or I swear to God, I'll do for you!'

In a sudden move that left her buckled against the door, he threw Daisy aside and, grabbing hold of the woman, wrapped his hands about her neck. 'So! You'll "do for me", will you?' he laughed. 'Well now, let's see you try, eh?' Wrenching the poker from her hands, he grappled her to the ground. There then followed a lot of shouting and threats as they tore at each other with blind hatred.

Suddenly there was a bang on the wall, and a neighbour yelled, 'If you don't stop the racket this minute, I'm fetching the police!'

'See what you've done now, you silly, jealous bugger!' As he continued to bear down on her, Daisy's mother fought like a tiger. 'You'll be getting us thrown out on the streets with your shenanigans!'

'Aw, come on, tek no notice of them buggers next door.' Stroking her breast he gave a knowing grin. 'What say we make up, eh?'

In a matter of minutes, the two of them were rolling about on the floor, laughing and teasing, and blatantly petting each other.

'You make me sick!' Disgusted with what was now happening before her eyes, Daisy ran to the scullery where she sobbed for a while. Then she washed her face, tidied her hair, straightened her tight little dress and checked her stocking seams, then, going out the back door, prayed the neighbours would not stop her as she ran down the street.

'I hate them!' she muttered. 'I wish they'd kill each other!'

Twenty minutes later, she stepped off the bus at the market square, where Amy was patiently waiting under the clock.

'Daisy!' Catching sight of her, she ran forward. 'Where in God's name have you been? I began to think you weren't coming.'

Daisy hurried to meet her. 'No you didn't,' she teased. 'You thought I'd forgotten and gone to the wrong place again, didn't you?'

Amy laughed. 'The thought did cross my mind.'

'Well, I'm here now,' Daisy told her, 'so stop nattering and let's get going.'

Amy hesitated. In spite of Daisy's jolly manner, she could see she'd been crying and, knowing how Daisy was sometimes reluctant to talk about what was going on at home, Amy offered all the same. 'You can tell me what happened if you like?'

Daisy shrugged. 'Who says anything happened?'

'I can see for myself. All I'm saying is,' Amy gently assured her, 'if you want to talk about it, I'm here for you.'

On the way to the shops Daisy outlined the cause of the trouble. 'It's always the same. He keeps accusing her of having a fella in the house when he's not around. Oh, I'm not defending her, because she's a disgrace—one man after another, and no shame to go with it. But she never brings

142

them home . . . not as far as I know, anyway.'

'Why don't they split?' It seemed a natural solution to Amy. These were two people who already seemed to live separate lives, with each carrying on with whomever they fancied. Yet they fought over each other like a pair of crazed animals, with poor Daisy caught in the middle of it all.

'They'll never split,' Daisy answered. 'They love each other—at least that's what they say.'

'But it doesn't make sense.' Amy had never been able to understand it.

Daisy was quiet for a time, then in a sombre voice she confessed, 'Sometimes, Amy, I hate them so much it frightens me.'

Then suddenly, and before Amy could answer, Daisy was running ahead. 'Come on, slowcoach!' she cried. 'Let's get a move on, or the shops will be shut before we get there.'

Realising it was Daisy's way of telling her she didn't want to talk about her parents any more, Amy went along with her. 'Race you to the Co-op!' she called, and the two of them ran down the street as though everything was right with the world.

They wanted new dresses to wear to a dance that evening. But the Co-op, even in the town centre, didn't carry much stock, so could not really help.

'We haven't got such a big dress selection,' the assistant told them, 'but we're looking to move to larger premises soon, and when we do, we'll have much more room for a clothes department.'

Leading the way, she ushered them into a small area at the back of the shop. 'There.' Pointing to the rack of garments, she said confidently, 'I'm sure you'll find something suitable.'

143

As the assistant walked away, Daisy sniggered. 'Bloody Nora! Now *there's* a frightening sight, I must say.'

Amy discreetly glanced at the woman. 'As long as she helps us to find what we want, she's all right by me.'

Though Amy had to admit she hadn't felt altogether comfortable in the woman's company. With her straight black skirt, starched white blouse and her dark hair scraped back so tightly it threatened to spring from the roots, the woman really did look quite unfriendly.

It didn't take long for the girls to realise they would not find what they wanted here. After fifteen minutes of rummaging through the rack, they had seen and tried all the frocks, and none of them was right.

'Have you found anything suitable?' The woman was back, arms folded and a grim look on her face, as though she was ready for a fight.

Amy shook her head. 'Sorry, but there's nothing there we fancy.' It was no use beating about the bush, she thought.

The woman was not pleased, and it showed. 'If that's the case, you might as well leave, because that's all we have, I'm afraid.' That said she turned her back on them and began straightening the dresses, all the time muttering and complaining.

'I wouldn't like to meet *her* on a dark night,' Daisy said as they made their way out.

'Happen she wouldn't care to meet *you* neither!' Amy quipped.

They were in merry mood as they burst into the second-hand shop.

'We're looking for party dresses,' Daisy informed

the proprietor. 'We'd like something pretty and cheap, with no stains or holes.'

'Well, now . . .' Bald-headed and round as a pumpkin, the man looked like a leprechaun perched on a stool. 'You've come to the right place, ladies.'

When he showed them through to the back room, they were confronted with three racks of dresses in all sizes, colours and styles. He left them to browse.

'We're gonna have a good time here, lass!' Laughing, Daisy wasted no time in sorting out four dresses to try.

'They've all been cleaned and pressed,' the odd little man informed them on his return. 'So don't go wiping lipstick and powder on 'em, or I'll have to charge you for the cleaning!' With that he loped out and left them to browse further.

Daisy and Amy had the time of their lives trying on the dresses. 'What do you think to this one?' When Daisy came out from behind the curtain, Amy almost collapsed in hysterics. Tight across her stomach and loose about her chest, the crimson dress clung to her backside, and when she bent down Amy could see her knickers.

'Put it back, for God's sake!' Amy urged. 'If you go out like that, you'll get arrested!'

'Does that mean you don't like it?' Daisy groaned, feigning disappointment.

'Trust me,' Amy laughed. 'Wear that and you'll have a trail of dogs behind, wherever you go.'

Daisy giggled naughtily. 'Men-dogs, or dog-dogs?' she asked.

'Both!' Amy answered.

For a bit of fun, Amy tried on a green dress with

145

a trailing hem that reached halfway across the room, and a feather boa.

'If you keep messing about we'll never find what we want,' Daisy chided. 'Let's get on with it.'

'Are you ladies all right in there?' the leprechaun enquired from the front room.

'We're fine,' Amy answered. 'You've got so many, it's difficult to choose.'

'I knew you'd be pleased,' he replied smugly. 'Take your time; we don't shut for another hour.'

In the end, Amy chose a straight, pale blue dress with stand-up collar and belted waist, which fitted as if it was made for her.

Daisy too was delighted with her find: a pink floating thing with low neckline, and also with belted waist, it fell to a swingy hem that kicked out as she walked.

'I feel like a film star,' she told Amy, and Amy was glad to see she had forgotten her troubles, at least for now.

When the dresses were parcelled and paid for, they thanked the little man and left.

'I'd best get the bus,' Daisy said. 'So, what time d'you want to meet at the Grand?'

Hearing a tone of regret in Daisy's voice, Amy told her, 'You don't have to go home if you don't want to.'

Daisy's smile returned. 'Really?'

Judging by the relief in Daisy's voice, Amy knew she had done the right thing. 'Yes, really. I'd love you to come home with me. By the time we've had a bite to eat, we'll need to get ready, and then it'll be time to make our way into town.'

'But what will your mam say?' Daisy knew what her own mother would say, if she took a friend home unexpectedly. 'Won't she be angry?'

'Course not! She'll say exactly what I've said—that it seems silly you spending money on the bus fare to go all the way home, when you're already here.'

'But I haven't got any lipstick. And I need to change my shoes and all that . . .' She would have gone on, but Amy stopped her.

'You take the same size shoes as me, so borrow a pair of mine. And I'm sure you'll find the right colour lipstick, because you've borrowed it often enough when we've been out. Oh, come on, Daisy, I promise you'll look beautiful . . .' She chuckled. 'Well, passable, anyway.'

She got a playful dig in the ribs for that cheeky remark, but Daisy was grateful that she wouldn't be going home just yet. 'By the time I get home tonight, they'll have calmed down,' she said, and if Amy needed any convincing that she had done the right thing, that remark did it.

Linking arms they walked home together, with Amy wishing she could change things for Daisy; and Daisy thanking her lucky stars, for having found the best friend in the whole wide world.

*   *   *

Amy was right. Marie and Dave welcomed Daisy with open arms. They had their tea: thick meat butties of home-made bread, and a delicious apple pie with ice-cream to follow.

'I'll be so full I'll not be able to dance,' Daisy groaned, tucking in happily none the less.

Afterwards the girls went up to Amy's room.

'Oh, Amy, I do like your room.' Daisy had seen

147

it before, and never failed to admire it. Pretty as a picture, with its rose chintz curtains and a cream-coloured rug, the room was furnished with just a wardrobe, bed and dressing table. Being at the back of the house it was not the lightest of rooms, but the light painted walls and the lovingly chosen seascape paintings created a sense of space and light that belied the smallness.

'One of these days we'll decorate *your* room,' Amy promised, 'if your parents will let me through the door, that is.' Last time Daisy had taken her home, there had been a terrible row and ever since then, Amy had been reluctant to visit.

'Thanks all the same, but you needn't bother,' Daisy replied. 'As soon as I can afford a place of my own, I intend leaving that house for good.' And from the tone of her voice, Amy knew she meant it.

'Right then!' Taking Daisy by the arm, Amy propelled her towards the dressing table. 'You don't want your room decorated, so we'll have to see what we can do with your face instead.'

'I don't want to be looking like a clown,' Daisy declared fearfully.

'Now, would I do that?' Amy's mischievous little grin got Daisy worried.

'I mean it, Amy! If you make me look ridiculous, I won't set foot outside this room.'

Ignoring her protests, Amy found enough make-up to suit Daisy.

A few minutes and a lot of grumbling later, she looked especially pretty. Her lips were lightly painted in the softest pink so as not to clash with the vibrant colour of her hair; a thin coating of powder on her skin and just the merest touch of mascara against her lashes and she was finished.

'Now then, what do you think?' Amy asked. 'Have I made you look like a clown, or have I made you pretty as a picture?'

Daisy was delighted with the result of Amy's handiwork. 'It's lovely,' she said, 'but what can we do about this?' Pointing to the marks on her neck, she reminded Amy, 'The dress has a low neckline, so folks are bound to see the bruises.'

Amy had not realised the extent of Daisy's injuries until now. 'Oh God, Daisy. That looks nasty.' She lowered her voice, although no one would hear. 'Did your father do that?' she gasped. It beggared belief that a man could do that to his daughter.

Daisy nodded. 'He had me pinned to the wall with the crook of his arm.' Under her breath she uttered the word, 'Bastard!'

Amy knew about Mr Robertson's temper but hadn't realised he was so vicious. She squeezed Daisy's arm in silent but helpless sympathy. Then: 'Don't you worry, sunshine.' She had an idea. 'Stay there a minute.'

Going to the wardrobe, she took out a box and from that she withdrew a pretty necklace. It had been a present from her father, something to help cheer her after Don left. Thick-banded with dangling pink stones, it was perfect for what she had in mind. 'This will not only go with your frock, it'll hide the blemishes as well,' she pointed out.

Draping it round Daisy's neck she fastened it at the back. One look in the mirror told her that it had done the trick. 'There you are. Now stop your moaning!'

Daisy gave a sigh of relief. 'You're a clever little bugger, aren't you?'

Amy chuckled. 'I do my best. Now, come out of my seat and go and get your frock on. It's time for me to get myself ready.'

'I'll not be long.' Taking her frock with her, Daisy went away to the bathroom. When she returned a few minutes later, her wild, wavy hair was brushed to a golden shine, and she looked so lovely, Amy leaped out of the seat and, coming to turn Daisy round and round, she told her, 'By! Every bloke in the room will want to dance with you.' Tutting loudly, she grumbled, 'The rest of us won't even get a look in!'

'Are you telling me the truth, Amy?' Over the years Daisy's parents had dented her confidence until, now, she needed constant reassurance. 'Do I look nice? Do you really mean it?'

'Of course I mean it, Daisy,' Amy answered warmly. 'You look *beautiful*.'

She observed Daisy's bouncy mop of auburn hair and the pretty freckles that danced about her nose and eyes, and she meant every word.

At half-past seven, looking pretty as two pictures, they came down the stairs to a round of applause.

'You look a treat!' Dave was proud of them both.

Marie was so impressed, she vowed to visit the second-hand shop next time she went into town.

'Mind you behave yourselves!' Marie fussed as they went out the door. She made them put on a coat each and warned, 'It'll be chilly by the time you come out of there. And don't be back late,' she told Amy. Addressing Daisy she offered, 'If you want to come back and stay the night, you're very welcome, lass.'

'Better not,' Daisy declined gratefully. 'My dad

might take it into his head to come looking for me, and I wouldn't wish his presence on anybody.' Staying out until the early hours was one thing, but staying out all night would cause trouble and she daren't risk it.

Chatting excitedly, the girls set off for the Grand. 'I wonder if there'll be any good-looking blokes there?' Daisy mused aloud. 'Somebody who's rolling in money and looking for a girl like me.'

'You'll not find anybody rolling in money in this town,' Amy declared, 'except the mill-owners and businessmen, and they're all fat, bald and married.'

'Not all,' Daisy corrected her. 'I've heard that Luke Hammond is a real knockout.'

Amy was surprised. 'Dad works for Hammonds, but he never talks too much about his work, or his boss.'

'Men are useless!' Daisy declared scornfully. 'The poor devils just don't know how to gossip. All I know is what I were told, and they say he's a real good-looker.' Her eyes widening with anticipation she glanced about. 'D'you reckon he comes in here?'

'I shouldn't think the poor man goes anywhere, what with running the factory and then his wife to look after. Remember she was beaten up, and needs constant care?'

Daisy felt little sympathy. 'He's rich, isn't he? And if he's as caring as you say, I'm sure he's arranged for her to have the best of everything.'

'I'm sure he has.' Amy felt both sympathy and curiosity. 'It's a terrible thing, though, don't you think—him having such a burden, and for his wife too . . . It can't be easy for either of them.'

151

Daisy agreed, though she had to have the last word. 'It's a damned sight worse if you've not got money. My old grandad fell over one Friday night. Drunk as a lord he were . . . broke both his legs and lost his false teeth down the grating. Months he had to wait for a new pair. His sodding legs were mended afore he got his new teeth.' She laughed. 'Two crutches and no gnashers—what a state to be in!'

As always, Amy had to laugh. 'You're a wicked bugger!' she chuckled. 'Anyway, what were we saying?'

Daisy reminded her, 'We were saying how all the rich blokes are either fat, bald, or wed.'

'That's true, an' all,' Amy replied. 'So, even if they do cast an eye in your direction, they'd only be after one thing, and we all know what that is, don't we?'

Daisy gave a knowing wink. 'It means they'd be after a bit of "how's your father".'

'Right,' Amy confirmed.

'I'm not really sure I'd mind either,' Daisy answered. 'I'd mek the buggers pay top whack for their entertainment. Then I'd get my own place a damn sight sooner!'

'Behave yourself,' Amy told her. 'We both know you wouldn't sell yourself like that. Look, we're here now, and don't make eyes at every man in the room, or they'll get the wrong idea.'

'Trust me,' Daisy said.

Linking arms with Amy, she pushed her forward. 'I don't want no trouble. I'm just here for a good time. All right, lass?'

'So make sure you stick to that,' Amy said. She knew from experience that when she and Daisy

152

went out together, the evening could end unpredictably.

As they went through the doors and into the bar, Amy glanced at Daisy, who was already casting her net for any good-looking, unattached young men.

She smiled inwardly. Daisy was Daisy and try as you might, you would never change her.

'By heck!' Daisy gave Amy a sly little dig with her elbow. 'Look, lass!' Grabbing Amy, she then drew her aside, at the same time pointing to the two young men at the bar. 'It's *them*!'

Following Daisy's gaze, Amy heart sank when she recognised the two blokes they'd tangled with last spring. 'You're right,' she whispered. 'It's them all right.'

Daisy began backing away. 'We'd best get out of here, before they see us.'

'No!' Standing her ground, Amy declared, 'We're not leaving. We've as much right to be here as they have.'

Daisy couldn't believe her ears. 'Bloody hell, lass,' she groaned. 'Have you forgotten what happened?'

'I haven't forgotten,' she replied defiantly, 'nor have I forgotten what that devious little squirt was up to when I interfered. For all I know he meant to have you by any means he could, and if I hadn't dived in, he probably would have done. No, Daisy. We're staying! If anybody needs to leave, it's them.' With that she marched forward to the bar, with Daisy clinging on to her arm for all she was worth.

In a strong, clear voice Amy ordered, 'Two sarsaparillas please, barman, and a packet of pork scratchings.'

Daisy whispered, 'What did you order them for?'

153

'Because we always have pork scratchings.'

Daisy groaned. 'Well, you can pay for 'em, and you can eat 'em. I ate enough food at your house to last me all week.'

Addressing the barman, Amy said, 'Forget the scratchings. We'll just have the sarsaparilla.'

Grumbling and groaning he replaced the packet of scratchings on the shelf. 'Women!' he muttered. 'Never can mek their mind up.'

Catching sight of the two young men out the corner of her eye, Daisy tugged at Amy's sleeve. 'Don't look now, lass, but they're coming this way!'

Wishing they had given the Grand a miss tonight, Amy told her, 'Ignore them, and they'll go away.'

But they didn't, and a moment later they were standing before the girls; the tall one looking unsure of himself, and the other one braving it out as though nothing had happened. Amy couldn't believe the nerve of them.

'Well! Would you believe it?' It was the short one who spoke first. 'We meet again, eh?' Encouraged by the twinkle in Daisy's eyes, he reminded her, 'I'm Roy Williams.' Gesturing to his friend, he addressed himself to Amy. 'This 'ere's my mate, Jack Tomlinson.'

Angered by his bare-faced cheek, Amy confronted him. 'I think you'd best clear off,' she answered haughtily, 'before I call somebody to have you thrown out.'

His mate quickly stepped forward. 'There were misunderstandings on both sides. What say we call a truce?' Looking from one to the other, he waited for an answer.

'Depends.' Daisy spoke out. It was clear she was

154

still attracted to the other young man, who by now was giving her the wink.

'On what?' Appraising Daisy from head to toe, the smaller man smiled confidently.

'On two conditions.'

'And what might they be?'

'Firstly, you apologise for what you did.'

Looking uncomfortable, he dropped his gaze to the floor. 'I was carried away. I didn't mean anything by it.'

'That's not an apology!'

'All right! I'm sorry.' He turned to his friend. 'We're both sorry.'

'That's right,' Jack readily agreed. 'We're sorry about what happened. It ruined what seemed like the start of a good relationship.'

'Now then! Is that enough for you?' Roy asked Daisy.

'Yes. Your apology is accepted.'

'So we can be friends, can we?'

'Not yet,' Daisy reminded him. 'I said there were *two* conditions.'

'So, what's the second?'

Daisy surprised them all with her quick smile and her bold answer. 'Now that you've apologised, you can dance with me.'

'DAISY!' Drawing her aside, Amy was flabbergasted. 'What the devil are you playing at?'

'Look, Amy, if they want to make friends, why can't we?' Giving her glass of sarsaparilla to Amy, Daisy reasoned, 'I think they've learned their lesson.'

'Well, I don't! That Roy fella is arrogant as ever.'

'Don't worry, lass,' Daisy whispered. 'I can handle him now.'

Amy couldn't help but worry and said so.

Daisy wasn't listening. 'I've seen the other blokes on offer round here,' she said, 'and I wouldn't give 'em house room.'

Just then the music struck up; Roy asked her if she wanted this dance, and like the devil-may-care creature she was, Daisy fell into his arms and quickly led him onto the dance floor.

'Well, I never!' In spite of a niggling worry in the back of her mind, Amy had to smile. 'I can talk till I'm blue in the face, and she takes not one blind bit of notice.'

'And what about you?' Suddenly, Jack was standing before her, his warm gaze inviting. 'Fancy a twirl on the dance floor, do you?'

'No, thanks all the same.' She had a feeling he was genuine in his apology but she felt embarrassed about the whole incident and didn't want reminding.

Excusing herself, she walked the few paces to a nearby table where she set the drinks down.

He followed her. 'Do you mind if I sit beside you?'

She was annoyed yet curious. 'Sit where you like,' she said, 'but don't think you're forgiven for what you and your mate did.' Best to face it out, pretend she hadn't panicked.

He sat down. 'Can I ask you summat?'

Taking a sip of her drink, Amy shrugged. 'Ask away.'

'Will you please tell me what I did wrong that night?'

'What d'you mean?'

He explained, 'Just now, you said I mustn't think I'm forgiven for what me and my mate did. So. All

156

I'm asking is, what exactly did I do that was so wrong?'

'When he was attacking Daisy, I thought you went in to help him,' she answered lamely. But even at the time she hadn't been certain that was the way it had happened.

'You're wrong.' He sounded sincere. 'Like you, I saw what was happening and needed to put a stop to it. When I got between you it wasn't to help Roy, believe me. It was your friend I was trying to help.'

'If that's the case, I'm sorry for what I did,' she admitted reluctantly. She'd felt embarrassed about it long enough. It was time to make amends.

He gave a wry little laugh. 'You're a dangerous woman, though.' He observed her slight build, the mop of brown hair and those bright blue eyes, and his heart turned over. 'I would never have guessed you could throw like that,' he said admiringly.

Amy smiled, aware that he was teasing her. 'Neither did I.' Under his intense scrutiny she felt neither embarrassed nor angry, but curiously warm inside.

'You managed to put me out of action for three days,' he told her, exaggerating so she knew he was laughing with her. 'What's more, I had to lie to my boss. If I'd told him what really happened, the men would have taunted me mercilessly.'

As he talked and smiled and looked back with amusement at what she'd done, Amy began to see a different, pleasant side to him. 'I might have been a bit too quick in throwing that brick,' she confessed. 'But I really thought you were as bad as your friend.'

His smile was all-embracing. 'You don't think that now, do you?'

Amy shook her head. 'I'll admit, I'm beginning to see you in a different light.'

'Is that good or bad?'

'Good . . . I think.' In fact she had thought about that night often, and each time she was increasingly certain she'd got it wrong where he was concerned.

'So, will you dance with me?' he asked, and Amy agreed.

In spite of Amy's earlier worries, the whole evening was surprisingly enjoyable, and by the time they were preparing to leave, their relationship was developing fast.

As for Daisy, her attraction for Roy was strong as ever. 'I'm as much to blame for what happened,' she told Amy in the toilets. 'I must have given him the idea that I wanted it every bit as much as he did.'

'That's no excuse for coming on like he did.' Amy wasn't happy that Daisy had forgiven him so easily. 'If you ask me, there's a darker side to him than meets the eye. I know I can't tell you what to do, but I'm asking you to stay on your guard. Will you do that for me?'

Daisy groaned but promised all the same. 'All right, mother hen,' she quipped cheekily, 'I'll stay on my guard.'

Then she laughed her impulsive, hearty laugh, and Amy couldn't help but laugh with her. 'You're incorrigible!' Amy said, and Daisy told her she didn't even know what the word meant.

When they returned to their table, Jack was at the bar getting more drinks, while Roy was impatiently pacing the floor. 'At last!' He threw out his arms in frustration. 'Whatever it is you women do when you go to the toilets together, it seems to take you one hell of a long time! What *do* you do, anyway?'

'That's for us to know and you to find out!' Daisy retorted.

'Hmm! You're a brassy bugger and no mistake!' He had fallen for Daisy hook, line and sinker.

They drank their drinks and danced until their feet ached. When the last waltz was over, they made their way outside.

'Which way are you headed?' Jack asked Amy.

'Let's just walk.' Heading off in the direction of the marketplace, Amy wasn't altogether happy about telling them where she lived. Since Don Carson had let her down she'd got out of the habit of trusting men. 'Me and Daisy will soon have to make our way home,' she warned amicably.

As they walked they chatted, and the more they chatted the more they found friendship.

'What kind of work are you two in?' Jack asked the girls.

Amy hesitated while Daisy answered in a rush, 'Amy runs Atkinsons' Corner Shop with her mam, and I work at Tooley's Café.' Puffing out her chest, she added proudly, 'I'm in charge most of the time, on account of Ma Tooley's forever gadding about. She likes the men, y'see? Goes off for days on end and leaves me to it. Mind you, I like being on my own. That way I don't get nagged at every five minutes. Besides, when she's not there, I get to use the old chip pan an' grill.'

'Use the old chip pan and grill, eh?' Roy laughed out loud. 'I can't think of anything more exciting.'

'Hey! Who asked you?' Daisy gave him a sharp dig in the ribs for his cheek.

Jack smiled down on Amy. 'So? You run a

159

corner shop with your mam, eh?'

Amy wished Daisy hadn't told them, but now there was no use denying it. 'That's right,' she said.

'What about you two?' Giving Roy another nudge in the ribs, Daisy asked, 'What work do *you* do?'

'We both work at Hammonds, only I'm a mechanic and he's the foreman, lucky bugger! And if yer don't mind, I'd like you to keep yer elbows to yerself. I'll be black and blue all over if you keep digging me in the ribs!'

'I'm not a "lucky bugger", as you put it,' Jack protested half-heartedly. 'I've worked hard for what I've got, and anyway, you've only been there for a year, while I've been there ever since I left school. All you have to do is knuckle down and your time will come.'

'Hmm! Like hell it will.' Roy had no self-worth.

Because of Roy's complete lack of confidence in his future, Jack confided a snippet of information. 'You're already in the manager's good books. I know for a fact he's had a word with Mr Hammond on your behalf.'

Roy's face lit up. 'You're kidding, aren't yer?'

'No,' Jack answered, 'you've been noticed. So from now on, you'd best watch your p's and q's.'

Having now arrived at the meat-pie stall alongside the marketplace, Roy dug his hand in his pocket and drew out a cache of coins. 'Right! Meat pies all round, is it?'

Amy and Daisy declined politely, exchanging secret looks of horror at the idea of more food.

A few minutes later, they were all seated on one of the empty stalls, swinging their legs, the two men chewing on their meat pies with Roy slavering all the way.

'Ugh! You mucky pup!' Daisy gave Roy a playful push. 'You've dripped gravy all down your front!' The gravy ran from his chin to his shirt and over part of his lapel.

Wiping his hand over it and making matters worse, Roy turned to Jack. 'Has he really had a word with Hammond?'

Jack nodded. 'I've already told you. I heard him saying what a good worker you'd turned out to be. According to him, it wouldn't be too long before you were moved up a notch or two.' He wagged a finger. 'But you don't know anything about it, all right? I never told you.'

As a rule he would never have divulged such privileged information, but he had long suspected that Roy was ready to pack the work in and look for something else, and he needed encouragement to carry on. 'Keep on the way you're going, and there's a future for you at Hammonds, that's all I know.'

Roy grinned like a Cheshire cat. 'Right, matey! Enough said.'

Daisy put paid to his grinning. 'Look at that, you sloppy devil!' Pointing to his shirt, she groaned, 'Now, there's a lump o' meat stuck to your collar.'

He slid an arm round her. 'So, I'm a sloppy devil. Does that mean you don't love me any more?'

'Gerroff!' But this time she didn't push him away, so he kept his arm round her shoulders, delighted when she didn't complain.

Daisy too was secretly delighted. We're two of a kind, she thought, and was happier than she'd been in ages.

'I can't believe you both work at Hammonds,'

161

Amy told them. 'My dad works there, driving wagons. He travels so far, he doesn't usually come home during the week.'

'Well, I never! That's what I want to do,' Roy informed her. 'I'd really like to drive the wagons. I've asked for training, but I'm last in the line, seeing as I was last into the factory.' Plucking the lump of meat pie from his collar he popped it into his mouth. 'I thought I didn't stand a cat in hell's chance, but after what Jack just told me, I'm over the moon. What's more I wouldn't care if I was out all week.'

Daisy didn't think much to that. 'What about your sweetheart?' she asked. 'How do you think *she'd* feel about that, eh?'

'I've not got a sweetheart,' he said cunningly, 'so it won't matter, will it?'

Searching for some reassurance as to her own standing, Daisy was reluctant to let the matter go. 'You might not have a sweetheart now, but what about in the future?'

'I don't expect I'll have one in the future,' he winked, 'unless o' course, *you're* offering to be my sweetheart?'

Daisy's eyes shone. 'We'll have to see, won't we?'

'Looks like those two were made for each other,' Jack whispered in Amy's ear.

Amy agreed. 'They got off to a shocking start,' she said, 'but you're right. They do seem to be getting on really well.'

She had believed Roy to be a bad lot, but now, she wondered if maybe Daisy had been honest when she said how that first evening had ended was as much her fault as Roy's. Even so, she told herself now, that wasn't to say he was an angel.

Recalling the previous conversation between herself and Amy, Daisy saw the chance to get an opinion from Roy. 'What d'you think of Luke Hammond?' she asked.

'He's all right,' Roy said casually. 'Mind you, we don't see much of him on the shop floor. He tends to get on with other things, though he does walk through the factory every day, talking to the foreman and managers and such. He's not one o' them bosses who leaves others to do his work. He likes to know what's going on . . . keeps his finger on the pulse, as they say.'

'That's right,' Jack readily agreed. 'And if there's ever any trouble he soon sorts it out, when nobody else can.' He lowered his voice in respect. 'If you ask me, he's got more than his fair share o' troubles at home. I expect you've heard how his wife got beat up and now she's got some sort of brain damage . . . has these weird moods . . .'

'Aye, that's right,' Roy chipped in. 'Once she came round the factory, looking for him, asking questions and causing trouble. Stunning-looking woman, though. You'd never think she were round the bend.'

Choosing to change the subject, Amy asked, 'So you think Luke Hammond is a nice bloke?'

'The best boss I've ever worked under,' Roy said. 'He keeps the factory rolling and keeps his workforce informed as to what's happening. I expect your dad's told you how we all thought we were for the high jump some time back, but it was exactly the opposite. When work got tight, Hammond went out and snatched a contract from under the noses of the big boys; enough to keep all of us in work for the foreseeable future. He gets my vote, I can tell you that!'

Curious about Amy's father, Roy asked, 'What did you say your Dad's name is? Atkinson?'

'What's that got to do with anything?' Amy thought it was one thing them knowing where she and Daisy worked, but it was another thing discussing her father.

Sensing a deal of hostility, Roy realised he had not yet redeemed himself in Amy's eyes. 'Just curious, that's all.'

Feeling uneasy, Amy turned to Jack. 'I'll have to say good night,' she said. 'It's time me and Daisy were headed home.'

But Daisy had other ideas. 'If it's all right with you, lass, I won't be coming home with you tonight.'

Amy didn't like what she was hearing. 'So, where are you going?'

When Daisy hesitated, Roy answered, 'She's coming home with me.'

Amy's fears grew. 'Won't your mam and dad have summat to say about you bringing a stranger home without warning?'

'I've got my own place,' he said. 'But don't you worry. She'll be all right with me.'

Seeing how worried Amy was, Daisy assured her, 'It's all right, Amy . . . really.'

Amy didn't like it. 'I'd be happier if you came home with me, Daisy.'

Daisy shook her head. 'Not tonight, lass. Me and Roy have a lot to talk about.'

As always, whatever Amy said, Daisy's mind would not be changed.

Jack also had a word with Roy, but he and Daisy were adamant. 'We're not kids. We know what we're doing.'

Amy and Jack watched them walk away. 'I'm really worried,' Amy said. 'He tried to go too far with her once before. He could easily do it again, and we won't be there to help her.'

'He won't do it again.' Jack was certain. 'The two of us have talked often about that night and I know he regrets it. Deep down he's a good sort. I've never known him take to anybody the way he's taken to Daisy.'

Unconvinced, Amy was all for going after them, but he stopped her. 'Trust me,' he said, 'he respects her. He won't harm her.'

'How well do you know him?'

'Well enough.' Cupping his fingers about hers, he took the liberty of tucking her arm through his.

'You feel cold,' he told her, and though her first instinct was to draw away, she found herself leaning into him. It was a curiously comforting feeling.

*   *   *

Strolling down the street, Daisy and Roy had already agreed to forget what happened that night. 'I overstepped the mark,' Roy explained. 'I honestly don't know what came over me.'

Every time he looked at Daisy, he felt a surge of need he had never felt with anyone else, but it wasn't like before, when he had wanted to rip off her clothes and take her where she stood. Now, however, he had a deal of respect for her. There was something special about Daisy, he told himself. And somewhere beneath the laughter and bravado, he sensed a frightened, nervous creature who needed taking care of.

'Amy thinks you're trouble,' Daisy remarked slyly. '*Are* you?'

Roy smiled. 'You've got a good friend there,' he evaded answering.

'So, *are* you trouble . . . like Amy said?'

'I can be, yes.'

'Should I avoid you then?'

'I hope not.'

'Give me a good reason?'

'Is *this* good enough?' Grabbing her by the shoulders he kissed her on the mouth, a rough, exciting kiss that sent her weak at the knees.

Taking a moment to catch her breath, she laughed. 'It'll do for starters.'

With his arm round her shoulders he drew her backwards to the wall. 'I've done some bad things,' he hesitantly confessed. 'I've fought with everybody who ever disagreed with me . . . even put a fella in hospital once. I've stolen other fellas' sweethearts just to prove I could, and I've led girls on, just to get what I wanted . . . if you know what I mean? I've broken into houses and stolen, and I've lied through my teeth whenever it suited me . . .'

Now, as he saw how she was beginning to pull away, he held on to her. 'NO! Please, Daisy, hear me out.'

'Amy's right!' Daisy cried, struggling. 'Yer really are a bad lot! Gerroff me, yer lying git!'

'LISTEN TO ME!' There was desperation in his voice. 'Why d'you think I'm telling you all this? I wouldn't do that if I was only after one thing, would I? I've tekken a real liking to you, Daisy . . . you've got to believe me.'

'Why should I?' For one glorious moment she had thought he was everything she'd ever wanted

166

and now she was finding out he was a worthless good-for-nothing. 'Go on!' she challenged. 'Tell me why I should believe a single word you say?'

For a moment he held her, his hands clamped round her shoulders and his gaze melting into hers. 'I think I'm falling in love with you,' he murmured. 'I've never felt like this about any girl before. That's why I need you to know the truth about me—so that if you hear it from somebody else, you'll know I've told you all there is to know.'

Daisy wondered if she should walk away before she got hurt. Then she looked at his face and read the truth in his eyes, and she knew she could never walk away.

'Why?' she asked softly. 'Why did you do all them bad things?'

'I don't know . . .' He shrugged. 'Anyway, what does it matter?'

'It matters to me,' she said. 'If you're being truthful with me, I need to know all of it. What made you so bad? Tell me.'

'I can't . . .'

Daisy was angry. 'Why not?' she demanded.

'Because if I do, you'll walk away. You'd be crazy not to.'

Daisy smiled. 'I can be crazy at times, or haven't you noticed?'

Her smile was infectious. 'Yes . . . I've noticed.'

'So, tell me.'

He told her how his father had been mixed up in a robbery. 'I knew nothing about it until afterwards, when Mam told me. It was an organised gang, who had already pulled off a number of jobs. The police had been after them for some time, but they always managed to get away.

167

This time, though, the robbery went wrong and they all went to prison.'

His voice fell to a whisper. 'In the prison, there were accusations and threats among them. One day a fight started and my dad was stabbed to death—a piece of metal, they said, straight through the heart.'

'God Almighty, how awful!' Daisy was shaken. 'It must have been a terrible shock to the family.'

'There's no family,' Roy corrected her, 'just me and Mam. Mam was in a bad way when she heard—shouting and crying . . . desperate she was. After a while, she went upstairs, packed a bag and left. She never came back, and I never found out where she'd gone. I was twelve years old.'

Daisy began to understand. 'No wonder you turned bad,' she said. 'How did you manage? What did you do? Did they let you stay in the house, or did you go to relatives?'

'Relatives didn't want to know,' Roy said sombrely, 'so I took off. I had no idea where I were going or what I might do. I managed to get work here and there—told them I were fifteen and nobody questioned it. I managed to pay for board and lodgings and didn't go hungry.'

He smiled, but it was a poor, lonely smile. 'I even went looking for my mam, but I never did find her. After a time I gave up and just got on with my life.'

'Didn't you have any friends?'

'Just one,' he said. 'I was seventeen and in with a bad lot. Don was one of 'em, but he turned out to be a good mate. If it hadn't been for Don, I might have got into even more trouble, but he watched out for me. Then we parted ways and I didn't see him again until just recently. We bumped into each other at the pub and got talking. I told him I needed a regular place to stay, and he got me a room in a house near to him, in Johnson Street.'

Daisy had a reason for being curious. 'What does he look like, this Don?'

'He must be about twenty-five, I reckon . . . fairly well built; kinda handsome, in a rough-looking way.' He smiled. 'He's good at charming the ladies, so I won't be introducing him to *you*, that's for sure.'

Daisy's curiosity grew. 'What's his surname?'

'Carson.' He gave her a quizzical look. 'His name is Don Carson. Why are you so interested?'

'Don . . . Carson.' Her eyes grew wide and bright as marbles. 'Bugger me, Roy, it's *him*! Don Carson is Amy's ex-fiancé. They were due to be wed and he dumped her days beforehand, the swine!'

Though shocked that Daisy should know of his old friend, and that he was once engaged to Amy, Roy was not surprised.

'He's not the marrying kind,' he told her. 'What's more, if you ask me, Amy had a good escape. He'd make the worst husband imaginable. He likes a drink and he loves the ladies, and, as far as I know, there's never yet been one woman that could hold him.'

'Well, I never!' Daisy couldn't get over it. 'I wish you hadn't told me now.'

'It were you that asked,' Roy protested light-heartedly.

'I know that, and I wish I hadn't.'

'Will you tell Amy?'

'I don't know,' Daisy answered. 'If I did, what purpose would it serve?'

'None that I can see, except for her to realise

what a lucky escape she's had.'

'Oh, look, all that aside, I'm sorry I forced you to tell me all those other things . . . about you and your dad and that. But I'm glad you told me,' Daisy said. 'I understand you a lot better now.'

'I'm glad too,' he replied. In truth he was relieved to have told her.

Daisy went on, 'You have to believe that what happened was not your fault. I know what it's like for parents to do bad things that frighten you, and sometimes you get the blame. It makes it difficult to think you can rely on people, but, you know, you can trust me, Roy.'

He gave a small, harsh laugh. 'Don't be so quick,' he urged. 'You don't know me well enough to think I'm worth the effort yet.'

'What else is there for me to find out?' Daisy asked. 'You haven't murdered anybody, have yer?'

'No.'

'And you haven't set fire to anybody's house, have yer?'

'Not that I know of,' he laughed. 'Though I've slept in a few places where burning them down might be an improvement.'

'And is there anything else you need to tell me?'

'You've heard it all,' he promised. 'And I can see from your expression that you don't like what you've heard.'

'You're right there,' she answered honestly, and looming in her mind was Don Carson.

Roy's face crumpled. 'I knew it would turn you against me. That's why I didn't want you knowing,' he groaned. 'I knew you'd run a mile, the minute you heard what a bad 'un I've been.'

Raising her hand to touch his face, Daisy asked

170

softly, 'Do you see me running?'

When he looked at her now, she could have sworn there were tears in his eyes. 'No.' Wrapping both his arms round her, he held her. 'So why *aren't* you? I'm no good, Daisy. Happen I never will be. So why aren't you off down the street, like a cat with its tail on fire?'

'You're right,' she admitted. 'If I had any sense that's what I'd be doing all right—putting as much distance between you and me as I could. But then, I've never been known as a sensible person, so I'm not running and I don't know why, so don't ask me. But I'll tell you something,' she went on. 'You mustn't feel sorry for yourself, and you mustn't think you're the only one who's ashamed of their parents.'

Now it was time for her to confess. 'Mine fight and squabble all the time. They swear at the neighbours and they hurt each other until they draw blood. They're selfish, shameful, and half crazy, and sometimes I wish I was a million miles away.' Inclining her head to observe his reaction, she asked, 'Is that all my fault, d'you think?'

He shook his head in disbelief. 'Is it true . . . about your parents?'

'True as I stand here.'

'It's not your fault,' he murmured.

'That's right,' Daisy agreed, 'same as what happened to you is not *your* fault.'

'D'you know what I think?' he whispered, placing his hand on her shoulder.

'I expect you'll tell me.' Reaching out, she laid her hand over his and kept him there.

He smiled appreciatively. 'I think you and me were made for each other.'

'You could be right,' she said. 'We'll have to wait and see, won't we?'

Now that the air was cleared and they understood each other, they went off down the street hand in hand, making plans together—and beginning to fall in love.

*   *   *

Not too far away, Amy and Jack had also been getting to know each other.

'It's good that we're friends again.' Ever since leaving the Grand he had longed to take her in his arms, but there was something about her that warned him off. 'You do trust me now, don't you, Amy?'

'I think so,' she answered, smiling up at him. 'I can't say you've done anything tonight to make me think bad of you.'

'I'm glad about that.' He smiled down at her.

She wasn't the prettiest girl he'd ever walked home, he thought, but she was lovely. She was kind and thoughtful, and very caring; he had seen that side of her when she was so concerned about her friend Daisy. There was a warmth about Amy that shone through, and those deep blue eyes were enchanting. No, he thought, she had more about her than mere prettiness.

'I'd like to see you again . . . if that's all right with you?' he asked tentatively.

Amy nodded. 'I'd like that, yes.'

Before he could go on, she drew to a halt. 'We'd best part company here.' They were already at the foot of Montague Street. From here it was only a step or so to Derwent Street, and though she

172

thought she liked him, she didn't want him to know where she lived, at least not yet.

'I don't like to leave you in the dark like this,' Jack said worriedly. 'Why don't you let me take you all the way home? You never know who's about this time o' night.'

Touched by his concern, Amy assured him, 'I'll be fine. I've walked up this street in the dark so many times I've lost count, and I've never yet been worried.'

Her remark brought a smile to his face. 'I'd chase you at the drop of a hat.' Looking at her now, he thought he'd gladly jump in the River Ribble for just one kiss.

'Besides, I only live five minutes away.'

'Are you ashamed of me?' he asked.

Amy was taken aback. 'No. What made you say that?'

'Because this is the first time a girl hasn't let me take her right to the front door, so there has to be a reason. Either you're ashamed of me . . . or you still don't trust me. Which is it?'

Amy laughed. 'I've no reason to be ashamed of you,' she answered.

'Ah! So that means you still don't trust me.'

'It might,' she admitted. 'Oh, look, it's just that, for now, it might be better if you didn't know where I lived, that's all.'

'What? So I'll not be able to come knocking and worrying you to go out with me?'

She laughed again. 'Something like that.'

'What if I followed you?'

'You won't.' She had learned enough about him to know he wouldn't stoop to such a thing.

'No, you're right. I wouldn't do that. If you don't

want me to know where you live, that's an end to it.' Placing his hands on her shoulders, he asked hopefully, 'You will see me again, though, won't you?'

'Yes, I'd like that.'

'All right . . . when?'

She gazed up at him, her heart beating fast as their eyes met. He had such sincerity, she thought. 'I'm not surprised you made it to foreman,' she remarked. 'I'm sure with your dogged attitude it won't be long before you make manager.'

'Next year,' he remarked casually, 'I intend making manager next year.'

'Oh? So you've set yourself a target, have you?' Amy was impressed.

'Aye,' he declared confidently. 'And one day I'll have my own factory, you see if I don't!'

'I expect you will,' she said mischievously. 'Happen you'll have more than one—happen you'll have them across the length and breadth of Lancashire.'

Throwing back his head he laughed out loud, a deep, musical laugh that made the hairs on the back of her neck stand up. 'One thing at a time, if you please,' he said. 'Let's not run before we can walk.'

They set off walking again, but slower this time, with Jack persisting, 'You didn't say when we could meet again?'

'Next Saturday?' she suggested. 'Unless you're busy doing something else?'

Again, he drew her to a halt. 'If I was—though it happens I'm not—I'd cancel whatever it was,' he promised. 'To tell you the truth, Amy, I don't think I can wait a whole week before I see you again.'

'Well, you'll have to,' she replied firmly. 'Saturday is the best time for me, so it's that or nothing.'

'Then it'll have to be Saturday,' he conceded. 'And will you change your mind about letting me walk you home?'

She smiled. 'One thing at a time,' she mimicked, wagging a finger. 'Let's not run before we can walk.'

His face wreathed in a gentle smile, he nodded. 'You've got me there,' he acknowledged.

'Good night then, Jack.'

'Good night, Amy.'

As Amy turned away he laid his hands on her shoulders and tenderly swung her round. He didn't say anything and neither did she, but she knew he wanted to kiss her, and she wanted the same.

When he bent his head towards her, for a brief moment she remembered the man who had kissed her and betrayed her, and she wanted to turn away, but a deeper instinct kept her there. She raised her lips to his and when the softness of his mouth was pressed against hers, she enjoyed the experience to the full.

When it was over, he dropped his arms to his sides, his voice tender. 'Good night, Amy.'

Amy nodded, and walked on, her heart beating fifteen to the dozen and her lips tingling from Jack's kiss. 'That was nice,' she murmured. But that's all it was, she thought. At that vulnerable moment the image of her ex-fiancé had come into her mind. She wasn't ready for a serious relationship just yet. She quickened her steps.

'AMY . . . WAIT!'

Coming to a halt she turned to see Jack running

175

after her. 'I forgot to ask . . . where will we meet?'

She'd forgotten as well. 'I'll be up Corporation Park . . . about half-past two,' she laughed. 'Oh, and don't forget to bring a bag o' bread when you come.'

When he looked at her in disbelief she explained, 'We often feed the ducks on a Saturday, me and Johnny.'

'Who's Johnny?'

'A fella I know. Good-looking and fun to be with, he is.'

'And I'll get to meet him on Saturday, will I?' The tiniest hint of jealousy showed in his voice.

'You'll like him,' she went on. 'He's not the easiest of people to get on with. He's a bit wary of strangers, y'see? If he likes you, he'll be your friend for life. But if he doesn't take to you straight off, he'll have nothing to do with you at all.'

'Hmm! He sounds a moody sort of a fella to me.'

Amy left him wondering. 'See you Saturday,' she said, and hurried towards home smiling to herself all the way.

She wondered what Jack would think of little Johnny and, more to the point, what Johnny would think of *him*.

CHAPTER NINE

It had been a hot day and now the night was unbearably humid. Unable to sleep, Luke threw off the bedclothes and for a moment he just lay there, arms above his head, eyes closed, and the tiredness seeping through his every bone.

176

His mind, though, was alive with all manner of thoughts and emotions: pride in his work and the new contract he had managed to secure in spite of heavy competition; anxiety about Sylvia, who had been increasingly difficult of late. The dark, uncontrollable thoughts came with ferocity, lasted a moment or two and fell away just as quickly.

It pained him to see her suffering like that. He wanted to do more. He wanted her to be the vibrant, shrewd woman she once had been. But that woman was long gone, and he could do nothing to help her. No one could.

As always when he felt tired and lonely, his thoughts shifted to Amy. He recalled her warm, bright smile and those pretty eyes that twinkled even when she wasn't smiling. In his painting he had caught the very essence of that smile, and more, he had caught her spirit, strong and brave. 'Amy . . .' He relished the sound of her name. 'If only things had been different . . . if Sylvia and her lover had made a life together, you and I might have had a chance to get to know each other.' But things were not 'different', and they never could be.

Through the open window, he viewed the galaxy of stars and was mesmerised by their sparkling beauty. 'I wonder if she's looking at these same stars?' It was a curiously comforting idea that they could be sharing this view. Luke thought of his cabin in Bowland Forest, nestling in the shadows of the fells. The sky there would be darkest black, not faded by the reflection of any streetlamps, and the stars would be piercingly bright in contrast. How he longed to share that night sky with Amy—the lovely, laughing, spirited girl, not an oil painting. Seeing her on Tuesdays at Tooley's Café, then

177

escaping to the peace of the cabin, he saw her as inextricably part of his private world. If only she could make the journey to the cabin too. Somehow, this would be so *right*.

With thoughts of Amy came a warm feeling, and then tiredness began to swamp his consciousness. After a time he closed his eyes and drifted into a deep sleep.

He did not hear the door open, nor did he hear the soft tread of footsteps as they came across the carpet to his bed. When she leaned over him, he had no idea she was there. Even as she climbed into bed beside him, he did not feel her presence.

In his sleep he began to dream, and the dream was of Amy. One minute she was in the painting and the next she was stepping out, into his arms, the soft touch of her hand on his body making him tremble.

Beside him, Sylvia gently stroked her hand over him; touching the curve of his chest, savouring the feel of those strong vibrant muscles beneath her fingertips. Now she was reaching down, slipping her hand into the dip of his groin. When he seemed to respond, she pressed herself close to him.

'Love me,' she whispered, and as he turned to draw her closer, she gave herself up to him.

Greatly aroused he lay along her length, his member standing tall as he prepared to enter her. 'I knew you'd find me . . .' His voice softly caressing her, he slid his hands beneath her buttocks, tenderly arching her into him. 'You're lovely,' he kissed her neck, her ears, savouring the taste of her skin on his tongue, '. . . so lovely . . .' He wanted her with every fibre of his being.

In that moment she began screaming, shocking

him awake. 'LEAVE ME ALONE! GET OFF ME!' As he rolled away, she leaped on him, her fists pummelling his chest and face. 'GET AWAY FROM ME, YOU BASTARD!'

There was no let-up, and he, reeling under the blows, could not seem to hold her off until, with one mighty effort he took hold of her arms and, swinging her away, rolled off the bed.

'SYLVIA!' Somewhere between dream and consciousness he had imagined it was Amy in his arms. 'What are you doing here?'

Suddenly she was like a child, desperately clinging to him. 'Don't punish me,' she sobbed. 'It wasn't me . . . I didn't do it.' Her fear was so real, he could almost taste it.

'I would never punish you. Be still. Ssh!' As he reached out to comfort her she drew away like some frightened animal to cower against the pillow.

'Where's Edna?' she said, her wide scared eyes scouring the room. 'Please . . . I want Edna.'

Trembling inside, his senses scrambled, he swiftly assessed the situation. It was clear she had wandered in here, looking for comfort . . . maybe even looking for love. After all, it wasn't all that long ago they had been man and wife in every sense.

Turning on the bedside lamp he grabbed his robe from the back of the chair and, slinging it on, tied it tight around the front. 'It's all right, sweetheart . . .' Holding out his hand he gave a sigh of relief when she took hold of it.

Sliding off the bed, she asked meekly, 'Will you get Edna for me?'

'In the morning,' he promised. 'I'll fetch Edna in the morning.' He lifted her gently into bed and covered her over. 'You'd best stay here tonight,' he said. 'I won't be far away.'

'You won't leave me, will you?'

'No, I won't leave you.'

He stayed by her as promised, moving his armchair beside the bed, while she lay, quiet now, slipping gently into a calming sleep. 'It's all right,' he said as she twice opened her eyes. 'I'm here.'

Soon she was sound asleep. 'Oh, dear God, Sylvia, what's happened to you . . . to *us*?' He looked on that beautiful face, and his heart went out to her. To his mind there was no point in apportioning blame; it had all gone far beyond that.

He thought of Amy again, and his mouth twisted in a smile.

Amy was his dream and Sylvia was his reality.

He was still thinking of Amy when the soothing waves of sleep overwhelmed him.

In the morning, while Sylvia was sleeping soundly, he got quickly dressed and summoned Edna on the telephone he'd had installed at her home.

'You can't go on like this,' Edna chided. 'Just look at the state of you! You look terrible—dark rims under your eyes and a haggard look about you that tells the world you've not slept a full night in goodness knows how long.'

'I'll be fine,' Luke protested. 'A bath and a good breakfast, and I'll be good as new.' Though having slept in the chair all night had not helped his poor bones, which ached in every direction.

Edna threw aside his protests. 'How in God's name d'you think you can run a factory without a good night's sleep, tell me that?'

'I do all right,' he answered. 'There's no need for you to worry on that score.'

'Oh, aye! You might well "do all right", as you say, but for how long, eh? How long will it be afore you fall ill, or your brain won't function because it's half asleep? What then, eh?'

'Stop nagging me, woman!' he groaned, but fondly. 'I'm fit as a fiddle, and my brain's as sharp as a tack. The factory will be fine and so will I.'

'I've a suggestion to make,' she persisted. 'Let me move in.'

Taken aback he wanted to know, 'And what would poor Harry think about that?'

'He'd welcome it; says my snoring keeps him awake at night.'

Luke chuckled. 'So, you want to come here and keep *me* awake, is that it? I'm grateful to you,' he said, 'but there's really no need.' It seemed too extreme a measure.

Edna nodded. 'All right, if you're sure. But will you promise me . . . you'll ask me to stay if you're ever worried, or if she's disturbed your sleep too often?'

'She hardly ever disturbs my sleep, as you know, Edna. Once Sylvia goes to her bed, she usually sleeps soundly enough.'

'Not lately she hasn't.'

'She's going through a bad patch right now,' Luke said. 'I'm sure she'll settle down.' In fact things seemed to be getting worse, but he didn't want to worry Edna unduly.

'So, will you promise?'

He gave her a kiss on the cheek. 'You're a bossy devil and no mistake,' he said. 'And, yes, I promise, if I find I can't manage, we'll talk about you staying

181

over. Now, is it all right with you if I go and get my bath? I don't want to be late this morning. We've a big delivery to get out to a new customer. It's a huge order and could lead to more business, so I'd like to oversee it personally.'

Edna was satisfied. 'You get yersel' ready,' she told him. 'Mrs Hammond's still sleeping soundly, so I'll start your breakfast. It'll be on the table when you come down.'

'What would I do without you?' he asked, and she replied, 'I've no doubt you'd manage. Meanwhile, shift yerself or you'll be late.'

As he went up the stairs he called out wryly, 'Sometimes I wonder who's the boss in this house, you or me!'

'It's *me*,' she called back, 'and just you remember that!'

Luke went into the bathroom, chuckling. 'Edna, you're a gem, what are you?'

She didn't hear him. She was too busy throwing the bacon into the pan; followed by a handful of sliced tomatoes and a couple of mushrooms.

Pretty soon the delicious aroma of bacon cooking filled the house. 'Yer may be short on sleep,' Edna chunnered to herself, 'but while I'm about, you can be sure of a good breakfast afore you leave this house. A man in your situation needs feeding up. Haunted at home, haunted at work . . . By, it's a wonder you're not stark-staring mad!'

*   *   *

'I hate Monday mornings!' Roy always started the day shivering, whatever the weather. 'Jesus! It's bloody freezing in here!' Having taken off his

182

jacket he soon put it back on again. 'It's colder in here than it is outside.'

Jack looked at his mate, a small, shivering wreck. 'You could do with more fat on your bones,' he said. 'The sun's shining and it looks like another glorious day, and here's you shivering like a jelly. If you're that cold, run up and down for a minute or two,' he added with a grin.

Roy wouldn't have it. 'The boiler can't be on,' he argued through chattering teeth.

'Come here!' Like a mother-cat with a kitten, Jack got the little fella by the scruff of the neck and marched him to the wall. Pointing to the large, round meter attached to an army of pipes, he said, 'There y'are. Up and working and warming the place as we speak. Leave your coat on, give it half an hour, and you'll be warm as toast.'

Jack was right. Half an hour later the large open area was heated to the right temperature. The men were at work and Roy had taken off his coat and was looking much more comfortable.

From his vantage point at the top of the stairs, Jack oversaw the workforce. To his left, the men were waiting by the lorries and to his right, the rows of machine-hands, producing the many different brushes to be quickly stacked, were ready for inspection.

Deciding to take another look at the production line, he went down the stairs and across the loading bay, to where Amy's father, Dave, along with two other drivers were waiting for the word.

'Ready when you are, Jack.' That was Dave. 'We're all back from the station run, and now we're waiting on the brush delivery. The wagons are swept out and clean. All we need are the loads on,

183

then we'll be away.'

'You did well getting the distribution orders out on time,' Jack acknowledged. 'I know Mr Hammond appreciates you all turning in extra early to get it done.'

'So long as the appreciation shows up in us wage packets, that's all right,' Bert, Dave's friend, who was a loader, laughed.

'So, how long d'you think it might be afore we can be away with this new brush order?' Dave asked.

'Not too long,' Jack promised. 'Mr Hammond will be here shortly. As soon as he approves the quality, we'll have them packed and loaded.'

Since meeting Amy and realising Dave was her father, Jack had been amazed at how alike they were; not in looks but in mannerism—both homely creatures with no pretence about them, and bright, ready smiles. He didn't want to let Dave know that he had met his daughter. That was up to Amy, but only if and when she wanted to.

At the brush production line, the men were eager too.

'He can examine 'em all he likes,' an old workhand told Jack, 'but he'll not find a single misshapen base or one loose bristle. Matter o' fact, I'll go so far as to say, me and the men have taken more care with this little lot than we've ever taken . . . and that's not to say we've not *allus* been vigilant in turning out the best brushes in Lancashire.'

'I already know that, Will,' Jack assured him, 'and so, I'm sure, does Mr Hammond. But you know how important this contract is—a new outlet, at top prices, and the promise of even more

184

business to follow.'

'Aye, we know that, Jack, and we'll not let him down, 'cos if we do, it'll be like letting ourselves down.'

'You're right!' Jack agreed, 'especially as Mr Hammond is pulling out all the stops—new machinery, new wagons and even a new boiler system. He intends taking us up and up. No matter how good we've already proven our merchandise to be, we're on trial with every new customer. One shoddy piece of merchandise and it's back to square one.'

One of the newly started young men stepped forward. 'He'll not find any shoddy workmanship here.' Unlike the other men, he did not appreciate the fact that Jack had come straight to Hammonds when not much more than a bairn. From the start, he had been a quick learner and dedicated to his work. He knew the business inside out, and was fast becoming Luke Hammond's right-hand man.

All this envious young upstart could see was that Jack was not much older than himself, yet he wore the foreman's brown overall. 'Like Will 'ere says, these brushes must be the best in the whole of Lancashire. Tek a look and see for yourself.'

And because he knew Luke Hammond would do the very same, Jack did exactly that.

A few moments later he told the men he was well satisfied. 'But it's not me who needs to be satisfied,' he reminded them, 'it's the big man, and I'm sure he will be.' That said, he thanked them and set off towards the office.

'Cocky bugger!' The young man's envy was written all over his face. 'It's not right, somebody in his twenties telling you men what to do—'

185

He would have gone on, but was interrupted. 'You don't know what yer talking about, son!' A big ruddy-faced man spoke for all of them. 'Jack deserves the foreman's overall; he's earned it. What's more, he deserves a bit more respect from the likes of you. He knows more about these machines and this business than you'll ever know! We might be older and wiser than him in many ways, but he's been here longer than many of us and Mr Hammond knows his value.'

The other men nodded in full agreement, but it was young Roy who spoke for them, 'Aye, and it wouldn't surprise any of us, if Jack weren't running things round here one day.'

Unaware of these exchanges, Jack collected the paperwork from his office. Coming back down the stairs, he saw the supervisor enter through the main doors. He was a thin, sour-faced man who, because of his habitual lateness and lack of enthusiasm, was already under warning from Luke Hammond. He gave Jack the sign that Mr Hammond had turned into the outer gates.

Intending to have a word with him about not being around when he'd searched for him earlier, Jack merely acknowledged him for now and made his way to the main doors, where Luke was already in sight.

'Morning, Mr Hammond.'

'Morning, Jack. The men briefed, are they?'

'They are, sir. They're well aware of how important this new order is and, if you don't mind me saying so, I think you'll find they've done you proud.'

Luke smiled. 'It sounds as though you've already inspected the order.'

'I have, and I think it's a fine batch of brushes.'

Luke nodded appreciatively. 'Good! Right, let's have a look, shall we?'

With Jack following, he walked along the line of brush machines, talking to each of the twelve operators as he went.

His first stop was the broom-heads, where he dipped at random into the stacks, to check both quality and bristle quantity. Next the scrubbing brushes and miscellaneous, then the small hand brushes, and finally the large yard broom-heads.

With each one he turned the brush over, checking for bristle quality, possible missed holes, and that the bristle bunches were driven deep into the holes. When that was done he turned the broom-head sideways to check the straightness of the cut, and that none was misshapen.

Finally he thanked the work hands and returned to the office with Jack, where he told Jack that he needed a word with the supervisor.

'I'm not happy with him,' Luke said. 'He's turned out to be shifty and lazy, and he's never on time. The men see it all and it isn't good. He's already had too many chances and doesn't seem to take a blind bit of notice.'

In a matter of minutes, Jack tracked down the thin, sour-faced individual.

Luke outlined the man's lack of enthusiasm for his work, and his inability to take instruction, either from Luke or Jack. 'The men are aware of what's going on,' Luke continued, 'and it's not acceptable. You'll be paid a week's wages and leave straight away. There's no reason for you to serve out your notice, especially not when you haven't the slightest interest in what you're doing.'

The man swore and cursed and made many a threat, and even as Jack escorted him to the main doors, he was struggling, making it necessary for Jack to manhandle him roughly out of the building.

'You'd best keep an eye out for that one,' Luke told Jack. 'He can be a nasty piece of work.'

He also asked Jack to search out a new supervisor.

'I think we should look in the ranks of men we've already got,' Jack suggested and, trusting him to make the best choice, Luke told him to use his own judgement.

After Luke had gone, Jack had a brief idea that he might train Roy as supervisor, but his better instinct told him that Roy was not yet ready, and that one of the older, more experienced men would serve the firm better.

Later, during tea-break, he told Roy how he had been half tempted to train him up.

Roy replied exactly as Jack might have expected. 'I'm not ready. And besides, like you say, it wouldn't go down well with the other men.'

'That was my thinking,' Jack admitted. His first concern was always the company, and both men knew that. 'Your time will come, though,' he promised Roy, and Roy's confidence swelled a mile.

'I'll wait until you get your own firm,' he told Jack with a wink. 'I've a feeling it won't be too long afore we see you as yer own boss.'

'That's a long way down the road yet,' Jack answered. Though, in his heart it was all he wanted: to be his own boss, with his own business, and—the idea shot fully formed into his head—the lovely Amy to come home to every night.

That was his dream and he would settle for nothing else.

*   *   *

At six p.m. a whistle signalled the end of another working day. Roy lingered to wait for Jack, and they walked part-way home together.

'I'm seeing Daisy tomorrow,' Roy revealed with a confident little grin. 'I think she really likes me.'

'If that's true, try not to mess it up this time,' was Jack's friendly advice. 'She's a decent lass.'

'I know that now,' Roy said. 'She's better than I deserve, and I'll try never to let her down again.'

'Oh no, that won't do!' Jack cautioned him. 'If you want to keep her, you'll need to do more than "try".'

For a while, the two of them walked along, their heavy boots clattering against the flagstones and their minds filled with private thoughts.

'What about Amy?' Roy asked presently. 'It looked to me as though you were making a good impression there.' He grinned mischievously. 'Fond of her, are yer?'

'*More* than fond,' Jack replied, his voice dropping to a whisper. 'To tell you the truth, I reckon I'm falling in love.'

Roy whistled. 'Bloody hell, Jack. Steady on!'

Reluctant to discuss Amy any further, Jack skilfully changed the subject. 'So? You really want to make a go of it with Daisy then?'

'Yes, I'm hoping so. What's wrong with that, eh?'

'So you're determined to mend your ways, are you?'

Taking offence at Jack's comment, Roy brought

189

himself and Jack to a halt. 'What's the matter with you? What are you getting at?' Though he already had an idea of what Jack was referring to.

'You've some shady friends, that's all,' he said.

'What about 'em?'

'D'you intend to carry on seeing them?'

'Not all of 'em, no. I'll admit I've met some devious devils,' he confessed, 'and I know they got me in more trouble than I could handle, but they're long gone. I don't hear from them, and I don't want to.'

'But what about the one who lives down your street?' Jack persisted.

'Y'mean Don Carson?'

Jack nodded. 'Will you go on seeing him?' Roy almost always confided in him, so he knew Roy still paid him a visit now and then. He also knew that the fella was a close pal of Arnold Stratton, the man who had been gaoled for badly beating Luke Hammond's wife.

'I know what yer thinking: that I might get Daisy involved in summat bad, and that Don Carson is every bit as evil as Stratton. Well, he's not all bad. He's a rough diamond, sure enough, with an eye for dodgy deals and fast women, but he's tried to go straight so many times. Trouble is, he's easily tempted. One time he was even going to settle down and get married. I don't know what went wrong, but I reckon Don just couldn't manage the responsibility. But he's been a good friend to me, helped me when I was down, and I'll not snub him now.'

The irony of mentioning Don's former fiancée to Jack in this way did not escape Roy, but it wasn't Amy he was defending.

Always wary, Jack warned, 'I know it's none of my business, Roy, but if you're as serious about Daisy as you claim, then you need to think long and hard about this: the truth is, the company you keep might well turn out to be the company *Daisy* will keep. Don't forget that.'

Given food for thought, Roy remained silent until he and Jack parted company at the bottom of Penny Street. 'Are you seeing Amy tonight?' he asked of Jack.

'I'd like to,' Jack answered, 'but she and Daisy are doing "girlie" things—and don't ask me what that might be, 'cos I don't know.'

Roy suggested it might be something to do with Daisy telling him she was having her hair trimmed. 'I told her I liked it the way it was,' he said, 'but it didn't seem to matter what *I* thought.'

Jack laughed. 'Never interfere with a woman and her hair,' he advised. 'It's one of those mysterious things men are supposed to know nothing about.'

'See you in the morning then?'

'You will.'

'Good night then.'

'Good night,' Jack called after him. 'And don't be late!'

While Jack's journey home to the top end of Penny Street was a mere ten minutes or so, it took twice that long for Roy to get to Johnson Street.

By the time he closed the door to his bedsit, it was already going on for seven o'clock.

A sparsely furnished part of a large Victorian house, his living accommodation consisted of one long, wide room, the bottom of which was curtained off as a bedroom.

In the bedroom part was a narrow bed, a sturdy

191

if unattractive chest of drawers, which also served as a dressing table, and a chair that, with well-worn, dipped seat and sagging upholstery, had seen better days.

The rest of the room was furnished with a grubby old sofa, a small table with drop-down leaves and barley-twist legs and, standing proud on top of a tall slim cupboard, a handsome wireless.

There was also a horsehair-stuffed armchair, from which a multitude of black bristles protruded, and a green rug covering a greater part of the linoleum floor.

To one side of the room was a makeshift kitchen, consisting of a gas stove and a cupboard. There was a small wooden pantry containing a packet of tea, a half-used bag of sugar, a small uncut loaf and a pat of butter. The hinged drop-down lid served as a worktop. The bathroom, which was situated out on the landing, was shared with four other tenants.

The flat wasn't much, but it was his home and, sparse though it was, Roy considered it to be far more welcoming than the one he had shared with his parents. But that was a long time ago. He had always intended to better himself, but as yet he had not encountered the fortune he believed was waiting for him round every corner.

After washing and shaving, he devoured a cheese sandwich with a mug of tea, then he sat on the chair with his feet up on the table and, eyes closed, listened to the evening music on the wireless.

He was tired yet excited. He thought of Daisy and he couldn't sit still, so he put on his coat and departed the building.

Don Carson lived on the same street, just a few doors away. Roy visited him often, but had not seen him since he met Daisy again. Tonight he could hardly wait to tell him about his new girlfriend.

After Roy's three knocks on the front door of Don Carson's humble abode, Don answered the door.

Unshaven and wearing only his vest and trousers, he looked as if he'd just got out of bed. 'Oh, it's you!' Running his hand through his tousled hair, he stepped back to let Roy shove past. 'You'd best come inside,' he invited wearily.

Having followed Don along the passage and into the back parlour, Roy threw himself into a chair. 'What's up with you?' He observed how tired the older man looked, and how he was neither shaved nor properly dressed. 'I've never seen yer look such a mess!'

'Well, thanks, that's all I need!' Taking a long, noisy sigh, Don explained, 'I've been out all day, looking for work, but soonever I mention I've been in gaol, they don't want to know.'

'Why don't yer lie to 'em?'

'What's the use o' doing that?' the other man asked. 'They'd find out sooner or later.'

'Work for *yersel'* then.'

The other man sat down, his sharp eyes trained on Roy. 'Oh, yeah, doing what?'

'Don't ask me,' Roy shrugged. 'You've allus found summat in the past. Rob a bank or summat.' He laughed at his own suggestion. 'That's it,' he cried jubilantly. 'Rob a bank, why don't yer?'

'Don't be so daft, man!' Don snapped. 'I wouldn't know the first thing about robbing a bank. That's right out of my league. Besides, the last thing I need is to get thrown back inside. I've had enough of gaol to last me a lifetime.'

'D'yer want me to keep my eyes and ears open?' Roy was eager to make amends. 'They sometimes take folk on at building sites with no questions asked. I'll mek a few enquiries if yer like?'

'Thanks all the same, but I don't fancy working outdoors . . .' Don chuckled. 'Being in the nick seems to have spoiled me. Still, I'm not destitute yet,' he claimed. 'I do a bit here and there—buying and selling and such—but it won't last for ever. And lately it hasn't brought in the money, so I will need to get permanent work. I know that.'

Thinking about gaol, Roy asked, 'Do you still visit Arnold Stratton?'

'Course I do!' Don answered angrily. 'I'm not one to abandon a mate in trouble.'

Ready to change the subject, he regarded Roy with a degree of curiosity. 'Talking about Hammonds—as we kind of were—you seem to be settling down really well there.'

'Aye, an' I'm doing all right,' Roy revealed. 'I reckon if I stay on the straight and narrow, I might even be up for supervisor afore too long.'

Don laughed. 'Bugger me! You really are knuckling down.' He wagged a finger. 'There's got to be a girl involved somewhere,' he declared with a grin. 'That's it! You've got tangled up with some girl and gone all broody.'

Blushing to the roots of his hair, Roy said, 'All right, don't get too clever.' His face creased in a smile. 'Her name's Daisy and she's a good sort.'

'Daisy, eh?' Don made an expression of approval. 'And do you intend settling down with this Daisy? Is that the reason for your sudden

194

enthusiasm in working for a living?'

'And what if it is?' Roy asked sharply.

The other man apologised. 'Don't tek it so serious,' he said kindly. 'I were only joshing. Matter o' fact, I'm interested in a certain woman meself. Smart as a tack and twice as handsome.' His grin widened. 'The name's Helen . . .' he laughed again, '. . . or so she says, but I've a feeling she's lying, for whatever reason.'

'What! You mean you don't know her real name?'

'It's not her *name* I'm interested in,' Don replied with a wink. 'Besides, it's not a serious thing . . . not like you and this Daisy. We're just having a bit o' fun, if you know what I mean?'

From his friend's manner and the way he was looking at him, Roy sensed there was more. 'Have I met her?'

'Nope.'

'Am I going to?'

'Not if I can help it, no.'

Roy began to understand. 'She's wed, isn't she?'

'She hasn't said, and I'm not asking,' came the reply. 'All we want is a good time. Like I said, we're not looking to settle down. It makes no difference to me one way or the other. She arrives, we play around, and then she goes. And that's the way I like it.'

Roy was curious. 'Can I ask you summat?'

'You might as well. You've done nowt else since you got here. So, what else do you want to know?'

Roy took a deep breath. 'D'you know a young woman by the name of Amy Atkinson?' He had been curious ever since Daisy told him that Carson was Amy's ex-fiancé.

There was a long, unsettling pause, during which Roy thought he should never have mentioned it, because now the other man was staring at the floor as if he'd gone into some sort of trance.

Eventually Don looked up, his expression surprisingly soft. 'Yes,' he nodded. 'Amy and me were once engaged to be wed. How do *you* know her?' he asked sharply. And before Roy could answer he added quietly, 'You're not messing with her, are you?'

'No, I'm not messing with her, as you put it,' Roy was quick to explain. 'And neither is Jack.'

Carson was suddenly alert. 'And who might Jack be?'

Roy thought he might have touched on a jealous streak. 'Jack and Amy are seeing each other,' he said. 'I don't know how serious it is, but I have to say, they do seem to have hit it off together.'

There was another moment of silence, before the other man remarked softly, 'As long as he looks after her, it's none of my business.' Looking Roy straight in the eyes, he explained, 'Like I say, we were engaged to be wed. In fact, we got as far as booking the church and all that stuff.'

'I see. And what happened then? Why did you never get wed?'

'I hadn't told her I'd been in prison, and it got as I *couldn't* tell her. I was trying so hard to go straight when I met Amy, and she was part of that— something good to aim for and live up to. But I set my sights too high. I got to realising I could never keep it up, and one day my grubby little past would all come out, or I'd let her down and fall into my bad old ways. I'll allus be a drinker and a two-timer and a ruffian—I know that now. I liked her mam

196

and dad too. I couldn't hurt them all. I kept putting off mekking the break. Then suddenly the wedding was just a few days away and I had to do it before it was too late.

'Luckily they all work long hours so I know they're not around Blackburn much during the week, but I've been very careful to avoid anywhere I might bump into them.'

'Crikey!' Roy thought it must have taken some guts to back out of a wedding as close as that. 'And have you no regrets?'

'Well, of course I have! Amy's a lovely person, as good and kind as the day's long. I hurt her bad by trying to avoid hurting her even worse.' He took a minute to remember. '*That's* what I regret most.'

Suddenly he was on his feet, and demanding in a harsh voice, 'So what's this Jack like?'

'He's all right,' Roy told him. 'He won't hurt her. You've no need to worry on that score.'

Roy's answer seemed to calm him. 'How did they meet?'

'Me and Jack were out on the town when we just sorta met up with Amy and Daisy. Then another time, we met up again.' He wisely made no mention of his own shameful part in that first meeting. 'Me and Daisy get on like a house on fire. In fact, we're even talking about getting wed.'

Don laughed at that. 'You didn't mention me to Amy, did you?' he asked then.

'Nope.'

'Don't!'

'Why not?'

'Because there's no point. When I left her in the lurch it was a cruel thing. I'm not proud of what I did. What's done is done and can't be undone, so keep your mouth shut.'

'Don't worry, my lips are sealed.' And he meant it.

Carson glanced at the clock. 'You'd best soon make tracks,' he said. 'I need to get washed and changed.'

Roy understood. 'Got a woman coming, have yer?'

'I might have,' Carson admitted, 'so you can bugger off and make yourself scarce.'

'Helen, is it?' Roy licked his lips teasingly. 'I might like to introduce myself.'

Carson laughed. 'I thought you were already gone, on your new girlfriend?'

'I am. I've met the one I want, and she's more than enough.'

'Just as well then, because Helen's a different kettle of fish altogether. I doubt if you could even move in her circles.'

'Oh, I see . . . a rich bitch, is she?'

Smugly, Carson nodded. 'Rich, handsome, and needing to be satisfied on a regular basis, if you understand my meaning?'

Coming across the room he threatened to manhandle Roy out of the door. 'I've told you, I need to get washed and changed. Sometimes she gets here too early and catches me in the rough. I don't like that. I have my pride like any man.'

'All right, keep your shirt on. I'm leaving, I'm leaving.'

As he went he told Carson from a safe distance, 'Enjoy yourselves, and don't worry about me. I'll call round tomorrow and you can give me a full account.'

'Sod off!' Carson gave him a final shove out the

door. 'Get and find your own entertainment,' he suggested with a sly little chuckle.

As Roy crossed the street he was almost run down by a cab in a hurry. 'Watch where you're going!' Roy yelled as the taxi passed by. 'You nearly 'ad my bloody feet off then!'

When the taxi slowed down, Roy considered tackling the driver for his carelessness. Instead his curiosity was aroused when the taxi came to a halt outside Carson's place.

The woman who stepped out of it was exactly as Carson had described: well-dressed and well-built in all the right places, she was more than a cut above the rest.

But there was something else about her that intrigued him, yet for the life of him, he couldn't think what it was.

He watched her walk up the path, and he saw her knock on the door, and now, as she seemed to sense him there, she turned and smiled at him.

It was then that he realised who she was, and he could hardly believe it.

'My God!' Excitement coursed through him. *'It's Luke Hammond's sister-in-law!'*

He had seen her twice; once when she came to bring Hammond some documents from the house, and once when she came to collect her sister, Sylvia, who had come looking for her husband and thrown a tantrum when he was out on business.

He continued to watch her. Even before she had turned back towards the door, Carson was there to usher her inside.

Still reeling from the shock, Roy hurried away. 'It's just as well Carson doesn't know who she is,' he decided. This rich bitch really was roughing it.

He gave a whistle. 'I wonder what Arnold Stratton would say if he knew Carson was mixing with a Hammond?'

As he walked on, shock soon turned to amusement. 'Luke Hammond's sister-in-law, roughing it with a man like Carson!' He rolled his eyes. 'By! It's a turn-up for the books, and no mistake!'

Unable to contain himself, he made his way straight to Jack's place. The small house in Penny Street was furnished better than he himself could afford, a step up from his own humble abode.

'I thought I'd seen the last of you till tomorrow.' Jack was just beginning to settle down for an hour of music on the wireless, before getting an early night. 'Tea or coffee?' he asked, inviting him inside.

'Ain't you got nothing stronger?'

'No.'

'Coffee then. I can't abide tea . . . especially not when *you* make it. I put up with enough dish-water at the factory,' he grumbled, 'I don't see why I should put up with it in my own free time.'

'That's where we differ, you and me,' Jack informed him.

'Is that so?' Always at home in Jack's place, Roy sat himself down. 'And how d'you mek that out?'

Turning to answer, Jack paused at the kitchen door, 'Because you tend to see your time at the factory as being forced on you, in order to earn a living.'

'Too bloody right I do!'

Understanding Roy's point of view, Jack admitted, 'There was a time early on, when I felt like you . . . hated getting up in the morning and seeing it as precious time wasted, but now I see it in a different way.'

Roy had always known there was more to Jack than met the eye, so he wasn't surprised to learn he had a plan. 'So, what changed?' he wanted to know. 'How d'you see it now?'

Jack answered in simple terms, 'I used to see it as me working for somebody else and making them well-off. Now though, I look on it as all good experience . . . it's learning time, in preparation for my *own* business. The more I learn, the better I'll be, and the better I am, the quicker I'll get somebody to believe in me . . . say a bank manager, or a backer who'll take a risk on me.'

Roy nodded in agreement. 'By! If I had the money,' he declared boldly, 'I'd back you myself.'

'Honest? Would you?' Knowing Roy's wicked sense of humour, Jack never knew when to believe what he said. 'Or are you just having me on?'

'Am I heck as like!' Roy was genuinely indignant. 'Any fool can see you'll have your own business one day, it's just a matter o' time.' He gave a knowing wink. 'I dare say once you get your own premises, you'll be away with the best. And what's more, I'll be right there . . . your right-hand man, looking out for you all the way. Ain't that what best friends are for?'

Jack laughed. 'Looking out for *yourself*, you mean,' he chided, before adding in a serious voice, 'It's allus been my dream, to get my own premises. And when I do, I promise you hand on heart, you *will* be alongside me, and we'll look out for each other. How does that suit you?'

'Suits me just fine.' Roy was thrilled. 'I'll be the first in my rotten family to be a foreman.'

'Hey, don't get carried away! I never said you'd

201

be foreman.'

'You'll not be able to refuse,' Roy was confident. 'I'd work my socks off and learn the trade inside out. You'd be proud of me so you would. What! I'd be the best foreman you ever had.'

'All right then,' Jack laughed at his brashness, 'I'll think about it.'

While Jack made the coffee, Roy made himself comfortable. 'D'you want to know a secret?' he asked tantalisingly.

Jack popped his head round the kitchen door. 'What have you been up to now?'

'I've not been up to nowt! It's just that I know summat you don't.'

Jack returned to making the coffee. 'What's that then?'

'I've just been round to see Don.'

'So?' Returning with the coffee, Jack declared, 'There's nothing mysterious about going to Don's place,' he said. 'You visit him most weeks that I know of.'

Lounging in the chair, Roy took a leisurely sip of his coffee. 'I just thought you might be interested in what I've just seen.'

'Now, why would that be?' Settling into his armchair, one long leg dangling over the side of the chair and the other stretched out to the hearth, Jack waited for an answer.

Roy placed his cup in the hearth and leaned forward, his eyes aglow as he imparted his newly discovered secret. 'He's got a new woman friend.'

Jack stopped him right there. 'Aw, look, I've no interest in the man's love-life, for God's sake. Why would I want to know a thing like that, eh?'

Undeterred, Roy continued, 'She told him her

name was Helen, only her name *isn't*. It's Georgina.'

'Helen, Georgina . . .' Jack shrugged. 'It doesn't matter to me either way. Now then, is there another reason why you've foisted yourself on me tonight, because if there isn't and you intend talking about Carson's new woman-friend, I can think of a thousand better ways to use my time.' Standing up, he headed for the kitchen. 'So, you might as well drink up and head for the street.'

Roy's voice followed him. *'She's Luke Hammond's sister-in-law.'*

Stunned, Jack spun round. 'Your gaolbird friend . . . and Hammond's classy sister-in-law? What kind o' sad joke is that?'

'It's no joke,' Roy said, 'and there's more.' Having now caught Jack's interest, he deliberately paused, a look of mischief curling his face. 'Oh, I forgot! You don't want to hear about it, do you?'

Intrigued, Jack returned to sit down again. 'What else do you know? You've got this far, you might as well tell me the rest.'

Roy took his time, before revealing his own thoughts on the unlikely relationship. 'Think about it, Jack,' he urged. 'Don Carson is pally with the man who attacked Sylvia Hammond. I know for a fact Don visits Stratton in gaol.'

Again he paused to let his words sink home. 'And now her glamorous sister is on the scene . . . making up to Don like there's no tomorrow.'

Realistic as ever, Jack mused aloud, 'Happen they just fancy each other?'

'It's all too convenient,' Roy insisted. 'My bet is she must have found out that Don was pally with the man who damaged her sister.'

Thinking on it, Jack slowly chewed on his bottom lip, as he did when something bothered him. 'It doesn't make any sense, does it?' He wondered if it was a cruel twist of Fate, or simply animal attraction. Besides, even if she did know the connection between Carson and her sister's attacker, there was nothing much she could do about it.

'I must admit it's an odd coincidence, though,' he went on. 'This Georgina is not short of a bob or two; she's attractive and desirable by anybody's standard, so why would a woman like that want a man like Carson?'

Roy had the answer. 'To get even for what happened to her sister.'

'But the man who attacked her sister is already behind bars.'

Roy nodded affirmatively. 'I know that,' he replied, 'and I don't know how she means to get her own back, but for the life of me, I can't see any other reason for her to come after Don.'

'I can!' Like a light had switched on in his mind, Jack had seen something Roy couldn't see, or didn't want to.

'What's on your mind, Jack?'

'Your friend, Don.'

'What about him?'

'You're not his only friend, are you?'

'You know I'm not. He's got a lot o' good friends.'

'Ex-convicts like himself, are they?'

Not too comfortable with his line of questioning, Roy demanded to know, 'What are you getting at, Jack?'

Jack revealed his thoughts. 'I'm wondering about

Georgina,' he said. 'I'm wondering if she's the kind of person who would want her sister's attacker done away with, and if she did, who better to go to than an ex-convict, with contacts who might well be prepared to carry out a sort of execution . . . for a price?'

Against his better instincts, Roy could see the feasibility of what Jack was proposing, and was shocked by it. 'Jesus! Are you saying she might ask Don to put out a contract on Stratton?'

Throwing out his hands in a gesture of helplessness, Jack asked, 'What do I know? But look, mate . . . you have to admit, it's not beyond the realms of possibility. Is it?'

'You must be bloody mad!' Scrambling out of the chair, Roy slammed his half-empty cup onto the mantelpiece. 'You don't know him like I do!' Shock trembled his voice. 'All right, I'll admit . . . Don Carson spent time in gaol, so he's an ex-convict and keeps in touch with others of his kind. But I'm an ex-con too, and I keep in touch with Don, so you could say we're out of the same mould.'

'I never said any such thing!' Getting out of his chair Jack confronted him. 'All I'm saying is, this woman might not be what he thinks. After what he did to her own flesh and blood, she might want Stratton taken out for good, if you know what I mean?'

'You might be right,' Roy agreed, 'but even if you are, there's nothing *I* can do about it.'

Jack disagreed. 'If you think Carson is a genuine mate, and not capable of organising a hit man, then tell him to check her out. Tell him who she is, and—'

'I'm telling him nothing!' Roy snapped. 'He wouldn't thank me for it, and I wouldn't blame him. Besides, you're wrong about him. You said yourself, you know nothing about the man, while I've served time alongside him; slept on the bunk above him and talked well into the night about nothing and everything. We've ate garbage at the same table; slopped out together and looked out for each other.'

He paused, remembering how it used to be, and hating every last minute he'd wasted of his life. 'I reckon I know Don Carson well enough to be sure he'd never get mixed up in what you say. He might be a petty thief and he might like to use his fist when he's had a drink or two. But he wouldn't entertain murder . . . not for a woman, nor a wad o' money, however tempting. He just wouldn't do it!'

Jack nodded. 'All right, matey, forget what I just said. Happen she just fancies him after all, eh?' Placing his two hands on the smaller man's shoulders, he smiled to ease the tension. This was the first time he and Roy had exchanged such strong words. 'Happen he gives her what she can't get from her other men, eh? A bit o' rough and tumble.'

'Mebbe.'

'I didn't mean anything by what I said. You asked me what I thought and I thought wrong. OK?'

Calmer now, Roy nodded, 'OK.'

'So, will you finish your coffee or what?'

'No, I'd best make my way back.' Needing to clear his head, he made his way to the door. 'G'night, Jack.'

'G'night, Roy.'

Following him to the door, Jack watched him go down the street, shoulders hunched and hands thrust deep in his pockets. 'I think you're getting out of your depth mixing with Carson,' he mused, 'but you'll need to find that out for yourself, because I'll not risk our friendship by interfering.'

Another startling thought occurred to him. 'Unless o' course you're in danger. If I thought there was a chance you might be hurt . . .' his expression darkened, 'o' course, that would be a different kettle of fish altogether.'

*   *   *

Hurrying along, Roy heard the door close behind him. He looked back but Jack was already gone.

The chilling air seemed to clarify his thoughts, making him consider what Jack had said.

Now that there was a distance between himself and Jack, and the cool air had sharpened his reasoning, he could see the sense in at least some of what Jack had said. 'I suppose it *would* make sense if she was planning to have Stratton done away with,' he voiced his thoughts in a harsh whisper, '. . . considering what he did to her sister. But if she *is* keen to have him out of the way for good . . . and I'm not even sure about that . . . why would she go after Don? As far as I know, they go back a long way and they've allus looked out for each other.'

He tried to work it through in his mind. 'If she's done her homework . . . and she looks like the kinda woman who would, then she must know the last thing Don would do is to arrange for Arnold Stratton to be murdered. They're best buddies for

207

Chrissake!'

All the same, Jack's warning was strong in his thoughts, and now, he was made to see things in a different light. 'She *is* getting to him though,' he admitted reluctantly, 'even I could tell that. By! She's the kind o' witch who could worm herself all the way into a man's soul if he wasn't careful.'

He thought of the way Don looked when he spoke of her . . . kind of proud and excited all at the same time; wanting to look his best when she turned up, yet not complaining if she unexpectedly turned up early, when he was still in his rough.

'It looks to me like she's already twisting him round her little finger,' he muttered. 'If she can make him behave like a lovesick schoolboy, then what else can she do to him, eh?'

And back came the answer, 'She could work on him, until he's ready to do whatever she asks.'

He couldn't believe what he was thinking. 'Would Don really have his best friend done away with?'

He hated himself for even entertaining the idea. 'No.' The thought was abhorrent to him. 'He wouldn't. Never!'

He dismissed the notion from his mind as quickly as it had entered it.

CHAPTER TEN

September had been such a glorious month, it came as something of a shock when October arrived with a vengeance. For three days and nights the heavens opened and drenched the earth below.

Today was the first Tuesday of October. The heavy downpour had mellowed into a steady, soaking drizzle, but the wind was still strong.

'Bugger me, Mrs Tooley . . .' With a clatter and a thump, Daisy fell in through the door, her umbrella inside out and her hair standing up like the rag end of a floor mop, 'it's like all hell's cut loose out there!'

Mrs Tooley remained firmly behind her counter. 'Don't you dare come near me dripping wet!' she exclaimed, holding her hands up in protest. 'I'm wearing my best clothes.'

Her smile all teeth and wrinkles, she proudly informed Daisy, 'Mr Leyton has invited me to dine with him,' she giggled like a dizzy girl, 'at the Royal Hotel, no less.'

Wet to the skin and unable to muster any excitement on Mrs Tooley's behalf, Daisy took her time in answering. She shook her brolly all over the floor and threw off her wet coat and hat, which she then hung over the radiator, and now she came forward, sneezing and coughing and frightening Ma Tooley into retreating a few more paces behind the counter.

'Don't you think that's wonderful, Daisy?' Mrs Tooley persisted, desperately needing to be told how clever she was at having secured a date with the man who owned two ironmonger's shops, and wore suits from Jacob's tailors.

'Well, I never, Mrs Tooley!' Daisy answered, in a manner that had the older woman bristling. 'Aren't we the lucky one. Ooh! The Royal no less! Bleedin' hell, whatever next, eh?'

'Hey!' Incensed, Mrs Tooley dared to venture near. 'I'll not have you talking to me with that

209

attitude, young lady. Moreover, I will not have someone working in my café who can't keep a civil tongue in their head.' Giving Daisy one of her commanding stares, she asked, 'Do you understand what I'm saying?'

Daisy understood, and was mortified at her own rudeness. 'I'm sorry, Mrs Tooley,' she answered meekly. 'It's terrible out there. The tram was late, then I stepped off into a puddle. The wind drove the rain right at me all the way here, and now I'm soaked to the skin and freezing cold. I didn't mean to be cheeky, honest.'

'Hmm!' Mrs Tooley took note of Daisy's red nose and bedraggled hair and the way her feet squelched as she walked, and she felt a wicked feeling of satisfaction. 'So, it won't happen again, will it?'

'No, Mrs Tooley, it won't happen again.'

As Mrs Tooley turned away with a condemning comment, Daisy put out her tongue, only to swiftly retrieve it when Mrs Tooley suddenly turned on her heel to tell Daisy, 'I'm being collected in less than an hour. I've seen to the till and filled out the shelves and that's my little bit done for today.'

'Yes, Mrs Tooley.'

'Go on then, young lady. Get a move on. Into the back and get yourself straightened up. You'll find a new towel hanging on the loop, and make sure you replace it with a clean one when you've finished.'

'Yes, Mrs Tooley.' Half-tempted to curtsy, Daisy managed to contain herself. She didn't want to risk losing her job, at least not yet. 'I'm on my way, Mrs Tooley.' Silently mouthing, she started off towards the back room.

'And be sharp about it,' Mrs Tooley called after her. 'It's market day. The customers won't be long before they start arriving. They'll be queuing for breakfast if you're not careful.'

Daisy went away mimicking her. 'Queuing for breakfast, my hat!' she sniggered. 'I've never known there to be a queue for *anything* in this place, not since the day I started.'

All the same, she was thawed and dried and ready for work in a matter of twenty minutes. 'I'm all right now, Mrs Tooley. So you can go whenever you like.' Thinking: the sooner the better, you miserable old cow!

Mrs Tooley was impressed. 'There's a good girl,' she purred. 'You look the part now.'

Daisy had on her blue overall with a white pinafore over, and her hair was enclosed in the white mobcap Mrs Tooley insisted upon—and which the minute her back was turned would go into a drawer.

Mrs Tooley smiled sheepishly. 'Do I look smart, Daisy?'

'Yes, Mrs Tooley. You look . . .' Hesitating, Daisy searched for the right word, but for the life of her, she could not find one to describe the sight before her eyes.

The over-painted Bertha Tooley was not a pretty sight. Dressed in a brown bouclé two-piece with overlong arms, too tight a skirt and too loose a jacket, she had a spotted green blouse underneath and a yellowing pearl necklace enclosing her rubbery neck. Her hair had been permed so tight it resembled a scouring pad, and her crimson lipstick, which had partly spread over her teeth, was now melting into little rivers at the corners of her mouth.

'You look . . . er . . . you look . . .' Again she couldn't find the words, so had to finish, 'Good grief, Mrs Tooley! I do believe Mr Leyton won't know which way to look.'

'Oh, Daisy, I do hope you're not just saying that to please me?' Mrs Tooley's chin dimpled in a surprisingly pretty smile. 'Well, I never!' She even blushed a slight shade of pink. 'Do you know, Daisy, I actually think I might have found the right one, in Mr Leyton.'

'That's very nice, Mrs Tooley. I'm pleased for you, I must say.'

Every man over the past year had been 'the right one'. Until the inevitable day when Mrs Tooley would march in, moaning and complaining about how men were not worth the ground they stood on, and however could she forget what monsters they all were.

Then the outrage would pass and she was on the rampage again, searching for the poor unsuspecting soul who would give her the attention she craved.

At half-past ten, a cab arrived, and Mrs Tooley sailed out in all her glory. 'I'll see you later,' she told Daisy. 'Mind you take care of the place while I'm gone.'

'Don't you worry, Mrs Tooley,' Daisy assured her. 'It'll still be in one piece when you get back.'

After setting out the teacakes and flapjacks and turning on the oven for the sausage rolls and pies, which were bought in, delivered to the back door and needed only reheating, Daisy was ready for serving. All she needed now were a few likely customers.

'I hope Amy comes in early,' she sighed, leaning her elbows on the counter. 'I've a feeling it's gonna be a long, quiet day.' Still, at least the Tuesday man would be in, though since the blossoming of her relationship with Roy, he didn't feature in her daydreams so much these days.

* * *

Not too far away, Amy was happily meandering round the indoor market, buying some elbow patches, elastic and a potted chrysanthemum—all things Atkinsons' Corner Shop didn't stock.

Running a few steps ahead, little Johnny was having a wonderful time. Amy sometimes took him with her on her Tuesday bill-paying and shopping trip now, finishing with a treat at Tooley's Café. Johnny and Maureen had become friends with Daisy, and the little boy was charmed that Daisy worked where cakes were sold.

Maureen, who had had numerous unsatisfactory jobs over the last few months, was, she had explained this morning, going to look for a job in the Brookhouse area of Blackburn, north of the town centre, so Amy had been happy to include Johnny in her Tuesday routine.

'Don't go too far,' Amy called as he rounded the wet fish stall, 'or I won't be able to keep tabs on you!'

After pausing beside the hot-potato barrow, the boy came running back. 'Can I have a potato, please, Amy?'

'Best not, sweetheart. We're on our way to the café to see Daisy. We'll get summat to eat there.'

Johnny gave a half-smile. 'I like Daisy.'

213

'So do I.' Smiling, Amy took him by the hand. 'It's only a few minutes now,' she promised. 'D'you think you can last till then?'

Johnny looked up, his big eyes round and wondering. 'Can I have a cream cake?'

Amy laughed. 'If you like.'

When they emerged from the market, it was still raining. 'I hate this drizzly weather!' Juggling with her shopping, Amy managed to put up her umbrella. 'Hold on to me, Johnny,' she warned. 'The weather's got worse, since we've been inside.'

Johnny liked the rain, because he could stamp in the puddles and send the water up in sprays, though Amy told him not to. 'We're already wet from before,' she smiled. 'We'll steer clear of any puddles now, if you don't mind.'

As they went down the busy street, Amy had to grab him close because of the vehicles driving near to the kerb and splashing their feet. After a time, she swapped her shopping bags into one hand and, holding the umbrella with the other, she told the boy to hang on to her skirt. 'Come round this side,' she instructed. 'I don't like you being too close to the kerb.'

It was when Johnny let go of her hand to come round her that he saw the long, meandering puddle, which for an excited little boy was too good to resist. To Amy's horror he gave a skip and a jump and landed right in the middle of it. At that moment a beer wagon came hurtling down the street straight towards him.

'*God Almighty! JOHNNY!*' Horrified, Amy dropped her bags and made a desperate grab for him.

But someone else was quicker.

214

'You're all right, sonny.' Thanks to the passer-by, the boy was snatched away only a second or two before the wagon would have come thundering down on him.

Amy grabbed Johnny into her arms. 'Thank God you're not hurt!' She had been so frightened by the incident, she could hardly breathe, but once she realised he was unharmed, her fear evaporated and anger took its place. 'That was a stupid thing to do!' she chided. 'It's a wonder you weren't killed!'

'I think your son has probably learned his lesson.'

At the sound of the man's voice, both Amy and the boy looked up. Amy was mortified. In her panic she hadn't even looked at him, never mind thanked him. Embarrassed and astonished, now she recognised the rescuer as the man Daisy referred to as 'the Tuesday man'. His dark hair was covered by a flat cap, which was drawn down low, and over his heavy work cords, he had on a thick black coat done up to the neck. His smile, though, was warm and handsome, and now as he looked at her with those intense eyes, she felt as though they had known each other for ever.

'Oh, look, I'm sorry,' she apologised. 'I don't know how to thank you.' It didn't register that he called Johnny her son.

'There's no need to thank me,' he answered quietly. 'I'm just glad to have been of help.'

He looked at the sodden shopping bags where she had dropped them to the ground. 'Let me help you,' he said, collecting them up. 'How far are you going?'

'No, thanks all the same, but I'll be fine now. I can manage well enough.'

215

'If you're sure?'

'I am . . . thank you.'

Reluctantly, he handed her the bags. 'Then I'll be on my way.'

* * *

Luke bade them goodbye and strode off, his mind in turmoil. He had just spoken to the young woman in his painting. Close to, she was even prettier than he'd imagined—not *exquisitely* pretty, he thought, but reliably, unforgettably pretty, which was different. He'd imagined being with her so often—together at the cabin, walking in the woods arm in arm, her face lifted to the sun where it filtered through the trees, laughing . . . Or in the cabin, the only light from the log fire, the silent wood dark around them—they'd be sitting together, their hands lightly clasped in one another's, relaxed in peaceful and instinctive understanding.

Now they had met—and it wasn't in circumstances Luke had envisaged at all. How could he bridge the gulf between these long-held dreams and this unforeseen reality?

For one mad, inexplicable moment he wanted to go back. He wanted to look into those mesmerising dark blue eyes and talk with her, just to be near her and hear her voice.

'You're not making sense,' he told himself. 'She's married, with a child.' And the disappointment he felt was like a physical pain inside him.

* * *

Deeply shaken, both by Johnny's narrow escape

216

and the brief meeting with Daisy's 'Tuesday man', Amy watched him walk away.

'That man likes you.' Johnny said it as he saw it.

Thankful that the boy couldn't see her blushes, Amy asked, 'How do you know that?'

'Because I do, that's all.'

Amy laughed. 'You're an old head on young shoulders, that's what you are.'

'That's what Mammy says.'

'I know,' Amy admitted. 'And now I know *why* she says it.'

'I'm hungry.'

'I'll get you some food soonever we get to Mrs Tooley's.'

'Who's Mrs Tooley?'

Amy was used to the boy's constant questioning, but she was delighted by it because it told her he was losing his nervousness and wanting to know more about what went on around him. 'Mrs Tooley owns the café where Daisy works,' she informed him. 'Now put your hand in my pocket and don't let go!'

Walking close to the shop windows she did not give way for anybody as they set off in the direction of Tooley's Café. Even when a woman with a big pram tried to get between her and the wall, Amy would not budge. The last thing she wanted was for Johnny to get close to the road edge again.

Daisy was delighted to see them. 'Look at the pair of you!' Grabbing Amy's umbrella she shook it and left it in the porch. 'You'll catch your death o' cold.' Ushering them inside, she took Amy's bags and went ahead to the table by the radiator. 'I'll be back with a pot o' tea in a minute,' she declared, marching off in a hurry. Meanwhile, Amy and

Johnny took off their coats and hats, and draped them over the backs of the two chairs nearest the radiator.

By the time they were settled, Daisy was back. 'How does that do yer?' she asked, planting the tray on the table. 'One giant pot o' tea.' She gave Amy a wink. 'I reckon I'll join yer,' she said, 'being as there's not much on at the minute.'

Amy smiled to herself. Whenever the café was quiet, and even when it wasn't, Daisy always invited herself to sit down. 'Mrs Tooley's out then?' That much was obvious.

Flopping into the chair, Daisy drew it up to the table and began to pour. 'She's off for lunch with Mr Leyton,' she answered, rolling her eyes. 'The way she's tarted up, anybody would think she were off to the palace for a meeting with His Majesty.'

She poured three cups of tea—one with more milk to cool it quicker, and this one she put before Johnny. 'Sup up, lad,' she encouraged with a friendly little grin. 'It'll warm the soles of yer feet.'

Johnny took the cup, wrapping his hands round it. 'But my feet aren't cold,' he told Daisy.

'Oh, aren't they?' Giving Amy a wink, she asked the boy, 'Where are you cold then?'

'I'm not.'

Daisy feigned surprise. 'My word, yer a brave little thing aren't yer, eh? You've been outside in all that rain and you look like a drowned rat, and you're not even cold.' She gave an almighty shiver. 'I would be.'

Johnny made a disappointed face. 'I'm just hungry.'

'Well!' Staring at him in astonishment, Daisy's

eyes grew round as marbles. 'Why didn't yer tell me that before,' she asked incredulously, 'because I think I can help you there? Y'see, I've got some big fat pork sausages just waiting to be fried. Would you like that?'

Clapping his hands excitedly, the boy jumped up and down in his chair. 'Ooh! Yes, please . . . and a chukkie egg and a buttie?'

'Right! I'll have it back here afore you can finish that tea. Bacon buttie is it, lass?' she asked Amy.

'That'll be lovely, Daisy, thanks.'

While Amy and the boy supped their tea, Daisy got to work, and it wasn't long before she was back. 'Get that down you,' she said, dishing out the food between the three of them. 'I thought I'd join you.'

The buttie on her plate was thick as a doorstop and oozing with butter and, like Amy's, it was packed with crispy, fried bacon and thick slices of tomato. Now, as Daisy bit into it, the butter trickled down her chin, only to be licked up with the length of her pink tongue. 'Though I say it meself, I can mek the best bacon buttie in the whole of Lancashire.' Picking out a sliver of pink wavy bacon, she popped it into her mouth and quickly devoured it.

'You say Mrs Tooley's gone to *lunch*?' Amy asked. 'It's a bit early for that, isn't it?'

Daisy nodded. 'That's what I thought, but she's probably gone to have her nails done or summat, or the lines on her legs painted straighter.' She chuckled. 'Honest to God, lass, I don't know why she can't lay out a bob or two and buy herself some proper nylons. You should have seen the way she painted them lines . . . went down her legs like crooked tramlines.'

Amy thought it was a shame. 'You should have told her.'

'Naw. Why should I? The old cow makes my life a misery, so what should I care?' She laughed out loud. 'Besides, if she thinks to fool that fella of hers into thinking she's got a fancy pair o' nylon stockings on, he'll soon find out when he gets his hand under . . .' Remembering Johnny was there, she dropped her voice to a whisper. 'Once they get at it, if you know what I mean, there won't be any lines left to talk about, will there?'

Amy shook her head. 'You're wicked, you are.'

Half an hour later, warmed and fed, Amy and Daisy were talking of their next dates with Jack and Roy, while Johnny played round the tables.

'It's not raining now,' the boy told Daisy.

'That's good.' Daisy hated the rain.

'Can I have another sausage?'

Daisy nodded. 'I think I can manage that. You sit yourself down and I'll get started on it, eh?' And the boy slid onto his seat where he patiently waited. Then, as Daisy was returning, the door opened and all three heads turned to see who it was.

'It's *him*!' Amy whispered, and before he had taken off his cap and coat, she had managed to fill Daisy in with the bare bones of what had happened earlier. 'If it hadn't been for him, Johnny might have been badly hurt,' she finished.

Daisy was full of admiration, and a few minutes later, on taking his order, she told him so. 'My friend thinks the world of that little chap,' she said. 'It would have devastated her if anything had happened to him.'

Luke smiled appreciatively and told her how anybody would have done the same thing. Then he gave his order and, as always, concentrated hard on his newspaper, while all the time taking quiet little glances at Amy. He saw how loving and protective she was with the boy and he thanked his lucky stars he had been there when it mattered. Now, though, his deep attraction to Amy was marred by the belief that she was not only married, but the mother of a child.

He was acutely aware of the fact that though he had a marriage in name only, he was not free either, but somewhere in the back of his mind, he had dared to entertain the idea that, at some time in the future, he and Amy might form some kind of friendship, if not a closer relationship.

That was all out of the question now, he thought. And, for many reasons, it was just as well.

But it did not stop him from admiring her, and sneaking a glance whenever he thought she was not looking.

He watched her now as she walked towards the cloakroom. He thought how easily she moved, with a kind of gentle sway and a proud, pretty manner. Her clothes were ordinary and well worn but she wore them with easy grace, and her girlish hairstyle complemented her happy, unmade-up face. The ease of her friendship with the brassy little waitress and her love for the angel-faced child shone through in her warm smile and laughing blue eyes. He so much wanted to know her better, to talk with her, and walk with her, and learn about the things she liked most.

One thing was certain: he imagined she was not the kind to place much value on jewellery or material things. Not like Sylvia, who had always put them above all else, preferring jewels and furs, even more than the love and affection he had always generously given. Sylvia's clothes were always stylish—they came from the smartest shops in Blackburn and Manchester—and her hair and face were immaculately maintained. But she lacked Amy's natural warmth.

While Amy was away, Daisy kept a wary eye on Johnny. But he had noticed Luke and was quick to recognise him.

'There's the nice man who helped me,' he told Daisy, and Daisy mischievously suggested that he should 'go and thank him'.

To her astonishment, Johnny promptly ran across to Luke's table. 'Daisy said I have to thank you,' he announced proudly. 'She said I'm a lucky boy.'

'Did she now?' Breaking his own golden rule never to let anyone interfere with his Tuesday freedom, Luke invited the boy to sit beside him. 'What name do you go by?'

'Johnny.'

'Well, Johnny, I'm glad I was able to help out back there, but you must remember in future, never to go into the road like that. You gave your mummy a terrible fright.'

Confused, Johnny looked up. 'She's *Amy*,' he said. 'She's my best friend, not my mummy.'

'Really?' Thrilled at the news, Luke told the boy, 'Well, in that case you really are a lucky boy in more ways than one.'

'Why?'

'Well, because it's nice to have a best friend.'

Wriggling in the chair, the boy warmed to the conversation. 'Have *you* got a best friend?'

'I suppose I have, yes, but she's not like your

Amy.'

'What's she like then?'

'She's very small and very beautiful, with big brown eyes, and she comes to see me every week.'

'Where does she live?'

'In the woods.'

'What's her name?'

'I don't know her real name, but I call her Velvet.'

'When does your friend come to see you?'

Folding his newspaper and laying it down, Luke concentrated on the boy. 'It's always on a Tuesday.'

'Why?'

'Because every other day, I have too much work to do, but on Tuesday I can do whatever I like.'

He thought about his precious hideaway, and for a moment he was tempted to explain to the boy, but as yet his privacy was too precious and instead he talked about his 'friend'. 'Sometimes, when I'm sitting on my steps, she comes and sits with me, and we talk for a while. Then she goes away, to be with her family. But she always comes back another time.'

At that moment, Luke caught sight of Amy. 'I think you'd best go back now,' he suggested.

Emerging from the cloakroom, Amy was intrigued to see Johnny and Luke in earnest conversation and, knowing how the stranger preferred to be left alone, she hurried across to them. 'Johnny! Don't pester the man.'

When Johnny clambered off the chair and came to her side, she said to Luke, 'It seems I owe you another apology. I didn't know he might come over to you or I would never have left him.' She felt herself blushing under his smile. 'He's not usually

223

so friendly,' she added. 'He normally shies away from people.'

'He's good company.' Luke thought she looked especially fetching when she blushed.

Johnny piped up, 'He's got a best friend like you, and I want to see her.' Without taking a breath he turned to Luke. 'Can I see her, can I, *please*?'

'Johnny!' Amy was horrified. 'Come on now. Your mammy will be back soon.' Holding out her hand she waited for him, but ignoring her, he turned to Luke instead. 'Can we see Velvet,' he persisted, 'me and Amy?'

There was a moment of silence, when Luke wondered if this once it might not hurt to let someone like Amy and the boy into his special, secret world. But then it wouldn't be secret any more, he cautioned himself.

And yet, Amy was already there, in the painting he had hidden away, and she was in his heart too, another deep, wonderful secret that kept him sane when life was overwhelming.

Looking from the boy to the man, Amy felt her emotions spinning. Something magical was happening, she thought, something she could not explain. She wanted to sit down with this man she hardly knew. She needed to talk with him, to know him, and yet she was half afraid, of him, and of herself.

'I've never seen him take to a stranger the way he's taken to you,' she told Luke now. And to the boy she said, in a firm voice, 'We have to go now, Johnny. Thank the man and say goodbye.'

Some short time later, Luke left, leaving the money on the table, as usual.

'You lost your chance there, lass,' Daisy

reprimanded. 'I saw him looking at you, and I know he fancies you.'

Amy laughed, but it was a quiet, hesitant laugh. 'I thought you wanted him for yourself,' she teased, 'and here you are, trying to get me together with him.'

'That's because I've got my Roy now,' Daisy said, all dreamy-eyed. 'He's what I've been looking for . . . somebody to make a home with, to have babies and make his dinner every night, and sit with him by the fireside of an evening.'

Now, when Daisy looked up, Amy was amazed to see there were tears in her eyes. 'All I want is a real family, and a home, where people don't shout and scream at each other, and I need never be afraid.' Her voice hardened. 'That's my dream, and I know in my heart of hearts Roy can make it come true for me—for us both.'

Realising she was showing her deeper feelings, Daisy gave a nervous little laugh. 'There! I'm getting carried away.' She surreptitiously wiped away her tears.

'I want to see Velvet,' the boy declared. 'She's pretty, like Amy.'

Amy shook her head. 'I don't suppose we'll get any peace now,' she told Daisy jokingly. 'All he'll go on about is Velvet—whoever she is!'

Noticing a customer on the way into the café, Daisy stood up. 'Well, whoever this Velvet is, I wouldn't mind meeting her myself,' she told Johnny.

'But Daisy can't see her. Only you and me can see her,' he told Amy.

Wisely dismissing his comment, Amy ruffled his hair, and they waved cheerio to Daisy and left. The rain had stopped and the wind seemed to be settling.

'When's Mammy coming home?' Johnny skipped down the street; but having been frightened by the earlier incident, Amy was careful to keep him on her inside.

'I expect she'll be there when we get back,' she promised, 'and she'll want to know all about your shopping trip, you'll see.'

*   *   *

Arnold Stratton was desperate. 'I don't know how much more I can take in here,' he told Maureen. 'There are some bad buggers in this place . . . worse than ever I've messed with.' Running his hands through his thinning fair hair, he looked up, his blue eyes stricken. 'I don't mind telling yer, I've been tempted to finish it once or twice.'

Maureen was shocked. 'What d'you mean, "finish it"?'

'What d'you think I mean?' he asked impatiently. 'String myself up, o' course, an' have done with it!'

Maureen was angry. 'That's a dreadful thing to say!' she chided. 'May God forgive you.'

He seemed to be deep in thought for a minute, but when he looked up he shocked her again with his next statement. 'I've been thinking,' he grunted. 'God knows there's not much else you can do in a place like this.' Leaning forward he lowered his voice so it was almost inaudible. '*I reckon it were her husband—Luke Hammond.* For years she's carried on with one bloke after another . . . they say Luke Hammond were the only one who didn't know.

226

Happen he found out about us, and went for her—meant to kill her mebbe, only it all went wrong and now he's lumbered with a mad woman.'

Maureen was afraid. 'Keep your voice down, Arnie. You're saying a dangerous thing, and you never know who's listening.'

'No, no, lass. I mean it!' He gave a deep groan. 'Mind you, since I've been in this damned place, I've blamed everybody that ever knew her. This time, though, I'm almost certain. Look, lass, if I were guilty, I'd serve the time and be done with it, same as I did afore. But I'm damned well innocent of this one! I'm telling you, there's somebody out there as knows who did the crime. And why was I fitted up—that's what I'd like to know? Who did it to me? What reason had they?'

Maureen didn't want to be dragged into this conversation. She knew her husband's tendency to overdramatise. Sometimes it could be fun; now, though, it was self-pitying. 'I'm sorry, Arnie,' she said. 'It's time to go. They're coming to show us out.' And sure enough the two officers were already descending on them.

As the guard led him away, Arnie blew her a kiss. 'See you next time, lass.'

'Keep your chin up,' she told him. In a minute he was gone and she was being given her umbrella, which had been confiscated on entering. Without fuss or favour, she was then ushered outside.

Feeling low as always whenever she came to see him, Maureen stood by the gates for a time, her mind full of the conversation she had shared with her husband.

'It must be hell,' she muttered, 'to be locked away.' As a husband Arnie had been less than a success, especially when his temper was on him. Clumsy, often tired, late with his tea, losing things and sometimes nagging . . . she listed her faults. He'd always had an eye for other women but perhaps he had needed to look elsewhere because of her. If she'd just tried a bit harder . . .

She looked up and down the street as though expecting someone to leap out and march her back inside to share her husband's punishment.

'Where to, lady?' A cabbie drew up alongside her, seizing his opportunity.

'I don't need a cab, thank you very much,' Maureen told him, 'not when there's a perfectly good tram service.'

'How much is the tram compared to my cab?' he asked. 'Not much more than the price of a cuppa tea, I'll bet.'

'So, how much will it cost me to Derwent Street?' she enquired.

The cabbie looked her up and down. He saw how she was down at heel and straight out from visiting some poor sod in gaol. 'Go on then,' he answered. 'I'll run you there for a tanner. How's that?'

Maureen did a mental calculation and realised he was doing her a good enough deal. 'All right, Derwent Street it is.' Taking a great gulp of fresh air she climbed in.

All the way there he talked: about the state of the nation and how, unless the heads of government got their thinking together sooner rather than later, they'd all be heading for a second world war. He talked about a recent visit to London, and how horses and carriages were becoming rarer and rarer. 'Soon, there won't be a horse on the streets, and that'll be a proper shame,' he complained.

'There are still horses and carriages round here,' Maureen observed. 'And we still have the milk brought round by horse and cart.'

He had an answer for that too. 'Ah, well,' he commented smugly, 'this is the North, and they do say as the North is allus lagging behind. But I'm glad of it, and so should you be. Things are changing too damned fast, if you ask me.'

Before they reached Derwent Street, Maureen was informed of the 'crippling, rising prices'. 'These days, if you want a smart suit for going out somewhere special, you've to pay as much as two pounds. And look at the picture house. Only last year, you could sit through a three-hour picture for sixpence. Now you've to pay eightpence. Prices never go down, they allus bloody well go up, if you'll excuse the language . . .'

By the time he dropped her off, Maureen would have 'excused' him anything to let her out of his cab. 'I don't suppose you can afford a tip as well,' he griped, holding out the fare in the palm of his hand.

'Sorry,' she said. 'I can't afford tips.'

'Well, then, good luck to you, and mind how you go.'

'You too.' She waved him off with a smile on her face. 'It was a good try, I'll give you that,' she told the rear end of his cab as he went away up the street. Then she hurried into the shop.

'Hello, Maureen.' Marie was at the till, serving a customer. 'Our Amy's in the back, if you want to go through?'

After thanking Marie and enquiring about her

busy day, Maureen made her way to the living quarters.

'Mammy, Mammy!' On seeing her in the doorway, little Johnny ran to her. 'Me and Amy went to see Daisy, and the man who got me out of the road was there and he told me about his friend . . .'

He would have gone on, but Maureen quietened him down. 'Not so fast,' she laughed. 'What's all this about the man "getting you out of the road"?' That was the one remark that registered. 'What were you doing in the road in the first place?' She raised a quizzical gaze to Amy, who quickly explained.

Once she was armed with the facts of the matter, Maureen could see that it was no one's fault really. 'It's a good job this man was there,' she said. 'And as for you, lad,' she wagged a finger at her son, 'you'd best do as you're told in future and stay close to Amy.'

Uncomfortable, the boy looked from one to the other. 'I won't run out again,' he promised.

'Now then, what's all this about a friend?' Maureen gave him a hug.

Growing excited, Johnny explained, 'She's called Velvet, and one day me and Amy are going to see her. You can come too if you like?'

'I should think the poor man has seen enough of you, without taking you to meet his friend,' Maureen said. 'And here you are, inviting me and Amy into the bargain.'

'The man won't mind,' Johnny assured her. 'He's nice.' He then returned to his toy train and Amy made Maureen a cup of tea.

They had just settled down for a long chat, and

Amy was coming round to ask Maureen if she'd found suitable work, when Marie came rushing in. 'The shop's getting busy,' she told Amy. 'I'm sorry, love, I know I gave you the day off, but I'd appreciate your help just for an hour or so.'

Amy leaped up. 'Aw, Mam, you should have called me earlier.'

Marie sighed with relief. 'Thanks, love. Oh, I nearly forgot, Maureen,' she added. 'There's a man in the shop to see you. I think he said he were a cabbie.'

Leaving Johnny to his playing, both women followed Marie out to the shop, Amy to help serve the customers, and Maureen to see who wanted her.

On seeing Maureen come across the room, the taxi driver stepped forward. 'I found this. I knew it must be yours 'cos you were the last fare I picked up.' Handing her the umbrella, which she had not missed, he went on, 'It was caught up in the offside door . . .'

Shifting his gaze to Amy, who had just dropped a packet of sugar, he told her with a grin, 'Your mate here were in a right state when I picked her up from outside the prison. All white and shocked she were, as if she might faint any minute. No wonder she weren't thinking right when she climbed into the cab.'

Deeply shamed, Maureen none the less had to thank him. 'Do I owe you anything?' All she wanted was to be rid of him. She propelled him towards the door. 'I mean, what with you having to come back and all . . . how much d'you want?' All she had in her pocket were two small coins, but he could have them if only he'd bugger off, she

231

thought angrily.

'Keep your coppers in yer pocket, it's all right,' he answered. 'I were in this neck o' the woods anyway. Got a fare to collect from Penny Street.' With that he bade her goodbye and hurried off 'to earn a crust or two', as he put it.

It wasn't only Amy who had been in the vicinity when he mentioned how Maureen had been to the prison; it was also Marie and the customer she was serving—though Mr Wagner was deaf as a post, his hearing destroyed by a shell explosion in the war, and he wouldn't hear the ceiling come down, not even if it fell right on top of him.

After the customers had all gone, Amy saw that Maureen was close to tears.

'Is it all right if we go into the back, Mam?' she asked, her arm round Maureen's shoulders.

Marie could see the turn of events and her heart went out to the other woman. 'Aye, lass, you two go on. It's quieter now. Yer can send Johnny out to help me sweep up the sugar, if yer like.' It was Marie's way of letting Amy and Maureen have the little chat they obviously needed.

A short time later, with her son out in the shop, Maureen apologised to Amy. 'I should have told you the truth before,' she said tearfully, 'only I were that ashamed, I couldn't bring myself to speak of it. I thought if you knew my Arnie was in prison, you would never want me or Johnny anywhere near you again.'

Amy was mortified. 'I would never turn you and little Johnny away,' she said. 'I love you both, like my own family. And if you don't want to tell me your troubles even now, it's all right. You don't have to.'

Maureen took Amy's hand into her own. 'You're a lovely lass,' she said, wiping her tears away with her free hand. 'I reckon you've known all along there was summat I had to hide, but you've never pressed me, and I'm grateful for that.'

Amy could see how this whole sorry business was too painful for Maureen, and she didn't really know how to help her. But she could listen, and she could offer support. 'Like I say, Maureen, if you feel it's something you're not able to discuss, then don't. But if you can trust me, you know I'll keep your confidence and I'd like to help, if I can.'

'I know you would,' Maureen acknowledged, 'but it's not summat anybody can help with.'

'Try me,' Amy urged. 'You never know.'

Nervously, Maureen confessed how she had been deceiving everyone. 'When I told you Arnie was working away,' she began, 'I was lying. He isn't working at all. He's serving ten years in gaol, for attempted murder.' Glancing about, she lowered her voice. 'His name is Arnold Stratton; the man who was convicted of attacking Sylvia Hammond.'

'Good God!' Amy could hardly believe her ears. 'No wonder you've had to move from place to place. No wonder you didn't want anybody to know.' She began to understand now.

'Langdon is my maiden name,' Maureen explained. 'I don't want people making the connection with Arnold Stratton, particularly for Johnny's sake. We've come to like living round here, and Johnny thinks the world of you,' she went on. 'You and Marie are the first friends we've had in a long time. It would break his heart, and mine too, if we were thrown out of Derwent Street.'

Taking both of Amy's hands in hers, Maureen

clutched them tightly. 'That's why you mustn't say anything,' she pleaded. 'I know Marie heard just now, and I know I can trust her like I can trust you, but don't tell nobody else. Promise me that much, Amy. Please? For Johnny's sake, if not for mine.'

'Your secret's safe with us,' Amy promised. 'Does Johnny know about his daddy?'

'No, and I don't want him to. Arnie has a terrible temper on him—but he can't help himself. His imprisonment has brought shame on us both. I'm terrified that me and Johnny will be tarred with the same brush.' She wiped away a tear. 'It would hurt the lad too much if he found out. So far, thank God, he doesn't know the truth of why we've had to keep moving on, and I pray he never will.'

'He won't learn it from me or Mam,' Amy declared. 'You need have no fear on that score.'

Maureen took her friend's hand and squeezed it in silent gratitude.

'You say he's known to be violent?' said Amy.

'That's right! He'll think nothing of lashing out with fists and feet, and anything else that comes to hand. He threw a vase at me once and cut my forehead, look!' Shifting her hair aside, she displayed a crooked scar across the top of her hairline. 'A couple of inches nearer and he would have blinded me for sure!'

Amy shook her head in disbelief. This was the kind of thing she heard about Daisy's parents. 'And he's confessed to having had an affair with Sylvia Hammond?'

'Aye, that's right enough, lass—her and several other women that I know of!'

She saw what Amy was getting at and now she could see it herself. 'Why! The bugger's led me a

234

merry dance these years.' She gave a harsh laugh. 'An' there's me half believing his self-pitying and his moaning, instead of him taking his punishment like a man. He's bullying me even from inside prison.'

When a moment later Johnny came back into the room, Amy took it as a sign that her mammy was waiting for help in closing up the shop for lunch.

'Thank you, Amy.' Maureen was grateful for Amy's sympathetic ear. 'You'll not breathe a word of what we've discussed, will you . . . except to your mammy o' course?'

'You know I won't.' Amy saw her and the boy out to the doorstep. 'Mind how you go,' she gave them each a hug, 'and remember, I'm here if you need me.'

When they were gone, and Marie's curiosity was satisfied, she came to the same conclusion as Amy. 'It seems the man's a bully and a brute and, if you ask me, he's in the right place.'

What Maureen had told Amy was still playing on her mind after she went to her bed that night.

Poor Maureen. Amy tried to imagine what it might be like to be married to a violent man—a man who had been in prison—to live in fear of violence and bullying.

Then her mind ran to the other victim of Arnold Stratton's violence: Sylvia Hammond. Why had she turned to this dreadful fella when she was married to someone so widely admired? Amy's father, and others, had first-hand experience of Luke Hammond and had only praise for him. She could not believe a man like that would ever deserve to be betrayed. If his reputation for fair-mindedness, even generosity, for sympathy and humanity, even despite his sharp business mind, were anything to go by, he sounded like the kind of man any woman would be glad to spend her life with.

PART THREE
November 1933
Twist of Fate

CHAPTER ELEVEN

'Well done, Jack. You've done a good job.'

Trusting his own judgement, Luke Hammond had given Jack more responsibility than usual, and as always, the lad had not let him down. 'I wanted the buyers to get a good impression when they came to look round. They went away more than satisfied, and now I'm hopeful we'll get that big contract.'

Jack appreciated the praise. 'If there's any chance of them using us to store and deliver their merchandise, we can't let them slip through our fingers.'

That was Luke's thinking also. 'You never cease to amaze me, Jack,' he said thoughtfully. 'You're a born businessman, if ever I saw one. I wouldn't be at all surprised if one of these fine days, you'll be up and away to start your own company. Am I right?'

'I won't deny it, Mr Hammond,' Jack answered cautiously. 'It's allus been my ambition to have my own factory. But I reckon it's a long time away yet.'

'I wouldn't be too sure of that if I were you. You're not a man to sit on his backside while the competition takes over,' he told Jack. 'You'll want to be up there with the best of them. I've no doubt about that.'

Suspicious that Luke Hammond was preparing to be rid of him, Jack assured him, 'It all teks money, as you well know, so I dare say you'll not see the back of me for some time yet.'

Luke nodded. 'You're right about the money.

You'll get nowhere without it, that's for certain, but it isn't everything. If a man's got drive and commitment enough, he'll always find a way. That's why I know you'll do it, and when that day comes, it'll be a bad one for me, I'm aware of that.' He smiled warmly. 'Happen the customers will move over to you. Then again, happen they'll stay loyal to me. We'll have to see who's the better man, won't we, eh?'

Made nervous by Luke's last remark, Jack asked pointedly, 'Now that you know I mean to have my own business one day, I expect you'll be wanting me out now.'

Luke looked him in the eye. 'The fact that you have a mind to be your own boss has only strengthened my faith in you. If I were to get rid of a man like you, I'd be the biggest fool this side of London town.'

Jack was astonished. 'How's that, Mr Hammond?'

Luke took a moment to observe the younger man: that tall, confident stance and the aura of conviction. 'You remind me of myself when I was that bit younger.' He laid a hand on Jack's shoulder. 'You know what you want and you'll not rest until you get it. You work hard and plan hard, and head towards your dream until it becomes hard reality.' His face crinkled into a deep smile. 'I admire that in a man.'

'You've got me bang to rights,' Jack admitted. 'I've allus known what I want. And even if you were to send me on my way now, I'll never lose sight of my ambition, nor will I ever give up!'

'Do you think I don't know that?' Luke went on to explain his thinking. 'I've no intentions of sending you on your way. I want you here with me, where I can keep an eye on you.' He took a deep breath. 'Think about it, Jack. I'd be sending you straight to the competition, and that would be the act of a very naïve and stupid man . . . which I hope I'm not.'

Jack nodded. 'I see what you're getting at.'

'Good man! But that's not the only reason I want you here.' He paused to formulate his words. 'I'm sure you've already realised how fast we're expanding. Work is taking off at such a rate; the orders are pouring in and it seems before too long, I'll have need of another warehouse and a couple more wagons. That means I'll have more management work than a man can handle on his own, and that's where you come in.'

Jack was intrigued. 'In what way?'

'I have plans for you, Jack,' Luke replied. 'Plans that will give you a free hand, and put you in good stead for the day you captain your own company.'

Jack was secretly delighted. 'You seem to have a lot of faith in me, if you don't mind me saying.'

'I have,' Luke confirmed, 'but only because you've earned it.'

With that he moved away. 'Best start closing up.' Glancing up at the clock he saw it was already ten minutes to six. 'It's been a long day. Happen tomorrow will be a bit easier.'

'Good night, Mr Hammond.'

'Good night, Jack.'

Having secured his own office, Luke made his way out to the car, leaving Jack to close up the factory.

'I hope she's in a better mood than when I left her this morning,' Luke said aloud, speeding his way home.

Lately he'd got into the habit of talking to himself, which wasn't surprising when he had no one else to confide in. Even Edna could never understand what was in his heart . . . all those futile hopes and dreams and broken ambitions, of raising a family and growing old with the woman he had loved and married.

Now they were all gone. And there were times when he felt like the loneliest man in the world. Having drawn up to the house, for a minute he was tempted to turn the car round, drive away and never come back. For too long now, his life had been a roller-coaster ride. There were times when he could hardly bear to leave Sylvia behind in the mornings. Other times he wished himself a million miles away. Or at least in the cabin in the woods— starting a new life, more peaceful and possibly less lonely . . .

Knowing he had no alternative but to face the certain chaos Sylvia's mood this morning foretold, he nosed the car into the driveway and drew it to a halt. For a long, aching moment he folded his arms across the steering wheel and, resting his head on them, briefly closed his eyes. He was tired, drained, devoid of energy.

He consoled himself with the knowledge that tomorrow was Tuesday. Out there in the wilderness he could breathe, and smile, and feel the weight of his burden slip away.

He locked the car and went inside the house, his feet like lead, and his heart too.

He braced himself for what was coming. He had never shirked his responsibility, and he would not shirk it now.

'I'm glad you're home, sir.' On her knees, beginning to clear away the crumbs of an apple pie, Edna looked frazzled. 'She's been unsettled all day.'

He glanced around the kitchen. There was no sign of Sylvia, but the oven door was wide open and there were pieces of broken earthenware scattered from one end of the room to the other. He was very familiar with the results of Sylvia's rages.

'What happened, Edna?'

'It's all right,' she answered, 'I've managed to persuade her upstairs. She took her medication and I watched her until it was all gone. She's getting sly about it again—says it makes her too tired, and I suspect she's been pouring it away although she swears not. I've tucked her in. I expect she'll be sleeping like a babe when you go up.'

With an inward sigh of relief, he thanked her. 'You look all in, Edna. Go home and put your feet up. I'll take over now.'

Edna did not argue. It had been one of those days when she would be glad to get home.

'Thank you, sir,' she said. 'If you need me, you know where I am.' Sylvia was like a child to her and, weary or not, she would remain on call, any time, day or night. Then she was quickly gone, though not to 'put her feet up', as Luke had suggested. Instead she would cook the dinner and clear up behind her, before starting that enormous pile of ironing. By then her joints would be aching and her feet swollen like new-made bread.

Sylvia slept quietly throughout the night.

Occasionally checking that she was all right, Luke alternately paced the floor and slept fitfully.

243

On Tuesday morning, he couldn't wait to get out of the house. No factory, no noise or people, no fretting over Sylvia, just peace and quiet in the heart of God's creation, where he could think straight and not be disturbed.

That humble cabin in the heart of the woods was his only sanctuary. If he didn't have that, he believed he might go out of his mind.

At seven thirty, washed, shaved and looking every bit the businessman, he went down the landing to check on Sylvia; she was still fast asleep, hair across the pillow and arms akimbo—like a child, he thought.

Half an hour later, just as he was clearing away his breakfast things, Georgina arrived, looking stunning in a dark green, tight-fitting two-piece and her hair superbly groomed and shining.

'You should have waited,' she chided. 'I would have cooked your breakfast, you know that.'

'I know.' He poured her a cup of tea and placed it on the table. 'I've been up and checked Sylvia and she's still sleeping. Leave her be for now,' he suggested. 'She was unsettled yesterday and needs her rest.'

'And what about you?' Georgina had already observed the hollow eyes and listless mannerisms as he wiped the flat of his palms across his face. 'You look shattered. Can't your Tuesday meetings wait till tomorrow?' She was angling for information again.

'No.' One word, but it was a firm, decisive word, and for a moment she was silenced.

The moment passed. 'But you look exhausted.'

244

Coming closer, she gazed up into his dark eyes. 'Kept you awake, did she?'

Reaching for his jacket from the back of the chair, he gave a wry little smile. 'You could say that.' He recounted the previous evening's fiasco. 'It seems Edna made her an apple pie, which, as you know, was always Sylvia's favourite. Sylvia asked her to bake it for her, then insisted on helping and, of course, Edna agreed. But when it came to taking the pie out of the oven, she could see how worked up Sylvia had got so she refused to let her do it in case she burned herself.'

He put on his jacket and began to move away. 'You can guess the rest,' he remarked cynically. 'Sylvia threw one of her best tantrums. When I got home the pie was all over the floor. Edna had managed to get her upstairs and give her the medication.'

He then confided how concerned he was about Sylvia, and Edna's worries about her not taking her medicine. 'She's due to see the consultant in a fortnight,' he reminded Georgina. 'I've been wondering if I should bring the appointment forward.'

'Why?' Georgina was suddenly alert. 'You're not thinking of having her put away, are you?'

'Good God no!' Anger flooded Luke's face. 'What kind of man do you think I am?'

'A tired man,' she replied. 'A man who could be at the end of his tether. A man whose wife has some kind of brain damage, and now she's a burden to you . . . dangerous to herself and others.' She cunningly tested him. 'If you wanted her locked away, no one would blame you.'

Unable to suppress his anger, he took her by the

245

shoulders. 'I don't want to hear you talking like that again.' The hardness of his fingers pressed into her flesh. 'Sylvia is my wife. I made my vows before God: "in sickness and in health". So you see, it's my duty to take care for her, and I will. As long as she needs me, I'll be here.'

'I believe you.' Feeling his hands on her body, however innocent, was a wonderful thing.

But she had to know what was on his mind. 'There must be times when you feel lonely.' Reaching up, she laid her hands over his. 'A man has a need,' she whispered huskily. 'I can fill that need . . . if only you'll let me?'

He gazed down into those deep, inviting eyes set in that porcelain-smooth face. Her scent was heady and very feminine, like lilies, and for a moment his resolve began to slip. She was right. He was more lonely than anyone could ever imagine. It wouldn't be so bad, would it, if he took her in his arms and satisfied that deep-down need that never seemed to go away?

He thought of Sylvia and of how it used to be: her soft nakedness merging with his flesh, the warmth of mingling bodies and that great exhausting passion that swept them along and took all their energy.

Sylvia was no longer part of him in that way. But here was Georgina, offering herself, so why shouldn't he take her? After all, he was only a man, with all a man's strengths and weaknesses.

Almost without him being conscious of it, he drew her to him, gently, tantalisingly, his mouth half open to hers, so close he could taste her sweet, warm breath, mingling with his.

Then suddenly he thrust her away. 'I'll check on

246

Sylvia, then I'd best make tracks,' he said abruptly.

As though nothing out of the ordinary had happened, he pointed to the telephone table. 'You know where Edna's number is, though I don't think you'll need it. You know how Sylvia is: she has a bad time, then it goes away and leaves her drained for a while. I'll see you later.'

Georgina acknowledged with a nod. She knew he had cut that moment between them out of his mind, and it told her that he was either very cunning to have rejected her and was playing a long game, or he was genuinely still in love with his errant wife.

'Don't worry, Luke, I'll see to it,' she assured him. 'Mind how you go.' In a way she was glad things had not gone too far. There would be time when Sylvia was off the scene. In the meantime, Don Carson was satisfying her appetite with great energy, though she'd have no compunction in dropping him when she became bored with him.

A moment later, she could hear Luke running up the stairs and then the faint sound of a door squeaking open. Then he was running back down. The front door opened and closed, and he was gone.

She ran to the window where, engrossed in watching his car as it drove away, she almost leaped out of her skin when a voice whispered close to her ear, 'He's gone to see his sweetheart.'

Swinging round, she saw Sylvia. Still dressed in her flimsy nightgown, and with her hair wild about her shoulders, she looked like a mad woman.

'For God's sake, Sylvia . . . you'll catch pneumonia, running about like that.'

Wrapping her arms round her sister's shoulders,

Georgina led her gently back upstairs. 'First we'll get you dressed, then I'll make you a hot breakfast . . . egg and bacon with tomatoes and toast,' she suggested tenderly. 'Would you like that?'

Sylvia nodded. 'Then what?'

'Well, if you feel like it, we'll think about going out. We could buy you a new fur hat if you want, or a pair of boots to keep you warm.'

'Oh, yes, I'd like that.'

Perfectly lucid now, Sylvia chatted eagerly. 'Remember the last time we went shopping?' she asked with a grin. 'I saw this beautiful blue scarf in Hatton's window. I might go back and buy it.'

They talked about the scarf and other items of clothing that Sylvia might fancy, and as they walked into the bedroom, the two of them were laughing and joking, just as they had done when they were young and fancy-free, on the days when Georgina suppressed her jealousy and insecurity and sisterly love was allowed to flourish.

'I need to visit the bathroom.' Sylvia turned back towards the door. As she went she called out, 'Why don't we have breakfast in town? There's that lovely restaurant down from the church.'

'Whatever you want,' Georgina replied. 'As long as we leave enough time for shopping afterwards.'

Relieved that all was normal again, and hopeful that it would turn out to be a good day for them both, Georgina softly sang as she busied herself, tidying the room.

'Honestly, Sylvia,' she called out, 'you really are a sloppy devil! You've always been the same. I remember when Mother used to blame me for the mess, and it was you all along, but you never did own up—'

She might have finished the sentence if at that moment some sound behind her hadn't made her whip round. Sylvia was standing in the doorway and the look on her face was of pure hatred.

'It was *you* who used to make a mess, *you* who spilled things and broke things on purpose to try to get me into trouble.'

'Come on now, Sylvia, you know that wouldn't have worked. You were always our mother's favourite,' said Georgina, trying to jolly her along.

'You lied,' insisted Sylvia, working herself into a frenzy. 'You lied and you cheated. You stole my clothes and my pearl necklace. You even tried to steal my boyfriends, but they wouldn't have you. You're no better now than you were then. You told tales, and they weren't true—horrible lies you told to Mother. You even lied about me to her when she was dying.' Sylvia launched herself at her sister like a wild animal.

'YOU BASTARD!' Lashing out with her fists, she caught Georgina a hard blow on the side of her face. 'You always told tales on me, even when I asked you not to. Tell-tale tit, that's what you are!'

Screaming like a banshee she let up with the blows, only long enough to grab the curtain cord. Yanking it down, she threw it round Georgina's neck. She began to pull tighter and tighter, all the while laughing like a crazy woman. 'I said I'd pay you back,' she hissed softly, 'and now it's time.'

Terrified for her life, Georgina fought hard. The cord was rough and scorching her neck, and Sylvia was strong in her wild rage. After a desperate struggle Georgina managed to loosen her sister's hold on her. She threw aside the cord at the same time as twisting Sylvia's arm nearly out of its socket. Sylvia screamed and leaped back, the spitting Fury transformed to an injured animal in a moment.

'I'm sorry . . . I'm sorry!' Sobbing uncontrollably, Sylvia cowered away. 'I didn't mean to hurt you . . . please, Georgina, don't tell on me, will you? Please don't tell Mother.'

Georgina couldn't speak; her throat felt as though it were on fire. Backing away from her sister, she ran to the bathroom where she locked the door and for a moment stood with her back to it, terrified in case Sylvia followed her.

'She's mad!' The words issued in a harsh, broken whisper. 'Stark, staring mad!'

Emblazoned on her mind was the unbelievable. *Her own sister had tried to kill her!*

In the mirror she saw her neck was marked by the cord. Still trembling, she splashed cool water over her face and neck; she scooped it into her hands and drank it, every gulp feeling red-hot in her throat.

'Georgina!' Sylvia's quiet, pleading voice sounded close to the keyhole. 'Please come out. I won't hurt you any more. I never meant to do it. Please, Georgina . . . I'm so sorry.'

Georgina ran the tap faster and faster so it might drown out her sister's voice. Time and again she scooped up the water and drank it down, groaning with each mouthful yet determined to ease the fire inside.

'Please, come out, Georgina. I'm really frightened . . .'

Georgina turned the tap full on. She sat on the floor with her back to the door and listened to her sister pleading. Shocked rigid by the incident, she made no attempt to open the door, or to reply. Instead she kept very quiet, hardly daring to breathe.

Presently the pleading stopped and there was no sound from the other side of the door.

Now the tables had turned again. 'Sylvia?' Georgina's voice issued in a harsh, rasping sound. 'Are you there, Sylvia?'

No answer.

'Sylvia?'

Still no answer.

Clambering up, Georgina turned off the tap and put her ear to the door.

The silence was eerie.

Softly now, she inched open the door and looked up and down the corridor. Sylvia was nowhere to be seen.

Quickly and soft-padded as a cat, she made her way downstairs to the sitting room.

'Sylvia?' The soft sound of crying sent her towards the sofa. 'Where are you, Sylvia?'

It took but a moment to find her. Crouched down behind the sofa, Sylvia was crying like a bairn, arms folded across her face, and her hands tugging so viciously at her hair, it was likely to come out by the roots.

On seeing Georgina she looked up, her eyes red and swollen, and her mouth quivering. 'I'm insane, aren't I?' she asked. 'They'll lock me away now, won't they?'

Going gently forward, Georgina slid to the floor beside her. All her fear had evaporated when she found the pathetic weeping wreck of her sister. 'No one's going to lock you away,' she whispered, her heart softened—at least for now. 'I won't let them!'

251

'When you tell Mother what I did,' wide, confused eyes stared up, 'she'll *make* them lock me away.'

'I won't tell,' Georgina promised. 'I can't.'

'Why can't you?'

'You *know* why.'

Reality was never far away, and somewhere in the darkest corner of her mind, Sylvia remembered. 'Mother isn't here any more, is she?'

Georgina shook her head. 'No . . .'

'She's with Daddy, isn't she?'

'Yes.'

Sylvia was quiet for a time, before declaring sadly, 'They can't come back, can they? They're *never* coming back?' The sadness flickered and was quickly replaced with a half-smile. 'So, you can't tell on me, can you?'

Georgina slid her arm round those trembling shoulders. 'Are you all right, Sylvia?' she asked. 'Has the anger left you now?'

Sylvia nodded. 'I know what I did, but I couldn't stop. I'm sorry. Really sorry.'

'It's all right now, Sylvia. It's over.' She feigned a bright smile. 'Maybe a little sleep would do you good?'

Sylvia returned her smile. 'Yes . . . I'm tired.'

Georgina nodded. 'Come on then. I'll help you upstairs.'

As they climbed the stairs, Sylvia began to speak at length about Luke. 'One minute I'm convinced he's got another woman, and the next I'm ashamed even to think it. He does love me, I know that.' Her voice trembled. 'I wish I didn't make life so difficult for him.'

'You can't help the things you do,' Georgina

assured her. 'You've been very ill.' Leading her into the bedroom, she settled her on the bed, and sat beside her.

'I know that,' Sylvia admitted, 'but it's my own fault. I cheated on Luke and now I'm being punished.'

Leaning sideways, she laid her head on Georgina's shoulder. 'I thought Arnie was exciting, but he was just violent.' Hatred marbled her voice. 'I'm glad he's in gaol. He should rot there!'

The look on her face bespoke the loathing she had for Arnold Stratton. 'I'll never forgive him for what he did to me!'

'Hatred is a bad thing.' Holding her tight, Georgina could feel the rage in her sister. 'You need to rest now.' Gently laying her back against the pillow, she told her, 'I'll come up later and see how you are. Sleep now.'

'I will.' Letting herself be covered over with the eiderdown, Sylvia slid deep into the bed until she was comfortable. 'Just for a minute or two,' she said. 'Then I'll be ready to go shopping.' She smiled dreamily. 'I do love him so. I hope they haven't sold that scarf. I so much want Luke to see me in it.'

Georgina waited and watched, until Sylvia had drifted into a deep, restful sleep. She saw how Sylvia had drawn her arm out from under the clothes and gently covered her over again. 'You're my only sister,' she murmured. 'We've had our differences over the years, but it hurts me to see you like this. What use is Luke to you now—or you to him? He wants you to be better, but that's not going to happen. And he doesn't want me at all . . .'

Strolling round the market square, Luke did not feel the biting wind as it tugged at his face and blew open his jacket. After spending most of his time in the factory or at home, it was always a pleasure when Tuesday came and he could be outdoors, in the fresh air.

Dressed in his forest clothes of brown cord trousers, thick dark jumper and heavy boots with his cap pulled well down over his ears, he was unrecognisable as the suave young owner of Hammonds, and that was the way he wanted it to be.

After leaving Sylvia with Georgina, he had gone straight to the cabin, and only realised he was out of paraffin when he'd wanted to light the stove. That meant he could not cook, so somewhat reluctantly he had left the cabin in the late morning to come to Blackburn market to pick up a drum of paraffin. After that he would make his way to Tooley's Café for an early lunch, and, hopefully, a glimpse of Amy and the boy.

On the other side of the market, Amy had pulled Johnny into a nearby doorway. 'The wind's getting up strong,' she said, fastening the top button on his coat. 'We don't want you catching a chill, do we, eh?'

The boy stood patiently while she tightened his belt and drew his cap down low over his forehead. 'Are we going to see Daisy?'

'Later,' she answered. 'First I need to get a few things from the market. We won't stay out long, though. It's much too cold for a bairn like you.'

Glancing up at the dark clouds, she tutted. 'If I'd

254

known it was going to be as bad as this, I'd never have brought you out.'

'I like coming out.' Johnny slid his hand into hers. 'I don't like it when you leave me behind.'

'Well, that's all very flattering, lad!' Stepping out on the cobbles again, Amy tickled him under the chin. 'I thought you liked staying in the shop.'

'I do,' he said, 'but only when you're there.'

She laughed. She really enjoyed Johnny's company, and whenever she could, she would take him with her, if only to give Maureen time to visit her husband in prison—a secret between them—or to hunt for some suitable job to which she could take Johnny, and which continued to be difficult to find.

'Come on now, Johnny.' Grabbing him by the hand Amy tugged him out of the doorway. 'Let's get the shopping done, then we can go and see Daisy.'

They hadn't gone far when they came face to face with Luke. He had purchased his paraffin and was also on his way to Tooley's Café.

'Hello, young man.' He addressed himself to Johnny, but it was Amy he really wanted to speak to.

Johnny was thrilled to see him again. 'Oh, Amy, look!' He began jumping up and down on the spot. 'It's the man.' He stopped jumping to ask Luke wondrously, 'Have you got your friend with you?' He stared about. 'Can I see?'

Luke shook his head. 'I'm sorry, son,' he smiled. 'She won't come out of the forest. She doesn't like people very much.'

'She might like me?' Johnny's face had fallen with disappointment. 'I won't frighten her.'

255

'I know that,' Luke acknowledged. 'As a matter of fact, if she was ever going to make a new friend, I'm sure it would be you,' he humoured the little fella. 'Only she won't come out of the forest, you see, not for anybody.'

Johnny's disappointment melted into a bright, eager smile. 'We can go to her.' He looked up at Amy with pleading eyes. 'We can, can't we, Amy? We can go to her, and she'll make friends with you as well?'

Amused, and pleasantly comfortable in Luke's company, Amy refused. 'I'm sorry, Johnny. We can't go to the forest,' she told him gently.

'Why not?'

'Well, for a start, we haven't been invited, and it's rude to invite yourself.'

'Consider yourself invited,' Luke interrupted; though why he had said that, he didn't know, because he had never yet invited anyone to the cabin, and had no intention of doing so. And yet here he was, inviting Amy without a moment's hesitation. Suddenly, and quite unforeseen, he realised that, if he could manage to persuade her to visit, in a strange kind of way he would be living his dream—or at least beginning to. From an inauspicious start suddenly this Tuesday would indeed be special.

'See, Amy!' The boy was delighted.

Amy was flustered. 'It's very kind of you,' she told Luke, before addressing Johnny. 'Sorry, sweetheart, but we can't go. I haven't done my shopping yet. And, anyway, your mammy will be expecting you back soon.'

'Mammy won't mind,' his face dimpled into a mischievous little grin, 'so long as you don't run away with me.'

Amy laughed. 'No, I won't do that,' she promised. 'But I do need to go and see Daisy . . . I told her I'd be there, and you know how she watches for us.'

Having pleaded with Amy and got nowhere, Johnny turned to Luke. 'Please, Mr . . . tell her, will you?' he urged. 'It'll be all right . . . tell Amy it'll be all right.'

Luke put out his arms in a gesture of hopelessness. 'It looks like your Amy doesn't want to come to my log cabin.' He turned to her. 'We're not ganging up against you. Only, like Johnny here, I really would like you to come back with me, if only so you could meet my special friend.' Gesturing to the paraffin, he added hopefully, 'I've got my paraffin, so I can promise you the best cup of tea you're ever likely to get.'

Dangerously tempted, Amy looked from one to the other. 'I don't know . . . I did promise Daisy . . .' The Tuesday man had such a gentle but sad face, and he was so good with Johnny that Amy instinctively felt safe with him. Besides, hadn't he already saved the little boy from serious harm?

'Please Amy! Please!' The boy's voice cut through her thoughts. 'Daisy won't mind, I know she won't.'

Sshing him, she asked Luke, 'If we were to come with you—and I'm not saying we will—we'd need to be back here within a couple of hours.' I must be crazy, she thought. What am I thinking of? Yet she really did want to go.

Excited by the possibility of having her near for even a short time, Luke answered assuredly, 'Fifteen miles either way, and twenty minutes at the

257

cabin. There's time enough.'

'Oh, please, Amy!' Sensing that she might be weakening, the boy couldn't keep still.

'I don't even know your name,' Amy told Luke. 'We've hardly met.'

'You can call me Ben.' Though he had impulsively invited Amy and the boy to his sanctuary, he wasn't yet ready to let his name be known. 'I'm quite amiable, and I really do make the best cup of tea in Lancashire. Moreover, I'll have you both back here so you'll still have time to do your shopping and see your friend Daisy. But, it's up to you. If you agree to come along, that would be wonderful. If you refuse, I would understand, and there would be no hard feelings.'

'Are you sure it would be all right for me and Johnny to come to your cabin?' Amy asked worriedly. 'What would people say?' She was thinking of Jack and Daisy in particular.

'None of their business,' he answered firmly. 'Besides, you and the boy are the only two who know about my hideaway, and I would ask that you don't divulge it to anyone.'

Amy readily agreed to that. 'As you say, it's none of their business. In any case, from what you say, I expect we should consider ourselves highly honoured. Should we?'

When she softly laughed he laughed with her. 'You most certainly should!' he declared. 'And when you see my humble cabin, I hope you'll give me your honest opinion.'

His laughter felt companionable to her and, warming to him by the minute, she conceded, 'All right! Me and little Johnny would be happy to come with you, as long as you get us back here within two hours.'

'Agreed.' His whole face lit up and Amy knew he was genuinely delighted. Gesturing towards the perimeter of the marketplace he told them grandly, 'Your chariot awaits.'

As they climbed into the car, Johnny was excited, and Amy was amazed at such luxury: smooth carpet and red leather seats, and even a soft blue rug to cover their knees. She'd already begun to realise that Luke was not in any way an ordinary working man, despite his workaday clothes. His voice was a bit posher than her father's or Jack's, and his hands were smooth, with neat nails.

'This is a lovely vehicle,' she said. Making sure Johnny was comfortable in the back, she climbed in beside him and wrapped the rug round them both. 'Sit tight, sweetheart,' she told him, 'and don't touch anything.' She had frightening visions of him opening the door and falling out.

'Ready, are you?' Disappointed that she had preferred not to sit in the front with him, Luke switched on the engine and slipped into gear. A gentle touch on the accelerator and they were away down the street.

When, a short time later, they began passing familiar sights to leave Blackburn behind, Amy couldn't help but feel excited. The industrial outskirts of the town grew less dense, the streets were wider and already the air was cleaner.

As if concerned that she might be uneasy, Luke slightly turned his head to ask, 'You're very quiet back there. You're not sorry you accepted my invitation, are you?'

'No, course not!' Amy was quick to reassure him,

259

'I'm just wondering how far it is now, that's all?'

The gloomy, overcast day was quickly sliding into a kind of twilight. A moment ago they had turned off into a country lane; unlit and eerie, it made her nervous, though Johnny appeared to be loving every minute of the ride, with his nose stuck to the window, while giving her a detailed account of everything he could see.

'There's lots of water,' he told her now, when they were speeding along through the countryside. 'And stones and trees, and everything.' He laughed with excitement. 'I'd like to play down there.'

'That's the brook,' Luke enlightened him. 'It means we're only half a mile from the cabin, but you'll not be able to see very much from here on as the woodland thickens, so much so that the daylight is shut out in places.'

'I don't know if I like the sound of that,' Amy said. 'It must be gloomy in winter.'

'I love it,' he told her, 'but you needn't worry. I created a large clearing before I began to build. There's plenty of sky and space immediately round the cabin.'

Amy was impressed. 'You mean you built the cabin yourself?'

Luke smiled at her through the rear-view mirror. 'Isn't that what men do . . . build things?'

Amy gave a cynical little laugh. 'Not the men *I* know.'

Intrigued and a little perturbed by her remark, he asked, 'And how many men have you "known"?'

Amy explained. 'None to speak of. There's my father, who's the loveliest man in the world. He can drive a wagon and sell snow to Eskimos, but I doubt if he could ever build a cabin. Then there's

260

the only other man who ever seriously meant anything to me, and he would tell you himself, he couldn't even build a fire.'

Her mind went back to the days when she and Don were happily making plans to be man and wife, and all too soon those plans lay in ruins. 'No. You'd never see the day when Don Carson would tackle building a cabin.' Suddenly she wanted to talk about Don to this kind, gentle man who had invited her to share his private place. It was a way of finally exorcising Don from her life as a bad thing and turning him into a bit of a joke, a harmless, slightly foolish figure without the power to hurt her any longer.

One small memory made her chuckle. 'He once put up some shelves in my parents' shop. When it was finished, our mam put a few containers of biscuits up there and the whole lot fell down, taking half the wall with it.'

In a quieter, more serious voice, she revealed, 'Me and Don were to be wed, but he backed out at the last minute.'

Not knowing what to say, Luke answered limply, 'I'm sorry.'

'No! It's all right.' Mortified at having confessed to something so private, Amy replied in a brighter voice. 'Happen it was just as well. I'm not sure I'd like shelves and cupboards falling down round my ears.'

They laughed at that, and then fell silent.

Amy considered herself fortunate to have got over the trauma of what Don had done to her. She had learned to be philosophical about it. What was done was done, and there was no changing it now, even if she wanted to, which she didn't. In some ways, she thought, she had had a lucky escape. She'd loved Don, yes, but she'd never quite been *comfortable* with him. It was as if she had felt he was holding something of himself back from her. And now, of course, she had her romance with Jack, who was open and honest as a man could be, and with whom she felt entirely comfortable—although not deeply in love.

Concentrating on skirting the many puddles in the lane, Luke reflected on what she had told him. He had no right to feel envious of this man Don Carson, but he did. In fact he thought the man was a fool for not going ahead with the marriage. To his mind, Amy was the loveliest person he'd ever met and, given half a chance, he would have been proud to take her as his wife. While Amy's face was open and honest and readable, Sylvia could, even before her illness, be such hard work. She liked to manipulate and her motives were often unclear. She was intriguing, beautiful and never dull, but nor was she, increasingly since he'd married her, entirely comfortable to be with.

'Well, here we are.' Slowing the car to a crawl, Luke manoeuvred down the narrowing trackway, and the further he went, the further behind them seemed the daylight skies.

Above them, the isolated pockets of light flickered through the tree-tops, creating little specks of dancing brilliance, and Johnny, like Amy, thought it was magical.

Then suddenly the trees that had blocked their path and made the going difficult, seemed to open a way before them, and they were in a large open clearing surrounded by woodland. Just within sight came the glimmer of water as it skipped and tumbled its way through the forest.

'Oh, it's just beautiful!' Peering through the window, Amy was mesmerised.

Luke drew the car to a standstill and pointed to the wooden building ahead. 'There she is,' he cried, 'my pride and glory.'

Clambering out of the car behind Johnny, Amy took stock of the cabin. Larger than she had imagined, it was like a miniature house, with a front door of sizeable proportions, and long, small-paned windows either side. The slightly crooked chimney only added to its charm, and the wide, beautifully built veranda was a visual delight, with its rustic table and chairs and a deep frill of wood, which went the whole way along the entire cabin roof.

Amy laughed out loud. 'I love it!' Taking Johnny's hand, she walked towards the cabin, her eager gaze enveloping it. 'And you say you built all this, on your own?'

'That's right.' Walking beside her, the can of paraffin in one fist, Luke spread the other large, capable hand before him. 'Built it with my own two hands, a great deal of cursing and God knows how many mistakes, before it all finally seemed to fall into place.'

Climbing the steps he led them onto the veranda. 'It's not what you might call grand,' he warned, 'but it does for me.'

Leaving Amy and the boy to take in the view from the veranda, he quickly hurried inside the cabin, where he surreptitiously slid Amy's portrait from the wall and hid it, back outwards, behind a large basket of kindling wood. Then he opened the many shutters to let a measure of light inside, before lighting the fire in the hearth. Soon the flames were licking and spitting and, to be safe, he arranged the fire screen across it.

'There,' he said. 'It'll soon be warm as toast in here.'

'I can understand why you've kept all this to yourself.' Amy had never encountered anything like this place. Deep in the heart of the forest, it was like something out of a fairy tale. 'It's so beautiful.'

'I think so too.' Although seeing Amy there in his secret place, having her so near, was another 'beautiful' thing.

'What do you think of my furniture?'

Amy glanced about, surprised at how sparse the cabin was inside. And though the furniture was bulky and slightly crude, it was sturdy and wonderfully unconventional, and it was enough for his needs. 'It isn't what you might call grand,' she said with a wry little smile, 'and I dare say you'd get next to nothing for it at market. But it's kind of special.' Her quiet smile warmed his heart. 'I imagine you spent many long, enjoyable hours putting it all together.'

Deeply moved by her sincere words of approval, Luke sensed something more. He felt a kindred spirit in Amy, a kind of understanding he had not experienced in anyone he had ever known.

Going to the window he gazed out, at the forest and the waters beyond and, as always, his heart was uplifted. 'Every time I leave the town behind and come out here, I feel like I've been set free. It's like I belong, if you know what I mean? I feel . . . part of it all.' He smiled with embarrassment. 'Sorry! You must think I'm some kind of oddity?'

How could he expect anyone—even Amy—to understand how he felt?

'I don't think that at all,' Amy answered. 'I think any other man, given the chance, would want the same as you have here.' In fact, there were times, she thought, when she too might have found peace and contentment in this place. One of those times was when Don dashed all her dreams and hopes, and she was as low as a woman could get. When she could see no way forward, the urge to run away and hide had been overwhelming. Was Ben running away, she wondered.

Just then, Johnny came rushing in, and the growing closeness between Amy and Luke was broken. 'Quick! Come and see!' Eyes alight with excitement, he jumped up and down on the spot, the way he did when he was so happy, he could not contain himself.

When they followed him outside, the excitement turned to disappointment. 'Oh, it's gone now.' Dejected, he sat on the veranda steps, his gaze reaching all around.

Amy and Luke sat down either side of him.

'What was it?' Amy asked. 'What did you see?'

'A dog.' He pointed to the trees. 'It was over there.'

Luke understood. 'That was my friend,' he said, 'the one I told you about. Remember?'

Johnny shook his head. 'No! It were a dog. I saw it, and now it's gone.'

Luke put his fingers to his lips. 'Ssh.' Pointing to the spot Johnny had indicated, he advised, 'If you're very quiet, she'll come back. It's just that she doesn't know you and Amy yet. But she's a curious little thing.'

For long, breathless minutes they sat very still, watching and waiting, until suddenly there she was—the most beautiful creature, slim and elegant, her body brown and dappled and her dark brown eyes wide and her face silky as she gazed at them with nervous curiosity.

She looked at Amy and the boy, and for an instant it seemed as though she might go away, but when Luke dipped into his jacket pocket and held out his hand, she took one hesitant step forward. A wary moment, then she took another. Johnny began to fidget. She stopped, eyes alert and frightened.

Luke whispered for him to stop fidgeting.

Slowly, the creature began to tread its way towards them again. Luke kept his hand stretched out and, murmuring words of persuasion, enticed her nearer, until she was only a step away.

Now, she was nuzzling Luke's hand, her soft, moist nose pushing against his skin and her eyes half closed as she tenderly took the corn treat. Slowly, Luke took Johnny's tiny hand and, bringing it to the creature's head, he tenderly stroked the length of her velvet-soft ears. 'It's all right,' he kept saying, 'it's all right.' And the deer knew they would not hurt her.

After a while she turned and walked away, leaving the three seated on the steps: Luke delighted that she had come out to greet his visitors, and the other two trembling with the wonder of what they had just witnessed.

'See!' Johnny was the first to break the wondrous silence. 'I told you I saw a dog.'

Amy gave him a hug. 'It wasn't a dog,' she said. 'It was a deer.'

'Can I have one?'

'No,' Amy laughed.

'Why not?' As always, Johnny wanted reasons.

'They couldn't live in a house,' Luke told the boy. 'They're wild, you see? The forest is all they know. It took me an age to gain her trust, and now she comes to see me whenever she can.'

The boy had put two and two together. 'Was that your friend?'

Luke nodded. 'She's my best friend in all the world.'

'Can I see her again?'

Raising his gaze to Amy, Luke answered, 'That's not for me to say. You'll need to ask Amy.'

Amy read his thoughts and her heart turned somersaults. 'We'll see,' she told Johnny. 'For now, though, we'd best be making tracks back to Daisy.'

At that, Luke clambered up. 'Not before you've sampled my tea,' he said hopefully. 'There's plenty of time yet.'

Amy agreed. 'But then we'll have to go,' she finished reluctantly.

Taking a bucket, he walked ahead. 'You can come with me to the brook, if you like?'

And so they went, and Johnny ran on ahead while Luke and Amy talked of the deer, and Luke's cosy cabin, and Amy revealed how pleased she was that he'd asked them along.

As they broke through the woods to emerge near a fast-flowing brook, Luke warned, 'Stay away from the edge, Johnny. It's dangerously slippery underfoot.'

While he filled his bucket with clean fresh water, Amy kept the boy a short distance away. 'I want to live here,' Johnny declared. 'We can bring Mammy

267

and all of us, and make a house like Ben's.'

'That would be nice,' Amy humoured him, 'only we have to work, or we won't have any money.'

'Ben lives here,' Johnny answered. 'He doesn't work, and it's all right.' And the boy's innocent remark got Amy thinking.

On the way back, while Johnny went forward towards the cabin, Amy took the opportunity to ask Luke about himself. 'I think I already mentioned that I work in my parents' shop,' she began.

'That's right.'

Curious, but needing to know more about him, Amy asked tentatively, 'Would it be too forward of me to ask, what kind of work *you* do?'

At her question he slowed his step, but he kept his gaze to the ground and remained silent for a time.

Her curiosity had set his mind racing. Should he tell her the truth about himself? And if he was ever going to confide in her, then surely this would be the best chance he might ever get.

But wouldn't that put him in a bad light with her? After all, he had blatantly lied, calling himself by the name of Ben. If he was now to reveal the truth, what would she think of him? What if it turned her against him? Oh, he didn't want that. He would never want that.

Amy waited for his answer. When he was hesitant, she suspected he might be angry that she should have asked about his business, especially when he was so obviously a man who valued his privacy. After all, he was evidently no woodlander but a man of means with a smart motor car and the time and income to indulge himself with this charming grown-up playhouse. Maybe he was well known in Blackburn—he seemed to know Blackburn well—and was hiding a very public identity. Whatever, Amy decided there was no sinister motive—Ben was much too kind for that—so he must just be an intensely private person and she had intruded with her question.

As they reached the clearing, Amy murmured, 'I'm sorry. I didn't mean to offend you.'

Luke's answer was curt. 'You didn't offend me.'

Taking hold of Johnny's hand, Amy followed Luke into the cabin. 'I asked what you did for a living, and it's none of my business,' she persisted. 'I had no right to ask. Forget I mentioned it, will you? Please?'

Luke turned to smile at her. 'It's forgotten.'

He then went to the drawer and, taking out a sheaf of drawing paper, gave it to Johnny. 'You can sit at the table and draw if you like?' He had his own reasons for wanting to keep the boy entertained.

Johnny climbed onto the chair. 'What will I draw?'

'Whatever you please. You can draw our little friend with her big soft eyes, or you can draw the boulders with the water tumbling over. It's up to you.'

'I'd like to paddle in that water,' Johnny declared boldly, 'but I might drown! That's what I think.'

Luke laughed out loud. 'You think right!' he said. 'But you won't drown while me and Amy are about, because we'd soon be in the water to get you out. But the water here is fast-flowing and dangerous. The best thing of all is to stay right away from it, at least until you learn to swim.'

269

While they talked, Amy stayed at the back of the room from where she observed them together. She saw how trusting Johnny was, and recalled how he had taken to Ben from the start. She saw how protective Ben was towards Johnny. And she was deeply moved by it.

When he turned to regard her with that deep, intense gaze, Amy felt her heart turn somersaults.

'*Have* you time for a hot drink before you go?' he asked hopefully.

'Thank you, yes. I'd like that.'

She offered to make the tea but he would hear none of it. 'You're my guest,' he said, and quickly set about boiling the water on the paraffin stove.

When the tea was made and he had poured three cups, one of which he left to cool for Johnny, he took the other two and went in search of Amy, who had gone outside.

Seated on the veranda steps, she had one wary eye on Johnny and the other on the distant brook. It was so unbelievably beautiful here, she thought. If she had not known different she could have imagined herself to be anywhere but in the vicinity of Blackburn.

In town, the sky hung low and ominous, while here, the sky seemed far out of reach. In town the streets were lined with lampposts and never a tree in sight, while here the trees stood tall and strong, with their branches stretching all around like a galaxy of giant umbrellas. Then there, just beyond, was the water, just as he had described, 'fast-flowing and dangerous'.

This countryside was all a new and splendid experience to Amy, and there was a glory about it that held her gaze and lifted her soul, and in that

270

moment, in the clear light, with the rustle of leaves and muted winter call of birds, when she seemed so much a part of it, she never wanted to leave. She would be content to stay for ever in this magical place.

Behind her, Luke stood holding the cups, his quiet eyes drinking in the sight of Amy, and his heart more content than he had known in an age. It seemed so right and natural that she should be here, and he could hardly believe it.

All this time he had gazed at her painting and longed to speak with her and share her smile, and now here she was, real and warm, and, if her expression was anything to go by, her heart, like his, was deeply touched by this very special place.

Not wanting to break the silence but knowing he must, he stepped forward and reaching down, handed her the cup of tea. Then he sat beside her.

'Just now, you seemed so far away . . . deep in thought?'

She nodded, her voice little more than a whisper. 'I was thinking how a body might well want to stay here, and never leave.'

'You're right,' he murmured. 'I've felt that way, since I first came to this little paradise.'

Amy was curious. 'How did you find it?'

He told her about coming here with his grandparents, who had owned the land, in his school holidays, and how the woods had become associated with those carefree times. Here he had learned to fish and survive a day at the hands of nature, to appreciate the beauty and solitude of this lovely part of Lancashire. Now the land was his.

Amy finished the tale for him. 'So, you made this

clearing and built your cabin, and now this is where you hide, when the weight of the world weighs you down?'

For a moment he did not answer. He looked into her eyes and there he saw a reflection of his own, deeper feelings. 'I do love it here,' he answered, 'and you're right: this is where I hide.'

He glanced back to see how Johnny was occupied with his drawing. 'Amy?'

'Yes?'

'Must you go?'

'You know I have to.'

'Will you ever come back, do you think?'

Amy shrugged. 'Who knows?'

'But you won't promise?'

'I can't promise.'

She so much wanted to come back here; even to leave little Johnny at home and be here with Ben, just the two of them. But she was afraid of the way he made her feel. There was something about this place, about *him*, that made her wary. She was fond of Jack, but she could not recall ever feeling like this with him. It was strange. And a little frightening.

Finishing her tea, she stood up to place her cup on the handrail. 'It's time we went,' she said. 'I'll get Johnny.'

As she brushed past him, he caught her by the hand.

'Wait!' A look of anxiety shaded his features. 'There's something you need to know.'

Amy sensed his concern and was afraid. 'What is it?'

'I lied to you,' he went on quickly before he might lose his courage. 'My name isn't Ben. It's . . .'

he hesitated, before finishing in a rush, 'my name is Luke Hammond.'

It took only a second or two to register in Amy's mind. *'Luke Hammond?'* Stunned, she stared at him. 'Luke Hammond, the factory owner?' The anger rose inside her. He had lied to her! Why had he felt the need to lie?

When he nodded, she turned from him without another word. Hurrying into the cabin, she felt a pang of fear when the boy was nowhere to be seen. 'Johnny?' When suddenly her eyes alighted on him, she gave a sigh of relief. Having wandered to the other side of the room, he was peering at something against the wall. She went across to him at a run. 'Come on, Johnny.' Taking him by the hand, she told him, 'We have to go.'

Having put the fire screen in place, Luke waited at the door. 'I'm sorry,' he said. 'I'll take you back now.' He cursed himself for not having told her the truth from the start. But he had been afraid to tell her. He had hoped always to keep his identity secret, because the man he was today was the man he desperately needed to be. It was not the man who ran the factory and held his life together with duty and responsibility. He had never wanted Amy tainted with all that. She was already, in his mind, a part of this retreat on the Tuesdays when the factory owner became a free man.

As they drove home, the silence weighed heavy.

No one spoke, not even Johnny, who sensed an atmosphere and instinctively curled himself into Amy's embrace. In a matter of minutes the gentle bumping of the car and the hum of the engine lulled him to sleep.

When the car drew up at the market, Luke

273

clambered out to open the back door.

'I'm sorry,' he told Amy. 'I should never have lied to you.' Reaching into the car he helped them both out, Johnny being still dozy from his sleep. 'Will you stay a minute?' Luke asked her. 'Let me explain?'

Amy shook her head. 'We have to go.'

Luke persisted. 'It doesn't matter, does it . . . who I am?'

She had been doing up Johnny's coat buttons, but now she paused and, looking up, took stock of him for a minute—that mop of dark hair, those intense, sad eyes—and she felt a pang of guilt. He had been nothing but kind and hospitable to her and Johnny—and had done them the honour of sharing his private retreat with them. 'No,' she answered. 'It doesn't matter. But we have to go now.'

Visibly relieved with her answer, he asked, 'Will you forgive me?'

She nodded. That was all. A curt, hesitant little nod, but it was enough for Luke. For now.

Amy finished buttoning Johnny's coat.

'Are we going to see Daisy?' Wakening fast, he smiled up at Luke. 'I like your friend,' he said. 'She's mine too now, isn't she?'

Luke ruffled his hair. 'She certainly is,' he said brightly, 'and I hope I'm your friend too . . . yours and Amy's?' He turned his attention to her, but she made no reply. Instead she wondered what kind of man he was, to lie like that, even to the boy.

'Thank you for a lovely time,' she told him, for it had been wonderful—until he spoiled it, she thought regretfully.

In a minute he was in his car and driving back

the way they had just come.

'You're a damned fool, Hammond!' he told himself. 'You should have been truthful from the start, especially with a woman like Amy.'

He thought about his situation and the way he was forever torn two ways. He thought about his unhappy, mundane life and the split between the man he was and the man he wanted to be, and he wondered if sometimes his fantasies got in the way of real life. He hoped not. For if that was the case, it might well be the first step to madness.

*   *   *

'Why aren't we going to see Daisy?' Johnny was bitterly disappointed. 'You said we could.'

'I know I did, and I'm sorry.' Having rushed the boy and herself across the marketplace, Amy had paid the tram fare and now they were in their seats and on the way home. 'We stayed too long away,' she said. 'It's too late to go to Daisy's.'

'Can we see her tomorrow?'

Amy recalled something Maureen had said that morning. 'I think your mammy said she was going into town tomorrow,' she answered. 'Maybe you'll see Daisy then.'

She wondered whether to tell Daisy about today, or if it might be better not to mention it at all. But then, Johnny was sure to say something. But even if he did, she mused, there was no reason why Daisy should know that the man involved was Luke Hammond himself.

The name was emblazoned in her mind. Luke Hammond. A wealthy man. *A man of secrets.*

Johnny busied himself looking out the window. 'I

275

saw your picture.'

Amy had been deep in thought. 'Sorry, sweetheart, what did you say?'

He turned to look at her. 'He had your picture. It was nice.'

Amy's heart skipped a beat. 'What do you mean, Johnny? *Who had my picture?*'

'The man . . . Ben. It was a nice picture.' He grinned shyly. 'I peeped.'

'Are you sure it was me?' she asked, trying to sound calm.

He shook his head. 'Don't know.' Now he wasn't so sure, especially as Amy wasn't very happy about it. 'I shouldn't have peeped, should I?'

Amy hugged him. 'It's all right,' she assured him. 'I expect it was something and nothing. We'll just forget about it. All right?'

Johnny had been drawing, and the drawing was left behind. No doubt he had drawn her likeness, as he had done many times before. It was of no consequence.

His quick, bright smile warmed her heart. 'All right,' he said.

And it was quickly forgotten.

For the rest of the journey, Amy turned her thoughts to Luke. Why had he felt the need to lie? And why would a man like Luke Hammond want a 'hideaway'?

Deep down she understood, because weren't there times when she too would like a hideaway where she could sit and think and let the madness of the world pass her by?

And why not a man like Luke Hammond; a man who worked as hard and long as he did, and when his work was done he had to go back to a reputedly

276

difficult and demanding woman, a woman who had cheated on their marriage? Of course he needed a sanctuary.

She had felt such a bond between them when they were at the cabin—a sense of growing friendship. She thought of his strong hands as he scooped the water from the brook with the bucket, his gentleness with the tame deer, and his delight in showing the creature to his visitors. She thought of his sad dark eyes, his handsome face and tender manner.

So he had lied about his name? But that was just to protect his privacy, and to avoid making her feel uncomfortable, wasn't it? After all, if he'd revealed that he was Luke Hammond at the outset, would she have accepted his invitation? Probably not.

It had been fun at his lovely woodland hideaway—until she'd spoiled things. Johnny was already asking to go back. But Luke Hammond would, she thought with a sudden rush of regret, not invite her to go again.

CHAPTER TWELVE

The following Tuesday, Amy, after much deliberation, decided she would go to Tooley's Café after she'd done her shopping. It was no use avoiding the place on account of Luke Hammond. Daisy would soon be demanding to know why she was staying away, and, anyhow, Luke might not be there at the time Amy was. They didn't always coincide. Possibly, she thought miserably, *he'd* stay away from the café, not wanting to see the ungrateful girl who'd got on her high horse after he'd shared the secret of his lovely hideaway with her.

When Tuesday came round, Maureen took Johnny with her to a new part-time job she'd taken, pushing a tea trolley round the town hall offices. Maureen thought it a poor job and was already talking about finding something better; Johnny was very pleased he'd be 'giving out biscuits, like Daisy does', and was rather keener than his mother.

Amy was half sorry not to have Johnny with her and half pleased in case he saw Luke and blurted out something to Daisy.

When Amy opened the door of Tooley's the first person she saw was Luke, sitting in the window, reading his newspaper. He looked up, smiled at Amy and then glanced quickly round the café. Daisy was nowhere in sight—evidently in the back, wrestling with the toaster, from the smell of charred bread pervading the steamy atmosphere.

In a moment Luke was on his feet. He dug some change out of his pocket, left it on the table and in two strides was beside Amy and escorting her back outside with his hand clutching her elbow.

'What . . . ?' she gasped, as he led her a few steps away down the street.

'Amy, I'm so glad to see you,' Luke said, releasing her. 'Sorry to drag you out like that but I didn't want to embarrass you in the café, and maybe make your friend curious.'

Amy saw the sense in this, and was, now she was with him, pleased at this excellent opportunity to make amends for her foolishness last week.

'I'm so sorry—' she started. 'Amy, forgive me—' he began at the same time, and they each stopped

278

and looked at the other and laughed.

'You first,' said Luke.

'I'm so sorry I got cross and spoiled everything last week after you were so kind to Johnny and me,' she said, looking him in the eye. Now she was with him her anxiety had evaporated. The gentle expression on his handsome face was making her apologising easier. She could see he was not angry now.

'Dear Amy, please don't apologise. You were quite right. It was wrong of me to deceive you. I should have known you would never condone even an innocent deceit. I meant . . .' he looked down, suddenly struggling for the right words, '. . . when I invited you and Johnny to come to see the cabin I didn't want you to be *put off* if you knew who I was. And I suppose, in a way, I didn't really want to be Luke Hammond then. I just wanted to be someone you saw at the café, a man from Blackburn who lives in a cottage in the woods and wanted to show you and Johnny that cottage. Does that make sense to you?'

Amy saw the truth of this in his anxious eyes. 'Of course,' she smiled. 'Let's just think it was a simple misunderstanding.'

'Quite right,' Luke agreed eagerly, also smiling, 'and if you'd like to come out to the cabin again sometime—' he raised an eyebrow questioningly— 'today, perhaps?—then I shall know I'm forgiven.'

Suddenly Amy realised this was exactly what she had been hoping for but had hardly dared to think. He really was a very nice man—and rather a lonely one too. There was no doubt that he genuinely wanted her to accept this invitation.

'Thank you,' she beamed. 'I'd love to come, but

just for a little while or Mam will be worried.'

'Is Johnny not with you?'

Amy explained about his new job as Maureen's assistant and Luke laughed as he led her to the car. This time Amy sat in the front seat next to him.

The journey, under winter sun, seemed to her shorter than before, and soon they were jolting up the final lane to the cabin. The little house in the woods really was exactly like something from a fairy tale, Amy thought, especially with the veranda.

'Come in, come in. I'll make us some tea as you've missed your elevenses.' Luke unlocked the door and swung it wide to let her go before him.

He lit the log fire, and they both went to collect water for the kettle.

By the brook he pointed out a mistle thrush, the weight of red berries on a dark-leaved holly bush, and the patch that, in just two months, he'd expect to be covered in the first snowdrops. He knew how to share his enthusiasm for the countryside and for this particular place, and told a couple of stories about his childhood holidays here that made Amy laugh. By the time they had drunk their tea, Amy was thoroughly relaxed.

They put on their coats again and went to sit on the veranda steps to see if Velvet would visit. Just when Amy, but not Luke, had almost given up hope, she appeared tentatively and walked slowly towards them. Amy saw how the little deer trusted Luke, and she was enchanted by it.

So this is the real Luke Hammond, she thought, watching as Luke hand-fed the deer. This is the man with a good head for business, who employs so many people in Blackburn—Dad, Jack and Roy included—and who has such a troubled life at home.

How could she have thought there was anything odd in having the hideaway and anything other than a wish to be more a part of this other life in his reluctance to reveal who he really was?

Velvet trotted away and Luke turned and smiled at Amy. It was a smile that lit his whole face and she could see that he was truly happy.

'That was beautiful,' she said, recalling how the deer had fed so trustingly from his hand.

'Beautiful,' he agreed, but it was her he was looking at.

A moment passed between them and then Amy looked away. 'I have to go now,' she said.

'Amy . . . not yet, please?'

Something in the tremor of his voice, or it could have been the lonely look in his eyes, made her hesitate. Before she knew it he had wrapped his arms around her and the warmth of his body was pressing against her. At first his kiss was hesitant; then, when she did not reject him, his arms tightened about her and his lips were more demanding.

Reaching up, she wound her arms round his neck, giving herself, wanting more than she should, but when the want grew to a desperate need she pushed him back.

'No!'

'Amy–'

'No, Luke, we mustn't . . . I can't. Please, you know it's wrong.'

'No, Amy, it's not wrong. Don't you see—'

'You're married!' She raised her voice and stepped away as he made to hold her again.

Though her voice had broken on the words she knew she had to go on and say what she felt. 'You're a dear, kind man. I've had a lovely time today, but now I have to go home.'

'But, Amy,' he took a step towards her and took her hands in his, 'here's where you belong. Here, with me.'

'Luke, you know that can never be,' she said softly. 'You *know* . . .'

Dejected, he swallowed and cleared his throat.

'Yes, yes, of course. I'm sorry. It was stupid of me even to think . . .' He looked away, out to the woods. After a minute or two in which they both stood in silence, he turned back to Amy. 'Come on, let's get you back. Your friend Daisy will have missed you this morning, and I don't want you getting into trouble with your mam either.' He smiled a brave smile and hand in hand they walked back inside the cabin to make the fire safe before leaving.

*   *   *

It was, Amy thought that night, lying in bed and reliving every moment, like the most wonderful dream—right up to the moment when she pulled away from the kiss.

And a dream was what it must remain, she had told Luke gently as he'd driven her back to Blackburn. She would not go to the cottage again.

She snuggled down in her bed, straightening her thoughts and her resolve. He was Luke Hammond, wealthy businessman, married to a wife who wasn't well. She was Amy Atkinson who worked in a corner shop. She must never again behave as if he wasn't married.

Oh, but the kiss had been so tender, so *loving* . . .

Amy chided herself, don't you start thinking of kissing Luke Hammond any more. It can lead nowhere except to unhappiness.

*   *   *

Dim November ran into December and, to everyone's relief, the weather took a turn for the better. 'It's like a summer's day out there.' Ted Fogarty was crooked as an old bent tree and twice as gnarled. 'If I were thirty year younger, I'd be tekking you out on a picnic.' He winked at Amy, who laughed at his cheek.

'If you were thirty years younger, I wouldn't even be born,' she said.

'All right then,' he conceded, 'fifteen years.'

'That's no good neither,' Amy teased, 'because fifteen years ago, I'd be about ten, and you'd be had up for child-snatching.'

The old fella laughed out loud. 'I can see there's no winning with yer, so I'll be off.' With that he departed the shop, leaving Amy and Marie chuckling. 'I bet he were a randy old devil in his time,' Marie remarked.

'Nice, though,' Amy said dreamily. 'I can imagine he were a real gentleman. I bet he treated his women like china dolls.'

'Mebbe, but it wouldn't do for me,' Marie answered thoughtfully. 'I never did like a man who was afraid to be himself when he had a woman on his arm.' She straightened her shoulders and prepared herself for the next customer, who by now was approaching the door. 'I like to know that what

283

I'm getting is the genuine article, warts and all.'

She giggled like a schoolgirl. 'I remember the very night when I decided your father were the one for me.' A wave of nostalgia brought a little smile to her homely face. 'We'd been to the pictures and were strolling home eating fish and chips. There'd been a terrible downpour and the streets were riddled with puddles. A horse and cart went by and splashed your father from head to toe. Before I could stop him, he were running up the street, shaking his fist at the driver and using language I'd never heard afore in my life. By! It was enough to mek your hair curl.'

Amy was confused. 'And how did that make you decide to wed him?'

'I knew straight off,' Marie declared indignantly. 'I mean, I wouldn't have liked it, if he'd just carried on eating his fish and chips as though nothing had happened, dripping wet and silently fuming yet saying nothing, just 'cos I were there.'

Stretching herself to full height, she went on. 'He were angry and he let it be known. After he'd stopped the cart and given the driver a piece of his mind, he came back to me and apologised for the language. I forgave him there and then, took him home and lent him a set of my father's clothes. From that day on we never looked back. Y'see, lass, I knew what I were getting with your father, and I liked the fire in him.'

Amy understood. Honesty and trust were vital to a relationship. Luke's handsome face leaped into Amy's mind, as it had done many times in the month since she'd been to the cabin. As long as he was married there could be no honesty, indeed, no future in loving him. 'All I can say is, whatever

284

made you decide to wed our dad, it was the best thing you ever did.'

Just then the doorbell rang as the young woman breezed in; dark hair flowing and coat flapping open, she looked like she'd been through a wind-tunnel. 'I've run out o' Fairy Snowflakes,' she said breathlessly, 'I'll take two packets, one for now and one for the cupboard.'

'You look like you've been running,' Marie commented as she served her. 'Come far have you?'

'Far enough!' The woman was obviously not in the mood for conversation. 'How much is that?'

'Ninepence-halfpenny if you please.'

'Hmh! You're a penny dearer than the Co-op.'

'Is that so?' Marie had been in a good mood but now she was fighting fit. 'Well, I'm sorry, but that's the price. D'you still want it or not?'

The woman was positively bristling. 'Of course! How else can I do my washing?'

She thrust the coins onto the counter, snatched the two boxes of Fairy Snowflakes, and dashed out of the shop.

Amy was flabbergasted. 'You were a bit harsh weren't you, Mam?' she remarked. 'That might well have been a regular customer in the making, and now you've frightened her off.'

Marie chuckled, 'I don't know what came over me,' she said. 'It must be your father's influence.'

A moment later, the woman returned. 'I need a bar of carbolic,' she announced, 'I got all the way to Ackeroyd Street before I remembered.'

Marie was ready for an argument and before she got the carbolic she informed her, 'That'll be a tanner.'

285

'That's all right.' The woman counted out six pennies. 'This is a pleasant little shop,' she said looking around, 'I dare say I'll be back again.' Before hurrying away, she bade them each a friendly 'Good day.'

'There you are, lass,' Marie pointed out. 'That proves what I've just been saying. Folks get suspicious when you pretend to be something you're not. Besides, when she made that cutting remark about the Co-op, it got me off on the wrong foot.'

*   *   *

That evening after the shop was closed and tea was over, Amy went upstairs to get ready for her Saturday evening out with Daisy, Jack and Roy. According to Daisy 'the Tuesday man' hadn't been in the café since last month. Amy herself had stayed away on Tuesdays with the excuse that the shop was busier than usual in the run-up to Christmas, though she had been sure to meet up with Daisy in the evenings and at weekends, knowing how Daisy valued these escapes from her home life.

Amy thought again about what her mother had said. 'Folks get suspicious when you pretend to be something you're not.'

That was what Luke Hammond had done—pretended to be something he was not. He had pretended he wasn't married, and, however tempting, she must never again behave as if this were true.

She quickly brought Jack into her mind. He did not possess the same wealth or standing as Luke

286

Hammond, but as far as she could tell he had never lied to her. He had never pretended to be anyone but the man he was, and she respected him for that.

With Jack in mind, and the desire to look nice for him, she took her burgundy dress out of the wardrobe, clean underwear out of her drawer, and after deciding on her long brown coat, she laid it all out on the bed and took herself to the bathroom to get ready.

'By! You look good enough to eat, lass.' Having finished his tea, her father was stretched out in front of a cheery fire when Amy came down. 'Where are you off to then?'

Amy kissed each of her parents on the cheek. 'Daisy said there's a good film on at the Roxy,' she answered. 'We thought we might go there.'

'Oh, aye?' Giving Marie an aside wink, Dave said coaxingly, 'Are them two lads going with yer an' all?'

Amy had to smile. 'Have you two been talking about me?' she accused, wagging a finger.

Marie was unperturbed. 'Aw, go on with yer. O' course we have, lass. You can fetch the young man home, if yer like. Me an' your father would like to meet him, wouldn't we, Father?'

Dave nodded. 'Aye, we would that. Besides, I need to cast a wary eye over this young man o' yourn. I'll not have you taking up with a bad 'un like Don Carson.'

Amy chuckled. She could cope with the mention of her former fiancé these days. 'You've probably already "cast an eye" over him,' was her teasing, parting remark. 'After all, you see each other most every day.'

As she dashed away, she could hear him calling

after her, 'What's that supposed to mean? Hey! How do we see each other? COME BACK 'ERE!'

Amy chuckled all the way down the street. 'You'll know soon enough,' she murmured, 'and when you do, I think you'll agree that Jack's a good bloke.'

And the more she sized him up for her father's approval, the more she came to understand how fine a man Jack really was.

*   *   *

Daisy was waiting at the tram-stop as usual. Agitated and upset, she was pacing the ground, head down, and her thoughts still back at home with her feuding parents.

'I've decided,' she told Amy as they walked to the Roxy where they had arranged to meet up with Jack and Roy, 'I've had enough. I can't stand the shouting and fighting any longer. Soonever I can get enough money together for a deposit, I mean to find a place of my own to rent. There are rooms advertised in the *Evening Telegraph* that are perfectly respectable. Happen I can find a house where there are other single ladies.'

Amy was not surprised. She had long seen it coming. Time and again, Daisy had threatened to leave home and it had never come to anything, only this time Amy could see she meant it.

'Tell them what you intend doing,' she suggested. 'Happen it will make them see sense.'

Daisy poured scorn on the suggestion. 'It would be a waste of time,' she declared. 'They haven't got an ounce o' sense between them. They drink and fight, then make up, and drink and fight all over again. This time our mam broke the mirror and, according to some folks, that's seven years' bad luck. And look at that.' Rolling up her sleeve she showed Amy a long, deep cut over which she'd taped some gauze. 'When I tried to pick up the pieces of broken mirror, she went for me. Like a bloody wildcat she was.'

Amy was horrified. 'It looks deep to me,' she exclaimed, bringing them both to a halt. 'I think we should go to the infirmary and let them have a look at it.'

Quickly rolling her sleeve down, Daisy resumed walking. 'It'll mend. I don't need to go to no infirmary!' And try as she might, Amy could not persuade her.

Worried for Daisy's safety, Amy offered her a way out. 'Come and stay with us. The back room's going begging. You can have that.'

'Thank you. You're a good friend.' Daisy was visibly moved by Amy's kind offer. 'In fact you're my *only* friend. But I can't move in with you.'

'Why not?'

Daisy explained, 'For one thing I know your mam uses the back room for storage, and for another, it wouldn't be fair on her. She works hard in that shop, and the last thing she wants is to take me on, with my noisy ways and bad habits.'

Amy argued that her mam would have no objections, but Daisy was having none of it. 'Grateful though I am, lass, I prefer to do it my way.' She gave Amy a sly little wink. 'Besides, I've an idea that I might be getting wed afore too long. What would yer think to that, eh?'

'Has Roy asked you already?'

'Not in so many words, but I reckon it's on the

289

cards.' Daisy gave Amy a playful nudge. 'I reckon tonight's the night, love,' she chuckled, 'and I'll jump at the chance.'

'Don't get wed just so's you can leave home,' Amy warned. 'That's not a good basis for a long life together. Jump in with both feet and you might live to regret it.'

Daisy lowered her voice. 'Shall I tell you summat?'

'You will anyway, so go on. What's on your mind now?'

'If Roy asked me straight out to be his wife, the reason I'd say yes is because I love him.' Her eyes lit up. 'He makes me laugh, and when he kisses me, I shiver all over.' She shivered now just at the thought of it. 'I hate every minute when I'm away from him, and when I see him, my heart leaps and jumps and I'm all butterflies inside. That's love isn't it, lass?'

Amy laughed. 'Sounds like it to me.'

Arm in arm, with Daisy going on about how devoted she was to Roy and how lucky she was to have met him, they went down the street at a good brisk pace.

It wasn't long before Daisy wanted to know, 'How do you feel about Jack?'

Amy shrugged. 'I'm not sure.' At that moment, it was Luke Hammond who was playing on her mind.

'D'yer love him?'

Amy was visibly startled. 'Who?'

Daisy groaned. 'Who d'yer think? Jack, o' course! D'yer love him?'

Amy had to ponder that one, but not for too long. 'I like him a lot,' she answered, 'but I'm not sure if I love him—at least not in the way you seem

290

to love Roy.'

Daisy persisted. 'Does he make you laugh?'

'Sometimes.'

'Well then, yer halfway there, lass.' Daisy gave her a knowing nudge. 'You like him a lot. He makes you laugh. So, does he make you shiver when he kisses you?'

Amy blushed. 'Don't be so nosy.'

Undeterred, Daisy lowered her voice to a whisper. 'Have you two *done* it yet?' she asked shamelessly.

Amy shook her head. 'If we had I don't know as I would tell you, but we haven't.' She gave her a sideways smile. 'Sorry to disappoint you.'

'Bloody hell, lass! Yer do fancy him don't yer?'

'Of course. He's good-looking, I like him a lot, and he's probably everything I could want in a man.'

'So, why haven't yer done it yet then?'

Now, when Amy compared herself and Jack with Daisy and Roy, the answer presented itself. 'I'm not headstrong like you, Daisy. I can't go diving into things without working out the consequences. Besides, Jack is different from Roy.'

'I know what you mean about me diving in headfirst,' Daisy agreed, 'because that's the way I've allus been. But I'm not sure what you mean about Jack being different from Roy.'

Amy attempted to explain. 'The way I see it, Roy is much like you. You're like two sides of the same coin—light-hearted and game for anything. You seem to see life like a roller-coaster, up one minute and down the next, and you don't care what tomorrow might bring. Am I right?'

Daisy laughed. 'You know us only too well, love,'

291

she laughed. 'Live for today and let tomorrow tek care of itself, that's us.'

'Jack's a bit like me,' Amy went on. 'More cautious about life. I've been hurt once and I'm always afraid it might happen again. Oh, I know Jack would take care of me, and I'm sure he would make the best husband in the world, but I'm not sure I'm ready for all that serious stuff yet. I'm not even sure Jack is either.' And flitting through her mind numerous times every day was the look on Luke Hammond's face when he had taken her in his arms and bent to kiss her.

Daisy disagreed. 'I've seen you and Jack together,' she said, 'and you look like a good pair to me. It's clear he loves you, and from what you've just said, you've been eyeing him up as a possible husband. The truth is, I expect you've put him off, with your worries and your hesitating.'

Amy could not deny it. 'The truth is, I don't want to go rushing in, and then it all go wrong, like before.'

Suspecting that Amy might never find the courage to let herself love again, Daisy let her impatience show. 'Look 'ere, lass! It's time you forgot about what Don Carson did to you. For God's sake, if you don't let it go once and for all, it could bugger up your future for ever.'

'It won't,' Amy replied confidently.

All the same, her confidence in men had been wrecked since Don had deserted her like that. She had put the hurt behind her, and now felt indifference to the man, but even now, after all this time, there were still periods of panic, when she was haunted by the fear of being rejected.

'You do like Jack, though, don't yer?' Once

Daisy got her teeth into something she wouldn't let it go.

Amy groaned. 'I've said so, haven't I?'

'Has he asked you to marry him yet?'

'No . . .' Though there had been times when she had sensed him on the verge of asking her.

Encouraged, Daisy had a word of advice. 'If he does pluck up the courage to ask you, say yes.' She laughingly gave Amy a shove. 'Just think, lass, we could have a double wedding.'

As they turned the corner and saw the two young men waiting outside the Roxy, Daisy pointed out, 'Look at the way he's reaching his neck to see you.'

Waving to them she cunningly changed the subject to impart a snippet of information that she knew would shock Amy, yet give her little time to react. 'By the way, I've been sacked,' she announced casually. 'I did a silly thing. I told Ma Tooley exactly where she could put her bleedin' toaster and she finished me on the spot. So now I need a job, or I'll never be able to save for a deposit.'

'Oh, Daisy!' Amy's heart fell a mile. 'What am I gonna do with you, eh?'

Daisy had already thought of a solution. 'If yer want to help, yer can ask your Jack to give me a job at Hammonds.'

With that idea firmly implanted in Amy's mind, she skipped on ahead where, flinging her arms round Roy's neck, she greeted him in her usual cavalier fashion. 'Hello, handsome. Been waiting long, 'ave yer?'

Roy kissed her full on the mouth. 'I'd wait for ever if you asked me,' he said, and holding hands they went ahead towards the foyer.

Behind them, Jack took Amy's hands into his and, looking into her upturned face, he told her softly, 'It's good to see you, Amy.'

With Daisy's words about putting him off still large in her mind, Amy found a boldness she didn't even know she had. 'Aren't you going to kiss me?' she asked, her heart going fifteen to the dozen.

His slow, searching smile betrayed the love he had for her. 'I thought you'd never ask,' he whispered. Another precious moment of looking into her eyes, then, with his two hands cupping her face, he bent his head to hers.

Pressing his lips over her part-opened mouth, he kissed her with such intensity that she could hardly breathe.

'We don't have to go into the pictures,' he suggested hopefully. 'I mean . . . if you want to go somewhere else?'

Amy knew what he was meaning, and she was not ready for that. 'We'd best go after them,' she suggested. 'We can't just run off; they're bound to wonder where we've gone.'

Jack held her for a while, thinking how he so much wanted to sweep her away and keep her all to himself. He wanted to ask her to marry him and be with her for ever. But he sensed her nervousness and, taking her by the hand, walked her towards the other two, who were now waiting for them. 'Another time, eh?' he murmured, and when Amy gently squeezed his hand, he took that to mean yes.

Some two hours later, when they emerged from the cinema, Amy could hardly recall what *The Squaw Man* was all about. She remembered there were cowboys and Indians, but if anyone had asked her to describe the plot she would not have been able to answer, because all evening her mind had been on Luke and Jack, and whether one day she might find the trust and courage to let herself love again.

On the way to the hot-pie barrow, Roy and Daisy walked ahead, arms round each other and so much in love, while Jack and Amy followed on behind, hand in hand, each filled with a measure of contentment.

'Can I ask you something?' Amy had not forgotten Daisy's dilemma.

'You can ask me whatever you want, sweetheart.' Hoping it was to do with himself and Amy and their future together, Jack drew them to a halt.

His hopes were quickly dashed when Amy began, 'It's to do with Daisy. It seems she got hot-headed with Mrs Tooley. The upshot of it is that Daisy has lost her job, and she was wondering if you might be able to find her something at Hammonds?'

Saying the name made her feel slightly breathless.

Disappointed, Jack assessed the possibilities. 'I can't altogether promise, but I've got one lady leaving this week, so there's a chance I might be able to fit Daisy in—providing she doesn't mind standing at a machine, packing bristles into wooden bases for hours on end?'

Amy was thrilled. 'Oh, Jack, that would be great. I'm sure she wouldn't mind one bit.' They resumed walking. 'You see, she's not getting on too well with her parents and she's desperately trying to save enough money for a deposit to rent a place of her own. I've asked her to move in with us at home, but she refused.' Her affection for Daisy spilled over.

295

'She's headstrong and independent, and sometimes I could throttle her, but if she sets her mind there's no changing it. Oh, Jack, if you could only get her a job at Hammonds, I know she'd work hard. You wouldn't regret it, I'm sure of that.'

'As I said, I can't promise, but I'll see what I can do.'

When they'd got to the pie stand and were all seated on the wall eating their pies, Jack said, 'I'm told you're looking for work, Daisy?'

Daisy's face lit up. 'Oh, I am!' she declared, 'I am!'

'I've promised Amy I'll see what I can do to get you in at Hammonds.'

'Yer not having me on, are yer?' gasped Daisy. 'Is it true? Are you really gonna give me a job at Hammonds? Oh, wow! WOW!' And to the roars of laughter from the fat pieman, Daisy took up dancing on the spot.

'Don't get too excited!' Jack was shouting. 'I can't promise,' but there was no stopping her now. Dropping the remains of her pie into the bin, she skipped off down the street, doing pirouettes and shouting to the world, 'To hell with old Tooley! She can stick her job up her arse.'

When the excitement had died down, the four of them made their way to Corporation Park. As always, the park was closed through December, but Daisy and Amy knew that the side gate would be unlocked, as they had been through it many a time when lost for somewhere to go.

'I'd like to be married in a long white dress with flowers in my hair and six bridesmaids following me into the church.' Daisy described it all in great detail. 'Afterwards, I want four children, two boys

296

and two girls, and a house big enough for a couple of dogs to roam about.'

Roy laughed at her enthusiasm. 'You don't want much, do yer?'

At that she flung her arms round his neck. 'To tell you the truth, I just want you,' she said earnestly. 'The rest of it won't matter.'

But it did, and Roy knew that. 'If you want a long white dress, flowers in your hair and a big house to live in, well then, I'll just 'ave to work twice as hard.' And the joy shining in her eyes was enough to spur him on.

While Amy and Jack wandered off along the street, Daisy and Roy stayed on the wall, talking and laughing, kissing and canoodling.

'Look at them two,' Jack said. 'They're like two lovebirds.'

The sight of Daisy so happy brought a lump to Amy's throat. 'She deserves a chance at happiness. Ever since I've known her, it seems trouble and strife have just followed her about.'

'Well, she seems happy with her lot now,' Jack observed, 'and if I can fix her up with a good job and a decent wage, you know I will.'

'Do you really think they're right for each other, Jack?' Amy slid her arm through his. 'Only Daisy and men usually spell catastrophe.'

Jack had no doubts at all. 'I've known Roy a while now,' he said, 'and I've never seen him so smitten. If you ask me, they were made for each other.' Reaching down, he kissed her on the top of her head. 'So you can stop worrying.'

'HEY!' Roy's voice sailed through the night air. 'We'll see you two later.'

As Jack and Amy turned, it was to see the other

two running off like two playful children, Daisy in front and Roy chasing her across the street.

'Where are you going?' Amy wanted to know.

There was no answer; already they were out of earshot.

'Leave them be, sweetheart. I expect they need to be on their own.' Sliding his arm round her shoulders, he led her onwards. 'At least it gives us a proper chance to talk.'

'About what?' Amy had long suspected the depth of his feelings for her, and however much she tried not to, she found herself growing anxious. What if he asked her to marry him? Did she want to be his wife? Yet again, Luke entered her mind—was even the thought of Luke a betrayal of Jack?—and now Don, and once again she was reliving all the disappointments and heartache of rejection.

Jack's voice whispered in her ear, 'Are you all right, sunshine? You've gone very quiet.'

'I'm fine.' She smiled up at Jack and thought how fortunate she was, because he was a good man; a man any woman would give her right arm for, and yes, she did feel the stirrings of love for him.

As they walked on, Jack talked of all his hopes and plans for the future, and before they knew it, they had left the centre of town and were making their way along beside the railings of Corporation Park.

'Amy?'

'Yes, Jack?' They stopped walking and leaned against the railings.

'I so much want you to be a part of my future,' Jack murmured, sliding his arm round her waist, 'because now you've become more important than anything else. All the scrimping and saving. All those precious plans to build a business and be my own boss; to go from strength to strength until I'm the biggest employer in Blackburn . . . I never thought there could ever be anything more important than that.'

Leaning closer, he followed the curve of her mouth with the tip of his finger. 'The truth is, Amy, it means nothing if I haven't got you to share it with me.'

Placing his two hands on her shoulders, he gently drew her towards him, until her head was pressed close to his shoulder and his chin was resting against her hair. 'You know what I'm saying, don't you?' he whispered. 'Marry me, Amy? For pity's sake, marry me, before I go crazy.'

Tearing herself away, Amy was utterly confused. She had not visualised being married to Jack—for the rest of her life. It was such a big thing to ask of anyone—the biggest commitment you could make. Don had not been the right man and this time they must both be sure.

'Amy,' Jack persisted, 'will you say yes?' His tender voice murmured in her ear.

What should she say? Did she want it to happen, or didn't she?

Aware of her dilemma, Jack walked slowly on and took her with him. 'Think about it,' he suggested reluctantly. 'There's no hurry. I'd rather wait and get the right answer, than rush you and be turned down.'

Feeling warm and secure in the crook of his arm, Amy hated herself for the coward she was. It was on the tip of her tongue to say she would marry him tomorrow, if that was what he wanted. But she had to be sure. Maybe he was right after all. Maybe she ought to give it a deal more thought before committing herself.

All the same, she wanted to say yes. But fear got in the way. And Luke. And Don.

In no time at all, they were at the top of the rise. From here, they could see the silhouette of the lake; all silvery and shifting in the moonlight. 'I love it here,' she murmured, looking up at him. 'When I was little, our dad used to bring me up here and we'd sit on the grass and have a picnic. Afterwards we'd feed the ducks and watch them fight over the crumbs, then we'd run down the hill, laughing and screeching, until we got to the gates, where we'd keel over, exhausted and breathless. Then he'd sit me on his shoulders and take me home, and our mam would have the Sunday roast all ready.'

She laughed softly at the memories. 'Oh, Jack, it's so beautiful here.'

'So are you,' he whispered, and before she could say anything, he had her in his arms and was kissing her passionately.

She did not resist. Wrapped in his arms, all the fear and uncertainty didn't seem so daunting any more. Amy's doubts were not altogether gone, but she knew she had to conquer those doubts, or be alone for the rest of her life. 'I love you,' she murmured. 'I think I've known it all along.'

He laughed out loud. 'So you'll be my wife, is that what you're saying, Amy, is it?'

Amy's answer was to kiss him long and hard, and though she had not yet fully agreed to marriage, her ready kiss was taken as an acceptance.

'We'll find Daisy and Roy!' Jack exclaimed

excitedly. 'I want them to be the first to know.'

*   *   *

'Aw, come on, Daisy!' Roy was getting more and more frustrated. They had walked slightly out of town and the streets were very quiet. Daisy, however, was adamant. 'I'm no alley-cat,' she retorted. 'I don't make love in the street, and that's that!'

'Where then?'

'Wherever you like, but not in the street.'

'What about Hammonds factory?'

Daisy chuckled. 'Heck! That might be a laugh.' Common sense prevailed. 'Best not,' she said. 'If we're caught, you'll get the sack.'

Roy was adamant. 'We won't get caught, and besides, if Jack offers you work, it would be good for you to have given the place a once-over beforehand.'

'I don't know about that. All I know is that we could get into a lot of trouble, breaking into the factory like that.'

'We won't be breaking in,' Roy insisted, 'I know where there's a small window that's never completely shut. Oh, come on, Daisy. I promise you, we'll be in and out of there before you know it, and nobody will be any the wiser.'

'It's still breaking in, and it's against the law, or have you forgotten?'

Determined to show off his place of work, and make love into the bargain, Roy was eager to persuade her. 'If you don't like the look of the place, you can tell Jack you've got a job somewhere else. That way he won't put his neck on the line for

301

you, and you won't go to work on your first day all excited, only to be disappointed.'

'Oh, all right then.' Daisy was always ready for the next adventure; all she needed was a bit of persuasion. 'You've twisted my arm, so let's do it!'

A few minutes later, having successfully sneaked round the night-watchman, who was fast asleep in front of his cheery brazier, they crept along the back alley, over the low roof and in through the office window.

'Drop down softly,' Roy warned. 'We don't want you falling into the waste bin, do we, eh?'

*　　　*　　　*

Not too far away, there was another shadowy figure. Coming towards the factory by way of the canal, it hid for a time, knowing the night-watchman was on duty, and fearing to be seen.

Staying in the shadows, it peered towards the one who kept guard. Seated like a gnome on his stool, with his cap drawn low over his eyes and the flames from the brazier cradling him in its warmth, the old one was in a deep, contented slumber.

Reassured, the intruder ventured forward; in one hand it swung a length of rope. In the other it carried a can of fuel.

Breathing fast, afraid to be discovered, the silent figure went softly past the old man, down along the side of that great, familiar building and now, at the back door, it slid the key into the lock, inched open the door and slipped inside.

*　　　*　　　*

On the upper floor not too far away, Roy and Daisy had dropped to the ground without injury.

'Bleedin' hell, Roy!' Hopping and groaning, Daisy scrambled up. 'You didn't tell me it was such a long drop!' Vigorously rubbing her ankle, she complained, 'I could have broken my leg, for all you care.'

'Aw now, don't make such a fuss.' Roy slid his arm round her. 'I wouldn't let you get hurt. I'd rather break every bone in my body than see you break a leg,' he told her with a cheeky grin.

Daisy was not impressed. 'There! See! You're taking the mickey now.' She thrust him aside. 'Get off! Go on, get off.' With only the trickle of moonlight through the window to light her way, she searched for the door. 'Which way is it?'

'For God's sake, stop nagging.' Roy brushed himself down. 'This is the big man's office,' he imparted proudly. 'It's where he does all his business.'

Taking her hand he led her quietly past the large, neatly ordered desk. 'He may look quiet, and a proper gentleman,' he muttered, 'but there's no denying he can make things happen when he wants. One minute we're running short of work and the next we're flush with new contracts.'

Creeping along beside him, her hand fast in his, Daisy teased, 'D'yer reckon *you* can make things happen?'

He chuckled. 'Give me a chance an' you'll soon find out.'

'Be'ave yerself, yer randy dog.' She gave him a playful push. 'I didn't mean like *that*. I meant, d'yer think you could be as clever as he is?'

Roy shook his head. 'Happen not. Y'see, there

are them as were born to lead, and them as were born to follow, and I'm one o' the followers.' A serious note marbled his voice. 'But d'you know what? Lately, I've learned that if a man works hard and keeps his eyes and ears open long enough, he'll find summat worth going for . . . that extra mile, if yer know what I mean?'

Daisy followed him through the door, and down the iron steps to the lower floor. 'No, I don't know what you mean.'

Pausing on the step, he turned to her, his voice soft and his homely face creased in thought. 'It's like this,' he began. 'A man can slave all his life and not care to better himself. But if he finds a woman and a purpose, he might just discover that extra strength to lift himself above the rest.'

Daisy was impressed. 'Are you saying *you've* found a purpose . . . and a woman?' she asked wonderingly.

He smiled a quiet, sincere smile that touched her deeply. 'You know I have,' he answered. 'I've found you, and now I've got plans and ambitions that I never had afore. I want to be with the best. I want to be the one that men look up to.' He paused, his eyes shining into hers. 'Don't you understand, Daisy?' he asked. 'I need to make you proud of me.'

Without a word she slid her arms round his neck and kissed him—not the passionate, wild kiss he was used to, but a softer, gentle kiss that meant more to him than she could ever hope to know. 'I am proud of you,' she whispered.

For a long, beautiful minute he kept her there in his embrace, wanting never to let her go. Then he held her at arm's length and, with his usual cheeky grin, told her, 'Go careful down these steps, and keep hold o' me, or there's no telling *where* you'll end up.'

Hand in hand, finding their way through the maze of boxes and pallets and piles of merchandise, they emerged towards the back of the building, where the brushes were assembled.

'This is where you'll be,' Roy explained. 'Look!' Manoeuvring her, he positioned her in front of the machine. 'See them wooden bases?' He drew her attention to a dozen curved wooden brush-heads, ready for the bristles to be inserted. 'D'you know what they are?'

Peering hard in the dimness, Daisy thought she recognised the familiar curving of the shapes. 'They look like the tops of scrubbing brushes,' she said, 'and I should know, 'cos there's never a day passed when old Ma Tooley didn't have me down on my knees scrubbing the damned floor.'

'Yer right!' Roy laughed, but quietly, because they must not alert the night-watchman. 'Somebody's already put the shapes in place, but that'll be your job when you start. You take the shapes out of the boxes and fit them into the slots on the back panel, then you pack the bristles into the arm.' He pointed to a long metal arm open all the way along, but with short sides to keep the bristles in place. 'Then you work the machine and punch the bristles into the shapes . . . d'yer see?'

He now drew her attention to the many small holes in the shapes. 'When you've done that lot, you take them out and pack them neatly into a box, until you've filled the box with six dozen scrubbing brushes, all smart and ready for the customer. Now then, Daisy, me darling, 'ave you got that all straight in your head?'

Daisy took a moment to consider the workings of it all, before she gave her indignant reply. 'Course I have! I might not be the brainiest woman on God's earth, but I'm not the thickest neither!'

Roy agreed. 'Right! So, yer well pleased then? You reckon you'd be happy standing here nine hours a day, punching bristles into holes? Mind! You'll get a fifteen-minute break morning and afternoon, and an hour between.'

Daisy clapped her hands. 'I'm gonna love it,' she said. 'Better than working for that miserly, moaning old Tooley. Honest to God, I'm glad to see the back of her.'

Having done what he promised, Roy now wanted what Daisy had promised him. 'Off with 'em!' he chuckled.

Daisy played the innocent. 'Off with what?'

'You know what,' he whispered.

'No, I don't!' Stifling her laughter, she told him sternly, 'Anyway, we'd best get out of here, before somebody finds us.'

'Why, yer little sod . . .' Playfully struggling her to the ground, he looked into her twinkling eyes, and gave a groan. 'Are you playing games with me?'

She winked. 'I might be.'

He kissed her tenderly. 'You know how much I love you, don't you, Daisy?'

Her answer was to climb away from him, and when she had his full attention, she began to strip off, first her top, then her skirt and now her undies one after the other, slowly, teasingly.

'I'm yours, if you want me.' Naked as the day she was born, she slid to the ground and, wrapping herself round him, began taking off his clothes,

306

only this time there was an urgency that neither of them could contain.

A moment later, with their clothes strewn about, they made love fiercely, possessively.

There followed a few intimate moments when they held each other; they talked of their dreams, and their plans, and discovered a kinship they had never known before and oh, the contentment of being together.

Then a moment of wonderful silence, before their passions overwhelmed them, and they began making love for a second time.

It was Roy who noticed it. 'There's a burning smell!' He sat bolt upright. 'Bloody hell, Daisy, I reckon there's summat on fire.' Getting to his feet, he made a grab for his trousers. 'Can you smell that?' He sniffed the air. 'Stay here!'

As he went forward, Daisy made a playful grab for his leg. 'Don't be daft,' she coaxed. 'I can't smell anything. If there's summat on fire, it must be you.'

'Quiet, Daisy!' Her laughter disturbed him.

For a moment he stood perfectly still, sniffing at the air, his ears cocked for any sound. Suddenly he was frantic. 'Get dressed!' She hesitated, preferring to tease him. 'Daisy! Get dressed NOW! There's a fire somewhere. I can smell it in the air.' Making a grab for Daisy's clothes he threw them at her. 'Hurry up!'

While he quickly drew on his trousers, he glanced about. There was no sign of smoke, but he could taste it. He knew there was a fire somewhere and it wasn't too far away. 'I've an idea it might be that new boiler; we've had nothing but trouble with it. Look, Daisy, I want you to go back the way we

307

came. Keep to the right as you go. Then up the steps to the office. Wait for me there. I'll just go and take a quick look.'

Daisy was terrified. 'Don't leave me here,' she pleaded. 'I need to be with you. I'll stay close. Just don't leave me?' Having realised the urgency, she was now dressed and ready to follow him.

With Daisy tagging on, Roy headed straight for the back area, where the boiler was housed.

By now, the intruder was almost done. Because the boiler was too hot to get close to throw the petrol over, the rope was a means of allowing time to get out.

With one end of the long rope tied to the handle of the boiler door, the other end was stretched out as far as it would go. Tipping the petrol can upside down, the arsonist doused this end of the rope until it was thoroughly saturated. With the rope being a simple soft twine, it would soon suck the petrol along its entire length, until it reached the boiler.

Stepping back, the intruder gave a grim, satisfied smile. 'That should do the trick.' A lit match, dropped to the rope end, and a moment to make sure the flames were licking along the twists and turns, and then the intruder was fleeing.

'Hey!' Roy rounded the corner just as the shadowy figure ran out of sight. 'Oh Jesus!' Seeing what was about to happen, he stamped at the flames with his feet. 'GET BACK, DAISY! GET AWAY FROM HERE!' Grasping the rope with both hands, he tugged at it with all his might, but it wouldn't budge and now there was no more time. 'RUN, DAISY! FOR GOD'S SAKE, RUN!'

As they ran, the flames licked at everything around. The boxes of bristles were set alight; the billowing smoke was like a grey fog all around, hampering their getaway.

'I can't see where I'm going!' Daisy began to panic.

Roy called out, 'Stay calm. I'm right here. Keep to your right, Daisy . . . along the wall. Then up the steps. Daisy, are you all right? Take my hand . . . oh God! DAISY, WHERE ARE YOU?'

Having already strayed from the path, Daisy had no idea where she was. She couldn't keep to the right, because she could feel no wall beside her; neither could she see more than a few inches ahead. So while Roy fled one way searching for her, she fled another until, stumbling against a steel contraption, she was flung headlong to the ground, and the contraption was toppled. As it fell, it caught the side of a stack of wooden boxes and sent the entire load tumbling down.

Unwittingly, Daisy lay straight underneath and by the time she realised the danger, it was too late. She screamed once and no more, for the crates were tumbling down on her one after the other, until she was buried deep beneath.

She did not hear the sound of the explosion; nor did she see the flames licking at the wooden crates. By this time, Daisy knew nothing of what was happening.

*　　*　　*

Inside was mayhem; outside was panic.

'I sent for the fire brigade as soon as I saw the flames.' The night-watchman was frantic as he and a passer-by tried hard to keep Roy from going back inside. 'They'll be here any minute.'

Fighting like a tiger to free himself, Roy was frantic, 'I've got to find her!' Though suffering badly from the effects of smoke and fumes and with the flesh of one arm torn from top to bottom, his only thought was for Daisy. 'I couldn't find her,' he sobbed. 'All hell was let loose. I looked everywhere . . . oh, God! She ran the wrong way. I couldn't see her.' He tore at the two men. 'LET ME GO, YOU BASTARDS!'

'What's happening?' Leaping from the fire engine, the first fireman came running towards them. 'Is there anyone inside?'

'The lass!' The night-watchman and his helper kept a tight hold on Roy. 'He says there's a lass in there.'

Just then, Roy broke free but was quickly hauled back by the fireman. 'Leave it to us, son,' he warned. 'It looks to me like the whole bally lot is about to come down.'

Roy was beside himself. 'You've got to save her.' He was distraught. 'She's all I've got. Get her out. Please God . . . get my Daisy out of there!'

The fireman understood. Already the hoses had been unrolled and the men were dashing towards the building. 'Listen to me.' He gave Roy a gentle shake of the shoulders. 'Trust me, son. We're trained for this sort of thing. If she's inside, then we're her best bet. We'll get her out. I can promise you that.'

And then he was running after his men towards the building, which by now was like an inferno.

Though the next few minutes stretched away like a lifetime to Roy and the others who watched, the first fireman kept his promise and soon emerged with Daisy's limp body.

'DAISY!' Sick with relief, Roy ran to her.

He ran beside the stretcher as they carried her to a waiting ambulance, and while he held her seemingly lifeless hand, he talked to her. But she did not answer.

He could see her blackened face and burned clothes, and his heart sank like a stone inside him.

He dared not believe what his eyes were telling him.

CHAPTER THIRTEEN

In the month following the fire, Luke Hammond had to fight tooth and nail to hold his business together. Today, the fourth of January 1934, brought yet another meeting. Luke needed to persuade an old colleague to help him through what was proving to be one of the most difficult times of his life.

With Luke's help in the early days, Leonard Wrightson had climbed the ladder of success, but now, when the boot was on the other foot, he was not an easy man to deal with.

'You know you can trust me.' Luke felt he had bandied words long enough with the portly man seated behind the desk. 'Christ Almighty, Leonard! Have you forgotten how I kept you going when others wouldn't even give you the time of day? I carried you when money was short. There were times when I had to wait weeks for my payment, and I bent my own rules to store your goods when the warehouse was already full to bursting!' Angry at being doubted, he paced the floor. 'There's no risk,' he reaffirmed, 'so why the hell you're hesitating I don't know!'

The older man took out a cigar and, having lit it, he sucked hard on it while he studied Luke. 'You're not in danger of losing it all, are you?' he asked suspiciously. 'Don't tell me you were not insured?' Luke was not a man to neglect such an essential, but he did seem unusually keen to have him in his corner, Wrightson thought.

Luke's anger burst. 'Well, of course I was bloody insured. You know what a stickler I am for things like that.'

'In that case, you'll survive without my help.'

'Maybe I will. Maybe I won't!' Striding forward, Luke pressed his point. With his hands spread out on the desk and his face so close that the other man instinctively shifted back in his seat, he explained, 'It's nothing to do with insurance or how much money I've got in the bank. That is not my main concern.'

The fellow took another leisurely drag on his cigar. 'If it's not money, what is it then?'

'It's my *business* we're talking about. Thankfully, I've got most of my customers behind me now, but there are others, much like yourself, who forget too easily and need more convincing.'

Leonard was growing nervous. 'I hope you're not about to get nasty. If you are, then there's the door and you'd best leave right now, because I will not be bullied!'

Realising he might appear menacing, Luke stepped back. 'I'm no bully,' he protested. 'I'm a man who's spent years of hard work building a business I'm proud of, and if I don't fight my corner now, there'll be nobody else to fight it.'

312

Seeing how Luke was genuinely distressed, he had to admire his restraint, because if it had been himself that was in this position, he'd have smacked someone in the mouth. 'I can spare you a few minutes,' he said, 'but I'll promise nothing. So, if you're prepared to accept that, then I'm prepared to hear you out.' In fact, he was enjoying every minute of it.

Encouraged, Luke went on. 'Like I say, the insurers have paid out, so there's no problems in that direction. If I can only keep my customers happy, I'll soon be on top again. On the practical side, I'm renting a sizeable warehouse while mine is rebuilt, and, thank God, three of the wagons went unscathed as they were out on deliveries, so as you can see, I'm just one wagon down, but I'll soon rectify that. You know me, Leonard,' he declared confidently. 'I never hang about.'

'It's true,' he grudgingly admitted. 'You're one of the few men I know who can keep one step ahead of the competition.'

'Oh, is that right?' Agitated, Luke banged his fist on the desk. 'So, if you know that, why the devil are you playing games with me?'

Leonard Wrightson took another, longer drag on his cigar. 'The thing is . . .' he blew the smoke out of his nostrils, '. . . I've got strict deadlines to meet, and my own customers to satisfy. I'm sorry you've had this setback, but you'll come up smelling of roses.' He could not disguise his envy. 'You always do.'

'I asked you what game you were playing, and now I'm beginning to see just what you're up to.' Luke snorted with indignation. 'You mean to set up against me, is that it?'

Shifting uncomfortably in his chair, the older man answered hesitantly, 'I've been offered a large, empty warehouse at a fraction of its value. It's made me wonder whether I might be best off storing my own goods . . . and happen poaching a few o' your customers into the bargain. I could even go into the delivery side of it. After all, I'm doing well in my own field, and I've got spare money enough to buy a couple o' wagons. Matter o' fact, I might even make you an offer for your three, if you're looking to sell.' He took another drag on his cigar. 'You started out small. What's to stop me from doing the same?' His smile was evil. 'You know what they say . . . all's fair in love and war.'

As if he had been smacked between the eyes, Luke reeled backwards. He stared at Wrightson for a long minute thinking deeply on the other man's words. Then he saw what to do. Nodding his approval, he surprised Leonard. 'Why, there's not a thing in the world to stop you,' he answered. 'You're entitled to do what you please, and good luck to you, Leonard. I hope you do well.' He nodded in a friendly fashion. 'As there's nothing else to discuss, I'll bid you good day.'

In an instant the other man was on his feet and chasing after Luke, who had already started his way towards the door. 'Hang on a minute. There's no rush, is there? I mean . . . we haven't finished our conversation.'

Luke turned with a smile. 'Oh, I'm sorry, I thought we had.'

Realising he might have just made a formidable enemy, Wrightson invited hurriedly, 'Look here, Luke. Come back and sit down.'

'Thanks all the same,' Luke replied, 'but I've got

things to do.' Smiling quietly to himself, he turned to leave.

Puzzled and a little afraid, the other man asked, 'What are you up to?'

'I'm not "up to" anything.'

'So you're not intending to turn the tables on me and poach my customers, are you?' He was well aware of Luke's respected standing among the local businessmen. Also, the very fact that most of them had vowed to stand by him was proof enough of the influence he carried.

Luke could almost read the other man's mind and he was delighted, yet when he answered, it was in a calm, cool manner. 'Like yourself, I cannot promise anything,' he said. 'I've already explained how I've worked long and hard to build up my business, and you know it isn't altogether the money. It's keeping alive what my father started many years ago . . . keeping it alive and building on it. I've always meant Hammonds to be the biggest company in this part of the world, and I mean to see it through . . . with or without you.' He paused before finishing, 'I'm not a devious man, but having said that, you can depend on me to do what I have to do, in order to get the business up and running full swing.'

Taking Luke's meaning, the other man was uncomfortable. 'And does that include stealing my customers?'

Luke answered carefully. 'I hadn't thought of that, but, like you said yourself, Leonard, all's fair in love and war. And who am I to argue?'

'No, no!' The other one laughed nervously. 'You've got me all wrong. I'm content enough with the work I've got.'

He knew he did not command the respect that Luke did, and he also knew that if Luke moved into his own area of expertise, he could soon be the loser. 'What happened to you could have happened to any one of us, and of course we should always support each other.'

'Oh, really?' It was all Luke could do not to laugh out loud, but he maintained an indifferent manner, asking casually, 'So, does that mean you want to retain my services?'

'Well, of course. Isn't that what this meeting was all about?'

'You're right, Leonard,' Luke readily agreed. 'That was my idea when I came to see you. Only, now that I think on it, I'm not certain I can accommodate you. You see, the temporary warehouse isn't as big as the old one. Of course, it'll be different when the new one is built, but it'll be tight for a time. It'll mean a bit of juggling here and there, but if I made the effort, I dare say I could accommodate you—if I put myself out a bit, that is.' He feigned a worried expression. 'In fact, I'm beginning to think I should never have come to see you at all. I mean, what with the old customers keeping faith with me, I'm not really sure I could altogether handle your contract as well.'

Fearing he had done himself more harm than he had done Luke, Wrightson gently argued his case. 'Look, I need to keep my stock on the move. I haven't got time for fitting out a new warehouse, and I'd have to find capable, trustworthy drivers, not to mention new wagons and other workers. No! On reflection it would be foolish to lay out that sort of money, especially when I don't have to.'

Luke showed no pity. 'I'm sorry. I don't see

316

how—'

'Listen to me.' Interrupting Luke, Wrightson stubbed out his cigar in the ashtray and, taking a deep breath, he offered, 'An extra two per cent on top with every transaction. What do you say to that?'

At last, even though it was not in the way he'd intended, Luke had him where he wanted him. It was a good feeling. 'Three per cent!'

'Two and a half.'

Luke held out his hand. 'Done!'

Leonard Wrightson gave a sigh of relief. 'So, we're back in business, and no more nonsense about poaching each other's work,' he laughed. 'We've more than enough burdens on our backs as it is, wouldn't you say?'

Luke didn't 'say'. What he did was to draw up a rough, binding contract on either side and when that was signed by both parties in front of the secretary, he shook hands to conclude the deal.

'I'll be in touch,' he promised as he prepared to leave.

As he strode from the desk, the other man stopped him. 'Have they found the culprit yet?'

'Not yet, no.'

'And have they no idea who did it?'

Pursing his lips, Luke took his time in answering. 'If they have, they're not telling me.'

'I know the police are calling it arson, but what's *your* thinking on it?' Wrightson quizzed. 'Was it a deliberate act to put you out of business or an unfortunate accident?'

Luke was suddenly on the defensive. This turn of conversation was beginning to touch on deep issues that he would rather not think about. 'Your guess is

317

as good as mine.' Disgruntled, he turned away for the second time. 'Still, I expect they'll get to the bottom of it before too long.'

He was almost at the door, when he was pulled up sharply by the other man's casual remark. 'Terrible shame about that young woman.'

Dropping his head as though in shame, Luke did not turn round. Instead he answered, almost inaudibly, 'Yes . . . dreadful thing.'

'What was that?' The other man began his way to the door. 'I didn't hear what you said?'

Luke strode on, through the door and into the outer hall. 'I've said all I mean to say on the matter,' he called out angrily, 'and I suggest you do the same!' With that he was out of the building and hurrying away down the street as though the devil was on his heels.

Later that evening, he was ensconced in his study at home. He did not begin on the pile of paperwork that littered his desk, though much of it was urgent enough.

Instead, he paced the floor, sometimes pausing to stare out of the window, or at times hunched in the chair, head in hands, haunted by what had happened.

First, there was that poor blameless girl Daisy. Oh, the shock of discovering that the injured young woman trapped in the burning factory had been the little waitress from Tooley's Café.

Inevitably this made Luke think of the waitress's best friend, Amy. Thank God it had not been her in the blaze. Since the fire, whenever he went to the cabin, which was less and less as outside pressures increased, Luke had spent hours staring at Amy's lovely face in the painting. Did she still go

318

to Tooley's, he wondered. Since she'd come to the cabin that second time he had stayed away from the café so as not to embarrass her. She was more than ever a part of the Tuesday dream now. He must see her again.

Then there was the truly chilling thought that the factory fire had been started deliberately and that someone hated him and wanted to destroy him that much. He had no idea who could have done such a thing.

When the knock came on the door he almost leaped out of his skin. 'Who is it?' His voice shook. 'I'm busy!'

The door inched open. 'It's only me.' For some unknown reason Sylvia had been unusually quiet these last two days, avoiding him at every turn, whereas in the immediate weeks following the fire, she had been dangerously agitated; so much so that the doctor had had to sedate her on several occasions. 'Can I come in?'

Before he could answer, she was inside. Closing the door behind her, she stood against it, her arms behind her back and a look of wildness in her eyes. 'It was you, wasn't it?'

Sensing trouble, Luke leaped out of the chair. 'What the hell are you talking about?'

She smiled, that evil little smile he had come to recognise so well. 'I know what you did.'

He looked her in the eye. 'Do you now?' He wondered how much she really did know.

She started forward. 'You thought I was in the building, didn't you? That's why you set fire to it.' She began trembling, her face alight with excitement. 'You tried to kill me, just like you did when you crept up behind me in the alley.'

319

Nodding her head vigorously, she began gabbling, 'You think I don't know who it was that attacked me that night, but I do . . . it was *you*. You wanted me out of the way, so you could be with your fancy woman.' Wagging a finger, she had the look of someone demented. 'Ah! You didn't think I knew that, did you? You didn't think I'd seen you in the alley but I did! It was you! YOU WANT ME DEAD!'

'Calm down, Sylvia,' Luke said gently. 'You don't want to get all worked up.'

In the wink of an eye her mood changed. 'Don't kill me,' she sobbed. 'I didn't mean to do it. I'll never do it again!'

Desolate, he came forward, arms open wide. 'Come on, I'll get you a hot drink. You'd best take your tablets and go to bed.'

When he laid his hands on her, she shrank from him. 'Don't punish me,' she whimpered. 'I'm sorry. I'll be a good girl. I will.'

'It's all right,' he coaxed. 'Everything's going to be all right.'

But he knew it wasn't.

*   *   *

Amy was busy unpacking a delivery of soap and putting it on the shelves when Luke walked into Atkinsons' Corner Shop one Friday morning in early January. The shop was busy with people stocking up on groceries for the weekend, and heads turned to examine the smartly dressed stranger in a big black overcoat and a felt hat. One or two necks were craned to assess the shiny motor car parked outside the shop too.

320

Amy scrambled to her feet, flushing and looking confused.

'Good morning, Miss Atkinson,' Luke said, fixing her with a confident smile. 'I wonder if I might have a word with you about a friend of yours and acquaintance of mine—Daisy?'

'Of course,' answered Amy. She glanced at Marie, who, with Maureen—now helping in the shop at busy times, the tea trolley job missed only by Johnny—was efficiently getting through the queue of customers.

Marie nodded towards the living room behind the shop. 'Take the gentleman through, if you like, Amy,' she suggested. She would never show her own curiosity in front of the customers, particularly old Alice, whose eyes were bulging with the need to know what was afoot.

Amy showed Luke through, quietly closed the door behind them and turned to him with a mixture of both pleasure and anger at seeing him.

'What are you doing here?' she whispered fiercely, mindful of the thin wall.

'I told you, Amy, I've come to find out how Daisy is.'

Amy was immediately contrite. 'She's not well, I'm afraid,' she said. 'She's getting better, but slowly.'

'Will she be . . . scarred for life? I hear her injuries are awful.'

'Some won't heal entirely, some will. But she's so down. It's her mind tormenting her about her physical injuries that is making her so much worse.'

There was a long pause. 'I understand,' Luke said quietly. 'The mind can be so fragile.'

Before she knew it Amy had reached out and

321

squeezed his hand in silent sympathy. He imprisoned her hand with both of his and brought it to his lips. 'Dear Amy—'

'No, Luke,' she interrupted, pulling her hand gently away. 'I meant what I said last time. It can never be—you know that.'

Luke sensed that Amy could never be his. He had to accept that, and he did. 'All right, Amy—but we can be friends, can't we?'

Amy visibly relaxed. 'Of course we can.'

And so they discussed Daisy's injuries and Luke looked grave, especially when he learned he wouldn't even be allowed to visit her in the infirmary just yet. He promised to come by again to enquire after her progress.

'Won't you have a cup of tea before you go?' asked Amy as Luke gathered himself to leave.

'No, thank you,' he said. 'Better not.'

'I'm sorry about your factory burning down,' she said as they both moved towards the door.

'Thank you. Yes, I can hardly say fortune's smiling just now,' he shrugged, trying for nonchalance. 'Main thing is that Daisy gets better. I can always build another factory, but there's only one Daisy.'

'Too right!' agreed Amy. What a good man he was. 'Thank you for coming to ask about her. I'll tell her you did, when she's well enough to take it in.'

'Thanks.'

They stood awkwardly facing each other, unsure how to part. Suddenly Luke leaned over and planted a swift kiss on Amy's hair.

'Goodbye, Amy,' he said, and was through the door before she could reply.

When Marie came to look for Amy a few minutes later she found her looking suspiciously red-eyed.

'Don't worry, love. Daisy will get better,' she comforted, hugging Amy to her. But she had a feeling it wasn't just Daisy Amy had been crying about.

CHAPTER FOURTEEN

'Give her my love, won't yer, lass?' Like everyone who knew Daisy, Marie had been devastated by what had happened to her. 'Tell her we're all thinking of her.' Handing Amy the small posy of hot-house roses, she gave a deep sigh. 'God only knows, that poor lass needs all the support we can give her.' Marie said something like this every day, for her daughter was a daily visitor to Daisy's bedside.

Amy nodded. She didn't say anything. What could anybody say in a situation like this?

'Now you just mind how you go, lass, and don't worry about me and Maureen. We'll manage all right.'

'That's right, love.' These past weeks, while Amy had dedicated herself to keeping Daisy's spirits up, Maureen had taken on more and more in the shop, and was now as much Marie's right-hand woman as Amy.

Amy thanked them both. She glanced at little Johnny, who was playing with his toy train on the floor. 'See you later, Johnny.' When he ran to her, she gave him a hug. 'Be a good boy while I'm gone.'

And sensing the seriousness of the moment, the boy clung to her a while longer than was necessary.

A moment later, armed with flowers and other small gifts, she set off to see Daisy.

Amy was deeply troubled. Walking down the street she wondered how Daisy would be today.

Some short time later, seated on the tram, she tormented herself with what had happened just a few short weeks ago: Roy and Daisy trapped in a burning inferno; the terrible shock when the news came through, and that first time when she and Jack had gone to see Daisy at the infirmary.

There was never a conscious minute when the evening of the fire didn't play on her mind. And with it came the guilt.

That night, she and Jack should never have let Roy and Daisy run off on their own—but then they were not children; they were grown-ups with minds of their own. And what if the two of them had not gone into that factory? What if old Tooley had not sacked Daisy? Then there would have been no need to ask Jack if he could get her a job, and Roy would not have taken her into the factory to show her the kind of work she might be doing.

The most haunting question of all was who had set fire to the factory and why? Did they mean to hurt Roy and Daisy? Or was it a way of getting at Luke Hammond?

All the ifs and buts, and the reasons why, would not go away, and Amy wondered if they ever would.

The tram pulled into her stop and Amy disembarked for the infirmary. As she walked through the main doors, it seemed some kind of fracas was going on.

'I've told you time and again, I cannot allow you into the ward!' The matron was a formidable lady of some strength and size who, along with the two porters who had been summoned to her aid, was easily equal to the two louts whose way she was blocking. 'My first duty is to the patient, and I'd like you to leave at once.'

'Get outta me sodding way!' The scruffy burly fella hanging on to his wife's arm was so inebriated he could hardly stand. 'Yer can't bloody well stop us from seeing our own daughter!'

'That's right!' Screeching and yelling, his dishevelled wife lashed out wildly. 'So you'd best piss off out of it, the lot of you; or we'll 'ave the police on yer!'

There was a fierce scuffle and the exchange of a few harsh words, but in the end the pair were marched off the premises.

'And don't come back until you've sobered up!' Matron's voice followed them along the street.

In the frantic moment when they were manhandled past Amy, she recognised them as Daisy's parents. Wisely lowering her head, she quickened her steps to the receptionist's desk.

The kindly receptionist greeted her with a smile. 'Good morning, Amy, and how are you?'

Having seen Amy regularly since Daisy had been transferred to the ward from the burns unit, she had come to know her well. Her condemning stare went to the outer door. 'I expect you already know Daisy's parents, do you?'

Amy nodded. 'Though not very well.'

'Dreadful pair. They tried to barge their way in just now—drunk and violent, the both of them.' With a burst of pride, she squared her little pigeon chest. 'Matron threw them out.'

Amy gave an embarrassed smile. 'I know,' she said sheepishly, 'and I hope nobody intends telling Daisy because, I can tell you, she wouldn't be too pleased about them turning up in that state.'

'Don't you worry,' the receptionist answered. 'I'm sure none of us would want to add to Daisy's burden by telling her. Anyway, the nurse has just been down,' she told Amy. 'Apparently, Daisy's had her wash, nibbled at her breakfast and now she's got her eyes glued to the door watching out for you.'

Just then a small, round-faced woman in her mid-forties approached Amy with the long, confident stride of a navvy. 'Oh, Amy! I'm so glad you've arrived.' The nurse, Rita, was a friendly little thing, who had formed a warm relationship with Daisy, far beyond the call of duty. 'I've just been talking with her,' she told Amy. 'I hope you can cheer her, because I can't seem to.'

'I'll do my best.'

'I know you will.' Nurse Rita explained. 'She's so unhappy. She cried half the night, so I'm told, and today she's like somebody being made ready for the gallows.'

Amy was concerned. 'What's brought all this on? She was doing all right yesterday.'

'I'm told she had words with her boyfriend. In fact by all accounts, she sent him packing.' Gesturing towards the corridor, the nurse urged, 'You go along, dear. I know she's been waiting for you.'

As Amy began to walk away, the nurse noticed that Amy had gone ahead with a posy of flowers. 'I'm sorry, dear,' she called her back. 'You still can't take flowers in . . . risk of infection and all that.'

Accepting the flowers, she handed them to the receptionist, who promised, 'I'll put them aside until I've finished what I'm doing, then I'll put them in a vase. I'm sure they'll give pleasure to everyone who passes by.'

Amy merely nodded before, with Nurse Rita, she made her way towards the long corridor that would take her to the ward. Rita told Amy that Daisy was doing really well as far as her injuries were concerned. 'In fact, it wouldn't surprise me if the doctor allowed her home by the end of next week. Mind you, on the emotional and mental side of it, she's still got a long way to go.'

'Once we get her home, she'll soon be on the mend.' Amy tried to sound hopeful.

'She'll be coming home with you, will she?'

'That's the plan. We've taken on extra help in the shop so I can spend most of my time with Daisy. That way, hopefully she'll soon regain her confidence.'

'Well, I hope you can stop her from sliding into a deep depression,' the nurse remarked with a frown. 'I've seen it happen so many times before—the patient's physical wounds mend, but the mental scars don't heal so quickly.'

Lowering her voice, she admitted, 'I know it isn't very professional, but I've spent many an hour talking with Daisy—on and off duty—and I've come to know and like her well. What I'm trying to say is this: I'm so glad she has you to fall back on. Now tell her I'll be along later,' she said, 'though I'll expect her to be fast asleep by that time.'

With her heart in her boots, Amy wondered what could have caused Daisy to 'have words' with

Roy. Probably something and nothing, she thought. Besides, Daisy had been through so much, she could be forgiven for being touchy now and then.

At the door of the ward, Amy was told by the duty sister, 'Daisy is very low, I'm afraid. See if you can put a smile on her face.'

'I'll do what I can.'

The sister smiled her approval. 'You're the best medicine she could have,' and with a friendly wave of the hand she excused herself. 'I must away and tend to other duties.'

Left alone, Amy peered through the window to where Daisy was seemingly sleeping. 'Chin up, sweetheart,' she muttered. 'God willing, we'll soon have you out of here.'

Her heart was heavy as she went inside, but she would never betray that to Daisy, not for one minute.

As she approached the bed she saw that Daisy was in a deep slumber. Her eyes were tightly closed and now, as Amy came nearer, Daisy's arm went instinctively to her neck, and pushed away the blanket.

Quietly seating herself in the chair beside the bed, Amy's gaze roved over that familiar, beloved face, and her heart was sore.

Daisy had been hurt badly that night—first from the impact of the wooden crates as they fell on top of her, and then by the scorching heat and smoke as the flames licked all around. But thankfully, the fine scars on her face were now beginning to fade. The damage done to her lungs by the smoke had slowly repaired. Her hair, which had been shorn in order for the doctor to stitch the many smaller wounds, had grown back so that it was like a short, well-fitting cap over her head.

The worst wound, and by far the greatest cause of Daisy's anguish, was the wide, meandering scar that ran from her right ear down her neck and over the swell of her breast.

This was where the sharp, iron-clad corner of that first falling crate had torn a deep, jagged path through her flesh, leaving an unsightly wound that had later become badly infected, and subsequently taken a long time to heal.

The doctors had already informed Daisy that although it would fade in time, the scar would be a permanent one.

More times than she could recall, Amy had sat and watched Daisy while she slept, and each time, she had quietly cried.

She cried now. But the minute she saw Daisy stirring, she wiped away the tears. By the time Daisy opened her eyes, Amy's smile was brighter than a summer's day.

'Look at you!' she tutted light-heartedly. 'Lying in bed while some of us are flogging ourselves to death at work.'

'Amy!' As always, Daisy was filled with joy at seeing Amy's bright, familiar smile. 'I'm sorry, at first I thought it were Nurse Rita sitting there. Oh, Amy! I'm so glad you're 'ere.'

Daisy had news she could hardly wait to tell. 'Guess who came to see me after you'd gone yesterday?' And before Amy could answer, she went on excitedly, 'It were none other than Luke Hammond! I thought I were imagining things when I saw who it was—the Tuesday man from Tooley's! I kept thinking it were a dream or summat, but it really was him. Who'd have thought a posh fella like Luke Hammond would have been going to old Ma Tooley's café all this time and we never knew? And who'd ever imagine he would come to see me here? He were right kind. He brought flowers, but the nurse took them away, an' he said as how he were deeply sorry for what happened, and that I wasn't to worry about a thing. Whatever I needed, I was to let him know . . . but I told him I don't need nothing, 'cos you see to all that.'

She smiled knowingly. 'He said he thought you might, and that you seemed a caring young woman who would value a friendship more than others would.'

As Daisy ranted on, Amy couldn't get a word in. 'He said the police had been to see him, and I told him they came here as well, and that I didn't see nothing. He said I should never have gone inside the building, but that he would forget about that, and Roy's job was safe; though he did have to reprimand him. And after all, it weren't us that set fire to the place were it, lass? Anyway, they've not found nobody yet. And he says there's a job waiting for me if I want it . . .'

'Slow down, Daisy!' Concerned that she was getting too breathless and excited, Amy stopped her. 'I already know he would have been to see you,' she admitted. 'He came to the shop first and asked if that would be all right.' She also mentioned that it was not the first time Luke Hammond had called at the shop to check on Daisy's wellbeing.

'Anyway, how are you feeling today?'

Amy reached down to kiss her soundly on the forehead. 'By! You look better with every passing day.'

Daisy gave no answer. Instead she looked away as the tears rolled down her sorry face.

Amy had grown used to the tears, and she was ever supportive and sympathetic, while at the same time never letting Daisy's misery go unchecked. 'Hey! None o' that, my girl!' she chided. 'You'll have me thinking it's *me* that's making you cry. And besides, you'll get wrinkles if you keep on like that.'

When she turned her head to look at Amy, the tears had gone and Daisy was smiling. 'Oh, Amy, lass, you always make me smile,' she said. 'I can't tell you how much I miss you when you're not here.' Her voice broke. 'You're all I've got now, lass.' And as she silently wept, Amy's heart was deeply moved.

'It's all right,' she whispered. 'Aw, Daisy, I can't bear to see you cry, so from now on . . . no more crying.' Brightening the mood, she gave a wag of the finger. 'I want smiles and plenty of 'em, yes?'

Daisy gave a little heartening laugh. 'All right.' She wiped away the tears. 'Help me up, will you, lass?' Putting her two arms out, she let herself be guided by Amy.

After much gentle pushing and shoving, and Daisy wincing with pain when the scars in her neck seemed to take her body weight, she was sitting up against the pillow.

The tremendous effort had taken it out of her, but, as always, Amy would not let her slip into a mood of self-pity. 'You've worn me out,' she groaned. 'Move over an' mek room for a little 'un. I need to lie down.'

'Don't be daft!' Daisy laughed, though painfully. '*I'm* the one who's ill, not you!'

Amy corrected her. 'You're not "ill",' she gently

chided. 'You were badly hurt and now you're on the mend. That's the top and bottom of it. And never forget, me and Jack are here for you. And so is Roy.'

At the mention of Roy's name, Daisy fell silent.

'Hey?' Amy cocked her head to see into Daisy's face. 'What's wrong?' She had not been too unduly concerned when the nurse had said how Daisy sent Roy packing. It wouldn't be the first time Daisy had suffered severe bouts of depression since the night of the fire.

Daisy turned, her eyes bright and pretty as ever, and her pained expression wringing Amy's heart. 'I try not to feel sorry for meself, lass,' she murmured, 'but I can't help feeling bitter. I'm bitter about what's happened. I hate myself, Amy. I hate what I look like, and I hate my life. Sometimes, I think I'd be better off out of it!'

'No, Daisy.' Amy held on to her. 'Don't talk like that.'

'And why not?'

'Look, Daisy, I know it's terrible what's happened to you, and I wish to God I could turn back the clock, but I can't and neither can you. But hard though it is—and I can only begin to imagine how badly you must feel—it's not the end of the world. All right, I know you might think it's easy for me to say, with you in that bed and me looking on, but listen to me, please?' Leaning forward, she held Daisy's sorry gaze. 'It won't always be like this, sweetheart. The doctors have already said all the scars but one will heal, and the other . . .' she let her gaze fall to the neck of Daisy's nightgown, where the scar was like an angry tramline running out of sight, '. . . it *will* fade, Daisy, until you can

332

hardly notice it.'

'I'll always notice it, and so will everybody else!' Snatching away, Daisy gave vent to her anger. 'I don't care what they say. I'll *always* be scarred and ugly. I'll never be like I was before.'

'These are good doctors, Daisy,' Amy argued. 'You *have* to believe them. If they say it will fade, then it will. They deal with these kind of injuries all the time.'

Daisy was having none of it. 'Just look at me, Amy. The doctors have done what they can, and I still look like a freak! I'll spend the rest of my life buttoned up to the ears like some old woman in winter, just to cover up the wretched scar.'

Amy countered Daisy's anger with her own. 'You have to trust the doctors, Daisy. You're not on your own. I'll be there for you. And there are other folks who love you and want to help. My mam and dad . . . Maureen. Even Ma Tooley has asked after you every day. She said you can have your old job back if you want it—'

'Huh!' Interrupting, Daisy made a cynical, comical face. 'That *would* frighten the customers away, wouldn't it, eh?'

Choosing to let the remark go, Amy reminded her, 'Then there's the most important person of all, and that's Roy. He's hurting so much, Daisy. He loves you more than you could ever realise. He blames himself for taking you to the factory in the first place. Jack says there's never a minute when he's not talking about you, and making plans for the future. So you see, Daisy, you *have* got a future. And when you and Roy are married, you'll have a whole new, wonderful life to look forward to, with your own house and children, and everything.' She

333

recalled what Daisy had told her not so long ago. 'Can't you see, Daisy? It's what you've allus wanted. You'll be living the dream, the one you carried in your heart all these years, and never told anybody, until me.'

As she pleaded with Daisy, Amy's emotion spilled over. She had been alarmed by what Daisy had said about being 'better off out of it'. It made her realise how low Daisy had sunk. She had to make Daisy understand that life was a precious gift and whatever happened, it was worth living every last minute. She needed to make her realise how much she would lose by caving in, and how much more she could gain by being strong.

'Don't brood on it, Daisy,' she pleaded. 'Whenever you feel down, talk to me, please. And talk to Roy. He'll help you through this, you know he will.'

Daisy gave a deep sigh. 'I've sent him away. I don't need him.'

Amy sat bolt upright. 'What d'you mean, you "don't need him"?'

Staring at the sheet, Daisy twisted it between her fingers. 'I don't want to be with him looking like this. Oh, I know he wants to marry me, and that would have been wonderful, but not now.' She raised her stricken eyes. 'Don't yer see, Amy, he would only be marrying me out of pity because he's blaming himself? But it's no good. I don't want to wake up one morning to catch him sneaking a look at these ugly scars . . . and regretting the day he married me.'

Amy was visibly shaken. 'Is that what you told him—that you thought he would only marry you now out of pity?'

'No! I told him I don't love him no more. I said I could never marry a man I didn't love, and that he'd best find somebody else. He were here when the doctor told me about the scar.' Her hand touching the ugly scar running to her breast, she choked back a sob. 'I saw the look on Roy's face; he were horrified, lass. He couldn't even look at me. I knew then what I had to do, so I sent him away. I told him if he tried to see me again, I'd tell the nurses not to let him in.'

'Oh, Daisy, that was so cruel.' Amy knew how devoted Roy was, because he'd opened his heart to her more than once since this awful thing had happened. 'If Roy looked horrified, it was probably because he blames himself for what happened; not because he couldn't bear to look at your scars.'

Daisy would not be gainsaid. 'You weren't here. You didn't see the look on his face!' She closed her eyes in anguish. 'When the doctor had gone, he went really quiet, and soon afterwards he said he had to go for a walk. He was gone for such a long time, and I was thinking how he'd run off . . . that he couldn't even stand to be with me. When he finally came back, I told him it was all over.'

Hard-eyed and determined, she stared at Amy. 'If I remember right, they say you have to be cruel to be kind, and that's what I'm doing . . . being kind to him. Even though he might not think it now.'

Amy was helpless. 'You'll regret it, Daisy. When you realise what you've thrown away, you'll change your mind.'

'Think about it, lass,' Daisy whispered. 'Take a good look at me an' ask yourself what bloke in his right mind would want to make love to me, eh?' Her agonised gaze went to the scar and for a moment it was as though she was mesmerised by it. 'I'm marked for life,' she murmured, 'and like it or not, I'd best get used to it. I know I did right,' she declared, returning her gaze to Amy. 'It's best for Roy, and best for me.'

'All right, Daisy, if that's what you really want.'

Later, God willing, when she had thought it through, Daisy might come to realise that Roy was her best chance of happiness.

'Sleep on it tonight,' Amy suggested, 'and we'll talk about it tomorrow.'

'I don't want to talk about it any more. I won't change my mind.'

There was another image she could not get out of her mind. 'I wonder who it was that we saw running away.' She moaned as though in pain. 'I wish I could describe him, but it was so quick and the figure was too shadowy.' Her frown deepened. 'Why would anyone want to set fire to the place, knowing we were in there?'

Amy had no answers either. 'I don't know,' she said. 'Whoever it was hasn't been found yet, but he will be. I'm sure of it.'

Drawing up the collar of her nightgown to hide the greater part of her scar, Daisy imparted a confidence. 'A mate of Roy's reckons it might have been Hammond's wife who did it. God knows, she's crazy enough to do summat like that. Happen she's grown tired of him, and she wants him destroyed.'

Glimpses of the old Daisy peeped through. 'Happen that night they had the humdinger of a row. Maybe with her old lover behind bars, she took some other bloke to her bed and Hammond found out. They fought about it, and she stormed out and set fire to his factory to get back at him.

Anyway, that's what Roy's mate reckons, and so do I.'

Amy was curious. 'Who is this mate of Roy's? I thought Jack was the only mate he had?'

Cursing herself for being loose-tongued, Daisy tried to cover up. 'It's just some fella he sees now and then.' Deliberately avoiding Amy's quizzical gaze, she finished limply, 'That's all I know.'

She slid down in the bed. 'You'd best go now, lass. I'm feeling tired.'

'Daisy, what is it you're not telling me?' Amy gently persisted.

Knowing she had already said too much, Daisy reluctantly thought it best to tell the truth, and anyway, as far as she knew, Amy had long ago got over Don Carson . . . at least she hoped so.

'All right. You might as well know,' she conceded. 'It's Don Carson. He and Roy became friends when Don got out of the nick some time back and, apparently, Roy still goes round to see him once in a while.' Falling back against the pillow, she continued in a wearier voice, 'Roy mentioned his name soon after we met. I never told you because I thought it might be better if you didn't know.'

'Don Carson? Good heavens, I had no idea he was still in Blackburn. And he's been in gaol? How come he never told me he'd been in gaol? What did he do to end up there?'

'I don't know, Amy. I don't think he was there long, so maybe it wasn't much.'

'What do you mean? It had to be "much" for him to receive a prison sentence. Heck, he could have done summat awful. We could have been married and living on the proceeds of crime!'

'No, Amy, I don't think it were like that. I reckon he were a small-time crook and he's learned his lesson. Roy says he's straight now.'

'How come everyone seems to know about this but me, then?' Amy was angry and indignant.

'Just me and Roy know, lass. That's all. And I reckon Don were ashamed to tell you he'd been in prison. That's why he couldn't go through with the wedding—'cos he knew he'd not be able to keep his secret for ever and he thought you'd think badly of him. He thought so much of you that he reckoned he could never live up to your goodness and honesty, according to Roy.'

'Oh, so you've been discussing me, have you?'

'No, lass. It wasn't like that,' Daisy was quick to assure her. 'I were mad about Don too and Roy knew the truth and wanted to reassure me you'd not been thrown over 'cos, as you thought, Roy didn't rate you highly enough. It were the exact opposite.'

Amy gave a little sigh and then smiled. 'Honestly, Daisy, the longer I live the more glad I am that I'm not married to Don Carson,' she said. 'It's a surprise to find him still around, and a friend of Roy's, but I put all thoughts of what might have been behind me long ago. Now I'm with Jack, and he's a far better man than Don Carson could ever be.'

Daisy gave a mischievous little smile. 'You love Jack, don't yer, lass?'

Amy hesitated, as the memory of Luke Hammond's kiss shot into her mind. She firmly suppressed the thought before answering with a warm, shy smile. 'Yes, Daisy. I think I do.'

But Amy could not quite leave their former

subject. 'Where's Don living now?'

'Johnson Street, not far up from where Roy lives.'

'I see . . .' Noting how tired Daisy was beginning to look, Amy urged her, 'You need to rest now. We can talk about this tomorrow, if you like. Is there anything you need—another nightie? Some magazines?' Gathering Daisy's washing from the cupboard, she stuffed it all into her bag.

Daisy held her back. 'Don't go yet, lass,' she pleaded. 'Stay a bit longer, eh?'

Concerned that Daisy was tiring herself, Amy insisted, 'No, Daisy. You need your sleep. Like I say, I'll be back tomorrow.'

'Your friend is right, young lady!' An officious-looking nurse marched towards them. 'You've done enough talking for one day.'

Amy gave Daisy a kiss on the forehead. 'Take care, love,' she said. 'You need to get your rest like the nurse said.' She knew how much Daisy liked the pictures. 'When you're feeling up to it, I'll treat you to the pictures. There's a Clark Gable film advertised and it looks really good. What d'you think?'

Daisy smiled wistfully. 'Let's not make too many plans, lass,' she said solemnly. 'There are other things to think on first . . . like getting me home and settled.'

Realising that it might be a long time before Daisy ventured into public places, Amy assured her, 'Whatever you want is fine by me.'

A moment later Amy was on her way out. When she turned at the door to say cheerio, it didn't surprise her to see Daisy already sleeping. 'Sleep tight,' Amy murmured. 'God bless.' With that she hurried down the corridor and out of the building.

*   *   *

That evening, after Marie and Dave had left for the pictures, Amy rushed about titivating and preening herself, ready for Jack's arrival.

'You look tired and haggard,' she told herself in the dressing-table mirror. 'Bags under your eyes and hair as dull as dishwater—what's he gonna think of you, eh?'

Drawing a hairband over her hair to keep it back from her face, she patted on her face cream to make her skin smooth, and gently pinched her cheeks to make them rosy.

That done, she dabbed on a film of powder, putting extra on her nose, which had a natural tendency to shine anyway. Wetting the mascara brush under the tap in the bathroom rather than spitting on it, she blackened the bristles from the messy little block to paint on spiky eyelashes just like Jean Harlow. A light touch of dusky pink Max Factor lipstick, and twelve deep strokes with the hairbrush to make her hair bounce and gleam, and she was ready.

'Well, that's a bit of an improvement,' she viewed herself in the mirror from every angle, 'but you'll never look beautiful, not in a million years.'

Being somewhat plain was something she had learned to live with, and now it didn't worry her that there were any number of young women her age who could put her in the shade for looks. There were other, more important things in life than looking beautiful. Her dad said she had a lovely nature and her mam said she had a winning

340

smile, so if that was the case she had a lot to be thankful for. And anyway if, ordinary as she was, she could attract a man like Jack, what did it matter?

She'd also attracted Luke Hammond, she thought, allowing herself a rare moment of vanity. He'd kissed her with real feeling—and he was married to a very beautiful woman, so people said.

Yes, that was the point, she chided herself for the hundredth time: *he was married*. But the thought of him was a reckless, guilty pleasure, a secret she knew it was wrong to indulge in, but which sometimes, even now, after all she had said to Luke, she had not the willpower to resist.

By seven forty-five, Amy was as ready as she would ever be. She emptied a bucket of coal into the grate to set the cheery fire nicely burning, then drew the curtains to shut out the dark, and within minutes the homely little parlour was as cosy as could be.

Giving herself instructions, Amy made her way to the kitchen, where she set about the few more tasks she needed to complete. 'We won't want much supper, because we'll both have had our teas,' she muttered. 'Later on, though, he might be hungry so I'd best make some ham sandwiches . . .'

Happy that she was about to see Jack, and softly singing to herself, she cut half a dozen chunky slices from the loaf and filled them generously with ham, before lightly coating the ham in a thin layer of mustard. 'I hope he likes mustard.'

It suddenly occurred to her that she didn't know all that much about his taste in food, except he enjoyed a pint mug of tea, liked fish and chips straight out of the paper, and was partial to a meat and tatty pie from the barrow on King Street.

She smiled a happy smile. 'What I don't know about him, I'm sure I'll soon find out,' she murmured.

Arranging the sandwiches on two plates, she took them to the larder where she put them on the shelf and covered them over.

She then filled the kettle with water and put it on the gas stove. While that was coming to the boil, she resumed the singing, got out the large brown teapot and scooped four spoons of tealeaves into it.

Now it was a case of preparing the tray, with plates and knives, teaspoons, cups and saucers, sugar and milk, and a tea-strainer.

Just as the tray was dressed, the kettle began to whistle, so turning off the gas, she went to the window. 'No sign of him yet.' Her voice was marbled with disappointment.

She looked down the street. It was empty, save for a mangy dog and a group of girls twittering and giggling as they chased each other along the cobbles.

Returning into the parlour, she glanced at the clock. 'He should be here any minute.' She gave a deep, contented sigh. 'Until Daisy asked me, I didn't realise just how much I love being with him.' In fact, Jack was beginning to mean more to her with every passing day.

A few minutes later when she had only just finished clearing away the bread-knife and other paraphernalia, the familiar tap came on the window.

'D'you intend leaving me out in the cold all night?' When she ran to the window Jack's smiling, handsome face stared back at her. 'You're a wicked woman, you are!'

Hurrying to the door, Amy quickly drew him inside. 'I'm sorry,' she told him with a bright smile. 'I looked down the street only a minute or two since and there was no sign of you.'

He took her in his arms. 'Do I get a kiss or what?'

Her answer was to raise her face to his. 'You can have two if you like.'

He laughed. 'Hussy!' But he kissed her all the same; three times, each kiss as wonderful as the others.

With his gaze coveting her face, and his thoughts telling him what a lucky bloke he was, he told her how he'd been looking forward all day to seeing her. 'Matter o' fact, I haven't been able to think about anything else.'

Taking off his jacket, he hung it on the hook behind the door. Afterwards he walked her to the parlour with his arm round her waist and a look of admiration in his eyes. 'You look wonderful,' he said, laughing softly when she blushed bright pink.

Amy loved it when he laughed like that—kindly but heartily, and she loved it even more when he slid his arm round her, holding her tight as he could, as though he wanted never to let go of her. It gave her a warm, comfortable glow inside. It made her feel safe.

Yet the more she thought of serious, lifetime commitment, the more nervous she became. After all, when a woman had been let down as badly as she had, it seemed almost reckless to offer herself to another man; even a man as trustworthy and loyal as Jack. The habit of blaming herself could not be easily abandoned, despite what Daisy had told her at the hospital earlier.

The thought made her anxious, and the anxiety showed in her quietness.

'Penny for them?' Having returned from the cellar with a newly filled bucket of coal for the fire, Jack came across the kitchen to where Amy had finished setting the tray. 'I've been standing there watching you, my lovely.' His two arms closed round her waist from behind, and his voice whispered soft in her ear. 'Is there something troubling you?'

Startled, Amy swung round, still enclosed in his embrace and the quick, ready smile on her face belying her thoughts. 'It's summat and nothing,' she answered, giving him a kiss on the mouth.

Jack, though, was not so easily put off. 'I've come to know you pretty well,' he retaliated, 'and I know when you're worried. So, whatever it is, I'd like you to share it with me.' He gave her a quizzical look. 'You never know, I might even be able to help.'

Amy knew she could not reveal all the doubts she had with regard to their future, so she confessed to the other thing that had been playing on her mind. 'It's Don—Don Carson. He's a man I was once going to marry, but he broke off our engagement just before the wedding.'

Jack was stunned. 'Don Carson! I know of him. Good grief, Amy, when was this?'

'In the summer of 1931. It was awful, Jack. I thought he'd left me because I wasn't good enough for him. He was more worldly, had lived a bit, and I thought he'd seen me for what I was—for what I felt afterwards—a silly little girl, plain and homespun.'

'No, lass, never. You're the sweetest, kindest girl a man could hope to love. And Don Carson—he's a bad 'un. You're well rid of him. He's a friend of Roy's, but it's not a friendship I care to see flourish.'

Amy gave a little laugh. 'Well, I learned summat today that threw a new light on him, and, I have to say, you could just be right.'

'What? Where did you learn of this? You haven't seen him, have you?'

'No, don't worry, Jack. I haven't seen him and I don't intend to. He's past, done with, in my life. In fact, I didn't even know he was still in Blackburn. But at the hospital today Daisy told me about Don being a friend of Roy's—and that he'd broken our engagement because he had been in prison and was too ashamed to tell me. He thought I'd find out about the prison in the end and he couldn't face that.'

'Oh, love, I would hate to think of my gentle Amy with a husband like that. The only decent thing about him is that he saw he wasn't good enough for you—and even then he couldn't own up and tell you the truth.'

'I'm trying to get used to this new way of seeing things after feeling such a fool for so long,' Amy admitted.

'Fool nothing. The only fool is Don Carson. I'm right sorry you were hurt, and I'm glad you've told me all this.' He paused to consider, then asked tentatively, 'You don't feel the slightest thing for him now?'

'No!' said Amy. She looked straight into Jack's anxious eyes. 'No, nothing at all, I promise. But I wanted to tell you that I'd once been in love with

345

him, and going to be married, especially as he's still around Blackburn. Oh Lord, I'd hate to bump into him in the street. I just didn't want you to find out and be hurt because I hadn't told you, even though you've nowt to be hurt about.'

'Oh, Amy, you're a grand lass. You'd have been wasted on a ne'er-do-well like Don Carson, and I'm a lucky fella to have found you. Now you're sure there's nothing else worrying you? You're looking pretty tonight but I can see you're tired, even so.'

'It's Daisy.'

'What about her?' He knew Amy was deeply concerned about Daisy, for he had been with Amy every step of the way, and he was also concerned for Daisy, and for Roy, who had taken Daisy's rejection badly.

'Only that she's very down at the moment, saying she'd be better off dead and fretting about her big scar. I try to jolly her out of it, but I can understand her depression all too well.'

'But you've been telling me every time I see you how much Daisy's improving. She will get better— it just has to be got through. And maybe you're feeling down yourself, with all your hospital visits.'

'You're right—of course,' Amy smiled, but she still looked anxious.

Jack suspected the news of Don Carson being around was still weighing on Amy's mind. Maybe a tiny part of her still feared that the relationship between themselves might in the end go the same way as her previous one. He had no doubt at all that once he and Amy had embarked on their lives together, their love would only grow deeper and stronger.

Meantime, he would try and prove that all he

wanted was to love and care for her, and be the man she deserved because, in the short space of time that he had known Amy, he realised without a shadow of a doubt, that she was the only one for him.

Now, with the warmth of her body merging with his, he wanted her as never before. 'I love you so much, my darling,' he whispered. 'You know that, don't you?'

Amy knew it only too well. 'I love you too, Jack,' she answered, and when it came, the kiss was long and passionate.

They went to sit entwined together on the sofa, kissing and holding each other close, content in each other's company. They chatted and kissed and occasionally held hands, and it wasn't long before the conversation turned to Daisy and Roy, and the way Daisy had sent him on his way.

'D'you think they'll make up?' Amy was so concerned.

'I don't know about that,' Jack answered. 'The trouble is, they're both headstrong, and sometimes Roy has a clumsy way of showing his feelings.' He groaned. 'All I know is that he's been impossible all day—dropping things, forgetting things, a face like a wet weekend, and the look of a little lost boy. Poor soul.'

In reply, Amy revealed that Daisy had seemed the same. 'So, what can we do about it?'

Jack could see only one way. 'Try and get the pair of 'em back together, and make them see sense, that's all we can do. The rest is up to them.'

'I hope for their own sakes, they can make up,' Amy remarked. 'Daisy loves him so much, and still she seems determined not to talk it all through with him. She says he can't stand to look at her scars and she doesn't want him to end up hating her because of them. She says he's grown distant, but I told her, that's only because he blames himself for taking her to the factory in the first place. But she won't listen. She's determined it's over, and nothing I say will make her change her mind.'

Jack had seen the other side of it. 'Roy's thrown himself into work like a madman. He's determined to make good. Honest to God, Amy, he's besotted with Daisy.'

A moment of contemplation, then a smile from Amy. Climbing over the cushion to him, she entwined her fingers in Jack's. 'So . . . is that how you feel about me?' she asked in a murmur. 'Besotted?'

He gazed into her eyes and the look spoke for itself. 'You know I am,' he whispered, the tip of his tongue following the fullness of her mouth. 'Absolutely and totally besotted.'

Suddenly he curled his arm round her body and drew her beside him, holding her so tight she could hardly breathe. 'Oh, Amy! Won't you trust me?' With the tip of his finger under her chin, he raised her face so he could look directly into her eyes again. 'You know I would never hurt you.'

Now, as she let her gaze linger with his, there flowed between them a world of understanding. 'I do trust you,' she answered. Only now did it dawn on her that if she were to lose him for whatever reason, her life would be all the emptier for it.

He closed his eyes, took a deep breath, then in a strong, determined voice said, 'Marry me!'

Amy kissed him lightly on the mouth, her eyes smiling up at him, and her heart giving the answer

348

this time. 'All right. I will.'

'What!' He leaped up and, taking her with him, swung her round and round. 'D'you mean it?' he shouted for joy. 'You'll marry me? You really will marry me?' He laughed and danced, cherishing the moment. 'When?'

'Whenever you like.' Amy knew it was time. Time to start trusting again. Time to begin a new life, with Jack, the man she loved. 'We can name the day, if you like.'

Afraid she might change her mind in the cold light of day, Jack snatched the opportunity. 'Easter Saturday,' he urged daringly.

Amy was caught unawares. 'But that's only about ten weeks away!' But the moment of doubt was short-lived. 'All right!' She threw her arms round his neck. 'Easter Saturday it is,' she announced, 'and the sooner folks know about it, the better.' Like Jack, she had the smallest, sneakiest fear that if she didn't do it soon, she never would.

But there were two people that neither of them wanted to tell just yet. With luck by the time the happy news got to Roy and Daisy, they would have resolved their differences and be making plans for their own future.

Meantime, Fate had her own way of dealing with such matters. And the news that came through the following day was a blow to them all.

PART FOUR
February 1934
Hard Decisions and Repercussions

CHAPTER FIFTEEN

Saturday the third of February was a day of great excitement in the Atkinson household. At long last, Daisy was coming home.

'Anybody'd think royalty were coming to stay!' Dave too was delighted that Daisy was now considered well enough to leave the infirmary. 'By! You've worked hard, I'll say that for the pair of you. It looks grand in here.'

He roved his critical gaze round the back bedroom, and took stock of the soft cream-coloured walls, painted by Amy's own hand, and the new pale blue curtains made by his talented wife, Marie, and there on the floor a pretty flowered rug, almost identical in pattern to the bedspread.

'You did right in persuading her to come here with us,' he said. 'One thing's for sure, she can't go to her parents' house.' Rolling his eyes heavenward he commented angrily, 'Them buggers would drive her to drink inside of a week!'

'Going to her parents was never an option, Dad,' Amy agreed. Getting up from the hearth where she had been polishing the rose-patterned tiles surrounding the iron fireplace, she dropped her cleaning rags into the bucket. 'So! You think she'll like her bedroom, do you?'

It was Marie who answered for both of them. 'She'll love it, lass. When Daisy comes through that door, she'll be like a cat wi' two tails, you see if I'm not right.'

'Aye, lass!' Dave confirmed. 'She'll be coming

home in style, so she will.' He gave a winning, knowing grin. 'I can't wait to drive that grand little car of Steve's,' he chuckled. 'A Morris Oxford six, no less. By! He treats that car like a bairn. I never dreamed he'd let me behind the wheel, and here he is, offering it to fetch Daisy home. I told him my car were in the garage having the engine looked at . . . all that spluttering when I start it up! Still, all's well that ends well, 'cos when I mentioned how Daisy needed to be brought home from the infirmary, he didn't hesitate. Like the good man he is, he offered me the car there and then.'

Amy wagged a finger. 'I bet you didn't tell him that you could have taken the car in two days earlier, and still got it back in time to collect Daisy, did you, eh?'

'Never crossed my mind,' Dave chuckled. 'Mind you, he can't drive the car 'cos of his gammy leg, so the way I see it, everything's worked out for the best.'

Marie laughed. 'Except for his gammy leg.'

'You'd best mind how you go in it,' Amy warned. 'If you so much as scratch it, he'll have your guts for garters, and never mind all the favours you've done for him.'

Amy got herself ready, and half an hour later, she and her dad were on their way.

Dave still couldn't get over his good fortune. 'By! This is what you'd call a car!' Stroking the plush leather he almost drooled over it. 'By the time me and your mam retire, I mean to have one of these.'

Amy was also impressed—and not only with the red leather and the walnut dashboard. It surprised her how fast the little car travelled along, with the

354

speedometer showing no less than thirty-five miles an hour, and on a long straight it was even nearing forty.

'You'd best slow down a bit, Dad,' she warned. 'We need to get there safely for Daisy.'

At the infirmary, Dave stayed with the car in front of the main steps, while Amy ran up to the ward.

'I've come to fetch Daisy,' she told the friendly receptionist. 'I can't wait to get her home.'

So full was she of Daisy actually coming home with her, Amy didn't realise how quiet and nervous the receptionist was.

Fortunately Nurse Rita came along and was able to tell Amy the disconcerting news. 'She left early this morning,' Amy was informed kindly.

Amy stared disbelievingly at the nurse. 'Left? What d'you mean? . . . She can't have left.' A sudden thought made her smile. 'Oh, no! She hasn't left yet! She must be in the bathroom, collecting her bits and bobs. Y'see, Daisy's coming home with us this morning. I know you've been away for a few days and maybe you weren't told, but the arrangement is that we take her home today. The papers were signed and everything. Dad's outside now, so is it all right if I go and get her?'

Knowing what a very special friend Amy had been to Daisy, Nurse Rita was loath to tell her the truth, and there was no easy way to do so. She took Amy by the arm and, leading her to a nearby chair, sat her down.

'Daisy was waiting for me when I arrived first thing this morning,' the nurse began. 'The truth is, before I went on my short break, we had a little talk. Daisy told me how she needed to get right away from everything. Her life was in tatters— that's what she said—and if she didn't have time on her own, to think and plan, and decide what to do for the best, she believed things would never come right again.'

Amy couldn't believe it. 'I don't understand. She has *me*. I'll always look after her. She could have had all the peace and quiet she needed. I would never let her be hurt, not by anyone, and if she thought I would bully her into getting back with Roy, she must know I would never interfere. All I want is what's best for Daisy. I love her, Nurse Rita. She's like family to me. I just want to take care of her.' Amy's voice shook with emotion, but she swallowed the tears and regained her composure. 'Don't tell me her parents came and took her away?' she asked fearfully.

'No. They don't even know she's left the infirmary.' In a softer voice the nurse confided, 'Even if they did, I'm not sure they would care one way or the other!'

'I know you and Daisy got on really well,' Amy said, 'and I know Daisy trusted you . . .'

'Yes, she did.'

Amy hesitated, but had to ask: 'Do you know where she's gone?'

There was a moment's pause before the nurse answered, albeit reluctantly, 'Yes, I do.'

Amy felt a surge of anger. 'So, where is she?'

'I'm sorry, Amy,' Nurse Rita was genuinely apologetic, 'I can't tell you that.'

'Please!' Amy was desperate. 'I need to see her. I need to be there for her.'

'I know you do, Amy, but—don't you see?—

that's exactly why Daisy needed to get away. She knows how much you care for her, and more than anyone else, she knows how much of yourself you've given these many weeks.' She paused, tempted to tell Amy of Daisy's whereabouts, but reluctant to break a promise. 'Daisy feels that she's put on you enough. Now she needs the time and space to make decisions. You have to allow her that, Amy. You know it as well as I do.'

Reaching into her breast pocket she took out a small envelope, which she handed to Amy. 'She told me to give you this.'

Tearing open the letter, Amy read it through a blur of tears.

Dearest Amy,

Nurse Rita has found me a wonderful place where I can be alone for a while. I need time to think and work out what I really want. I need to accept the things that have happened to me, so I can decide which way to go.

I know I should have confided in you, lass, but you would only have worried. Now you needn't worry, because I know I have to do this myself, and maybe, after a time, I'll be able to live my life. I don't know, lass. All I do know is, if I can't be away from everyone and everything, I might do summat very bad, and I think you know what I mean.

You were right. I should never have sent Roy away. I love him so much, but right now I'm so confused, I don't know what I really want.

You and Roy have to trust me. Leave me alone. Please. I need this time on my own. Don't either of you try to find me, or you'll undo everything. I'll be

in touch.
Don't worry, lass.
Luv you.
Daisy XX

Slowly replacing the letter in its envelope, Amy asked, 'If I write a reply, will you see that she gets it?'

'Of course I will.'

Rita led Amy to the counter, where she gave her pen and paper before standing back. Amy wrote:

Dear Daisy,
I think I understand what you mean, and I promise, I won't try and contact you.

If Nurse Rita doesn't mind, I will write to you now and again, and maybe you'll send me a note to say how you're getting on. But, if you don't want to, that's all right.

I'm glad you haven't altogether pushed Roy out of your life, but if you did, then that would be your decision and nothing to do with anyone else, including me.

Take care of yourself, Daisy. I'll be thinking of you while you're away.
God bless,
Lots of love,
Amy XX

After folding the note into the envelope, she handed it to Nurse Rita, with her thanks.

Nurse Rita put the envelope in her breast pocket. 'Don't you worry now,' she said. 'I'll make sure Daisy gets the note.' With that she excused herself and made off down the corridor to tend her ever demanding duties.

Outside, Dave waited and worried, and when he saw Amy coming down the steps without Daisy, he jumped out of the car and ran towards her.

'What's happened?' he asked. 'Where's Daisy? There's nothing wrong, is there?'

Without a word, Amy handed him the letter.

While he read it, she watched his face. After a moment his changing expression told her that he was as shocked as she had been. 'My God!' Looking up, he asked, 'Did you ask the nurse where she'd gone? Did she tell anyone?'

'Daisy did confide in the nurse, but she wouldn't tell me,' Amy answered. 'Daisy made her promise not to tell anyone, me included.'

'I see . . .' Dave glanced back towards the main doors. 'I see.'

He said that once more, then he slid his arm round Amy's shoulders, and with his usual calm manner, told her sternly, 'You have to do as she says. You know that, don't yer?'

'I know.'

'And you'll have to tell Roy.'

'I'll tell him.' Though there was, at least, one consolation. 'She still loves him. She says so in the letter.' Amy smiled up at her father. 'Maybe Daisy's right, Dad,' she said. 'Maybe she does need the time to sort her thoughts out. Afterwards, who knows? Maybe she and Roy will get back together and Daisy will be happy again . . . like she deserves to be.'

Dave slowly nodded his agreement. 'D'you know summat, lass?'

'What's that?'

'I've come to the conclusion that our Daisy is a

wise old head on young shoulders.'

Amy couldn't help but be concerned for her hapless, lovable friend. 'Do you think she'll be all right, Dad?'

'She'll be fine. Like you say, give her the time she asked for, and I'm sure, in the end, she'll surprise us all.'

'You're right, Dad, and Daisy knows I'll do whatever she asks, as long as it's for her own good.'

Now when Amy looked up, her smiling eyes were swimming with tears. 'Ever since I've known her,' she gave a funny, broken little laugh, 'she's been nothing but trouble.'

Dave walked with her down the steps. 'Daisy's a lucky lass,' he murmured.

Amy was surprised by his comment. 'Why's that?'

With pride glowing in his face he answered softly, ' 'Cos she's got you, lass. The best friend anybody could ever 'ave.'

*   *   *

'Now then, young lady!' Mother Superior was a large, Irish, rosy-faced woman with hands the size of shovels and a heart as big as an elephant. 'There are three tings you need to remember while you're convalescing in this convent of St Mary Magdalene.'

She listed them off. 'Forstly, everyone pulls their weight, so they do! Unless they're too sick or useless to carry out even the smallest task.' Looking at Daisy with raised eyebrows she asked smartly, 'Would that be you now?'

Daisy was equally adamant. 'I'm not sick and I'm

not useless, and I'm used to hard work.'

'Good!' The nun went on, 'Secondly, we don't stand for fighting nor arguing in this establishment. You must understand this is God's house and we're only given charge of it! Do you foight?'

'No.' Daisy thought it a strange thing to ask. 'I usually get on with everybody.'

'Foine, foine!'

Mother Superior allowed herself a bit of a smile. 'And thirdly, we have to be disciplined, and we have to be respectful. D'you tink you could manage that?'

'I think so, yes.'

'Hmm! Well, I don't tink you can!' She elaborated. 'Forstly, I have a title, so I do! A title I might add, which has not come easy. The title is Mother Superior, and whenever anyone addresses me, that's the title I go by. So now, I'll ask you again.' Taking a deep breath she seemed to add another six inches to the girth of her already sizeable breast. 'I've told you the three tings that are important to us here. Now then, young lady, do you tink you're able to comply with *all three*?' She winked one eye and glared at Daisy through the other. 'Moind how you answer now!' she warned.

Daisy did 'moind'. 'Yes,' she said. 'I'm certain I can comply with all three things, thank you . . . Mother Superior.' She emphasised the last two words with slow deliberation, but not so slow she might seem disrespectful.

She must have done it right, because now the big woman was smiling from ear to ear. 'Report to Sister Charlotte in the laundry. Right away now, off you go. Down those steps and into the cellar wit you.' Pointing to the door at the end of the hallway,

361

she half turned, but then as Daisy was about to open the door, she called her back. 'Daisy?'

'Yes, Mother Superior?' Daisy was convinced it was a test. She was wrong, though.

'You have a scar, do you not?' The nun had been told of Daisy's problem, and though she thought it a heavy burden for a young woman to carry, she considered it her duty to make sure the burden was not a crippling one. After all, Daisy had come here for help, and help she would get.

Daisy was momentarily taken aback by the question, but then she realised that Nurse Rita must have given that as part of the reason why she needed to be here. 'Yes, Mother Superior,' she answered. 'I was in a fire.'

'Does the scar bother you?'

Daisy hesitated. 'Sometimes.'

'What was that you said?' The voice was sharp and reprimanding.

'Sorry, *Mother Superior*. No. It doesn't bother me—at least, not all the time.'

'That's no good, child. You mustn't let it bother you *at all*. Sure the Good Lord gives us only what we can deal wit and no more. Learn to be strong. Can you do that?'

Daisy nodded. 'I'll try, Mother Superior.'

Mother Superior nodded. 'So you will. So you will!' And that said, she ambled away, to good-naturedly torment some other poor unsuspecting soul.

On her way down the narrow, spiralling stone steps to the laundry, Daisy thought about the Mother Superior. 'That one would frighten the devil himself,' she muttered. Then she began to smile. The smile became a chuckle, and then a hearty laugh.

One thing was certain, Daisy told herself. If you needed a lesson in life, then this was the place to visit. Somehow, it put everything into perspective.

CHAPTER SIXTEEN

'I swear to God, I've never seen a man so changed.' Having popped into the shop on his way home, old Ted Fogarty raised the subject of Luke Hammond with Marie and Maureen. 'By! That poor devil must have been through hell and back, with all that's gone on. Working night and day, they say, trying to get the business up and running again, with nowt to sell and no vans to deliver it if he had.'

Marie agreed. 'It seems unfair that one man should have had so much of a burden.' She glanced at Maureen, who was sweeping up the cabbage leaves where they'd fallen from the crates. 'Drop 'em into a bag,' she suggested. 'Young Johnny can run 'em down to the Barnes' house. They've been given a floppy-eared rabbit, an' it's got the appetite of a full-grown donkey!'

'Yer right, Marie.' Ted was still preoccupied with Luke Hammond's situation. 'It's a bad thing. I thank the Good Lord it ain't resting on *my* shoulders, I can tell yer that for nuthin'!'

Marie gave him his wad of baccy. 'That'll be threepence,' she said, holding out her hand.

Ted rummaged about in his purse. 'First his wife is beaten up and left damaged beyond repair, and then his factory burns down. It's a terrible, shocking thing!'

Marie still had her hand out, waiting for his loose change, but her thoughts were elsewhere. 'I wonder what Luke Hammond will do now?'

Ted slapped a handful of coins into her palm. 'Sort that lot out, will yer, lass?' he said. 'I can't see a damned thing wi'out me specs.'

While Marie sorted out his loose change he addressed Maureen, who had now come to collect a batch of brown paper bags from beneath the counter. 'Yer seem to have settled down really well, lass,' he remarked. 'No doubt you'll be staying for good now, eh?'

Maureen smiled. 'I hope so,' she answered, pulling out the thick band of bags. 'Me and Johnny are more than content living in Derwent Street. Besides, Johnny starts school soon, so it looks like you're stuck with us.' Also Amy had heard Ma Tooley was looking to fill Daisy's old job at the café, and had mentioned Maureen to the old lady with some trepidation. Mrs Tooley had employed her straight away, saying she'd always wanted to have 'a more mature person' working for her.

'Aye,' Ted grinned his gummy grin, 'an' you're stuck with us, an' all.' The grin became a frown. 'All the same, it's a wonder all this awful business ain't made you want to run a mile.'

Maureen quickly dismissed his fears. 'This is our home now. But you're right in what you just said about Mr Hammond. He really has been through a bad time.'

She thought of her Arnie, likely to remain in gaol for some years yet. Funny that—Maureen realised she was able to accept that her husband was fully responsible for his violent temper and that he was being justly punished for it. She seldom

364

visited the prison these days. She had deliberately distanced herself from his influence and the bullying she suffered even when he was behind bars, with his suicide threats and his whinging. Now, living alone with her beloved son, surrounded by friends, working hard and gaining in confidence, she could at last see Arnold Stratton for what he was—a thug and a bully; a man who liked to have power over women. So let him rot in gaol. She was better off without him, and so was Johnny.

Maureen looked around the crowded little shop where less than a year ago she had been welcomed so kindly by Amy and Marie, who she had grown to love so much. No, she would not be moving on. This really was home at last.

Marie took Ted's baccy money and returned his change. 'Stop trying to frighten her away,' she said with a friendly wag of the finger.

'Aw, I wouldn't do that,' he replied. 'She's a grand lass, is Mrs Langdon.'

After he'd gone, Marie served a young woman who'd come in as Ted left and then went to help Maureen collect the cabbage leaves.

When she saw how quiet Maureen had gone, she blamed it on Ted Fogarty. 'You don't want to let him upset you with his alarmist talk,' she said. 'You know what he's like: one minute he's flirting, and the next he's putting the world to rights.'

But Maureen was thinking of Arnie, and the bad things he had done, so when she didn't respond, Marie put on her brightest smile, and changed the subject. 'Why don't you and little Johnny come round to us tonight?' she suggested. 'I'll mek us a nice tea. As you already know, our Amy's gone with Nurse Rita today, so she might have more news of Daisy. Jack will be here, and Roy too. It'll be like a little party. What d'you say?'

After what old Ted had said got her thinking, Maureen didn't feel like being amongst company. 'Thank you, Marie, it's really kind of you,' she answered graciously, 'only I thought I might take Johnny up the park, to feed the ducks before it gets dark.'

'Aw, that's all right.' Marie dropped the last cabbage leaf into the bag. 'You two go and enjoy yourselves. I'll cook plenty of everything, though,' she decided. 'That way, if you change your mind, you'll not go short on food.'

A few minutes later, Maureen and Johnny were ready to leave. 'Has Mrs Tooley offered you more hours yet?' Marie held her back for a minute or two.

'Not yet,' Maureen answered, 'but I reckon she will, 'cause the other girl she's taken on is absolutely useless—or so Mrs Tooley keeps telling me, in between giving me a detailed rundown on her latest romance.' She chuckled, but not unkindly. 'I tell you, Marie, it makes me curl up, the way she goes on about her randy old sweetheart, and how she has to fight him off.'

They laughed at that. 'But you have to give her credit,' Marie said. 'Old Ma Tooley is one of a kind. Here she is, sixty-eight years old if she's a day; running a business, and still keeping the men interested.'

Maureen agreed. 'There aren't many young 'uns that could manage that,' she declared, 'never mind a woman her age.'

'And are you happy working there?'

'Yes, and I've got Amy to thank,' Maureen

answered. 'If she hadn't gone to see Ma Tooley, I would never have got the work. But now, what with you giving me a few hours, and then the extra hours at Tooley's Café, I'm managing all right.'

She took hold of Johnny's hand and made her way to the door. 'We'd best be off now. Give my regards to Amy, and tell her I hope everything's all right with Daisy. If I don't come round tonight, I'll see you both tomorrow.'

Smiling to herself at the idea of Ma Tooley and her aged sweetheart, Marie locked the shop door while she got herself a sandwich.

When she opened up again, Amy still wasn't home. And, with Maureen and the boy gone, the little shop seemed uncomfortably quiet. It had been a real blessing the day Maureen and Johnny had first come to the shop. Marie now couldn't imagine life without the reticent and private young mother and her gentle little boy.

*   *   *

It was three thirty when Amy arrived at the infirmary to meet Nurse Rita. 'I don't know how to thank you for getting Daisy to see me,' she said gratefully.

'It wasn't too difficult this time,' the older woman answered. 'She seems ready to see you now.' She gave a wry little smile. 'Maybe I won't need to take letters backwards and forwards between you now, eh?'

Amy was excited at the prospect of seeing Daisy at long last. 'When can we go?'

'In about five minutes. My shift is finished, so if we don't get an emergency before I get my hat and coat, we can be off out the door, and you'll be seeing Daisy in about half an hour, if my reckoning is right.'

As it turned out her reckoning was spot on.

They came out of the building, caught a tram to Mill Hill to the south-west of Blackburn town centre, and from there they boarded a bus, which took them out of town and on towards Lytham St Annes. Halfway there, they disembarked.

'The convent is just five minutes' walk from here,' Nurse Rita said. 'Hopefully, once we arrive, they'll offer us a nice hot cup of tea and a scone.'

The narrow, meandering path up to the door of the convent was lined with early daffodils and as the visitors climbed, the way got prettier and narrower, and so steep that Amy wondered if they were climbing all the way up to Heaven.

Mother Superior's round red face greeted them with a smile. A younger nun, who was introduced as Sister Mary, hovered behind her. 'Ah! Will ye look at the two of youse, frozen to the bone, and stomachs rumbling, no doubt? Come in wit ye before ye freeze on the doorstep.'

Ushering them inside she introduced herself to Amy.

'I'll have scones and tea sent to you and your friend,' she told her, then addressing herself to Nurse Rita, she invited cheerfully, 'You can come along wit me.'

Knowing the heavy work burden carried by Mother Superior, Nurse Rita gracefully declined. 'Thank you, that's very kind, but I don't mind waiting out here . . . or I could go and have a word with the girls in the laundry, if that's all right with you?'

Mother Superior wouldn't hear of it. 'You'll do no such ting! Wit all the charity work you do on our behalf and all the kindness you've shown to the poor wretches who find their way through these doors, don't ye tink ye deserve to rest your weary feet?' She looked Rita up and down. 'Come straight from the infirmary, have ye?'

'More or less.'

'Ah, well!' Mother Superior's smile was a joy to see. 'There ye are then! Will ye come and sit wit me, and we'll have a little chat, so we will?' She gave the cheekiest wink. 'D'ye know what I'm tinking?' She lowered her voice. 'Sure I'm tinking . . . I might even have a little red wine, left over from a crisis we had last week.'

She then summoned Sister Mary to accompany Amy to the dayroom and, taking Nurse Rita by the arm, she marched her unceremoniously to her office. 'Sure I'll not take no for an answer.'

As they went from the hallway, Sister Mary gave Amy a knowing wink. 'Mother Superior likes to keep a little wine locked away,' she said with a chuckle, 'for emergencies and bad weather, or so she says.' She gave another, heartier chuckle. 'And if you believe that, you'll believe anything!'

Amy had to stop herself from laughing out loud. She thought Sister Mary was delightful. As a matter of fact she thought she wouldn't mind spending a day or two in this lovely place herself, it was so amiable.

It was also a beautiful, calming place as she observed when following Sister Mary along the corridors. Amy had never seen such beauty. The walls were panelled in richly carved walnut, and above them the ceilings dripped with beautiful

369

work by ancient artists. The daylight shone in through the many stained-glass windows, to illuminate the magnificent creations embedded in the glass: sun-rays and stars and Biblical figures, bathed in all the colours of the rainbow.

Beneath Amy and Sister Mary's feet the wood-blocked floors were lovingly polished, and as they walked along, the sound of their footsteps seemed to sing out in a peculiar, rhythmic melody.

'Ah! Here we are.' Swinging round the corner, Sister Mary pushed open the heavy wooden door. 'Daisy, here's your friend to see you.'

Thin and waif-like, Daisy was curled up on the window-seat, her gaze focused on the gardener as he went about his pruning. She didn't look up or speak, and made no move towards them.

Sister Mary had seen it all before and understood. 'Go to her, child,' she whispered in Amy's ear. 'If you need me, I'll be right next door, catching up on my paperwork. First door on the left as you leave this room.'

When Amy turned to thank her, she was gone, with the door still swinging shut.

Nervous, Amy ventured forward, her mind in chaos at the sight of Daisy looking so forlorn. Had she done right in coming here? Was it fair to force herself on Daisy before she was ready? And was she being selfish in wanting Daisy to hear of her engagement, and expecting her to be a part of the wedding celebrations? All the doubts began to flood in. But mostly, she desperately needed to know that Daisy was going to be all right, that she was stronger now, and more able to deal with things.

'Daisy?' Her voice sounded thin and weak, like

that of a tiny child, while her heart was beating fifteen to the dozen. She felt she had to leave, yet she needed to stay. For Daisy's sake she needed to be here, to help, and comfort. And so she continued across the room. 'Daisy?'

Daisy hardly moved a muscle. Instead, she kept her gaze averted, watching the gardener as he wheeled his barrow over the stony ground.

Another step, and Amy was both thrilled and surprised when Daisy turned to look at her.

'Are you all right, Daisy?' she asked tenderly.

Dropping her gaze, Daisy looked away.

Amy came closer until she could almost touch her. 'I so much wanted to see you, Daisy,' she whispered. 'I'm sorry. If you tell me to go, I will.' Her voice broke and the tears threatened. 'You know I'll do whatever you want.' When Daisy turned and looked directly at her, Amy's composure broke and the tears ran down her face. 'Oh, Daisy . . . I've missed you so much!'

Suddenly Daisy was in her arms and the two of them held on to each other, as though afraid they might be separated for ever if they were to let go.

They cried and laughed, and when Amy held her friend at arm's length, she saw how the scar on her neck had faded. It was still an intrusion to the eye, but it wasn't angry or vivid red, and Daisy did not have her collar turned up to hide it. 'Are you all right?' she asked her again, and Daisy nodded; but she didn't say anything about the scar, or her state of mind, or whether she had come to terms with what had happened to her.

Instead, she told Amy, 'I'm sorry I didn't want to see you before.'

Amy understood. 'I'm here now,' she said. 'You

can tell me how it's been, if you want to?'

Just then there came a tap on the door, and an elderly woman entered with a trolley on which was a selection of cakes and a pot of tea with all the necessaries. 'I was instructed to fetch this along,' she informed them. 'Is it all right?'

'It's lovely, Annie,' Daisy said quietly. 'Thank you.'

Annie grinned and went away, content to be appreciated.

'She was thrown out of her home when her son decided to get married,' Daisy told Amy. 'Now she'll stay here for the rest of her days.'

While Amy took off her coat, Daisy poured the tea, and as she did her hands were slightly trembling. When she handed the cup and saucer to Amy, the trembling seemed to worsen.

Amy took the cup and, wrapping her other hand round Daisy's shivering fingers, she murmured, 'It's all right, Daisy. I'm here with you now.' She decided there and then, not to tell her about herself and Jack and their wedding in a few weeks' time.

For a time, they sat together, these two old friends who had hated every minute apart, and when Daisy asked her what news she had brought, Amy deliberately did not mention Jack. Instead she concentrated on other things. 'Roy misses you dreadfully,' she said.

Daisy lapsed into deep thought and when she emerged from it, she remarked softly, 'I miss him too.'

Made hopeful, Amy asked, 'Do you love him still?'

Daisy gave a whimsical smile. 'I'll always love

him.'

'And will you see him?' Amy asked.

Daisy gave a long, solemn shake of the head. 'No, I won't see him. I can't.'

Amy did not persist. 'Everybody asks after you in the shop,' she told her, 'even old Ted Fogarty.'

Daisy chuckled at that. 'Randy old devil!'

Amy's mood was suddenly serious. 'Oh, Daisy, when are you coming home?'

Daisy looked her in the eye, and for a long moment gave no reply. Then when she did it took Amy unawares. 'I haven't got no home to go to,' she said.

'Oh, but you have!' Amy sat bolt upright in the chair. 'My home is yours. Wherever I am, you'll always be welcome.'

'No.' Daisy had thought it through. 'I can't move in on you like that. When I'm ready to leave here, I need my own place to go to.'

Amy reminded her about Roy and the dream they had shared. 'What about your dream?' she asked. 'The dream of a home with Roy, and children, and room enough for two dogs.'

Daisy gave a strangled kind of sob. 'It was just a dream.' She shrugged. 'People like me never have dreams come true.'

'Oh, Daisy, your dream will come true! If only you'll let it.' Getting out of the chair she went to Daisy and held her close. 'I don't think you realise how much you're loved. You have me and Jack, and my family; you have people who love you and want to help. And most of all, you have Roy, who loves you so much he's wilting away for the want of you. Not every woman has that kind of love, Daisy. Not every woman is fortunate enough to realise their dream. But you're lucky. You've got Roy! He would marry you tomorrow if only you'd give him the chance. Listen to me, Daisy. You know what I'm saying is true.'

Shrugging her off, Daisy gave her a searching look. 'Are you and Jack getting married?'

Taken aback by the directness of Daisy's question, and the way in which it was put, Amy hesitated for a moment. That was the very thing she had come to tell Daisy, and now, it was the very thing she feared would upset her—not because she was envious, but because she wasn't strong enough yet to see another woman enjoy what she believed was lost to her.

'Well? Are you and Jack getting wed, or aren't you?' Daisy persisted. 'That's why you came to see me—to tell me the "good" news?'

'No!' Amy was mortified. 'I mean . . . yes, and no! Yes, me and Jack are getting married. And no, it wasn't the only reason I came to see you. I've been desperate to see you since the day you left the infirmary, only you wouldn't let me.'

Beneath Daisy's stony glare Amy felt helpless and confused. 'I don't want to hurt you, Daisy. I just need you to know about me and Jack, because I so much want you to be my maid of honour . . .'

Without warning, Daisy leaped from her seat and fled out of the room, with Amy calling frantically after her, 'Wait, Daisy! Don't go, please . . .'

But Daisy was gone, and there was nothing Amy could do. With clenched fist she punched the windowseat. 'I should never have told her!' Angry with Daisy, angry with herself, she hurried after her.

She ran up and down the corridor, but there was no sign of Daisy, and when she returned, Sister Mary was waiting.

'Don't blame yourself,' she told Amy. 'Daisy is very emotional just now. She has a great deal to accept, and she hasn't yet found the way.'

Sister Mary escorted Amy to the hallway, where already Nurse Rita was waiting.

'How did it go?' she asked.

'I think I've just lost the best friend I ever had,' Amy murmured, her heart aching.

'I'm sorry.' Nurse Rita could say nothing else. 'Leave it a while, and she might come round.'

Amy didn't think so. 'In all the time I've known her, she's never looked at me like that before.' She recalled the stony glare, and the harsh words, and they cut her in two. 'I should never have come,' she said. 'It's too early. Daisy was right and I was wrong. She's been through so much; I should have given her the time she asked for.'

She followed Nurse Rita down the path to the road, where they caught the bus and began their way home. All the while Amy sat silent and thoughtful, sorry for the clumsy way she'd handled things, and praying that Daisy would find it in her heart to forgive her.

*　　　*　　　*

At the convent, Sister Mary was comforting Daisy, who had gone straight to her office when she ran from Amy.

'She came here to tell me about her and Jack being married,' Daisy told her. 'What kind of friend would do that, when she knows how lonely I am

375

without Roy? She can see for herself how ugly I am, and that no man would ever have me.'

'Good friends are hard to find,' the nun told Daisy, 'and I know that in your heart, you're very happy for her.'

But Daisy could only see as far as the scars on her neck, and whatever Sister Mary said, the girl would not be comforted.

*   *   *

When Amy got off the bus, she went straight to the factory site, where Jack and Roy were just locking up. The brush works was housed in a temporary building rather like a small barn, and situated right by the main gates, while a new permanent factory was being built on the now cleared site of the gutted one. These days, with Luke spending so much time seeing customers or finance people, Jack was becoming increasingly responsible for the security and day-to-day running of the Hammond business, such as it was.

'Hello, sweetheart.' Jack took her in his arms and held her for a while. 'How did your meeting with Daisy go?'

Roy too was desperate for news. 'Did she mention me?' he asked eagerly. 'Did she say she would see me? Oh, Amy! Did you tell her how much I miss her?'

Amy told them everything. She told them how quiet and uncooperative Daisy was in the beginning, and she relayed the snippet of conversation they had—about how much she missed Roy, but that she still believed that no man in his right mind would ever want her now that she

376

was scarred and ugly.

She told them of Daisy's reaction when she found out that she and Jack were to be married. 'She turned cold,' Amy said. 'She ran out on me, and I couldn't find her.' It was hard for Amy to relay all of this, but she believed they had a right to know.

'It wasn't your fault,' Jack said, 'and it isn't Daisy's fault either. She's not well enough yet, but she'll be all right, because at least she saw you, when she wouldn't even consider it before. Give her time, sweetheart,' he said, 'just give her time.'

Silent and thoughtful, Roy walked along with them for a while, and then as Jack and Amy clambered onto the tram, he told them he needed some fresh air, and that he would see Jack tomorrow.

He had one final question for Amy. 'Now that you know where Daisy is, will you tell me?'

For one insane, compassionate moment, Amy was tempted. But then she reminded herself it was not her place to give Daisy's secret away, and even if she did, with the way Daisy was now, what would happen if Roy turned up out of the blue?

'I want to tell you, Roy, but I can't,' was her answer. 'I'm so sorry, but if I told you, my friendship with Daisy might be ruined for ever. Besides, if things went wrong with Daisy because of me, I would never forgive myself.'

'But you have to tell me!'

Amy knew she could not and said so. 'Go to Nurse Rita,' she advised. 'Tell her I sent you. Let her know how you feel about Daisy, and that you need to talk with her.' It was the best she could do. 'She took my messages to Daisy, and in the end she was the one who talked Daisy round to seeing me. She might well do the same for you.'

He stood a moment, angry and frustrated, wondering whether to press the point, but even in his anger he could understand how Amy would not want to betray Daisy's confidence. 'All right,' he said. 'Take care, both of you.' And with that, he hurried away.

On the tram going home, Amy was concerned. 'Was I wrong?' she asked Jack. 'Should I have told him?'

As ever, Jack supported her. 'You did what you thought was right,' he assured her. 'You gave him a way to Daisy through the nurse. Now it's up to him. I'm worried about Roy,' he admitted. 'He's been like a cat on hot bricks all day long. This business with Daisy is driving him out of his mind. I wish to God him and Daisy could get back together again.'

'So do I.' Feeling vulnerable and disillusioned, Amy cuddled up to him. 'I don't want anybody else to be my maid of honour,' she said. 'I only want Daisy.'

Jack made a generous offer. 'Suppose we put the wedding back for a few months,' he suggested. 'Maybe by that time she'll be her old self again?'

Amy shook her head. 'We've got to live in hope—for Daisy to recover, but also for ourselves. Let's not change our plans unless we really must; let's just keep hoping and praying.'

*　　　*　　　*

Later that night Marie told Amy that, given time, everything would come right between her and Daisy. 'You've got too strong a friendship to let it

378

all slide away.'

Yet she had to prepare Amy. 'If I'm wrong, and Daisy has really taken against you, then you'll have to live with it, lass,' she warned. 'You have to remember that sometimes when a body goes through what Daisy's been through, it changes the personality. She's already finished with Roy and she's adamant that she won't change her mind, so the same could happen where you're concerned.'

As she spoke, she saw her daughter's face drop, and though it hurt Marie to say it, she finished, 'All I'm saying is, think on it, lass, just in case.' She hugged Amy hard. 'But, having said all that, I have a deep-down feeling it won't be that way at all. I'm keeping my fingers crossed, and hoping that once Daisy comes to see what she's throwing aside, she'll realise it's all too precious to lose.'

With Marie's warning, Amy shed a few tears. 'D'you think I should go and see her again, Mam?'

'No!' Marie knew that would be the worst thing of all. 'Let her think about it. She'll either go one way or the other, and whatever you do, lass, she'll still mek up her own mind.'

CHAPTER SEVENTEEN

Three weeks later Amy and Jack's wedding day arrived.

On this bright cold day in March, the crocuses and daffodils were still out, and the promise of spring showed in the buds on the trees and in the thickening hedgerows.

At quarter-past one in the afternoon, there were

only forty-five minutes before Amy and Jack walked down the aisle to be husband and wife, and the excitement in the little parlour behind Atkinsons' Corner Shop was growing. 'Where is she?' Dave was nervous as a kitten. 'It's tekkin' her long enough, ain't it?'

'Keep calm for heaven's sake!' Somehow, Marie had managed to control her nerves and was fully in charge. 'She were ready when I left her just now. All she had to do was slip on her shoes and that was it.' She was alerted by a noise above. 'Hey up! Here she is now!'

All eyes turned towards the door, and Amy walked in, to an appreciative gasp of admiration from all those gathered.

'By! Doesn't she look grand?' That was old Ma Tooley, whose own wedding was reputed to be on the cards. 'She looks like a reg'lar little angel!'

'Naw . . .' Maureen had tears in her eyes as she observed Amy in her long white gown decorated with forget-me-nots. The trailing, lacy veil was secured to her bouncy brown hair by an ornate mother-of-pearl pin that had belonged to Marie's own mammy. Her smile was wonderful and her eyes outshone the diamanté necklace kindly lent to her by old Ma Tooley.

'She looks just beautiful.' Marie choked back the tears.

'Do I really look all right?' Amy asked shyly.

'By!' Dave found his tongue. 'You look wonderful, lass,' he gasped. 'Every man in the land will envy me when I walk down that aisle with yer.' And his chest swelled at least another few inches as he walked her out the door.

Marie and old Ma Tooley were ready, while

Maureen applied the few finishing touches to the wedding tea.

As Amy appeared at the front door the crowd that had gathered outside clapped and cheered, and only one person whispered, 'Why is that little lad the only attendant?' Johnny looked a proper little gent in his light grey suit and dicky bow. 'Why ain't there no bridesmaids?'

Another neighbour had the answer. 'From what I know, she bought the dress and everything for her friend Daisy, hoping she might turn up, but she never did. Amy didn't want no other bridesmaid, only Daisy.'

It was that which played on Amy's mind as she climbed into the little black car.

'I wish Daisy had answered my letter,' she told her father sadly. 'I wish she was here to walk down the aisle with me.' As she turned to look at her father, the tears threatened. 'I miss her so much, Dad.'

'I know, lass.' Taking her hand in his, Dave patted it softly. 'We can none of us mek other folks do what they don't want,' he said. 'All we can do is be there for them when they need us.'

Amy gave him a fleeting kiss on the cheek. 'You're right,' she said, hiding her pain. 'You and Mam are here, and Jack will be waiting for me, and I know I'm luckier than most.'

She resolved then not to think of Luke Hammond any more. What might have been between them was a pipe dream. He was married, and very shortly she would be as well. She gave a little sigh, remembering the cabin in the woods, the gurgling brook, the pretty little tame deer and the kindness of that deeply troubled man. Well, let this

381

be an end to it all. It had been only a dream anyway . . .

Dave was looking at her curiously. 'All right, lass?'

She turned to him and suddenly beamed. 'Yes, Dad. Better'n all right. Come on, let's go.'

When they got to the church, there was another crowd of well-wishers to watch them in. The shouts of 'Good luck' and 'God bless' rang out, and, 'Ooh! Isn't she bonny!' 'Yer look lovely, lass!'

Grateful for the good wishes, Amy waved and smiled, and her heart was full.

When the music started and Jack, standing in the front pew, turned to look, his heart bounced inside his chest. Amy was the best thing that had ever happened to him. He loved her so much, it hurt.

Roy stood beside him, attentive, and, like Jack, dressed smartly in a brand-new dark suit.

The church was packed—with friends and neighbours and customers from the shop, and others who were there because they loved a wedding.

Linking her arm with that of her proud father, Amy went down the aisle, her smile bathing the faces of the many as they winked and smiled back, and mouthed their good wishes.

When she came to stand beside Jack, they exchanged glances and the love for each other in their eyes spoke more than words.

Suddenly, there was a fracas at the back of the church. When Amy turned, it was to the sound of people softly chuckling, and a breathless, dishevelled Daisy almost running down the aisle towards her. Dressed in the long blue gown that

382

Amy had bought for her, she was tripping over the hem and trying to straighten her tiara as she ran.

'I'm sorry, lass!' she called out. 'I almost didn't mek it!'

Amy couldn't believe her eyes. 'Daisy!' Crying for joy, she ran to meet her. 'Oh, Daisy! You didn't let me down after all.' She could hardly see her darling friend for the blur of tears as they hugged and held each other, with Daisy doing a little dance in the middle of the aisle.

'Hmm.' The vicar gave a little cough. 'Shall we get on?'

They 'got on' and, during the service, Roy and Daisy exchanged glances and Roy winked knowingly, for it was he who had contacted Daisy and persuaded her to forget her sorrows and come home, where she would always be loved.

Roy had been to speak to Nurse Rita, as Amy had suggested, and his pleading to be allowed to visit Daisy was relayed to the girl, but without success.

Then, last week, Roy had received a letter from Nurse Rita, asking him to meet her on the Saturday and she would take him to see Daisy, who had agreed to meet him at last.

They met in the room where Amy had seen Daisy. Roy stood in the doorway, twisting his cap in his hands, heart thumping, palms sweating and, maybe for the first time in his life, at a loss for words.

Against the light from the window Daisy's form was silhouetted where she sat on the windowseat, turned away from him. Slowly she moved her head, but Roy could make out nothing of her expression though he was all too aware that his own mouth was agape and he was holding his breath.

Then Daisy stood and walked slowly towards him, and as she approached him Roy saw tears spilling silently down Daisy's cheeks.

'Oh, Roy . . .' she said simply.

He gulped back his own threatening tears. 'Lass . . .' He reached a hand out towards her face.

'Why do you want to come here? What do you want with me now, with this scar and—'

Gently he placed his fingers over her mouth to silence her. 'Come home, lass,' he whispered. 'We all love you and miss you. And I love you most of all. Me, Amy, her mam—all your friends—we want you back with us, where you belong. We want to tek care of you.'

She looked at him for a long time with indecision in her face as more tears flowed.

'All our plans, Daisy,' Roy reminded her, his eyes never moving from her. 'All the dreams we have— let's get on now and start living 'em. We've no more time to waste.' He saw her face change as she struggled to contain her fears as he persisted gently. 'There's a wedding to go to next Saturday and—if you'll still have me—another to plan. Come home, lass,' he urged her softly. 'Please . . .'

'Yes,' Daisy said. 'You're right, Roy. And I love you too. Always have.'

'Oh, thank God, love.' With a sigh of relief he gathered her into his arms, kissing away her tears, holding her close and showing her she was indeed loved.

'But—'

'Shush, love. Put it all behind you. You were ill; now you're better and you're coming home.'

'Home? But where's home for me now?'

'You'll always have a home to go to, Daisy.' He laughed. 'Maureen and Marie are both desperate to welcome you into theirs. Come back for Amy and Jack's wedding and stay at Maureen's till then.'

'Are you sure that's all right with her?'

'O' course. She asked me to tell you, didn't she? By!' he grinned. 'Amy'll be made up when she sees you there to be her bridesmaid after all.'

And so later that week Daisy had come to stay at Maureen's house before the wedding, where she was welcomed with such love by all her friends who were in on the secret that she felt her confidence growing with every passing hour, and by that evening she couldn't think why she'd stayed away so long.

There was another unexpected guest at the wedding, but one Amy would never know about. Right at the back, hidden behind a wide stone column, Luke Hammond watched it all. He saw Amy go down the aisle, her arm linked with that of her proud father.

He saw Daisy's comical entrance, and listened throughout the service and sung the hymns along with everyone else.

But when it was over and Amy and Jack were pronounced man and wife, he waited until they began the short walk to the vestry where they would sign the register, and then, as quietly as he arrived, he quickly left; unseen and alone.

*　　　*　　　*

The wedding tea went down a treat and soon after that the music started, with old Ted Fogarty playing the piano left to Amy by her grandma. There

385

wasn't much room in the parlour, but it was where Amy had insisted on having the festivities; not least because she had enjoyed some of the happiest moments of her life in that little room.

Crowded though it was, there was dancing and laughter, and when Amy saw Roy waltzing with Daisy, with eyes only for each other, she was thrilled they were reunited at last.

When the evening was over, Jack took Amy into the front shop. 'You'll never know how much I love you . . . Mrs Tomlinson,' he told her. And she thought that whatever happened from now on, she would never, in her whole life, forget this one, very special moment.

'I love you too,' she whispered, and raised her mouth to his.

CHAPTER EIGHTEEN

Towards the end of May, after working twelve- and fourteen-hour days, Luke had his business back on track. His considerable achievements were partly due to his admirable reputation and his own sheer force of character, and now, at long last, he had managed to reassure and retain all of his old customers, and even recruit a few new ones along the way.

The insurance monies were through, and an even larger building than the old one was nearly completed at the factory site. As yet, there had been no breakthrough in the police investigation. It had been established that the fire had been started deliberately, but there was still no lead as to who might have been the culprit.

Over the past few months Luke had been so busy that he was reluctantly obliged to forgo his usual Tuesday escape. Consequently he was on edge, but managing to hold together both his business and his home life until he was in calmer waters.

Amy was married, and although this had happened several weeks ago now, the vision of her in her long white dress, the gauzy veil trailing behind her, beaming at her father, at Jack and at her friend Daisy, had stayed in his mind. Luke had, of course, been very pleased to see Daisy restored to health and vitality.

Amy had been so obviously happy that the sense of loss he himself had experienced at her marriage had struck him like a personal rejection and he could not shake the feeling off.

How he longed to escape to the cabin, to come to terms in solitude with this loss of Amy from his life. And how fate had conspired to deny him even that opportunity. Just to contemplate her portrait would provide some relief from his unhappiness. Maybe next week . . .

Sometimes he felt this thought was all that kept him going.

Throughout these difficult times, Sylvia had been unusually aggressive. As she was tonight. Her depression and mood swings were becoming more extreme, and her confidence reduced, so there was very little time now when her behaviour was normal.

'You're late again! Where've you been *this* time?' The minute he walked through the door, wearied and hungry for his dinner, she was on to him, her face distorted with rage and her fists lashing out. 'You've been with *her*, that's the truth, isn't it? Don't lie to me!' Before he could even reply she was raising her arm, then she brought her nails down on his face, leaving a narrow river of blood where the tip of each cut his flesh. 'You bastard! Who is she?' Screeching like a banshee, she threw herself at him. 'TELL ME WHO SHE IS!'

While he tried gently to fend her off, Edna came rushing down the stairs.

'NO!' Taking hold of Sylvia by the shoulders, she tried to take control, but for once, Sylvia was too much for her.

'It's all right, Edna.' Asking the housekeeper to move away, Luke forcibly took hold of Sylvia by the wrists. 'THERE IS NO WOMAN!' His angry voice, rising above the tirade of abuse, managed to calm her. 'Listen to me, Sylvia. There is no woman. There has never been anyone but you.'

That was the truth, and yet in his mind, he saw Amy's lovely face and his heart dropped. If only . . . he thought, if only . . .

Peering up at him with suspicious eyes, Sylvia allowed herself to listen, but even then she was not totally convinced. 'You do still love me, don't you?' she asked pitifully.

'I always will,' he answered simply, too worn for this kind of argument. And God help him, that was also the truth.

After a while, Sylvia was calm enough for Edna to lead her upstairs and put her to bed.

Later she returned to the kitchen where Luke was enjoying a well-earned cup of tea.

'Poor dear, she was worn out,' Edna informed

him. 'Miss Georgina was here earlier, and they got very lively, trying on dresses and hats. I think Mrs Hammond's got rather excitable, but she's sleeping soundly now.'

He thanked her. 'I really don't know what I would have done without you these past weeks,' he said, 'what with you helping out by staying with Sylvia so often, and hardly able to go home.' He gave a sorry little grin. 'It's a wonder your Harry doesn't come knocking at the door after me.'

'Aw, don't worry. He's an understanding man. Anyway, me and Mrs Hammond find plenty to do.' She chuckled. 'Although maybe I should never have taken her to the market on Saturday.'

Luke took a long, revitalising gulp of his tea. 'Maybe not,' he too was chuckling at the thought, 'especially after she had a fallout with the greengrocer and upturned his barrow in a temper.'

Edna laughed. 'It were his own fault,' she declared. 'He should never have hit the dog with a stick when it peed over the leg of his barrow. It were that which set Mrs Hammond off.'

'If you say so, Edna,' Luke conceded.

Going to the oven Edna took out the cottage pie she'd made for him. 'I cooked it late,' she told him. 'It's still piping hot, and the gravy is nice and rich.' With his place already laid at the table, she set the meal before him. 'And don't dare tell me you're not hungry,' she chided, ' 'cause I know you don't stop to eat, and these past weeks I've seen the weight falling off yer.'

He didn't argue. 'Thanks, Edna. And have *you* eaten—you and Sylvia?'

'We have. So tuck in.'

As he did, a voice called from the top of the

stairs. 'Edna!' It was Sylvia, and she sounded like a frightened child. 'Edna, where are you?'

Going to the door, Edna called back, 'It's all right, dear. You get back into bed. I'll be up in a minute.'

Luke made to get out of his seat. 'I'll go,' he said. 'You sit and have your night-cap.' If there was one thing he'd learned, it was that Edna was very fond of her late night cup of chocolate.

'You'll do no such thing!' she said firmly. 'You've been at work since seven o'clock this morning, and that was after a restless night because of Mrs Hammond and her nightmares. Besides, I had my chocolate only minutes afore you came in, so sit yourself down. I'll see to her. I'm ready for my own bed anyway.'

She bade him good night and hurried across to the door. 'Happen I'll lie with her for a while, at least until I'm satisfied she's hard and fast asleep.'

Luke was immensely grateful. 'Good night, Edna.'

'Good night, sir.'

She nodded and smiled, and was gone in an instant.

Luke ate his cottage pie and thoroughly enjoyed it. Afterwards he carried the used crockery to the sink, where he piled it up inside the porcelain bowl. Then he poured himself a small measure of brandy, which he downed in one gulp. He was not a drinking man, but lately there had been times when he'd felt the need of a drink; but never more than one, and never on a regular basis.

Going to the sitting room, he dropped his weary body into the wide-armed, well-worn leather chair and, stretching out his legs, he closed his eyes and quietly reflected on the tumultuous events of these past weeks.

How could he forget that heart-stopping moment when he stood before his burning factory, when everything he had worked and schemed for was being reduced to ashes before his eyes?

Then, when news broke that there were two people inside the burning building, and then that those same two people were Daisy and Roy, it was one of the worst moments of his entire life.

In fact, though he was working all hours God sent to keep his business running in difficult conditions, he didn't think it was the long, back-breaking hours that wearied him to the bone. Instead he believed it was the trauma of that night, and the searing question: who had set fire to his business? And, more importantly, did they realise that Roy and Daisy were trapped inside?

Luke could not imagine anyone setting that fire, for whatever reason. Time and again he had gone over the events of that night and the questions they raised with the police. How did they get in? Who else had access to keys? Why would anyone want to torch his business? Had he got enemies or competitors who might bear a grudge? Were there any former employees who might think they'd been badly treated?

Luke answered their questions as best he could. He told them how he had no idea how the arsonist had got in, although Roy had already admitted how he and Daisy had climbed in through a small window that had inadvertently been left open. As far as keys were concerned, it was only trusted employees who had access, such as his clerk and his manager, and as far as he knew they had no reason to burn down the building and jeopardise their own incomes with it. They were trusted men. And no, he did not know of any former employee who might think he had been badly treated; but he gave them a list of people who had formerly worked for him anyway.

He explained how his successful business would always have its fair share of competitors who might be pleased to see him cease trading, but he personally could not think of anyone who would stoop to such a terrible thing as burning down a factory.

The watchman couldn't help either because as he already told them, 'I nodded off, but only for a minute or two! It must 'a been then, when the buggers sneaked past me!'

And so the investigation was still ongoing.

Questions, questions, and none of them yet answered. And now, made drowsy by the brandy, Luke fell asleep, and still the disturbing questions played on his mind.

Some time later he woke with a start when a cold, soft hand touched his face.

'Luke?' Inside his head the whisper reverberated in an echo. 'Luke, it's only me.' Her velvet voice thrilled through him.

When he opened his eyes, she was so close he could feel her warm breath bathing his face. 'Georgina!' Leaping out of the chair he crashed against the fender, which then went backwards into the hearth and sent him off balance. 'What the devil are you doing?' A rush of alarm scrambled his senses.

'Ssh!' Putting her finger to her lips she calmed him. 'You'll wake them up!'

'But what are you doing here?' Shaking his head he gathered his wits. 'For God's sake, Georgina!' He glanced at the mantel-clock. 'It's nearly midnight!'

'I couldn't sleep,' she answered. 'I was so worried. I didn't leave here until way past eight o'clock, and you still weren't home. You're overdoing it, Luke. You've got to slow down. You can't turn back the clock and undo what's been done. It's bound to take time. You can't rebuild in weeks what took years to achieve.'

He began pacing the floor, not thinking straight. 'How did you get in here?'

She smiled, surprised. 'You gave me a key, remember?'

'You shouldn't have come out this time of night.'

She tutted. 'I need to check up on Sylvia whenever I'm worried, whatever time it is.' She looked at him from under her eyelashes, her smile flirtatious. 'In fact, it was very naughty of you to ask Edna to stay, when you could have asked me. After all, I am her sister.'

Luke turned to study her—always impeccably dressed, with her hair beautifully groomed and that smile, which though he begrudged saying it, always outshone her sister's. There was no denying it: Georgina was an extremely beautiful woman. 'How did you get here?'

'I walked.'

Shocked, he took her by the arms and gave her a little shake. 'You *walked*, at this time of night? That was a foolhardy thing to do. And all that way . . . whatever were you thinking of?'

'I was thinking of Sylvia,' Georgina said. 'And you. I was thinking how I'm the only family you've got, and I was thinking that we should look after each other. We don't need Edna. We don't need anyone.'

'Oh, Georgina! I'll never understand you.' Taking a deep breath, he blew it out through his nose. 'I don't understand your way of thinking, but there's no use taking you back now.' Ruffling his hair with his two hands as he did when troubled, he told her, 'You'd best sleep in the spare room.'

She smiled a slow, satisfied kind of smile, like the cat that got the cream. 'Is it all right if I warm myself by the fire before I go up?' she asked sweetly. 'I got so cold, walking all that way.'

If Luke had been thinking straight he would have realised that Georgina was not the kind of woman who would walk two steps if there was a taxi in sight.

'Of course.' Mortified at his own bad manners he offered, 'I'll put a few more coals on and make you a mug of cocoa. Then I must say good night. I've an early start in the morning.'

She watched him bring in the coals and stack them neatly into the grate, and she thought how wonderful it would be if Luke was hers and not Sylvia's. In that moment, as many times before, she imagined what it would be like with Sylvia out of the way.

There would be no one to stop them then . . . her and Luke. They might even become lovers. And oh, but wasn't that what she had wanted from the first minute she'd set eyes on him?

Rage flooded her senses. Sylvia had everything; even when they were children, it was always Sylvia, sweet, darling Sylvia, the quiet one, the delicate one. The one who smiled easily, and laughed at

394

silly things, just to please people.

She had always been in the way. She was in the way now, because Luke loved Sylvia. He had always loved her. Even now, when she was nothing but a burden, he took care of her like no one else could.

'Here we are!' Luke's voice shook her out of her reverie. 'I'll back the fire up, but don't forget to put the guard in front before you go upstairs,' he advised.

'Don't worry,' she answered sweetly, 'I won't forget.'

Like a cat with a mouse, she never took her eyes off him. She watched while he kneeled before the fire, shovelling new coals on the old, and revitalising the dying embers to create a warm glow. She studied his profile, that handsome, classic profile that she had studied so often before. She imagined herself kissing those lips, stroking her hands through that thick hair. Now, when she closed her eyes, she could almost feel his arms round her. She wanted him more than ever. She needed him, more than she had ever needed any man before, and there had been plenty.

Then she looked around the room. Like the rest of this beautiful house, it was grand and spacious, with expensive furnishings and a tasteful ambience. Sylvia was mistress of this house. But it should be *her*, Georgina, who was mistress, with Luke as master. Was it so impossible, she thought. Was it so unattainable?

Now, as Luke straightened himself up from the fireplace, a feeling of desperation overwhelmed her. In a moment she was behind him, running her hand up the inside of his shirt, her heart leaping and bounding and everything that made her a

395

desirable woman coming into play. 'I love you,' she whispered. 'I've *always* loved you!'

When he spun round, a look of shock and astonishment on his face, she grabbed him by the hair and, drawing him down, kissed him full and strong on the mouth.

He snatched away, the palms of his hands pushing against her breast. 'What the hell d'you think you're doing?'

She would not let go. 'Hold me, Luke.' She reached down, touching him where a man likes to be touched, and as she did so, her part-opened mouth found his and this time the kiss was softer, more enticing, and for one crazy, wonderful moment, he was tempted.

He did not pull away. Instead his arms came up to encircle her as he drew her to him, his mouth covering hers and his senses reeling. He was a man who, for too long now, had not enjoyed that intimate warmth and passion that a woman could give. Sylvia was out of his reach, but now Georgina was here—too beautiful, too close; deliciously stirring the manhood within him. His resolve began to melt, and for one mad, wonderful moment, he enjoyed the kiss.

But this was wrong. Sylvia was upstairs and it was Sylvia he loved . . . but what about Amy? *What about Amy?* But no, he must not think of her—he *must* not. The dream had become a habit it was hard to break.

In the moment Luke raised his arms to hold Georgina back, he heard a sound, looked up and was shocked to the core, for Sylvia was lunging herself at them. 'Jesus! Sylvia, NO!'

Too late! She snatched the poker and raised it

high. When it came down it hit him hard on the side of the head, flooring him, and all the time she was screaming wild, primitive screams that had Georgina running for her life.

The manic screams woke Edna. She grabbed her robe and, pushing her feet into the slippers, she ran down the stairs calling Sylvia's name. As she came down into the hallway, Georgina was already fleeing out the front door, and Sylvia was only steps behind.

'SYLVIA!' Edna's frantic voice fell on deaf ears.

From the corner of her eye she saw Luke, his body twisted across the tumbled fender, blood seeping from a wound in his forehead. 'Oh dear God!' Whether to go to him, or to Sylvia? Her instincts sent her towards the door. Sylvia was her baby. She had no choice.

Georgina was trying desperately to put some distance between her and Sylvia but, driven by what she had seen, and convinced that Georgina was the 'other woman' that Luke had long denied, Sylvia was rapidly narrowing the distance between them. By now they had reached the main road, quiet at that time in the evening. When in her frantic haste, Georgina tripped, it seemed there was no escape.

She was at Sylvia's mercy.

When Edna found them, Sylvia was sitting on the ground, rocking backwards and forwards with Georgina in her arms.

'Sylvia?' Edna ventured forward.

Sylvia continued rocking, whimpering, her stricken eyes looking up at Edna. 'I saw them,' she sobbed, 'kissing. He lied to me.'

Edna lowered her gaze, and what she saw chilled her to the bone. *Georgina's bloodied face was*

397

almost unrecognisable.

Suppressing the horror that threatened to engulf her, Edna held out her arms. 'Come with me, Sylvia,' she entreated. 'Come on, child. Get up from there.'

The whimpering stopped and Sylvia roughly pushed aside her sister's lifeless body. 'He lied to me!'

Edna nodded. 'We have to go,' she said, choking back the tears. 'We have to tell them.'

Sylvia stood before her like a frightened child, not rebellious, yet not content to go with her. 'Where are you taking me?'

Realising that Sylvia had completely lost her mind, Edna smiled encouragingly. 'It'll be all right, child. They'll understand.'

Sylvia took a step back. 'They'll . . . kill me!'

'No, they won't.'

Sylvia eyed the older woman with a curious, shifty glance. 'They don't know what I did.'

Edna glanced nervously at the ground, where Georgina lay crumpled and lifeless. 'I'll tell them if you like, my dear,' Edna suggested lovingly. 'I'll tell them about Georgina . . . how it was.'

Sylvia leaned forward, whispering intimately. 'She wanted to take him away from me. The factory took him away too, but I burned it.' She smiled, and slowly the smile curled into a grin and the grin emerged as a high-pitched chuckle that sent shivers through Edna's soul.

Shocked, but never cowardly and always filled with love for this poor injured creature, Edna continued softly to coax her. 'I'll tell them everything,' she promised, 'only I need you to be there when I tell them.'

Sylvia feverishly shook her head. '. . . Don't believe you . . . want Edna.'

'I'm here, child.' She had tried so hard, but now, with Sylvia unable to recognise her, Edna was devastated. She could not stop the tears that now ran down her face. 'I'll look after you,' she whispered. 'Trust me. I've never lied to you, and I never will.'

Reaching out, Edna managed to take hold of her, but Sylvia put up a fierce struggle as the night tram rumbled towards them. Realising Sylvia's intention, Edna fought with her. 'No!'

Sylvia twisted, Edna lost her grip and all she could remember later was the awful sound when Sylvia went under the iron wheels of the tram: a whoosh of brakes, the driver shouting through his window and Sylvia's screams.

Then the silence.

That eerie, unforgettable silence that was to haunt Edna for the rest of her days.

CHAPTER NINETEEN

Two weeks after the tragic event, both sisters were laid to rest in a peaceful churchyard high above Blackburn. There was a respectful presence of police officers, and local folks, who had been deeply moved by the sequence of events that had rocked the community, together with those curious bystanders who chose to peer over the fences and watch the service from a distance.

When it was over, the mourners dispersed leaving only two people: the tall, tragic figure of

Luke Hammond, his shoulders stooped and his face a mask of pain and disbelief; and Edna, that darling little woman whose grief was so crippling that a body would be forgiven for thinking that Sylvia had been her own flesh and blood.

They made an odd sight when eventually they walked away. The tiny woman's hat and veil covered the top half of her tear-stained face. The tall, dejected man had, until this very morning, lain in a hospital bed, recovering from an injury inflicted by his crazed wife. The doctors had told him that, if the deep jagged cut had been a mere half-inch further down, he would have lost the sight in one eye.

What happened that night played on Luke's mind over and over again. He was consumed with guilt at the easy manner in which Georgina had tempted him.

He did not blame Sylvia, nor did he blame Georgina, for the blame was his alone. What had happened was his fault.

Fate had given him choices and at every turn he'd chosen unwisely. Sylvia—so beautiful but always highly strung—how had he failed her that she needed to turn to a lout like Arnold Stratton for diversion?

Georgina—so like Sylvia as to be taken for her shadow—knowing Sylvia's waywardness, why had he allowed Georgina to come and go in his house? He'd always known she was dangerous, and so she had proved to be. Again, his fault.

But Amy—dear girl—not wayward or dangerous, but as sweet-natured and kind as it was possible for a woman to be—in Amy he had glimpsed what might have been his if fate had been less cruel. But the timing was all wrong and she could never be his now. His fault again, because he'd already chosen Sylvia.

Now, as he turned to close the heavy iron churchyard gate behind him, the strain showed deep in his still-handsome features. His eyes were hollow, and his face pinched and grey. Slow-moving, with his head down and his heart heavy, Luke had become an old man before his time.

He shuffled off to his car alone as Edna was embraced by her husband, who had ready a dry handkerchief and the promise of 'a nice cup of tea at home'.

Luke started the engine and drove out towards the forest. Since Sylvia's death he had gone to the cabin often. Now that she was laid to rest there was nothing to keep him in Blackburn at all, he realised. Jack Tomlinson was in charge of the day-to-day running of the factory; Luke was hardly needed there.

The cabin, which had been an occasional retreat, was already, even since Sylvia's death, becoming a home. Here, the perfect isolation brought Luke a measure of contentment, although he felt he would never be truly happy again. He had the birdsong and the trees, Velvet for company, the sound of the brook, his paints and, above all, the escape from noise and crowds and the responsibility of work that he had always craved. He even had Amy—in a way. The painting of Amy hung in pride of place on the wall. To gaze at her and think of what might have been, that was all his dreams had come to.

*   *   *

Coming out of the shadows, Don Carson made his way across the churchyard to where Sylvia Hammond and her sister, Georgina, were laid to rest.

For a long, poignant moment he stood, his gaze roving the oval mound in the ground, where the pretty posies and other floral tributes marked a sad ending to two vibrant, young lives.

Taking the newspaper cutting from his coat pocket, he opened it out to study the familiar picture of this woman he had known as Helen. Then, dropping to his knees, he turned the cutting towards the top of the mound. 'Y'see how your lies will allus find you out?' he whispered. 'Why did you not tell me the truth? Did you think it would have made any difference to me if I'd known you were the sister-in-law of a wealthy man? Did you think I might blackmail you . . . or him?'

He gave a gruff laugh. 'What does it matter now, eh? You're gone and I'm still here, and we none of us know why.'

He said a prayer, made a sign of the cross on himself and, straightening up, put his hand to his mouth and blew a kiss. 'God bless,' he murmured, and, dropping the newspaper cutting between the flowers, he quickly strode away.

*   *   *

Amy didn't see him, until she had turned the corner and was coming through the gate when he literally bumped into her. 'Don!' She was visibly shocked.

Don too was taken aback by her sudden appearance. 'Hello, Amy.' He felt a rush of embarrassment. 'Er . . . how are you?'

Amy gathered her composure. Involuntarily her hand went to her stomach as if to shield her, as yet, tiny baby from this man who had brought her so much disappointment. 'I'm well, and you?'

He nodded. 'Look, Amy . . .' he swallowed so hard his Adam's apple bobbed up and down, 'I did wrong to you, and I'm sorry. Sometimes we do things we regret, but once they're done there's no going back.'

Amy was astonished. She had never thought to hear him apologise. 'I understand.' Now that she had Jack, and was expecting a baby, everything had fallen into place. 'We had something for a time, but it wasn't right,' she explained. 'I can see that now. In the end, it was all for the best.'

She glanced back to the churchyard. 'This is a strange place to see you,' she mentioned curiously.

He gave the merest smile. 'I've been to see . . .' he too glanced back at the churchyard, '. . . an old friend.' His embarrassment betrayed itself when he now found it difficult to look into her eyes. 'Take care of yourself, Amy.' With that he was swiftly gone, leaving Amy to wonder about the 'friend' he had mentioned.

Hurrying across the grass, she laid her posy of spring flowers, and as she straightened up she spotted the newspaper cutting. Plucking it out, she saw that it was an article on the two sisters, with a photograph of each. 'That's odd.' She looked about the churchyard but there was no one to be seen.

Then, as a thought struck her, she turned her attention towards the gate and beyond, to where she could see the familiar figure of Don Carson hurrying away. 'I wonder?' Don had earned a reputation for enjoying the company of women friends; and why should he stop at the ones from his own class?

Before her thoughts ran away with her, Amy replaced the newspaper cutting where she had found it.

Jack and the coming baby were her life now, and she thanked God for what He had given her.

She stood a moment to murmur a prayer, then she went into the church, where she lit three candles, one for each of those young women, and the third for any poor lost soul who had no one else to light a candle for him.

CHIVERS
LARGE
PRINT
—direct—

If you have enjoyed this Large Print book and would like to build up your own collection of Large Print books, please contact

Chivers Large Print Direct

Chivers Large Print Direct offers you a full service:

• Prompt mail order service

• Easy-to-read type

• The very best authors

• Special low prices

For further details either call
Customer Services on (01225) 336552
or write to us at Chivers Large Print Direct,
FREEPOST, Bath BA1 3ZZ

Telephone Orders:
FREEPHONE 08081 72 74 75